Pan Tadeusz

The Last Foray in Lithuania

A Tale of the Polish Nobility in the Years 1811 and 1812
in Twelve Books

Pan Tadeusz

The Last Foray in Lithuania

A Tale of the Polish Nobility in the Years 1811 and 1812
in Twelve Books

Adam Mickiewicz

Translated into Prose
by Christopher Adam Zakrzewski

CHERRY ORCHARD BOOKS

2024

Mickiewicz Bust Sculpture by Pierre Jean David d'Angers,
The National Museum in Kraków, Poland.

LCCN 2024019937

ISBN 9798887196053, Paperback
ISBN 9798887196046, Cloth
ISBN 9798887196060, Adobe PDF
ISBN 9798887196077, ePub

Book design by PHi Business Solutions
Cover design by Ivan Grave
On the cover: illustration to Book 2 by Michał Elwiro Andriolli

Published by Academic Studies Press
1577 Beacon Street
Brookline, MA 02446, USA
press@academicstudiespress.com
www.academicstudiespress.com

For my father,
and in memory of poet and scholar Bogdan Czaykowski

Contents

Acknowledgments

The author and publishers express their gratitude to the following for permission granted to reprint, adapt, or otherwise make use of materials previously published:

The Polish Institute of Houston, Texas, for early translations of individual Books of *Pan Tadeusz* appearing in the *Sarmatian Review* 20, no. 2 (April 2000); 29, no. 2 (September 2008); 30, no. 1 (September 2009); 30, no. 3 (September 2010); 30, no. 2 (April 2010); 31, no. 1 (January 2011); 31, no. 2 (April 2011); 32, no. 3 (September 2012); 32, no. 2 (April 2012); 34, no. 2, (April 2014); 35, no. 3 (September 2015); 36, no. 1 (January 2016).

The Canadian Fellowship of Catholic Scholars Canada, for a reworked rendering of Book IV of *Pan Tadeusz* appearing in *Fidelitas* (Summer–Fall Edition, 2009).

The Polish Institute of Arts and Sciences of America, for an e-book of an earlier version of the entire work (2011).

Winged Hussar Publishing, Point Pleasant, New Jersey, for the "Zmok Books" popular edition of *Pan Tadeusz* (2019).

Grateful acknowledgement is due to Dr. George Weigel, Distinguished Senior Fellow of the Ethics and Public Policy Center, Washington, DC, for alerting publishers to the need for a fresh, annotated English rendering of *Pan Tadeusz*; Dr. Joseph Pearce, Series Editor of Ignatius Critical Editions, San Francisco, and Dr. Ewa Thompson, Professor Emeritus of Rice University, Houston, Texas, for their tireless advocacy on behalf of this undertaking; Dr. Andrzej Waśko of the Jagiellonian University of Kraków, Poland, for supplying this volume with an excellent scholarly essay; Dr. Kazimierz Braun, Professor Emeritus of the University of Buffalo, NY, for putting the author in contact with Dr. Waśko; the Polish Heritage Society, Barry's Bay, Ontario, Canada, for its generous financial contribution toward this project; and to the Kościuszko Foundation, NY, for a travel grant and stipend awarded the author in the spring of 1975, enabling him to work in the Institute of Literary Research (IBL), Warsaw, Poland, where the idea of translating *Pan Tadeusz* was first conceived.

The author further expresses his warm sense of obligation to his wife Wendy and sons for their forbearance and being always near and attentive when a word, a line, or a passage of the translation needed to be tested; to poet Fr. Janusz

Ihnatowicz, for his thoughtful criticisms and stimulating suggestions in the early stages of this project; to novelist and painter Mr. Michael D. O'Brien, for his unwavering encouragement throughout the whole process of gestation and development; to Mr. Vladimir Oslon, for the many delightful evenings spent together, comparing notes on translating Pushkin's and Mickiewicz's verse into French and English; to Dr. Daniel Frese, Acquisitions Editor of Academic Studies Press, for facilitating the labyrinthine process leading up to the work's acceptance and publication; to Mrs. Maria Henry and Mr. Konrad Bartul, for their assistance in formatting, editing, and proofing the manuscript in its various versions and stages of completion; to the faculty of Our Lady Seat of Wisdom College in Barry's Bay, for organizing public readings of portions of the translation; and finally, to the author's former Latin students at the College, who were never averse to taking an occasional break from the tedium of parsing a Latin sentence and lending an ear to a line or two from "The Polish Poem."

Adam Mickiewicz and *Pan Tadeusz*

Dr. Andrzej Waśko

Two centuries ago, the Publishing House of Józef Zawadzki abutting on the walls of the Imperial University of Vilna put out a first volume of poems composed by an obscure 24-year-old schoolteacher from the provinces named Adam Mickiewicz. The volume contained a cycle of Romantic poems entitled *Ballads and Romances*. No one could then have imagined that this first small book of verse would become the most groundbreaking work in the history of Polish literature—a literature which had already enjoyed several centuries of rich development along European lines, most notably, the Renaissance, known as Poland's "Golden Age," crowned by the lyrical verse of Jan Kochanowski, and the seventeenth century with its *pléiade* of metaphysical, pastoral, and epic poets, who documented in verse and in prose that century of wars which so beset the country. The vast Polish-Lithuanian Commonwealth encompassing the territories of modern Poland, Lithuania, Belarus, and Western Ukraine, had but one literary language apart from Latin, and that was Polish. Not even the crisis and decline of the Commonwealth in the second half of the eighteenth century halted the flourishing of consummate verse and prose that flowed out of the pens of Enlightenment writers like Ignacy Krasicki, Adam Naruszewicz, Franciszek Karpiński, and others. Only a poet of unique genius could have launched a new epoch in a literature boasting so rich a tradition. *Ballads and Romances* was a work of that order, and universal recognition came soon on the heels of its publication. So it is in Poland today: the ballads of that modest little volume remain masterpieces of Polish verse. They hold in Polish literature a position equal to that enjoyed by the ballads of William Wordsworth and Samuel Coleridge in English literature.

Adam Mickiewicz was born on December 24, 1798, into an impoverished noble family in Nowogródek in the Grodno region of what is now Belarus.

His father was a local lawyer, and the future poet and his three brothers were forced to make a living in accordance with the levels of their education. After the Third Partition of Poland, which took place shortly before the poet's birth, Mickiewicz's homeland—the territories of the former Grand Duchy of Lithuania joined in a centuries-old dynastic and political union with the Polish Kingdom to form a single state called the Commonwealth of Two Nations— found itself under the rule of Tsarist Russia. However, as the Empire's consolidation of power took time to come into full effect, the schools attended by the young poet and the University of Wilno in which he enrolled in 1815 remained Polish along with their language of instruction, text books, and professors. Thus, Mickiewicz's generation was the last to be educated in the Polish language according to the enlightened program instituted during the reign of the last Polish king, Stanisław August Poniatowski.

In 1812 Napoleon's Grande Armée marched through Mickiewicz's native district on its way to Moscow. The ensuing brief "Spring" of freedom enjoyed by his homeland, followed only a few months later by Napoleon's disastrous retreat, left a powerful impression on the future author of *Pan Tadeusz*. "Born in chains, enslaved while still in my swaddling bands, I have known but one such spring in all my life!"—he would write later in his epilogue to *Pan Tadeusz*. Dreams of freedom, of living in one's own country, of preserving the threatened traditions of the nation continued to be fostered in the hearts of Mickiewicz's fellow students at Wilno University. They formed secret cultural and political organizations: the Philomaths (the poet being one of its founders and actively taking part in it), the Filarets, and the Illuminati. It was out of the Philomath circle, a self-study group with ambitious scientific and literary plans, that Mickiewicz's *Ballads and Romances* sprang. Soon a second volume of Mickiewicz's poems appeared (1823). It contained the first two parts of *Forefathers' Eve*, a Romantic drama based on local folkloric motifs and the poet's idealized love of Maryla Wereszczakówna. The clandestine activities of the Polish youth did not escape the watchful eye of the Russian authorities. In autumn of 1823, Mickiewicz and his fellow Philomaths were arrested and imprisoned at the Basilian Monastery in Wilno. A long investigation, involving over a hundred accused parties, concluded with the poet being exiled to central Russia, where he was forbidden contact with existing Polish communities.

As it turned out, however, Saint Petersburg and Moscow where Mickiewicz and other fellow Philomaths found themselves in late 1824 were then themselves caught up in political and cultural ferment. Liberal views and Romantic poems were spreading among the fashionable Russian elite. Mickiewicz, an already recognized Romantic poet, became a prominent figure in their literary circles.

He formed friendships with a number of future participants of the Decembrist Revolt (1825), notably the poet Konrad Ryleev, who would soon be executed for his part in the rebellion. Naturally, the Tsarist police kept a close eye on the politically suspect Mickiewicz, but Moscow and Petersburg were also home to large Polish colonies which helped the poet to publish two additional books of poems, namely *Sonnets* (1826) and *Konrad Wallenrod* (1828). The first of these contained his *Crimean Sonnets*, sublime masterpieces of Romantic lyrical verse; the second, *Konrad Wallenrod*, a Romantic narrative poem expressing seditious ideas under a historical guise. These works were avidly read in Poland where they instigated a fierce critical debate known as the "Battle of the Classicists and Romanticists." Translations began to appear in foreign languages.

Mickiewicz's fame as an inspired poet spread quickly through Russia, where he was lionized and compared to Pushkin. By 1829, when he finally obtained permission to leave Petersburg for Europe, his literary reputation was firmly established. In Germany, he spent a week as the guest of Johann Wolfgang Goethe in Weimar. He visited the famous Romantics Ludwig Tieck and August Wilhelm Schlegel. In Prague he met Vaclav Hanka and other representatives of the Czech national revival movement. In Italy he made contact with several prominent literary figures, including Alessandro Manzoni.

Alas, this happy period of burgeoning literary fame and Romantic travels about Europe was short-lived. On November 29, 1830, an armed rebellion, known in Polish history as the November Uprising, broke out in Warsaw against Russia. Setting out from Italy, Mickiewicz traveled via Geneva to Paris and from there, on a false passport, through Germany to Poznań in Greater Poland, which was then part of the Kingdom of Prussia. Ultimately, however, he never crossed the border into his embattled country. The uprising fell in September of 1831. Thousands of its participants, soldiers, politicians, journalists, and writers sought refuge in France. For the next several decades Paris would become the main hub of Polish political and cultural life. Polish history refers to this period as the "Great Emigration." After a prolonged stay in Greater Poland and Dresden, Mickiewicz finally arrived Paris in late July of 1832, where he published his next major work: *The Books of the Pilgrimage of the Polish Nation*, a manifesto of liberationist ideas written in biblical prose. The work was soon translated into most of Europe's languages. In 1833 he published Part III of *Forefathers' Eve*, a continuation of the drama he'd published in Wilno. Georges Sand, in her *Essai sur le drame fantastique*, would later compare the work to Goethe's *Faust* and Byron's *Manfred*. It was in France also that he composed his ultimate masterpiece *Pan Tadeusz*, the first edition of which appeared in Paris in June, 1834.

Pan Tadeusz is unlike any of Mickiewicz's previous works or any other epic poem written at the time. Initially, Mickiewicz intended it to be a relatively short work: a poem of manners set in the pastoral region of the poet's child-hood around Nowogródek. In his private letters he compared it to Goethe's idyllic poem *Herman and Dorothea*. It was to be a tale of the life of the Polish provincial gentry, its romantic attachments, agrarian labors, and amusements. Commentators on *Pan Tadeusz* would later posit psychological reasons for the poet's nostalgic return to this subject-matter and literary form—a need to dis-tance himself from the debacle of the November Uprising and the uncertainties and bitter political quarrels dividing the Great Emigration. As the work pro-gressed, however, additional, less idyllic themes began to creep into the poet's yearning for Arcadia—the "land of his childhood years." He linked the poem's action to Poland's political situation under the Partitions and set it back (from 1814) to the year 1811—the eve of Napoleon's war with Russia, on which the Poles pinned their hopes of regaining independence. The love and marriage of the poem's young heroes, Tadeusz and Sophy, was intended to close the tale of two estranged families, the Soplicas and Horeszkos. But then Mickiewicz set this tale of a private family feud against a still larger background, weaving into it a conspiratorial plan of a national insurrection that was to co-opt Napoleon's imminent incursion into Lithuania. The plan was the brainchild of a mysteri-ous monk, Father Robak, in reality a Polish emissary and the disguised father of Tadeusz, Jacek Soplica. Thus, from a pastoral idyll, *Pan Tadeusz* became something more akin to a Walter Scott *Waverley* novel, only written in consum-mate verse and infused with sublime poetic descriptions and lyrical digressions. Mickiewicz would not stop there. Upon completing the manuscript of his tale of the provincial *szlachta* (nobility), now subtitled *The Last Foray in Lithuania*, he composed two additional cantos whose action unfolds in the year 1812—the opening days of the war that was to free Poland and Lithuania from Russian rule. These last two cantos rise to a level of sublimity transcending that of the preceding parts of the poem, and the heroes' fortunes take on a broader, sym-bolic and historic dimension consonant with the pivotal moment of Poland's (and Europe's) history there described. Thus, upon the appearance of the first German translation of *Pan Tadeusz*, the critic Wilhelm Häring would state the now generally accepted view that *Pan Tadeusz* represents a modern epic *sui generis*:

> This latest work of Mickiewicz is a perfect epic poem, a work
> whose form is unfamiliar to us, but whose very nature meets the
> most rigorous requirements set by our aesthetic critique of the

epic, namely its highest and, according to others, only variation. *Pan Tadeusz* presents a concise and comprehensive portrait of a particular nation and its characteristics at a given point in its history, a gripping plot rich in episodes; an equally interesting and informative retrospective on the historical past, masterly, evocative and pithy descriptions of places, relations, customs, and vivid still-life and living images of nature, boldly expressed—now in many words, now with the merest stroke of the pen—all aptly suited to the prevailing mood, and subject to the poet's needs.[1]

The story of *Pan Tadeusz* unfolds at Soplica Manor owned by Judge Soplica and the nearby ruined castle of the Horeszko family. As befits a Romantic tale, the castle is bound up with a tragic history. Its last holder, the Pantler Horeszko has a daughter who has fallen in love with the Judge's elder brother, Jacek Soplica, a mighty swashbuckler and leader of the local gentry but beneath the rank of the wealthy, aristocratic Horeszkos. Rejected as a suitor for his beloved Eva's hand, Jacek kills her father in an access of rage and despair. This occurs during Poland's preceding war with Russia during a siege of the Pantler's castle by the Muscovites. The unhappy Eva is given away in marriage to a wealthy bachelor and dies soon after being transported with her husband to Siberia. Thus perishes the Horeszko line. The Muscovites award the bulk of the family's estate to the Soplicas.

Twenty years pass. Jacek Soplica, who has left the country after committing his dastardly crime, lives on and directs his brother's affairs from abroad. On his behalf, the Judge rears Eva's orphaned daughter Sophy at Soplica Manor. Jacek's cherished aim is to wed Sophy to his son Tadeusz and thus restore to the heiress the Horeszko estate, thereby righting the wrong brought about by his crime. While abroad, the guilt-wracked Jacek experiences a conversion and reforms himself completely. He enters the monastic order of the Bernardines, assumes the lowly name of Robak [meaning "worm" in Polish—C. Z.], and becomes a secret emissary for the Polish Army serving with Napoleon. In his guise as a monk, he returns incognito to his native district where he hatches plans for an uprising against the Muscovites. In the course of events, however,

---

1   This article appeared in Leipzig in *Blätter für literarische Unterhaltung*, nos. 289 and 290. Its content and significance in shaping opinion on *Pan Tadeusz* is discussed in detail by M. Szyrocki and B. Zakrzewski in their essay "Wilhelm Häring o *Panu Tadeuszu*," published in the collective work *Mickiewicz. Sympozjum na Katolickim Uniwersytecie Lubelskim* (Lublin: Wydaw TN KUL, 1979), 227-236.

his plans are thwarted by Gervase, the Pantler's last remaining retainer who has sworn to avenge his late master's death. When Robak tries to organize an armed insurrection among the local nobility, Gervase gains their support and persuades them to mount a raid on Judge Soplica, whose good character he has impugned. The real reason driving him is the Judge's protracted litigation with the neighboring Count, a distant kinsman of the Horeszko family, over legal possession of the Pantler's castle, of which Gervase is the self-styled Warden. Gervase convinces the nobility that the lawsuit has been won in the Count's favor and that the Judge's title to Horeszko property is illegal. The situation can only be resolved by resorting to a "foray" (*zajazd*)—a legal recourse, long recognized in old Polish law, allowing an armed body of citizens to execute the verdict adjudged to the plaintiff. The law was abolished after the Partitions.

Of course, there is no question of the legality of the raid on Soplica Manor. This subtitular motif of *Pan Tadeusz* turns out to be a comedic adventure. (*Pan Tadeusz* is among other things a tale of high hilarity.) Tragedy comes only with the ensuing bloody battle between the Polish nobility and a detachment of regular Russian soldiers who arrive on the scene to restore public order. A *danse macabre* plays itself out in the hitherto peaceful precincts of Soplica Manor. The Russians are soundly beaten, but Father Robak takes a mortal shot while saving the life of the count—"last of the Horeszkos, albeit on the spindle side." On his deathbed, the Monk reveals himself to Gervase, the thwarter of his conspiratorial plans, and begs his forgiveness for killing the Pantler. Upon receiving the Warden's forgiveness, he dies. The fighting Polish nobility, including Tadeusz and the Count, seek refuge across the border in the Grand Duchy of Warsaw where the Polish Army, united with Napoleon, stands poised to invade Russia. The poem ends in the year 1812 with their return to Lithuania as Napoleon's soldiers. Soplica Manor holds a "last banquet in the old-Polish style" in which three generations of Polish patriots take part, thus marking a farewell to the old feudal order and the inauguration of a new era.

As in Scott's *Waverley* novels, the heroes of *Pan Tadeusz* are ordinary people whose lives are shaped by great historical events. The events shaping those of *Pan Tadeusz* are many: the Partitions, the Commonwealth's earlier attempts to reform itself, the Constitution of May Third, the Kościuszko insurrection, the nation's efforts to rebuild an independent state in the Napoleonic era. The wars and changes in social mores taking place throughout Europe after the French Revolution are seen through the prism of the various characters' biographies, their reminiscences, and the attitudes they hold and express. Always the author presents the historical panorama of the epoch with a painstaking realism accompanied by naturalistic descriptions of everyday life lived at the turn of the eighteenth and nineteenth centuries. The hunts, the court proceedings, the castle, the Polish nobleman's manor house, the Jewish tavern, the cookery, costumes and fashions—all these Mickiewicz depicts in the minutest detail, and always with the eye of a poet. The most ordinary things of everyday life, described in a poetic style replete with striking similes and cultural resonances, become endued with a magical light. Images of the sky and earth, the sunrises, the sunsets, the Lithuanian forest, the fields, meadows, streams, animal life and farm labor all have a lyrical character, full of painterly and musical effects. Always the microcosm of humble human affairs is presented against the monumental backdrop of nature, national history, folk legend, and myth.

Pan Tadeusz is written in the classical verse form of Polish literature. It consists of regular, rhymed 13-syllable lines with the caesura falling after the seventh syllable. The form was used by Franciszek Ksawery Dmochowski, among others, in his translation of *The Iliad*, the most popular Polish rendering of the classic in Mickiewicz's time. Mickiewicz's style contains many deliberate allusions and references to Homer; hence arose the generally accepted opinion that *Pan Tadeusz* represented an epic poem—albeit unique in all of modern European literature. The opinion is not unwarranted, but it is important to note that the literary method used here by Mickiewicz depends on the constant use of a variety of styles and literary conventions ranging from the most ancient (classical idylls, epic poems, etc.), to later typically indigenous forms (such as the Polish *gawęda*), to those of the Enlightenment (the comedy of manners, the mock heroic) and to the popular forms of the literature of the day (sentimental romances, historical novels, etc.). *Pan Tadeusz* is full of intertextual resonances, allusions, travesties and pastiches of literary genres and styles, humorous speech mannerisms, anecdotes, and other comic forms. Generically, therefore, *Pan Tadeusz* is a unique work, resisting conventional pigeonholing. Polish critics now universally accept Kazimierz Wyka's characterization of *Pan Tadeusz* as a "synthesis of literary genres."

The fact of such a profound, one might say *total* fusion of the poem's form with literary tradition is the more noteworthy in that *Pan Tadeusz* is for all intents and purposes Mickiewicz's last great work. Twelve years elapsed between the publications of *Ballads and Romances* and *Pan Tadeusz*. In the course of that time, the poet broke ever new literary ground, constantly overthrowing established conventions. Yet, having achieved this, having created new literary models worthy of imitation, he ended by returning to the tradition of the Enlightenment and rested the form of *Pan Tadeusz* on a deliberate—often parodic—travesty of the various literary genres and styles of his day. Contemporary readers, expecting from Mickiewicz further groundbreaking works in the manner of

Forefathers' Eve, Part III, failed at first to understand this return to a past literary tradition, nor did they perceive in *Pan Tadeusz* the poet's veiled assessments of contemporary life. This would come later. Only after several years did Zygmunt Krasiński and Juliusz Słowacki, Poland's greatest Romantic poets besides Mickiewicz, come to recognize the full grandeur of the poem. And only in the second half of the nineteenth century did *Pan Tadeusz* win universal recognition as Poland's national epos. Since then, *Pan Tadeusz* remains the most frequently published, most frequently translated work of Polish literature—a *carte de visite* and portrait of the Polish nation, her culture and character.

For Mickiewicz, *Pan Tadeusz* marked the close of his creative journey—a great artistic synthesis, not only of the works hitherto achieved by the author himself but of the entire gamut of possibilities of the Polish language, including those discovered in the poet's epoch and those of the literary traditions known to him and his time. From the standpoint of the literary revolution in which Mickiewicz participated and in large measure achieved singlehanded since 1822, all the poetic schools and genres of earlier times were obsolete. But this revolution, too, had effectively run its course, for it had triumphed, and having triumphed, it could not be continued. Yet all those genres and styles—those it had overthrown and those it had brought into existence—could be used again in a work that took as its theme and material a nation's traditions and a poet's childhood memories—a work in which these literary forms could be treated as part of the world represented, as objects of stylization, sui generis mediums of cultural memory among the many other mediums of memory.

And thus, after writing *Pan Tadeusz*, at the relatively young age of thirty-six and at the height of his creative powers, Mickiewicz put down his pen and stopped publishing new works. In a letter to a friend he wrote:

> It seems to me that historical poems and, in general, all old forms are now moribund and can be only be revived for the amusement of readers. The real poetry of our age has yet to be born; we can only see hints of its coming. We have written too much for amusement and paltry aims. Remember the words of St. Martin: *"On ne devrait écrire des vers qu'après avoir fait un miracle."*

In accordance with this expressed conviction, Mickiewicz's would no longer be the life of a poet but that of an intellectual and man of action: a professor of literature (in Lausanne and Paris), a religious activist (he having for a time joined the group of adherents of that strange mystic Andrzej Towiański), a publicist, and a Romantic fighter for national liberation during the Spring of Nations.

In all this, too, Mickiewicz played an outstanding role. His *Lectures on Slavic Literature* delivered at the Collège de France represent the first academic monograph comparing the main literatures of the Slavic peoples. In France, his role as poet and one of Romantic Europe's spiritual leaders is immortalized by Antoine Bourdelle's monumental sculpture of him that stands in Paris. The poet died on November 26, 1855, during the Crimean War, in Constantinople, where he had traveled on a political mission—much like Lord Byron, the hero and model of his literary youth, before him.

Naturally, not all the artistic riches of *Pan Tadeusz* can be captured in a translation. We need to bear this in mind, especially when reading it in prose. Lost in it are the rhythms and musicality of the original, features especially important for Mickiewicz and his era. These are, after all, constitutive elements of Romantic poetry. Still, *Pan Tadeusz* has more than once been rendered in prose (Paul Cazin's French translation being an earlier notable example) and there are good reasons for this. Although Polish culture has always been closely tied to that of the West and belongs, as it were, to the typical national cultures of Western civilization, it is still poorly known outside of Poland. This is especially true because of the peculiar features so strongly imprinted upon the culture by the *mores* of the Polish nobility (*szlachta*) and the social and political conditions prevailing in Poland during the seventeenth and eighteenth centuries. All this plays a key role in the action of *Pan Tadeusz* and is fundamental to the work's understanding. For this reason, though lacking perhaps the emotional evocativeness of a poetic rendering, a translation in prose can be both more intelligible to the non-Polish reader and even more effective perhaps in conveying the realism of the poet's depiction of Polish society. Despite its unique and poorly known history, despite its traditional dress which the Germans, the French, and the English did not wear, despite the traditional Polish dishes whose taste and very names remain untranslatable, this Polish world is not as foreign as might appear at first blush. Essentially, it is the same world in which everyone in the West has always lived, a world in which we live today, and in which—may we hope!—our grandchildren will continue to live.

Dr. Andrzej Waśko, Jagiellonian University, Kraków, Poland

Translator's Preface

Epics may be written in prose as well as in verse.
Cervantes

Beauty will save the world.
Dostoevsky

Pan Tadeusz has yet to be freed from its fiercely tight national orbit and claim its rightful place among the higher-orbiting luminaries of the Western canon. Wider recognition of the Polish masterpiece has always been hampered by a certain Quixotic eccentricity that sets the great poem apart from the main body of European classics. Perhaps no other classic—not even Dante's *Divine Comedy*, nor even Pushkin's own elusive "novel in verse" *Eugene Onegin*—finds itself more captive to the tongue in which it was written, bedeviling all attempts at translation, without which, needless to say, no work of literature can reach a universal audience.

Pan Tadeusz baffles categorization as a literary genre: it is neither, typically, an epic poem, nor a mock heroic in the eighteenth-century tradition, nor a pastoral idyll, nor a Romantic narrative poem, nor a realist novel in verse, nor yet a fairy tale. It is all these things—and much more. The integration of such disparate generic elements in an artistically sound whole is primarily a matter of striking the right style; and Mickiewicz was above all a master of style.

In *Pan Tadeusz*, Mickiewicz achieved in traditional verse what in our current age is arguably no longer achievable by even the great poets. This at least was the view of Polish poet Czesław Miłosz:

> [Mickiewicz] knew how to use conventional phrasing and, without straying beyond its limits, transform it into something completely new. That is not easy. Many poets maintain their standards only at the price of being unconventional, and drop into dullness as soon as they venture into traditional methods. Through a slight retouching of words, a genuine poet is able to invest a commonplace phrase with charm. But genuine poets are rare, and there are periods of history when such an operation is

impossible, because the use of a "common style" is then beyond the reach of even the great poets.[2]

Donald Davie, one of the few discerning English poets to have tried his hand at fragments of Mickiewicz's verse, agreed with Miłosz:

> These observations, and the implication behind them that Mickiewicz can today be an unusually fruitful model, are as timely and as apposite in London as in Warsaw. The example of Mickiewicz can be of great help to the English poet of today who is conscientiously trying to learn his trade. For English poets of today must be engaged just as their Polish contemporaries are ... in fighting their way back, from surrealism and *poésie pure* and belated Victorianism to a classical dryness and to the formula coined by T.S. Eliot and echoed by Mr. Miłosz, "the perfection of a common language."[3]

These words were written some six decades ago in a relatively benign literary context, yet if anything the intervening passage of time has only enhanced their relevance. One needn't be a close observer of contemporary "hyper-modernist" trends to be able to conclude that we have by no means put behind us the "period of history" alluded to by Miłosz. Indeed, the heightened historical moment in which we find ourselves compels even the most sanguine observer of culture to attach a darker significance to Miłosz's and Davie's words than these poets perhaps entertained, or at any rate intended.

We find ourselves enmeshed in a neo-Gnostic age when prevailing ideologically driven aesthetics and deconstructionist cultural forces conspire to propel not just poetic but all manner of discourse headlong in the very opposite direction of a true "common language"—by which I mean a language adequate to the task of expressing authentic human experience within the framework of the natural law. Generic language imposed by edict, "politically correct" newspeak, so-called "inclusive language"—all of which violate the particularity and synechdocality of words (and, in a deeper sense, are "exclusive" to the core)—are

---

2   See Donald Davie, "*Pan Tadeusz* in English Verse," in *Adam Mickiewicz in World Literature,* ed. Wacław Lednicki (Berkeley: University of California Press, 1956), 322.

3   Davie, op.cit., 322.

egalitarian atrocities amounting to an Orwellian assault on the referentiality and clarity of ordinary words.

What influence poetry can exert against the background of this powerful onslaught on the nature of language and thought is a crucial question today. The prevailing post-modern anti-culture, which denies the natural law and holds the meanings of words, logical discourse, and the very notion of objective truth in contempt does not respond easily to refutation of error by wise example or reasoned argument. At the same time, as the mirror held up to that infinitely differentiating thing called Nature, true poetic imagination finds itself fundamentally at odds with the current of procrustean thinking that prevails today. The "egregious" in the etymological sense of "standing out from the flock," the eccentric, the particular (as opposed to the generic), the strange, the mysterious—the things that constitute the very impulse of artistic creation—are precisely the things that the post-Marxian strain of "soft" ideological thinking abhors and conspires to eliminate by the process of praxis and progressive marginalization. Not surprisingly, then, genuine poetic art, the most effective means of countering the relentless and universal rape and truncation of language, finds itself increasingly marginalized, denied a significant audience and, consequently, rendered impotent.

Upon this flattened hyper-modernist landscape the art of Mickiewicz falls like something from a higher world. Mickiewicz's genius consists in his bringing to perfection a sublime Classical poetic style of utter simplicity. The hallmark of his poetic art is the *stark purity of his language*. With his Russian contemporary and friend Alexander Pushkin he shared that unique ability of packing powerful sentiment into the smallest compass (*multum in parvo*). We immediately recognize the same austere habit of mind, the same economy of expression and unerring sense of the native strength of the word. And yet here we have two distinct species of simplicity. If Pushkin's art achieves an effect of Mozartian 'lightness' and centrifugal 'amplitude' (Nikolai Gogol referred to the effect as an "abyss of space"), Mickiewicz's achieves the very opposite effect: a taut vigor and centripetal *gravitas* of the kind we find not in Mozart but in Beethoven and Tolstoy. Small wonder, then, that discerning modern poets in their preoccupation with stylistics have found in the poetic art of Mickiewicz material as profitable as that of Dante in their search for a common poetic idiom.

To its credit, the late modern era with its preoccupation with style and stylistics has done much to shed light on the "indivisibility" of the poetic utterance.[4]

---

4   See, for example, Yury Lotman's seminal study, *Analysis of the Poetic Text*, edited and translated by D. Barton Johnson (Ann Arbor: Ardis, 1976).

Like Pushkin's, though compassed by altogether different means, Mickiewicz's simplicity is great simplicity because it blurs the conventional distinction between the "form" and "content" of a poem. It constitutes an ideal dynamic fusion, a reciprocal straining of elements in which the form *becomes* the content and *vice versa*. While eminently capable of sublime poetical flights in which, as Davie puts it, "the prosaic statement is only a shaft of light through the foliage of metaphor" (and, in this sense, the Polish poet is much more like Shakespeare than Pushkin), Mickiewicz is equally capable of achieving effects that close the gap between poetry and prose in an incomparable generic synthesis. He is indeed the "poet of transformation," where the scope of the term encompasses not only the power of his protean imagination but also the very structures by which that imagination is expressed. All this contributes to the difficulty of classifying and fully appreciating his masterpiece *Pan Tadeusz*. With Mickiewicz, as Marshal McLuhan would have put it, the style is the "whole show"; the style *is* the poem. Thus, to expect from *Pan Tadeusz* a "realism" of the kind found in a conventional novel is to completely misapprehend the work and apt to disappoint the modern reader. Absent the subsuming dimension of its "style" (or "heterostylism," to use the term coined by the Russian critic Sergey Bocharov in his discussion of Pushkin's *Eugene Onegin*)[5] the reader of *Pan Tadeusz* is left with little more than a patriotic *cri de coeur* piggybacked on a sentimental tale of "a pair of star-crossed lovers." "The whole inflorescence," to use the poet's extended simile of the urchin blowing on a dandelion, "flies away like down on the wind, leaving behind in the hand of the fastidious observer a naked pedicel of grayish-green hue" (*PT*, Book III).

If nothing else, a fresh look at the art of Mickiewicz may give us occasion to pause and take stock of how far we have strayed from the notion and the reality of a genuine "common language." My overriding aim, then, has been to produce, within the limits and limitations of Standard English prose, a "close"[6] and readily readable translation of this still largely unknown masterpiece of European Romantic literature. In this, I am repeating what George Rappal Noyes sought to achieve in his almost century-old prose version of the poem.[7] That translation was never intended to be anything more than a bare, literal rendering of the original which might serve as a springboard for future, more creative experiments.

---

5   See Sergey Bocharov, "The Stylistic World of the Novel" in *Russian Views of "Eugene Onegin"* (Boomington and Indianapolis: Indiana University Press, 1988) 122-168.
6   See Walter Shrewing's use of the terms "close" and "free" in the epilogue to his admirable prose translation of *The Odyssey* (Oxford: Oxford World's Classics, 1998).
7   See George Rappal Noyes, *Pan Tadeusz* (New York: Everyman's Library, 1930).

My hope is that a new, more readable prose rendering will spur more translators[8] to undertake renderings of the Polish poem.

Needless to say, *Pan Tadeusz* ought, nay, *demands* to be translated into verse, this despite the formidable obstacle posed by the poem's having been written in a language with a phonology so foreign to that of English, or any other West European language for that matter. The fact that *Pan Tadeusz* is, fundamentally, an *epic* poem means that it shares that genre's characteristic fondness for genealogies and catalogues of personal and place names. The enterprising translator must therefore be prepared to contend with passages that, converted into English metrical form, cannot avoid stirring a veritable hornet's nest of dissonances. For, metric verse, be it rhymed, near-rhymed, or blank, *cries—qua* poetry—to be read aloud, and can only draw further untoward attention to the aural-visual dissonance of the myriad foreign names that obtrude themselves upon any translation of the Polish masterpiece.

It is of course too much to expect Mickiewicz's poetic art to attract translators in the Anglosphere to the extent that it has in Russia, for example, where translating the Polish poet became a kind of rite of passage. Pushkin, Kozlov, Viazemsky, Fet, Maikov, Bal'mont, Akhmatova, Khodasevich, Bunin and Nabokov all either translated, studied, or expressed deep admiration for Mickiewicz. But Donald Davie's sixty-year-old observation that Mickiewicz can be an unusually fruitful model, as timely and as apposite at home and abroad, still applies, and the aspiring English poet interested in perfecting his craft could do worse than to try his hand at rendering at least significant portions of *Pan Tadeusz*.

If Dostoevsky's dictum that "Beauty will save the world" holds true, then the poet still has a crucial role to play in the culture of our day. The degradation of cultural values and corruption of public morals resulting ultimately in the tragic loss of national sovereignty—circumstances that gave rise to Mickiewicz's masterpiece—resonate ominously with the distemper of our time. Finding herself already partially dismembered and on the brink of total collapse, the Polish-Lithuanian Commonwealth undertook sincere—alas, vain—efforts toward national renewal. Her Commission of National Education, the world's first ministry of education created by her Parliament and king in 1773, her Constitution of May Third, Europe's first and the world's second modern written national constitution adopted in 1791 (only three years after that of the United States), and the consequent erasing of a sovereign state from the political map of Europe are all matters of historical record.

---

8   For the most recent verse rendering of the Polish poem, see Bill Johnson's noble attempt, *Pan Tadeusz* (Brooklyn: Archipelago Press, 2018).

Can Western civilization yet muster the will and resolve to reach back into its authentic patrimony, recognize in it its salvific beauty, and achieve its own (*pace* J. R. R. Tolkien) "scouring of the Shire." Or will the poet's yearning for his then forfeited country, like Dante's for his beloved Florence, soon become the common lot of humanity?

Explanatory Notes

Explanatory notes are provided at the end of each of the poem's successive Books. Unless subsumed under my translator's note or, in the odd case, integrated into the poetic text, Mickiewicz's notes to *Pan Tadeusz* are indicated as "Author's note." The remaining notes are either my own or my more-or-less free adaptations of Dr. H. B. Segel's notes to Watson Kirkconnell's verse rendering (*Pan Tadeusz* [Toronto: University of Toronto Press, 1962]).

Extensive use is also made of Stanisław Pigoń's notes to the Ossolineum 1982 "Biblioteka Narodowa" edition of *Pan Tadeusz* as well as of the standard Mickiewicz concordances: *Słownik języka Adama Mickiewicza*, Wrocław 1962-1983, and *Słownik tematyczny języka poematu Adama Mickiewicza "Pan Tadeusz"* (http://nevmenandr.net/tadeusz).

A Note on the Poem's Title

Like *Don Quixote*, the title of the Polish masterpiece is best left untranslated. As an honorific title, Polish *pan* was traditionally reserved for hereditary noblemen and was roughly equivalent to "lord" or "sir" in English. In the nineteenth century it came to be used at all levels of society and may now be considered equivalent to the English "Mr." When prepended to the first name, the style suggests, as in Spanish, a genteel informality which stops short of the familiarity conveyed by the use of the given name alone. As to the Christian name *Tadeusz*, it is, like the name Jacek, very common in Poland even today. Apart from the eponymous hero, four Tadeuszes (Kościuszko, Rejtan, Korsak, and the chief steward) are introduced in the very first pages of the poem. Little is to be gained, and more lost, by englishing the name to the relatively uncommon Thaddeus.

A Note on the Polish Nobility

The term denoting the noble estate in Poland is *szlachta*. It has no precise counterpart in English, since the Poles made no distinction between nobility and gentry. "Every member of the *szlachta* was legally equal to any other: members addressed each other as 'brothers'; [in principle] no titles, such as lord or count, were allowed; any *szlachcic* could become a member of the Sejm [the Polish Parliament's Lower House] or even, at least in theory, be elected king. Only members of the *szlachta* were permitted to bear arms. Membership in this class was marked by possession of a coat of arms; the same coat of arms was often shared by several families, but unrelated people of the same family name could have different coats of arms" (Zdzisław Najder, *Joseph Conrad: A Chronicle* [New Brunswick: Rutgers University Press, 1984], 3).

In the historical period portrayed in *Pan Tadeusz*, the *szlachta* formed about a tenth of the population and was the only class to enjoy full political rights. Its members fell into several categories, from the great landowners or magnates, to smallholders and even landless squires serving as dependents in the households of the wealthy. While representatives of the upper nobility do appear in *Pan Tadeusz*, the poem deals mainly with the exploits of the petty provincial nobility, who represent, as it were, the collective hero of the epic. Thus, the present translation renders the term *szlachta* variously as "nobility," "minor nobility," "gentry," "petty gentry," "gentlefolk," "knighthood," and "squirearchy." The term *szlachcic* is rendered variously as "noble," "nobleman," "Polish lord," "knight," "squire," "born gentleman," or plain "gentleman."

A Note on Personal and Place Names

All Polish surnames in this rendering appear with their standard diacritic marks. Some common given names, such as *Zofia/Zosia*, Józef, *Maciej*, *Bartłomiej* have been anglicized to Sophia/Sophy, Joseph, Matthias, Bartholomew, etc. (The various diminutive forms are for the most part ignored.) Pronunciation tips have been provided only for the principal characters' names. These can be found in the notes in the order of the characters' appearance in the narrative. The rest of the names can be comfortably glossed over without serious impairment of the reader's pleasure. The few Russian personal names that occur have been transliterated directly from the Russian and do not appear in their Polish or polonized form (e.g. Suvorov not *Suworów*, Kozodushin not *Kozodusin*). For the most part, Lithuanian, Belorussian and Ukrainian place names are given in their Polish variant form with the contemporary toponym indicated in the note.

Christopher Adam Zakrzewski
Wilno, Ontario, Canada, 2024

List of Main Characters

PAN TADEUSZ (the eponymous hero; nephew of the Judge)

JUDGE SOPLICA (Tadeusz's uncle and younger brother of Jacek)

JACEK SOPLICA (the Judge's disgraced brother, nicknamed "Governor" and "Whiskers"; father of Tadeusz)

ROBAK (a Bernardine monk and alms quester)

THE PANTLER (Horeszko; the former holder of the disputed castle)

SOPHIA (Sophy; the Horeszko heiress; ward of Telimena)

TELIMENA (Sophy's guardian; a distant relation of the Judge; a notorious flirt)

THE CHIEF STEWARD (Tadeusz Hreczecha; kinsman of the Judge; skilled in the ancient art of knife-throwing)

THE WARDEN (Gervase Rębajłło; the last retainer of the Horeszko family; variously nicknamed "Old Boy," "Half Goat," and "Scarpate;" wielder of "Jackknife")

THE COURT USHER (Protase Balthazar Brzechalski; habitué of the hemp patch)

THE COUNT (a distant relative of the Horeszkos; an anglophile with quixotic leanings)

THE CHAMBERLAIN (president of the district boundary court)

THE NOTARY (Bolesta; nicknamed "Preacher"; owner of the greyhound Scut)

THE ASSESSOR (the acid-tongued owner of the greyhound Peregrine)

RYKOV (Captain Nikita Nikitich; an honest Russian soldier)

MAJOR PLUT (Rykov's superior officer; a renegade Pole)

JANKIEL (a Jewish innkeeper and Polish patriot; a maestro of first repute)

MATTHIAS (Dobrzyński; patriarch of the noble village of Dobrzyn; variously nicknamed "Weathercock," "Hipsmiter," "King Rabbit," and "Matthias of Matthiases"; wielder of "The Birch")

BAPTIZER (Bartholomew Dobrzyński; nicknamed *inter alia* "The Lithuanian Bear"; wielder of the battle club dubbed "The Sprinkler")

SACK, THE PRUSSIAN, WATERING CAN, RAZOR (all members of the Dobrzyński clan)

BUCHMAN (an estate manager from Kleck; weaver of sound political arguments and disciple of Jean Jacques Rousseau)

PAN TADEUSZ

Author's Note

In the time of the Polish-Lithuanian Commonwealth the execution of judicial decrees was not an easy undertaking in a country where the executive authorities had almost no police force at their disposal, and where powerful citizens kept household regiments, some of them, e.g. the Princes Radziwiłł, even armies of several thousand. So, the plaintiff who obtained a verdict in his favor had to apply for its execution to the knightly order, that is to the nobility (*szlachta*) with whom rested also the executive power. Armed kinsmen, friends, and neighbors set out, verdict in hand, in company with the court usher, and took possession, often not without bloodshed, of the goods adjudged to the plaintiff, which the usher legally made over or gave into his possession. Such an armed execution of a verdict was called a foray (*zajazd*). In ancient times, while laws were respected, even the most powerful magnates did not dare resist judicial decrees, armed attacks rarely took place, and violence almost never went unpunished. History records the sad end of Prince Dymitr Sanguszko and Stadnicki styled "The Devil." The corruption of public morals in the Commonwealth increased the number of forays, which continually upset the peace of Lithuania.

BOOK I

The Manor

___

Argument

The young master's return. A first encounter in a little room, a second at table. The Judge's weighty lesson on the polite arts. The Chamberlain's political reflections on fashion. Beginning of the dispute over Scut and Peregrine. The Chief Steward's lamentation. The last Court Usher. A glance at the political state of affairs in Lithuania and Europe of the time.

Lithuania! My homeland![1] You are like health—a precious gift, misprized until we lose you. Today I see your beauty and set it forth in all its radiant splendor, for I yearn for you.

O Blessed Maid, who safeguard the Bright Mount of Częstochowa! You who shine your golden light from Wilno's Ostra Gate! Protectress of Nowogródek and her pious citizens![2] In my boyhood, once, you healed me by a wondrous sign. My sobbing mother no sooner commended me to your care than I raised my lifeless eyelids and soon found myself able to walk unaided to your holy shrine where I offered my thanks to God. So, too, by a sign, shall you restore us to the bosom of our land.

Meanwhile, bear my yearning heart to those richly timbered hills, to those green meadows stretched far and wide along blue Niemen's banks. Bear it hence to that particolored patchwork of fields, daubed gold with wheat, silvered with rye, where the rape glows amber yellow, the buckwheat shimmers white as the snow, the clover mantles with a maidenly blush, and all this belted round by a green boundary strip where here and yon a solitary pear-tree stands.

Amid those fields, years ago, in a birchwood grove overlooking a small brook, there stood an all-timber manor house with cellars of solid stone. From a distance the lime-daubed walls shone the whiter against the dark-green backdrop of lombardy poplars that broke the autumn winds. The house, of modest dimensions, was spruce and trim. There was a mighty barn bursting with grain;

three surplus ricks towered beside it. Clearly, the region grew grain in super-abundance. From the sheer number of shocks that shone thick as stars across the length and breadth of the meadows, from the number of seasonable shares turning up the vast tracts of black loam left in fallow (all clearly belonging to the Manor and well-tended like garden plots)—from all this, you could tell that order and plenty made their dwelling here. The gate stood fastened back, a clear sign to passers-by that all were welcome, all received with open arms.

Even now a youth drove a single-pair britzka[3] through, made a turn about the courtyard, and backing up to the porch jumped out. Left unattended, the horses began to tug at the turf and strayed off in the direction of the gate. The house was deserted, the porch door locked—hasp fitted over the staple with a peg slipped through. Loath to run over to the servants' quarters and seek assistance, the traveler unfastened the door himself and burst inside. Great was his impatience to salute the house. He hadn't seen it for years, not since he'd left for the distant city to finish his schooling there; and now the long-awaited day had come.

Entering the house, he ran eager eyes over the dear old walls he knew so well. Before him hung the same furnishings, the same rich tapestries that had delighted him for as long as he could remember; true, they were smaller now, not quite as lovely as they'd seemed before. The same oils adorned the walls. Here stood Kościuszko[4] in his Cracow coat, sword raised in both hands, eyes upcast; such was the attitude he struck on the altar steps when he swore to drive the three great powers[5] from Polish soil, or fall on the point of his sword. Farther down sat Rejtan[6] in full Polish regalia, lamenting his nation's liberty, a dagger pressed against his breast; before him lay *Phaedo* and *Cato's Life*. Next: the handsome, sad-faced youth Jasiński[7] with his fast bosom friend Korsak[8] at his side. Knee-deep in bodies of slain Muscovites, they bestrode Praga's ramparts, hewing the foe while all around the city burned. Not even the old grandfather clock in the alcove escaped the youth's notice. With childish delight he pulled the cord to hear the chimes strike up the old Dąbrowski mazurka.[9]

On through the house he ran, seeking out the room he'd occupied as a boy ten years previous. On entering the chamber, he drew back; his astonished eyes swept the walls. Plainly, this was a woman's room! But whose could it be? His old uncle wasn't married, and his aunt had been away in Saint Petersburg for years. The housekeeper's? A housekeeper with a pianoforte! With music scores and books tossed over it in that careless manner? Happy disorder! Only tender hands could have tossed them so. Here, thrown over the arm of a chair, fresh off the peg, lay a white frock, all ready to put on. On the windowsills yonder stood fragrant potted plants—aster, geranium, violet, and gillyflower.

The youth drew up at one of the windows. A new marvel struck him there. Where stinging nettle had once run riot at the orchard's edge now stood a small path-sectioned garden, thick with clumps of mint and ribbon grass; around it ran a delicate cross-rail fence highlighted by borders of tremulous white daisies. The beds had just been sprinkled; yonder stood a full watering can. But where was the gardener? Clearly, she was here a moment ago; the gate-leaf, only recently nudged open, still swayed on its hinges. Nearby, distinctly visible in the snow-white, powdery sand, lay the shallow imprint of a dainty foot innocent of shoe and stocking. Light and nimble it must have been—a foot that scarcely grazed the ground.

Long stood the young traveler by the open window, gazing, musing, and breathing in the scent of the flowers. Turning yonder to where the violets grew, he ran curious eyes up and down the paths only to spy more footprints in the sand. Intrigued by these traces, he chanced to look up, and there, perched on the fence rails within hail of the house, stood a young girl in a white undergarment. The flimsy raiment covered her lissome frame from the bosom down, leaving bare her shoulders and swan-like neck. Seldom did maidens in Lithuania go about like this outside the early morning hours, and never with men present; even now, in the absence of spectators, the girl held her hands crossed over her bosom as if supplying the wanting veil. Her hair, the ringlets yet to be brushed out, was a mass of little knots folded into tiny white pods—a marvelous headdress, for it shone in the sun like the fiery nimbus enhaloing a sainted head.

Her face eluded the youth's eye; she stood with her back toward him, evidently seeking someone out in the fields far below. Descrying the party, she clapped her hands, burst out into a laugh, then alighting like a white bird from the fence fairly flew across the sward. Before the youth was aware of it, she'd threaded the rails, cleared the flowerbeds, darted up a plank that stood propped against the window ledge, and burst into the room—fleet, noiseless, radiant as a moonbeam! Trilling softly to herself, she seized her frock, ran to the mirror, and only then laid eyes on the lad. The frock fell from her hand; surprise and wonder drained her cheeks of hue. The traveler's face flamed red as when a cloud stands touched by the early morning glow. Half closing his eyes, covering them with his hand, the modest youth fumbled for a word of apology, then bowed and drew back. The girl gave out a faint, painful cry like a child startled in its sleep. The youth looked up in alarm, but she'd fled the room. Bewildered, his heart thumping in his chest, he made himself scarce, wondering if this strange encounter should cause him shame, amusement, or sheer delight.

Meanwhile, in the servants' quarters, the arrival of the new guest at the porch hadn't gone unnoticed. Even now the horses stood in the stable crunching on the ample portion of oats and hay that every decent country house provides. The Judge[10] wouldn't dream of boarding his guests' horses at the Jewish inn as was the fashion now. True, his servants hadn't run out to greet the caller, but it would be wrong to suppose they were lax in the discharge of their duties. They were waiting for the Chief Steward[11] to change his clothes after overseeing the banquet preparations at the rear of the house. As the Judge's kinsman and friend of the house, he stood in for the lord of the manor—to him fell the duty of greeting and minding the guests. Spying the new arrival, he stole back to the servants' quarters (he couldn't very well receive a caller in his homespun dust coat) and scrambled into the Sunday suit he'd laid out early that morning. Already then he knew he'd be dining in the evening with a large party of invited guests.

Recognizing the youth from a distance, the Steward flung out his arms with a cry and embraced him affectionately. Followed that rapid stream of muddled discourse in which the speakers strive to capture several years of events in a few disjointed words—scraps of narrative broken by queries, cries, sighs, then a fresh round of hugs. At last, satisfying his curiosity on many points, the Steward informed the lad of the day's events.

"Bravo, Tadeusz!"[12] he said. (They'd christened the boy after Kościuszko to honor the year of war in which he was born).[13] Bravo, Tadeusz! You could scarcely have timed it better, just when we have so many marriageable young damsels present. Your uncle has a mind to see you wedded soon, and we've girls aplenty! For days guests have been descending on us to hear the court settle our old boundary dispute with the Count. He'll be showing up at the manor tomorrow. The Chamberlain,[14] his wife and daughters have already arrived. Our youth are presently out for a leisurely shoot in the forest. The women and elders accompanied them as far as the neighboring field to inspect the harvest—they'll be waiting for the youngsters by now. Come, we'll walk down. Soon you shall see the Judge, the Chamberlain, the Chamberlain's wife, daughters, and the rest of the ladyships."

The Steward and Tadeusz took the road to the forest, chatting with insatiable gusto all the way. Meanwhile, the sun was nearing the end of his course across the heavens. Shining with less brilliance and shedding a broader beam, he glowed with the hale ruddiness of a plowman retiring home to his rest. The blazing disk settled over the forest. A dim mist arose, thickening limb and crown, merging the trees into a solid mass; the forest bulked black like a vast mansion with its roof set ablaze. At last, the sun sank below the tree-tops, flashed among the trunks like candlelight through a slatted shutter, and went out. The concert of sickles in the cornfields fell suddenly silent, the scraping of hay-rakes in the meadow ceased. Such were the Judge's orders: on his domain all fieldwork closed at sunset. "Our Creator knows best when to call it a day. When His toiler, the sun, retires from the sky, the farmer takes his cue and vacates the fields." So ran his maxim, and to the honest Bailiff the Judge's will was sacred. Even the wagons they were presently loading with rye returned to the barn half-filled, the oxen rejoicing in the unusual lightness of their load.

The entire company was returning from the forest. Despite their buoyant spirits, they went in orderly array. The children and their tutor led the train; the Judge and the Chamberlain's wife came next; beside them walked the Chamberlain and his family; the elders followed, and the young people brought up the rear—girls outpacing the lads by a half-step, as decorum demanded. No one compelled this observance of order, no oversight was needed. Men and women instinctively knew their place. The Judge clung to ancient custom. "Years, birth, rank, and wit should all receive their due regard," he was wont to opine. "All great races and nations observe order—without it families and nations die out." And so the rule of order came naturally to all the inmates of the manor. Relations, strangers or guests biding even briefly there soon fell in with the established practices of the house.

Brief was the Judge's greeting of his nephew: a solemn hand extended to his lips, a kiss planted on the lad's brow, a word of polite welcome. Constrained by the presence of the guests, he was sparing of words, but you could tell by the tear he swept away with the sleeve of his nobleman's robe that he held young Tadeusz in deep affection.

Forsaking harvest field, forest, mead, and pasturage, man and beast wended homeward together in the master's footsteps. A flock of bleating sheep ran squeezing into the lane, raising clouds of dust; behind them, brass bells clanking, ambled a herd of Tyrolean heifers; horses flew whinnying down from the freshly mown meadow—all made eagerly for the well where the wooden sweep, creaking non-stop, canted its bucket into the troughs, filling them to overflowing.

Though weary and busy with his guests, the Judge wasn't one to shirk the duties of the farm; he excused himself and made his own way down to the well. "No time like the evening for the farmer to inspect his stock," he was wont to say. He insisted on discharging the task himself, as 'nothing so fattened the colt as the master's eye.'

The Steward and the Court Usher[15] stood candle in hand at the manor door. They were at odds, having words. In the Steward's absence the Usher had ordered the banquet table removed and hastily installed inside the castle ruins which stood not far distant at the edge of the forest. Why the relocation! The Steward pulled a face and muttered his regrets. The Judge was stunned, but it was too late, the deed was done, past undoing—nothing for it but to extend their regrets to the guests and escort them to the ruins.

The Court Usher took full advantage of the opportunity to explain why he'd crossed his master's plans. The manor lacked room for so many honored guests, the castle hall was spacious, in good repair, the vault intact; true, there was a crack in one of the walls, no panes in the sashes, but this was summertime! The castle cellars were readily accessible . . . He prattled on, tipping winks to the Judge. You could tell by his look and mien that weightier reasons lurked in the back of his mind.

The castle, a splendid pile of imposing bulk, stood some two thousand paces back from the manor. It was the ancient seat of the Horeszko[16] family whose last heir had perished during the time of troubles.[17] State seizures, careless trustees, and awards of court had reduced the domain to rack and ruin. The bulk of the estate went into liquidation to pay off the numerous creditors; the residue fell to distant relations in the female line. No one cared to take the castle, the cost of its upkeep being more than the local gentry could afford. But then, having reached man's estate, the neighboring Count, a wealthy squire and distant relation of the Horeszkos, returned home from his travels abroad and took a fancy to the ancient pile. He made much of its Gothic architecture—no matter that the Judge produced papers to prove the builder was no Goth but a master builder from Wilno. His show of interest in the castle was all it took to set the Judge thinking along similar lines; no one knew why. Both laid claims at the district court.[18] The case went before the Senate. From there it worked its way back to the court then went before the Governor's Council; finally, after great expense and a dozen edicts, the case was remanded again to the boundary court.

The Court Usher was perfectly right. The castle had ample room for all the members of the bar and invited guests. Spacious as a refectory, its great hall had a high vaulted ceiling, sturdy pillars, a stone-flagged floor, and clean, spartanly appointed walls. Frontlets of stag and roebuck stood mounted all round with inscriptions recording where and when these trophies had been won; the hunters' names and arms stood carved into the wall directly below, and emblazoned across the ceiling, overarching all, stood the Half Goat, the Horeszko arms.

Entering the hall in orderly fashion, the party drew up in a circle around the table. The post of honor[19] rightfully belonged to the Chamberlain; it was the privilege of his office and senior years. Bowing in turn to the ladies, elders and youth, he advanced toward to the table; the Bernardine almsman[20] stationed himself beside him, the Judge next to the Bernardine. The Monk recited a brief benison in the Latin tongue, the men took vodka, whereupon they sat down one and all, and tucked silently into the beet-leaf soup, chilled Lithuanian-style.[21]

Despite his young years, the new guest was accorded a place at the head of the table along with the ladies and His Excellency the Chamberlain. The seat between his uncle and himself remained as yet unclaimed. The Judge kept glancing at it and at the door with an air of expectation. Tadeusz's eye followed his glances, darting now to the door, now back to the seat. Strange to relate! All around him sat a bevy of young demoiselles that no prince would have scorned, every one high-born and pretty; yet here was Tadeusz staring at an empty seat. The place was a puzzle, and youth delights in puzzles. Thus distracted, Tadeusz spoke barely a word to the Chamberlain's charming daughter seated next to him. Never once did he change her plate or charge her goblet, or seek to entertain the ladies with the courteous talk prescribed by table etiquette. The one empty seat in the hall held him spellbound; indeed, the seat was no longer empty, his thoughts had filled it; a thousand guesses thronged around it. Just so, in the aftermath of a cloudburst, the marsh frogs swarm over a solitary meadow. A lone figure holds sway among them, as when, on a calm day, the lily of the lake rears her pale brow above the waters.

The servants entered with the third course. Seizing the moment, the Chamberlain poured a finger of wine into Mistress Rose's glass and nudged a plate of salted cucumbers toward his youngest daughter.

"Alas, my dears" he remarked, "it is your old, fumble-fisted father who must wait on you." Instantly, several young men leapt up to serve them.

The Judge eyed Tadeusz askance. Adjusting the sleeves of his robe, he filled his cup with Hungarian wine and addressed the company:

"It's customary nowadays to send our youth to the capital to study. I don't deny that our sons and grandsons surpass their elders in book learning, yet I'm constantly given to observe how much they suffer from their lack of schooling in the domain of the polite arts. Time was when young noblemen went for periods of training in the courts of our great lords. I myself spent ten years as an attendant of the Royal Governor[22]—father of His Excellency the Chamberlain. (Here the Judge gave the Chamberlain's knee a squeeze.) It was he who groomed me for the public service and took such pains to make a man of me. My house shall always hold his memory dear. Every day I offer up a prayer for his soul. If I left his court to take up the tillage of our fields and profited less than others who stood worthier of the Governor's grace (they've since risen to our country's highest offices), at least no one here shall lay a lapse of courtesy or good manners to my charge. I say this without hesitation: courtesy's no easy art, nor is it of small account. Not easy, aye! for there's more to the art than giving a graceful leg or greeting all and sundry with a smile. Such fashionable manners may belong to the merchant class, but they are not the ways of Old Poland—or her nobility. Courtesy is owed to all," he went on. "Aye, but to each his own! A parent's love for his children is one form of courtesy, the husband's public regard for his spouse another, and the master's for his servant still another, yet each of these has its distinctive mark! Showing people their correct and due respect requires careful study. Not even our elders exempted themselves from this learning. Our great lords cultivated polite discourse as the living history of our land. The conversations of our landed gentry filled the pages of the county chronicle. Thus came our brother nobles to feel they were men of consequence, esteemed none too lightly; and so our nobility safeguarded their manners. Today you cannot ask, 'Who is he?' 'Of what parentage?' 'With whom has he lived?' 'What has he done?' So long as he's not a beggar or a government spy, he enters wherever he lists. As Emperor Vespasian cared little for the smell of his coinage or the hand or land it came from,[23] so no one troubles to take stock of a man's birth and manners. Enough that he have the heft and stamp of hard currency;[24] and so we value our friends as our Hebrew values his money."

While opining thus, the Judge eyed each of the guests in turn. Though he spoke with ease and made eminent sense, he knew today's youth were impatient and easily bored by long speeches, however eloquent; but the youth were all attention. He paused and glanced inquiringly at the Chamberlain who had been nodding quiet assent all along. The pause elicited another nod from the Chamberlain, whereupon the Judge charged both their cups, and spoke on.

"Now courtesy's no trifling matter. When a man learns correctly to value the years, the noble birth, the qualities and manners of his fellows, he comes to know his own importance. To gauge his weight, a nobleman must balance it against the recognized weight of another! But even more deserving of your attention, gentlemen, is the courtesy a young man owes the fairer sex, the more so, when substance and a noble house enhance her natural grace and merits. This is the path to the heart's affections. It paves the way to splendid alliances. So thought our elders, and yet—"

The Judge broke off; and turning to his nephew, he nodded sharply and fired him a stern glance; clearly, he'd come to the point.

The Chamberlain tapped his gilded snuffbox. "Come now, Judge," he said. "In former times things were worse. Presently, I'm not sure if the fashion isn't changing even us elders. Nor can I say our youth are better, but I see less scandal now. Oh, I recall when the mania for all things French first greeted our land. Fashionable young men fell upon us from abroad in a horde worse than the Nogai Tatars. They reviled our Creator, the beliefs of our forebears, our laws, our customs, and even our time-honored garments. What a sorry sight they were! Sallow-faced puppies drawling through their noses—often without noses!—brandishing all kinds of pamphlets and gazettes and espousing new-fangled religions, laws, and modes of dress. That horde held our minds captive, for when God sends chastisement down on a nation, he first robs its citizens of their reason. And so the wiser heads among us lacked the nerve to cross those fops; the whole country feared them like the plague, as now everyone felt the contagion's lurking germ. We inveighed against those dandies, yet we aped them nonetheless. We changed our religion, our manner of speech, our laws, our dress. A masquerade! A carnival of license, swift on the heels of which came the season of Lent—bondage![25]

"Though I was a mere lad then, I remember the Cupbearer's son fetching up in a French carriage before my father's house in Oszmiana district. He was the first in Lithuania to parade himself in the Frenchman's garb. Our people swarmed after him like swallows after a buzzard.[26] Envied the house in front of which his two-wheeled conveyance (*cabriolet* is the French word for it) stood parked! A pair of dogs sat on the trunk where the footmen normally sit, and on the boxseat towered a bizarre oddity of a German coachman—gaunt as a ghost, with long, thin shanks like hop-poles. He wore silk stockings, low shoes with silver buckles, and his queue hung encased in a bag.

"The sight of this equipage sent the elders into hoots of laughter. Our rustics blessed themselves, swearing a Venetian devil was abroad in an outlandish coach. The Cupbearer's appearance requires a story of its own. Enough to say he put us in mind of an ape or a parrot in a monstrous peruke wig, which he likened to the Golden Fleece and we to a plain case of the elflock.[27] Even if we thought our Polish apparel better than aping foreign fashions, we kept mum, for our youngsters would have decried us as enemies of culture, impediments to progress, and traitors to our land. Such was the sway of prejudice at the time.

"The Cupbearer's son declared his aim to refine our ways, to reform our system of rule, and bring in a constitution. Eloquent Frenchmen, he declared, had discovered that all men were born equal. Now hasn't Holy Writ always taught this? Doesn't every parish priest prate of it from the pulpit? The doctrine's old, its application, aye, there's the rub! But so befogged and beguiled were we then that we set no store by the older things of the world unless a French gazette should comment on them. For all his talk of equality, the Cupbearer's son took the title of marquis. Titles, as you know, originate in Paris, and marquisates were all in vogue. But fashion changed, and our marquis promptly became a democrat. When, under Bonaparte, the winds of fashion shifted again, our democrat returned from Paris a baron. Had he lived another year, the baron would doubtless have re-espoused the democratic cause. Paris prides herself on her frequent about-faces of fashion, and whatever France thinks up is sure to appeal to us Poles.

"Thank God that now when our youth go abroad, it's no longer to shop for fashionable clothes, or poke around printers' booths for new laws, or learn the art of speech in the coffeehouses of Paris. Now they've got Bonaparte, a clever, energetic man with no time for fashions and idle talk. Today we hear the roar of ordnance! Our old hearts swell with pride that our countrymen should again be the talk of the world. Our glory shines, and so our Commonwealth shall rise again! The noble laurel ever begets the tree of liberty! Yet alas that we should have to sit idle so long, and our boys always so far away. The waiting's long—even news is scarce. (Here, lowering his voice, he turned to the Bernardine monk.) Father Robak! I hear you bear news from across the Niemen. What of our troops?"

"No news. None!" said the Monk with a careless air; plainly, the talk unsettled him. "Politics bores me. The letter from Warsaw concerns our congregation's business. Bernardine matter! No need to discuss it at the table! It's of no interest to the laity."

Saying this, he glanced sidelong down the table at their Muscovite guest. The guest, whom the Judge had invited out of courtesy, was Captain Rykov, a seasoned old campaigner quartered in the neighboring village. Until now he had been eating heartily and taken little part in the talk, but at the mention of Warsaw he looked up.

"Ah, Chamberlain!" he said. "Always curious about Bonaparte. Mind always set on Warsaw![28] The Fatherland, eh? Rykov's no spy, though he speaks your Polish tongue. The Fatherland! I know these sentiments, understand them well. You Poles, we Russkies, eh? Right now we're not at war. We observe an armistice. We eat and sup together while our boys at the advance posts knock back vodkas and chum with the French. But when the huzzah breaks forth, get ready for a cannonade! We Muscovites have a saying, 'Love the one you love to thump. Clasp your crony close then dust him good and proper like an overcoat.'

"I say there will be war," he went on. "Just the other day, the staff adjutant called on Major Plut. 'Prepare to march,' says he. On Turkey, France, it's all the same. But Boney's a rare bird all right. With our Suvorov[29] gone, he may trounce us yet. When our troops marched on the French, word went out Napoleon had magic.[30] But Suvorov knew the black arts too, so it was spell against spell! On the battlefield once, we look around—where's Bonaparte! He'd turned himself into a fox. So Suvorov turns into a hound. Boney shifts shape again; now he's a cat, starts slashing with his claws, and presto! Suvorov's a racehorse. And what does Bonaparte do? . . ."

Here Rykov broke off and resumed eating.

A servant had just entered with the fourth course; at the same time, the side door swung open and a comely new guest swept in. Her sudden entrance, her carriage, beauty, and attire drew everyone's gaze. Everybody greeted her; clearly, all except Tadeusz stood acquainted with her. Svelte and charmingly endowed, she wore a low-cut frock of rose-colored satin with short sleeves and a thread-lace collar. In her hand was a gilded fan—a plaything to fiddle with, as it wasn't hot; when she whirred it, the bauble scattered a rich shower of sparks. Ornately coiffured, she wore her hair up in a cluster of ringlets interlaced with pink ribbons and a discreetly buried diamond peeping through like a star in the comet's tress. In a word: gala dress! All just too-too, muttered some, for a weekday in the country. Though her frock was short, her foot eluded the eye. She moved swiftly, or rather she glided along like the Twelfth Night puppets that little boys concealed in the booth slide across the stage.

Greeting the guests with a slight bow, she made for the seat reserved for her. Easier thought than done, for there was a general shortage of chairs. The guests were seated on four rows of benches at right angles to each other; either a whole row must move or she must climb over the bench. But she managed skillfully to squeeze in between two benches; then, gliding like a billiard ball around the table, cleared the corridor made for her by the guests. As she swept past Tadeusz, she caught her flounce on a protruding knee, stumbled and inadvertently steadied herself on the youth's shoulder. Begging his pardon, she plumped herself down between the youth and his uncle. But she ate nothing; she merely sat there, waving her fan, now twirling it by the stem, now smoothing her collar of Flemish lace, now running her hand lightly over her ringlets and knots of lustrous ribbons.

After a lapse of four minutes, talk resumed again, this time at the far end of the table, first in an undertone then loud enough to be heard. The men were discussing the day's hare course. A fierce, increasingly boisterous quarrel broke out between the Notary and the Assessor[31] over the former's bobbed greyhound. Passionately proud of his beast, the Notary insisted his Scut had brought the quarry to book. To spite him, the Assessor claimed the honor for his hound Peregrine. They appealed to the others; soon all were taking sides, some championing Scut, others Peregrine, some claiming to be experts, others eyewitnesses.

Meanwhile, at the opposite end of the table, the Judge whispered to his new neighbor: "My apologies, dear, we had to sit down. It was impossible to put off supper till later. The guests were hungry after our ramble in the fields. I thought you mightn't be dining with us tonight."

At this the Judge turned to the Chamberlain, and the two launched into a quiet political discussion over a full winecup.

With both ends of the table thus engaged, Tadeusz took leisure to study the stranger seated beside him. He'd suspected whose seat it was the instant he laid eyes on it. He felt the blood mount in his cheeks; his heart beat with unwonted vigor. So! the puzzle stood solved. Fate had ordained that the woman sitting next to him should be the very beauty he'd glimpsed in the twilight. True, now that she was dressed, she seemed somewhat taller (clothes have a way of enhancing or diminishing one's height). Her hair, it now appeared, was long and raven-black, not short and blonde; doubtless, the setting sun's rays and the reddish hue they imparted had caused him think so. He hadn't caught the gardener's face; she'd fled his gaze too swiftly. But the mind is apt to divine a lovely face. He'd imagined her with dark eyes, a cherry-red mouth, and a light-skin complexion; this one's eyes, mouth and face matched his image perfectly. Where the two appeared to differ most was in their age: the one in the garden had seemed a mere girl, while here was a woman of mature years. But youth is loath to probe into Beauty's birth certificate. To the eyes of a youth every demoiselle is young, every beauty his equal in years; to an innocent lad every sweetheart's a tender maiden.

Although Tadeusz was just shy of twenty years old and grew up in the great city of Wilno, he'd been entrusted to the charge of a priest who raised him in the stern rules of old-fashioned virtue, and so while Tadeusz brought home with him a pure soul, a lively mind, and an upright heart, there was also active within him a strong yen to break loose. Even before leaving the city, he'd vowed to taste the long-denied freedoms of country life. He was aware of his handsome looks, his youth and vigor. He came by his robust health honestly; after all, he was a Soplica,[32] and everyone knew the Soplicas were a strong and sturdy breed, apt at soldiering—less so at book learning.

Tadeusz brought no disgrace upon his ancestors. He rode ably, walked with a stout stride, and though he'd made but modest progress in his studies (the Judge having spared nothing for the boy's education), he was far from dull-witted. Shooting a gun and handling a saber were more in his line. He knew he was going for a soldier; such was his father's instruction in his will. And so all through school he'd yearned for the soldier's drum. But then, his uncle took a new mind. He recalled him home with plans for marriage and handing down the estate, first a small hamlet, then the rest of the domain.

None of these gifts and qualities escaped the observant eye of Tadeusz's companion at table. Taking due note of his tall, handsome build, his burly shoulders and ample chest, she proceeded to study his face, which flushed with lively animation each time his eyes met hers. By now he'd fully recovered from his initial shyness and was staring back at her with a bold, ardent eye. She returned his stare. Two pairs of eyes blazed opposite one another like *rorate* candles.[33]

She struck up a conversation with him—in French at first. Seeing as the lad had been at school in the city, she sought out his views on new books and authors. His replies elicited fresh queries, but then she launched into painting, music, dance—sculpture, even! Paintbrush, music score, printed page—she was equally at home with them all. Her show of learning rendered Tadeusz speechless. Terrified of being made an object of ridicule, he stammered out his answers like a schoolboy before his master. Happily, the master was pretty and lenient. Guessing the cause of his dismay, she turned to less taxing, less erudite matters— rural living, its tedium and bothers. She spoke of its diversions, of apportioning one's time so as to sweeten life in the country and render it more pleasurable.

Tadeusz's replies became increasingly bolder; before long, the pair were fast friends, partaking even in squabbles and jokes. Rolling three bread pills between her fingers, she placed them on the table before him: he must choose between three parties. He chose the nearest, whereupon the Chamberlain's two daughters signaled their displeasure with a frown. Tadeusz's partner chuckled, but refrained from naming the lucky pill.[34]

Meanwhile, the far end of the table was engaged in other games. Peregrine's champions had suddenly grown in strength and were mounting a furious assault on the Scuts. The contest ran high, the last courses stood untasted; both factions were up on their feet, shouting and draining their cups. By far the most impassioned among them was the Notary Bolesta. Given the floor, he went on like a millrace, gracing his speech with expressive gestures. He'd served on the bar where his habit of extravagant gesticulation earned him the nickname "Preacher." Just now he was concluding his account, his arms pulled in, elbows thrust back, two long-nailed index fingers representing the greyhounds' leads pointing forward:

"See-ho! Together we, the Assessor and I, slip our leashes like the hammers of a double released at the squeeze of the trigger. See-ho! They're off! The hare makes a sprint for the field, the hounds right on her bob. (The Notary ran his hands along the table, uncannily mimicking the dogs' movements with his fingers.) Right on her bob! In a trice, they head her from the forest. Then whoosh! Peregrine puts on speed. Aye, he's a fleet one, though hotheaded; he leads Scut by so much—by a whisker! But I knew he'd muff it. Rare game, our puss![35] She makes as if straight for the field, the hounds fast on her traces. Crafty puss! She no sooner senses the pack bunching up behind her than zip! she jinks to the right and turns a somersault. The fool dogs swerve to the right after her, but then after just two bounds, lickety-split! she jinks to the left and the dogs veer left after her. Now she's making her point to the forest—and that's when my Scut goes WHAP!"

Here, leaning over, the Notary ran his fingers to the other side of the table and roared "WHAP!" right above Tadeusz's ear. The outburst caught Tadeusz and his partner in the midst of a cozy *tête-à-tête*. Instinctively, their heads drew back like the crowns of close-set trees sundered by a gust of wind; a pair of hands lying close together under the table flew apart, and two faces broke out into a single blush.

Tadeusz strove to hide his distraction. "No doubt you are right, Mr. Notary," he said. "Your bobbed one's a handsome beast, no disputing. If he should be equally good at seizing his—"

"Good at seizing!?" bridled Bolesta. "My prize hound not good at seizing?"

Again Tadeusz expressed delight that such a handsome beast should be accounted faultless in every respect, but he'd only seen it when returning from the forest and scarcely had time to judge all its qualities.

Here the Assessor, trembling with indignation, dropped his cup from his hand and pierced the youth with a basilisk glance. Though shorter than Bolesta, of slighter build and less given to vociferating and gesturing, he was the awe of every ball, masquerade party, and regional diet. People said he had a sting in his tongue and could deliver witty jests worthy of citation in the almanac, all of them barbed and malicious. Formerly a man of wealth, he'd squandered away both his father's inheritance and his brother's fortune by cutting a figure in high society. Now he'd entered the government service to gain standing in the local county. He was immensely fond of the hunt, both for the sheer sport of it and because the peal of the horn and the sight of a ring of beaters recalled the days of his youth when he'd employed scores of hunters and kept a kennel of first-rate hounds. Of those hounds only two remained, and the reputation of one of these was now in question. And so, leaning over toward Tadeusz, slowly stroking his side-whiskers, he observed with a smile— a smile dripping with venom:

"A bobbed greyhound is like a nobleman lacking a berth. A tail, apart from its other assets, gives the hound a clear edge on speed, and you, sir, take its absence for a virtue! But why not put the case to your auntie? Though Mistress Telimena lives in the capital and only recently bides in our parts, I daresay she knows more about the course than the callow sportsman, for knowledge comes with years!"

Scarcely expecting such a thunderbolt, Tadeusz rose in dismay. For a moment he stood speechless, glaring at his rival with an eye that grew increasingly more grim and ominous. Fortunately, the Chamberlain chose this very moment to sneeze twice.

"*Vivat!*" they cried in a chorus.

Bowing to the guests, His Excellency beat a slow tattoo on his snuffbox. The article was wrought of gold and set with diamonds around a miniature of King Stanislas.[36] It had been His Majesty's personal gift to the Chamberlain's father, and now the son bore it proudly. A rap on the lid signaled his desire to address the company. The guests fell silent, all ears.

"Esteemed gentlemen! Brother nobles!" he said. "The field, the forest—these are the hunter's proving grounds. Such matters I do not decide indoors, and so I shall defer our session until tomorrow. No further rejoinders today! Mr. Usher, declare the case adjourned to the fields where the Count and his entire hunting party have agreed to join us. And you, my dear Judge and neighbor, shall ride with us, as will Mistress Telimena and the rest of our company. In a word, we'll organize a splendid day of sport as befits the occasion. Nor shall our good Steward deny us his companionship!" Saying which, he had his snuffbox passed down to the Steward.

The Steward, who sat with the hunters, had been listening in silence, squinting his eyes, resisting the efforts of the youth to draw him into the conversation, he being the most experienced hunter in the district. Long he held his peace, musing over the pinch of snuff in his fingers. At last, drawing the grains into his nostrils and sneezing with such violence as to send echoes reverberating through the hall, he shook his head and smiled a rueful smile.

"Ah!" he said. "How this saddens and astonishes an old gaffer like me. What would *our* hunters have said on seeing so large an assembly of lords and nobles having to adjudicate on a greyhound's stern? What would old Rejtan say, if he were raised to life? Why, he'd slink right back to his grave in Lachowicze! And what of old Niesiołowski?[37] Aye, the Governor—owner of the world's finest bloodhounds. Two hundred gunners and a hundred cartloads of nets he used to keep in the grand lordly fashion at his castle in Worończa! All these years he remains closeted in his hall like an anchorite, and no one's yet enticed him out for a hunt. Why, he even refused Białopiotrowicz himself![38] But what quarry would he be hunting on your expeditions, gentlemen? Some glory for a man of his stature to go haring after a jackrabbit as they do nowadays. In the sportsman's lingo of my day, it was the wild boar, the bear, the wolf and the elk that passed for noble game. A beast innocent of tusk, horn, or claw fell to the paid servant or manorial flunkey! No self-respecting nobleman took into his hand a gun bearing the indignity of firing small shot. True, they kept their hounds on hand in the event that on the way home they should spring a hapless hare from its covert; then, for mere amusement, they'd slip the leashes and watch the youngsters urge their hobbies after it, though, in truth, even then they scarcely bothered to watch much less argue over a hound. So, Your Excellency, pray revoke your command. Forgive me, but I cannot hunt this way. Never shall I take part in it! Hreczecha's my name, and no Hreczecha since the days of King Lech[39] ever went chasing after a hare . . ."

The young people's laughter drowned out the rest of his discourse. Meanwhile, the party was rising from the table. The Chamberlain was the first to leave; it was the privilege of his post and senior years. Bowing in turn to the ladies, the elders and youth, he made for the door. The Bernardine and the Judge went next. On reaching the door, the Judge offered his arm to the Chamberlain's wife; Tadeusz linked arms with Telimena; the Assessor followed suit with the Carver's daughter; and last went the Notary with the Steward's daughter.

Bewildered, angry, and dejected, Tadeusz walked to the barn with several of the guests. He was at pains to sort out the evening's events—the encounter at the house and dinner with his companion at table. Especially galling to him was the word 'auntie,' which buzzed in his ear like an irritating fly. He had wanted to learn more about Telimena from the Court Usher, but he hadn't been able to catch him. Nor had he seen the Steward, for directly after supper the domestic staff had followed the guests to the manor to prepare their night quarters. The women and the elders were sleeping in the house; the young men would bed down in the barn, and upon Tadeusz the host had enjoined the task of escorting them there.

Within a half-hour there had fallen over the entire Manor a hush as deep as when the cloister stands gathered for compline prayer. Only the night watchman's voice broke the silence. All slept. Meanwhile, the Judge burned the midnight oil, laying plans for the hare course and the breakfast to follow. Instructions went out to the overseers, foremen, farmhands, clerks, bailiff-mistress, shooters, and grooms. At last, after running his eye over the day's accounts, the Judge gave the Court Usher leave to undress him.

Protase unfastened his belt. It was a true nobleman's waist-sash, crafted in Słuck,[40] woven from strands of gold and hung with gleaming tassels, thick as helmet plumes. One side had a lining of gold brocade with purple flower designs, the reverse was lined with black satin stamped with silver checkers. The belt could be worn on either side, gold on gala days, black in seasons of mourning. None but Protase knew how to unfasten and fold the belt, and he was performing this very office as he closed his argument:

"So yes," he said, "I removed the tables to the castle. Show me the harm done. No one suffered as a result, and you may even profit by it. The whole case revolves around the castle. Now legal title is vested in us, and despite the strong contentions of the other side I aim to prove it. Whoever invites his guests to dine with him at the castle proves he holds possession there—or takes it! We'll even serve writs on the opposition to appear as witnesses. I recall similar cases in my day. . ."

But the Judge was now sound asleep. The Usher tiptoed into the hallway. Taking a seat beside a candle, he reached into his pocket and drew out a small notebook.

The article was a court calendar;[41] it served him like the daily missal[42]—at home or away, he was never without it. Recorded there were all the actions he'd called before the bench and many others he'd learned of later. To the layman, the calendar consisted of stark columns of names; to the Court Usher it conjured up a series of magnificent pictures. And so, leafing through the pages, he fell to reminiscing: Ogiński versus Wizgird; the Black Friars v. Rymsza; Rymsza v. Wysogird; Radziwiłł v. Mme. Wereszczaka; Giedrojć v. Rdułtowski; Obuchowicz v. the Jewish Kahal; Juracha v. Piotrowski; Maleski v. Mickiewicz; and, last, the Count v. Soplica. As he scanned the names, he recalled to mind the famous cases and the circumstances attending them. The court, the disputants and witnesses passed before his eyes. He saw himself attired in his white tunic and navy-blue robe, one hand resting on his saber, the other beckoning to the parties to approach the bench. "Come to order!" he bawled; and so he mused on. At length, after saying his night prayers, the last of Lithuania's court ushers nodded off to sleep.

Such were the sport and contests in Lithuania's rustic purlieus when the rest of the world foundered in a welter of blood and tears; when, compassed by a cloud of regiments, armed with field pieces innumerable, that Great One, that martial god, yoked both gold and silver eagles[43] to his war-car and winged his way from the Libyan sands to the lofty Alps, raining bolt after bolt upon the Pyramids, Tabor, Marengo, Ulm, and Austerlitz.[44] Victory was his van. Conquest his rear. Glory, swelling with countless deeds of valor, great with heroes' names, thundered northward from the Nile until, reaching Niemen's banks, she dashed herself like a wave on the rock of Moscow's host, a rampart of steel guarding Lithuania against tidings that Moscow feared like a pestilence.

And yet ever and anon, like a stone dropped from heaven, news came even to Lithuania. An old beggar lacking an arm or leg would appear at the door for a crust of bread. On receiving his alms, he'd cast wary glances around the courtyard. Once assured the place was clear of Russian soldiers, Jewish skullcaps, and scarlet collars, he made himself known: a legionary dragging his old bones back to his native soil which he could no longer defend. How the entire household, servants and all, choked back their tears and fell about his neck! Seated at the kitchen table, he related events far more wondrous than anything in a fairytale: of Dąbrowski[45] enlisting Poles in the Lombard plains and his attempts to reach Poland from Italy; of the victorious Kniaziewicz[46] issuing orders from the Capitol and the hundred bloody flags he'd seized from Caesar's scions then cast at the feet of the French; of Jabłonowski[47] and his Danube Legion venturing forth to exotic climes where the pepper was reared, sugar refined, and where, amid fragrant groves in the flourish of eternal spring, he rained destruction on the native folk and pined for home.

The old campaigner's tales would spread quietly through the countryside. A young lad who heard them suddenly vanished from his home. Pursued by the Muscovites, he beat a stealthy path through wood and slough, then plunging into the Niemen swam submerged to the other side—to the old Crown's banks where a friendly, 'Welcome, mate!' was sure to greet his ears. Only after scaling a rock and calling out, "Till we meet again!" to the Muscovite on the other side, would he walk away. Gorecki made it across. So did Patz, Obuchowicz, Piotrowski, Obolewski, Kupść, Rożycki, Janowicz, Brochocki, Gedymin, the brothers Bernatowicz, the Mierzejewski, and many others. They forsook their kin, their beloved land, and all their worldly goods, which the Tsarist treasury promptly seized and consigned to her coffers.

From time to time an alms quester arrived from a distant abbey. Upon acquainting himself with the manor holders, he would pull out the gazette he'd stuffed into the lining of his scapulary. Recorded in it were the muster and nominal rolls of every legion along with an account of the heroic feats or tragic death of each of the officers. And so, after many years, a family had first news of the life, glorious deeds and death of their son, and the whole house went into mourning. Whom they mourned, they shied from saying; the neighborhood could only guess. Silent sorrow or quiet expressions of joy were the gentry's only means of spreading the news.

Now it appeared that Robak was one such mysterious almsman. Not seldom was he seen holding private converse with the Judge. After each such meeting a fresh piece of news made the round of the district. Judging by his outward appearance, he hadn't always gone about in a hooded habit or spent his years within cloistered walls. From a point between his right ear and temple, the cicatrice of a cut traveled a handbreadth across the dome of his skull, and his chin bore the fresh wound of a grazing ball or lance; clearly, he hadn't won these from reading the sacramentary. Nor was it just the stern gaze and the scars; the very way he carried himself and his manner of address bespoke a martial air. At the Mass when with upraised arms he turned from the altar to the people, to say, "*Pax vobiscum!*"[48] he performed the action so smartly, so seamlessly, you'd swear he was executing a 'right about face' at the captain's command. He barked out the words of the liturgy in the tone of an officer addressing his squadron; so, at least, remarked the boys who served him at the Mass (indeed, he seemed far better versed in political affairs than in the lives of the saints). While questing for alms, he often tarried in the district town where he had a string of errands to run. Sometimes, he received letters, but he never opened them with strangers present. Sometimes, he dispatched messengers, but where he sent them and why, he wouldn't say. Often, he'd steal away at night to visit the manor holders.

He conferred endlessly with the gentry, paid frequent calls on the neighboring hamlets, and stopped by the taverns to chat with the rustics; invariably he spoke of events abroad.

So now, the Judge, who'd been asleep for an hour, was the object of such a visit; clearly, the Bernardine had news to impart.

NOTES

1. That Poland's great epic poem should open with an apostrophe to Lithuania has troubled readers since the day of its first publication in 1834. But Mickiewicz never changed this regional term; it expressed his strong sense of local patriotism. Mickiewicz was a posthumous child of the old Polish-Lithuanian Commonwealth whose final collapse and dismemberment occurred three years before his birth with the Third Partition of Poland (1795). The Grand Duchy of Lithuania, joined dynastically with the Crown of the Kingdom of Poland since 1385, and politically since 1569, included the ethnic territory of Lithuania proper as well as large parts of what is now Belarus, where in fact the Polish poet was born.

2. The references are to the wonder-working images of Our Lady of Jasna Góra in Częstochowa, Poland; Our Lady of Ostra Brama in Wilno (Vilnius), Lithuania; and Our Lady of Nowogródek (now Novogrudak) in Belarus. In his notes the poet also mentions the images at Żyrowiec (Zhirovichi) and Boruny.

3. A britzka (bryczka) was a long horse-drawn carriage with a folding top over the rear seat and a rear-facing front seat.

4. Tadeusz Kościuszko (pronounce: Kosh-_choosh_-ko) (1746-1817), Poland's most revered national hero. In 1776 he left Poland for North America where he took part in the American Revolutionary War as a colonel in the Continental Army. He won distinction in the defense of Saratoga and saw further service with the army of the South. Returning to Poland in 1784, he served as a general in the war of 1792 and led the insurrection against the Russians in 1794. After the failure of the insurrection, he was imprisoned in St. Petersburg until released by Emperor Paul who acceded to the throne of Russia after the death in 1796 of his mother, Catherine II. Kościuszko returned to the United States in 1797 but left when news of the formation of the Polish Legions at the side of the French reached him. From 1798-1801 he was in residence in Paris. Both Napoleon and Alexander I of Russia sought his services, but he resisted their attempts and played no direct role in the Napoleonic wars. In 1815, he appeared before the Congress of Vienna to plead Poland's cause, but his efforts to secure an honorable Polish settlement were doomed to failure. On October 15, 1817, he died in Soleure, Switzerland, where he had taken up residence. His remains now rest in the Cathedral of the Wawel in the ancient Polish capital of Kraków amongst Poland's kings and her greatest poets. The "Cracow coat" worn by Kościuszko (referred to as a czamara) was actually a sukmana, the white caftan of the common folk of the Kraków region.

5. Russia, Prussia and Austria, the partitioning powers of the Polish-Lithuanian State.

6. Tadeusz Rejtan (pronounce: _Rey_-tahn) (1742-1780); a participant in the Confederacy of Bar (1768-1772) and delegate to the Parliament of 1773, where he distinguished himself by his vigorous protest against the first partition of Poland. Later he fell into despair over the disasters that had befallen his nation and took his life by swallowing shards of crushed glass.

7. Jakub Jasiński (1759-1794), a soldier and poet who served as a colonel of engineers in the Russo-Polish war of 1792. He organized the insurrection in Lithuania and seized the city of Wilno. He was killed during the siege of Praga, a suburb of Warsaw.

8. Tadeusz Korsak (1741-1794); a deputy to the so-called Four-Year Parliament and a leader in Kościuszko's insurrection. He perished with Jasiński on Praga's ramparts during the siege of Warsaw.

9. Pronounce: Dom-*brof*-ski. Composed by Józef Wybicki in 1791, the piece was originally the song of the Polish legions in Italy under General Dąbrowski. A mazurka is a lively Polish dance originating from Poland's Mazovian Province. See also note 26 to Book XII.

10. [*Author's note*] The Tsarist government in conquered countries never overthrows their laws and civil institutions at once, but by its edicts it slowly undermines and saps them of their vigor. For example, in Little Russia [the parts of the Commonwealth annexed by Russia in the first partition of Poland—C. Z.] the Lithuanian Statute, modified by edicts, was maintained until recent times. Lithuania was allowed to retain her ancient organization of civil and criminal courts. So, as of old, rural and town judges are elected in the districts, and superior judges in the counties. But since there is an appeal to St. Petersburg, to many institutions of various standing, the local courts are left with but a shadow of their former dignity.

11. [*Author's note*] The chief steward or major-domo (*wojski*) was once an officer (*tribunus*) charged with the protection of the wives and children of the nobility during the time of service of the general militia. But this office without duties has long since become purely titular. In Lithuania, there is a courteous custom of bestowing on respected persons some ancient title, which becomes legalized by usage. For instance, the neighbors may call one of their friends quartermaster, pantler, or cupbearer, at first only in conversation and in correspondence, but later even in official documents. The Tsarist government has forbidden such titles, and would make mock of them, introducing in their place the system of titles based on the ranks of its own hierarchy, for which the Lithuanians still have great repugnance.

12. Pronounce: Tah-*deh*-oosh.

13 This would mean that Tadeusz was born in 1794, the year of Kościuszko's insurrection.

14. [*Author's note*] Under the Tsarist government, the chamberlain (*podkomorzy*), once a noted and dignified official (*princeps nobilitatis*), has become merely a titular dignitary. Formerly, he was still judge of boundary disputes, but he finally lost even that part of his jurisdiction. Now he occasionally takes the place of the marshal (*marszałek*) and appoints the district surveyors (*komornicy*).

15. [*Author's note*] The court usher (*woźny trybunalski*) or sergeant-at-arms (*generalis ministerialis*), chosen from among the landed gentry by the decree of a tribunal or court, executed writs, proclaimed persons to legal possession of property adjudged to them, launched inquests, called cases on the court's calendar, etc. Usually this office was assigned to one of the minor nobility.

16. Pronounce: Ho-*resh*-ko. The pantler's family name. No other name is revealed.

17. A reference to the period of Poland's partitions (1772-1795).

18. The court of the *zemstvo*, an organ of rural self-government throughout the Russian Empire; it adjudicated in local matters such as boundary disputes.

19. Evidently the central seat at the head of the table, since, as we discover later, the guests are seated on benches, not chairs.

20. In Poland and Lithuania, the Franciscan Friars Observant were known as Bernardines, after Bernardino of Siena.

21. A popular Lithuanian summer dish made of young beet leaves, dilled cucumbers, eggs, meat or crayfish tails, and sour cream. The poet calls the dish by its Belorussian name *chołodziec* (*холодец*), the standard Polish variant of which is *chłodnik*.

22. The royal governor (*palatinus*) was the highest authority of the province or voivodeship, the largest administrative unit of the Polish-Lithuanian state.

23. An allusion to Suetonius' *Life of Vespasian*. Among other things, the Roman emperor imposed a tax on public toilets.

24. A quibble on the word *ważny*, with its double meaning of "weightiness, importance" and "legal tender."

25. The reference is to the Third Partition of Poland (1795), which effectively erased the country from the map of Europe until its restoration by the terms of the Treaty of Versailles in 1918. The liturgical penitential season of Lent, beginning with Ash Wednesday, is preceded by Fat Tuesday (*mardi gras*), the last day of the Carnival, which was often associated with license and excess.

26. [*Author's note*] The buzzard (*raróg*) is a bird resembling a hawk. It is well known how a flock of small birds, especially swallows, will pursue a hawk. Hence the saying, to go swarming after a buzzard.

27. The *plica polonica* (pol. *kołtun*), a disease of the hair, in which it becomes matted and twisted together. It seems to have been a common condition among the peasantry in the northeast-ern border regions of Poland.

28. That is, the Grand Duchy of Warsaw, the rump state Napoleon had created by the terms of the Treaty of Tilsit. See also note 6 to Book VI.

29. Alexander Vasilyevich Suvorov (1729-1800), field marshal and later generalissimus of the Russian Empire; Tadeusz Kościuszko's nemesis. In addition to his brilliant Turkish and Italian campaigns he led two against the Poles: first, against the forces of the Bar Confederacy (1768-72); second, in 1794, to quell the Kościuszko insurrection during which he oversaw the siege of Warsaw and the massacre of Praga. He was famous for his gnomic expressions, which Captain Rykov evidently imitates.

30. [*Author's note*] Among the Russian common folk there were numerous stories current about the black arts reputedly practiced by Bonaparte and Suvorov

31. [*Author's note*] One class of notaries (*rejenci aktowi*) have charge of certain government offices; others (*rejenci dekretowi*) record verdicts; all are appointed by the clerks of the courts. The assessors form the rural police of a district. According to the edicts, they are in part elected by the citizenry, in part appointed by the government; these last are called the crown assessors. Judges of appeal are also called assessors, but there is no reference to them here.

32. Pronounce: *So-plee-tsah.*

33. The reference is to the early morning candle-lit masses during the liturgical season of Advent. "*Rorate*" (meaning: "Drop down like dew") is the first word of the opening verse of Isaiah 45:8 in the Latin Vulgate used during the pre-Christmas season in the divine liturgy.

34. The Polish-born English novelist Joseph Conrad who could recite large fragments of *Pan Tadeusz* by heart and occasionally interjected into his English works near vebatim citations from the Polish poem, was known for his habit of rolling bread pellets at the dinner table and flicking them in all directions, often striking his guests. See *Joseph Conrad As I Knew Him* (Doubleday, New York, 1927), 19-21. According to his wife, he acquired this bad habit at sea. But the connection with *Pan Tadeusz* suggests otherwise. Interestingly, this private amusement between Tadeusz and Telimena bears a certain resemblance to the "mystical intercourse" between Levin and Kitty in Leo Tolstoy's *Anna Karenina*. The similarity of these

scenes, and others (see note 4 to Book V), suggest that, in researching his grand subject, the author of *War and Peace* had also consulted Mickiewicz's poem.

35. The Polish term *szarak* (here rendered as "puss") stands for *zając szarak*, i.e. the brown hare (*lepus europaeus*). The English hunter's cant term is always feminine.

36. Stanisław II August Poniatowski (1732-1798), the last king and grand duke of the Polish-Lithuanian Commonwealth, ascended the throne in 1764 and ruled until the Third Partition in 1795.

37. Józef Count Niesiołowski (1729-1814), the last governor of Nowogródek, was president of the revolutionary government during Jasiński's insurrection. After its defeat he retired from public life.

38. [*Author's note*] Jerzy Białopiotrowicz (1740-1812), the last Secretary of the Grand Duchy of Lithuania, took an active part in the Lithuanian insurrection under Jasiński. He was judge of state prisoners at Wilno and highly honored in Lithuania for his virtues and patriotism.

39. The three mythical brothers, Lech, Czech, and Rus, are said to be the progenitors of the Polish, Bohemian and Russian nations.

40. Located south of Minsk in what is now Belarus, the town was famous for its manufactories, which supplied the whole Commonwealth with gold brocade and massive belts, or waist-sashes (*pasy kontuszowe*). They were owned by the fabulously wealthy Radziwiłł family.

41. [*Author's note*] The calendar of causes (*trybunalska wokanda*) was a long narrow booklet listing the names of the parties to lawsuits in the order of the defendants. Every advocate and court usher had to own such a calendar.

42. The Polish text gives *ołtarzyk złoty* (the golden altar), the generic title of devotional books commonly used in Poland in the eighteenth and nineteenth centuries.

43. That is, the golden eagle of Napoleon and the silver eagle of Poland. The Polish coat of arms bears a white eagle on a red field.

44. Napoleon's decisive military victories (1798-1805).

45. Jan Henryk Dąbrowski (1755-1788), outstanding Polish military leader and creator of the Polish legions in northern Italy. He saw service in the wars of 1792 and 1794, and participated in the Napoleonic campaigns of 1806-07, 1809, and 1812. After the fall of Napoleon, he returned to Warsaw where he served as a Senator-Governor in the Congress Kingdom, the Polish state created by the Congress of Vienna in 1815.

46. General Otton-Karol Kniaziewicz (pronounce: *Knyah-zheh-vich*) (1762-1842), another outstanding Polish military leader of the Napoleonic era. He participated in the wars of 1792 and 1794, and in 1798 commanded the First Legion in Italy. For a while he was commandant of Rome with his headquarters in the Capitol. In recognition of his victories he was entrusted with the commission of delivering the captured standards of the enemy to Paris.

47. Prince Władysław Jabłonowski (1769-1802), commander of Napoleon's Polish Danube Legion. At the latter's orders, he led his ill-fated expeditionary force to Haiti to quell a popular revolt led by Toussaint l'Ouverture. He and almost all his legion perished there.

48. Peace be with you (Latin).

BOOK II

The Castle

Argument

Coursing with greyhounds. A sightseer at the castle. The last of the Horeszko retainers recounts the story of his late lord. A glance at the garden. A girl among the cucumbers. The breakfast. Telimena's anecdote of Saint Petersburg. A fresh outbreak of hostilities over Scut and Peregrine. Father Robak's intervention. The Chief Steward's discourse. A wager. Let's go mushrooming!

Who among us can forget the days when as growing lads we'd shoulder a gun and strike out whistling into the fields? Neither ridge nor fence stood in our way. When we cleared a boundary strip, the thought of trespassing never crossed our minds. In Lithuania, the hunter is like a ship sweeping the seas; he goes where his fancy takes him, he roams the wastes at will. And when with searching eye he scans the heavens, he is like a seer reading the omens. No cloud but a host of visible signs! Or again, he is like a warlock communing with Mother Earth who, while aloof to the city-dweller, prompts the sportsman's ear with a vast array of voices.

The corncrake rasps in the meadow! Idle to seek him out; he glides through the grass like the jackfish in the Niemen. Overhead peals Spring's matin-bell—the meadow lark; plunged equally deep in the heavens, he soars unseen. Yonder sweeps the broad-winged eagle, spreading panic among the sparrows even as the comet alarms the tsars. There, too, the goshawk hovers in the cloudless sky, beating his wings like a butterfly impaled on a pin, then spying a bird or leveret in the meadow below swoops down on it from on high like a shooting star.

When will the Lord grant an end to our wanderings and resettle us in our native fields? Oh, to serve with a cavalry that rides against the hare! An infantry that marches on the birds! To bear no arms but the hook and the scythe! To scan no columns other than those of our household ledgers!

Morning had broken over the straw-roofed outbuildings of Soplica Manor; even now the sun was filtering into the barn. Flickering bands of golden light dropped like hair ribbons though chinks in the black thatch, flooding the dark-green, fresh-cut, fragrant hay on which the youth had made their beds. As a tender lass wakes her sweetheart with an ear of grain, so the sun played on the lips of the sleeping guests. Sparrows frisked and chirped among the rafters. Three times the gander gaggled. A chorus of turkeys and ducks answered back like an echo. The bawls of the pasture-bound cattle filled the air.

The youth were up and about. Only Tadeusz, the last to fall asleep, slumbered on. So much had last night's banquet upset him that the crowing cock found him still wide awake. All night long he'd tossed and turned in his bed, and now the heaped-up hay had closed like a wave over his head and borne him off. A sudden rush of cool air fanned his eyes as, with a loud crash, the creaking barn door burst open and in stormed the Bernardine monk Robak, swishing his knotted rope belt. "*Surge, puer!*"[1] he roared, and he lay into Tadeusz's back with the knots of his belt.[2]

The courtyard rang loud with the shouts of the gathering hunt. Stable grooms led out the horses. More carriages drove in through the gate. Scarcely could the yard contain such a throng! The bugles shrilled, the kennel gates flew open and out tore the hounds, yelping with joy. At the sight of the hunters' horses and leashes they began racing frenziedly around the yard; finally, running up to their masters, they eased their heads into the collars. All this promised a splendid run, and at last the Chamberlain gave the order to ride.

Slowly, in single file, the hunt rode out. Once past the gate, they quickened their pace and fanned out in loose array. The Notary and the Assessor rode two abreast at their head. Despite occasional glances of mutual loathing, they conversed in friendly fashion, like dueling principals on their way to settle a mortal quarrel; no one from their words would have guessed the rancor seething in their hearts. The Notary led Scut, the Assessor Peregrine; the women followed in open carriages with the young men cantering alongside, engaging the damsels in light badinage.

Meanwhile, Father Robak paced the courtyard with leisurely strides. He was finishing his morning devotions. Now and again, he shot glances in Tadeusz's direction, frowning one minute, smiling the next. At last, he crooked a finger for the lad; but when Tadeusz drew up, he merely tapped the side of his nose ominously. No amount of urging and pleading induced him to make himself clear. Refusing to answer the youth, or even favor him with a glance, he pulled up his hood and finished his prayers. With that Tadeusz galloped off to rejoin the hunt.

The hunters had just checked their hounds. The entire field stood dead in its tracks, waving silence. All eyes were fixed on a rock near which the Judge had halted. He'd spotted the game and was making signs with his hands. All understood him and stood perfectly still; meanwhile, the Notary and the Assessor advanced at a slow trot across the field. Tadeusz, who happened to be closer, reached the Judge first. Reining in beside him, he probed the prospect with his eye. It had been a good while since he was last in the field—not easy to spot the quarry in that gray expanse, the more so, as the ground lay strewn with rocks and stones. The Judge pointed to the spot. There sat the hapless hare, huddled against the rock, ears erect, red eye riveted on the hunters; alive to its plight, yet frozen by their gaze, it cowered in terror by the rock, motionless as the rock itself. Meanwhile, the dust cloud in the field drew steadily closer. Scut strained furiously at the leash, behind him sped Peregrine the Fleet; then hallooing as one, the Notary and the Assessor vanished in a smother of dust on the heels of their hounds.

Just as the hunt raced off in pursuit of the hare, the Count emerged from the woods by the castle. The whole district knew his lordship was incapable of showing up at the appointed hour. Once again, he'd overslept himself and vented his spleen on the servants. No sooner did he spot the hunters in the field than he gave his horse the head and galloped off after them, the skirts of his long white coat of English cut snapping in the wind. Behind him rode his men-servants. All sported shiny, black mushroom-shaped caps, short jackets, white pantaloons, and stripe-lined top boots; the Count insisted his house servants so costumed should be called "jockeys."[3]

As the mounted party rode down into the meadows, the Count caught sight of the castle and drew rein. Never before had he set eyes on the ancient pile so early in the day. Surely these were not the same walls, so much did the dawn light enhance and refresh their lines! The sheer novelty of the sight filled him with wonder. Thrusting up from the dew-mist, the turret seemed twice as high. The tin-sheeted roof shone gold in the sun. In the sashes below, remnant panes of glass broke the eastern beams into bows of prismatic light. Mist shrouded the lower floors, hiding the fissures and breaches. Now and again, the hunters' cries in the distant forest sprang back from the echoing walls. You'd swear those wind-borne voices hailed from inside the castle's walls, that, under the mantle of mist, the castle stood rebuilt and teemed once more with human life.

Now the Count was fond of rare and novel sights; he called them romantic, for he owned to a romantic cast of mind—in fact, he was an incurable crank. While riding to hounds or coursing hares, he was given to halting sharply and gazing upward with the mournful watchfulness of a cat eyeing a sparrow high in a pine. Not seldom he would roam the groves without gun or hound like a runaway recruit, or sit bowing over the marges of a brook and stare into the stream like a heron devouring the fish with its eye. Such were the Count's peculiar ways. The locals thought him rather an oddball, though they held him in high respect, for he was rich and well born, favorably disposed to the rustics, and friendly to neighbor and Hebrew alike.

The Count swung off the path, put his horse across the field and drew up alone at the castle gate. Heaving a sigh, he gazed up at the walls, then reaching for paper and pencil settled down to sketch. Suddenly, glancing aside, he noticed a man standing a short distance away—clearly a devotee of scenic prospects like himself, for the fellow had his hands in his pockets and was gazing up at the castle walls, as if counting the stones. The Count recognized him at once but had to call out several times before Gervase took notice.

Gervase[4] was of noble stock, a servitor of the former castle holder and the last living retainer of the Horeszko family. He was a tall grizzled old master with a hale, rugged face riven with creases, and a mien both stern and morose. Once famous among the nobility for his good cheer, he'd soured since the battle in which the last castle heir perished. No longer did he attend weddings and the annual fairs. Gone were the days when he amused others with his witty jests. No more did his face spread with smiles.

He always went about in the ancient livery of the Horeszkos, a yellow dress coat with a faded galloon trim (gold in its day) and embroidered all over in silk with the Horeszko arms, and thus the whole district knew the old nobleman by the nickname "Half Goat." Sometimes, too, they called him "The Old Boy" from the familiar address he was in the habit of using, and sometimes "Scarpate" from the many scars that seamed the dome of his skull. But his real name was Rębajłło[5] (his coat of arms was unknown) and he styled himself "Warden," since he'd formerly held that post at the castle. A hefty truss of keys still hung from his belt by a silver-tasseled cord. True, for years there was nothing to lock, as the doorways had been stripped bare; but, eventually, he found two leaves, repaired and hung them at his own expense; and so he amused himself each evening with turning the locks. He'd taken up quarters in one of the empty chambers. Though he could easily have lived on the Count's charity, he chose not to, as he was always pining for the old days and never felt well unless he could breathe the castle air.

As soon as he caught sight of the Count, he snatched off his cap and bowed to the kinsman of his lords, revealing to full view his great bald pate which many a saber-cut had scored like a battle club.[6] Stroking his head with his hand, he approached the Count, bowed profoundly again and addressed him in doleful tones:

"Greetings, old boy . . . young master! Forgive the address, my lord Count; it is my way, you know, no disrespect. All the Horeszkos used to say 'old boy.' My master the late Pantler said it all the time. Is it true, sir, you'd stint a penny for the litigation and cede the castle to Soplica? I shouldn't have believed it, but now everyone's noising it about the countryside." And gazing at the castle, he heaved a volley of sighs.

"It is no wonder," said the Count. "The expense is great and the tedium even greater. I dearly wish the matter were closed, but the tiresome old squire has dug in his heels. He knew he'd wear me out in the courts. Indeed, I cannot hold out any longer. Today I shall lay down my arms and accept such terms as the court awards."

"Terms!?" cried out Gervase. "Make terms with Soplica? The Soplicas! old boy? (He pulled a face, as if the very word confounded him.) Terms with the Soplicas? Come, my boy, you must be joking, eh? The castle, the ancestral seat of the Horeszkos, pass into Soplica hands! Only get you down from your horse, sir. Let us go into the castle. Come, see for yourself! You don't know what you're saying. Come! No shying from me! Dismount, I say!" And he held the stirrup for his lordship to dismount.

They entered the castle. Gervase halted at the threshold of the great hall. "Here—said he—the ancient lords and their retainers would lounge in their chairs after dinner. Here the Pantler settled disputes among the villagers. When in a good flow of spirits, he'd entertain his guests with beguiling tales or delight in another's yarn or jest; meanwhile, in the courtyard, the youth trained with wooden swords or broke my master's Turkish ponies to saddle."

They entered the hall. Gervase spoke on: "Count all the stones in this vast paved chamber and you'll still fall short of the number of wine casks we broached here in the old days. A summons to Parliament or the regional diet,[7] my master's name day, a hunting meet—name the occasion and our nobility would be lowering their belts into the vaults for a hogshead. On banquet nights a small orchestra stood in yonder gallery, playing airs on the organ[8] and sundry instruments. When we raised a toast, the trumpets pealed forth from the choir as on Judgment Day. The toasts followed in orderly succession: the first brimmer we raised to His Majesty the King, the second to the Primate,[9] the next three to the Queen, the nobility, and the Commonwealth respectively. Then came the sixth and final toast, 'Let us love one another! *Vivat!* A long life!' That was the rouse that never ended. Raised at sundown it rang forth clear until sunrise, when carriages and dogcarts would draw up to bear each guest to his lodgings."

They passed silently through several chambers. Gervase fixed his gaze now on the walls, now on the vault. A sad recollection struck him here, a pleasant one there. Sometimes, the words "Forever fled!" seemed poised on his lips. Now and then, he nodded his head sadly or waved his arm in the air—clearly memory itself was a torment to him, and he was at pains to keep it at bay. They fetched up in the old hall of mirrors upstairs. The mirrors had long since gone, the frames hung empty, paneless windows gave onto a gallery commanding a clear view of the castle gate. Entering thereon, the old man buried his head in his hands. When at last he looked up, an expression of intense sadness and despair had settled on his face.

Though mystified by what all this meant, the Count felt strangely moved. He stared into the Warden's face and squeezed his hand. For a moment neither of them spoke; then raising his arm the old master broke the silence.

"No terms, old boy!" he said, shaking his fist. "No peace between Soplica and Horeszko blood! Know that Horeszko blood runs in your veins. You are kin to the Pantler by your mother, the Royal Huntsman's wife. Her mother was the Castellan's cadet daughter, and he, as everyone knows, was my lord's maternal uncle. Now listen to this tale of your kith and kin. For it all happened here in this castle, in this very hall.

"My late lamented lord, the Pantler, was the first gentleman of the district, a man of family and substance. He had an only child—a daughter, the very picture of an angel. Young nobles and notables wooed her by the score. Among the nobility there was a roistering ruffian by the name of Jacek[10] Soplica. People nicknamed him "The Governor," and in truth, he wielded great influence in the province, for he had absolute sway over the whole Soplica clan and commanded their three-hundred votes as he pleased, yet all he had in the world was a land-holding of paltry size, a saber, and a pair of whiskers that spanned his face from ear to ear. Now the Pantler often invited this fellow to the castle and entertained him there, especially during the regional diets, as my lord's kinsmen and supporters found him amenable to their causes. Alas, their affecting of his company went to his head. Before long he was having thoughts of wedding the Pantler's lass. More and more he imposed himself on the castle; soon he'd settled in like one of the family. He was preparing to ask for her hand when they got wind of it and served him a bowl of black soup[11] at the table. Seems the lass had been sweet on him all along but hadn't breathed a word of it to her parents.

"Those were the Kościuszko days. My master declared for the Constitution of May Third.[12] He was mustering the nobility to go to the aid of the Confederates when, without warning one night, the Muscovites encircled the castle. We barely had time to bolt the lower doors and sound the alarm with a mortar shot. The sole occupants of the castle at the time were my lord Pantler, his lady and myself, the cook and his two turnspits (besotted all three!), the parish priest, the footman, and four stouthearted Haiduks.[13] So we seize our long guns and take to the windows. With a cry of 'huzzah,' the Muscovites come swarming across the terrace from the gate. We greet them with a fusillade, ten muskets strong, 'Back, you sons . . .' You couldn't see a thing outside; the servants poured a steady fire from the lower floors, and my lord and I sniped away from the gallery above.

"All was blowing great guns, though we stood in mortal peril. Twenty muskets lay right here on these very boards. We'd fire one, they'd pass us another; in this, our priest gave a good account of himself, as did also the Pantler's wife, his daughter, and her servant-companions. We were but three sharpshooters, but we never hung fire. The Muscovite infantry rained a hail of bullets on us from below. Our firepower was feebler, but we had height in our favor, and our aim was true. Three times the *muzhiks*[14] press up to the doors and each time three fall to the dust; so they leg it to the lumber house. Meanwhile, it was growing light. Gun in hand, the Pantler steps blithely out onto the gallery. The instant a Muscovite shows his pate from behind the lumber house my master lets him have it, and each time—for he was a dead shot!—another black shako goes tumbling over the grass. Soon they were loath to venture out.

"Seeing the foe in disarray, the Pantler decides to mount a sally. Seizing his saber, he barks orders to his men below, and turning to me yells, 'Come, Gervase, follow—' At that moment a shot rang out from beyond the gate. The Pantler's cry died on his lips. His face turned red then ghastly white; he tried to speak—and coughed up blood. Then I saw the wound; the ball had struck him square in the chest. He staggered back, pointing toward the gate. I recognized the knave—Soplica! Aye, I could tell him by his build and whiskers. It was his shot that felled my lord. I saw it! The villain still had his musket up, smoke was rising from the barrel. I drew a bead on him. The rogue stood motionless as a statue. Two shots I fired and twice I missed. Rage—or was it grief?—hampered my aim. The women screamed. I turned and looked. My lord lay dead!"

Here Gervase broke into sobs. Moments later he closed his tale.

"By now the Muscovites were hacking down the doors. With my lord Pantler dead, I stood helpless, insensible to what was passing around me. Fortunately, Parafianowicz arrived in the nick of time, he and two hundred Mickiewicz folk from Horbatowicz—a large noble family, stouthearted to a man and long-time sworn foes of the Soplicas.

"So perished a mighty, pious and upstanding man whose house boasted seats in the Senate, ribboned orders, and hetmans' maces.[15] Though a father to our peasantry and a brother to us nobles, he had no son after him to swear vengeance at his grave. But loyal servants he had! I smeared his blood over my blade, my rapier dubbed 'Jackknife.' You must have heard of my rapier. It used to be the talk of every parliament, regional diet, and annual fair. I vowed to notch it on every Soplica neck in the neighborhood. No session of parliament, no bazaar, no armed foray would I let pass without hunting them out. Two I hacked down in a brawl, another two in a duel, and still another I burned alive in a wooden shack during the raid on Korelicze with Rymsza. We baked him there like a loach! Those whose ears I lopped off don't enter into the reckoning. One Soplica has yet to receive a token from me: the born brother of that whiskered knave. He still lives and takes pride in his wealth. His land encroaches on the castle grounds, he enjoys the respect of the district, holds an office—aye, the Judge! And to him you'd yield the castle? Let his impious feet wipe the Pantler's blood from these boards? Not whilst I live! So long as Gervase has an ounce of courage in his veins and strength to match, so long as with one little finger he can wield his Jackknife, which hangs even now on the wall, Soplica shall never take possession of the castle."

"Ah!" exclaimed the Count, raising his hands. "What a good premonition my falling in love with these ruins! I hadn't realized all the treasures they contained. What dramatic events! What stuff of legend! Gervase, when once I seize from the Soplicas the castle of my ancestors, I shall install you as burgrave of its walls. Your tale stirs me deeply, only pity you didn't bring me here at the midnight hour. Draped in my cloak, I should have sat here among these ruins while you held me rapt with these tales of murderous deeds. Aye, pity you lack the gift of narration! Oft have I read and heard tell of such happenings. Every lord's castle in England and Scotland, every count's palace in Germany is a theater of slaughter and blood! Every ancient, noble and powerful family carries report of some perfidy or sanguinary deed whence vengeance devolves on the heirs; and now for the first time I hear of such a case in Poland. Aye, I feel brave-hearted Horeszko blood stir in my veins. I know my debt to glory and my kin. So be it! No more parley with Soplica, though it come to pistol or blade. Honor demands it!"

So saying he strode solemnly off, with Gervase following behind in profound silence. Still muttering to himself, he halted at the gate, then casting a last backward glance at the castle he leapt on his horse and closed his rambling monologue:

"What a pity old Soplica has no spouse or comely daughter with qualities stirring my deepest devotion. Loving her, yet prevented from seeking her hand. Aye, that would thicken the plot! Here the heart, there bounden duty! Here vengeance, there deep affection!" With that the Count dug in his rowels and sped off toward the manor.

Just then the hunt emerged from the far side of the forest. Now the Count was an avid sportsman. No sooner did he catch sight of the hunters than all preceding thoughts went by the board. Off he galloped to join the course. On past the gate, garden and fence he rode; then glancing aside on rounding a bend, he drew rein by the fence.

Here stood an orchard. Fruit-trees, planted in rows, shaded an ample field; below lay the kitchen garden. Here sat the venerable cabbage, bowing his tonsured head as if brooding over the fate of the vegetables. There, pods entwined around the carrot's green locks, the slender bean trained a thousand eyes upon his beloved. Yonder waved the maize her golden tassels, and here and yon, at the extremity of his vine, sat the stout-girthed watermelon. Far afield he'd trundled—a guest bulged in among the crimson beets.

Each bed lay parted by a ridge, and ranged like sentinels along each adjacent trench stood the cypresses of the cottage garden: hemp-stalks—silent, straight and green. Their pungent leafage served to ward off invaders. No snake dared press through it; the scent was lethal to grub and insect alike. Farther back, varicolored poppies lofted their whitish stems. You fancied a host of butterflies—wings trembling, iridescent, all a-shimmer like precious stones—sat balanced on their stalks. Even so the poppies' vivid diapason of hues beguiled the eye; and in their midst, like the full-orbed moon among the stars, the sunflower turned his fiery face from east to west.

Laid out by the garden fence ran long, narrow, mounded rows where neither tree, nor shrub, nor flower grew. Here lay the cucumber patch, grown to splendor, its great mass of leafage overspreading the beds like a rippling broadloom rug. A young girl dressed in white was even now wading knee-deep through the lush vegetation. Stepping down into the furrows, she seemed no longer to wade but to breast the leaves and bathe in their verdure. A straw-hat shaded her head; from under the brim fluttered a pair of rose-colored ribbons and the odd stray twine of flaxen hair. Eyes trained downward, she moved through the leafage, a wicker basket slung over her elbow, her right hand poised for the picking. Even as a bather stoops to brush away the minnows nibbling at her feet, so the girl, basket in arm, kept bending down to pluck up a fruit that grazed her foot or caught her eye.

The Count stood motionless, enchanted by the scene. Hearing his companions ride up from behind, he made signs for them to halt. They drew rein while he, craning his neck, resumed his watch. Even so the long-billed crane stands apart from his flock: balanced on one leg, he waits in ambush, eyes darting, a stone gripped in his claw to combat sleep.

Suddenly, a swish across the head and shoulders roused the Count from his reverie. Above him stood the Bernardine Robak, the knotted cords of his belt in his upraised hand. "So!" he cried. "It's cucumbers you want, eh? I'll give you cucumbers! Oh, beware, your lordship, these beds hold no fruitage for you; nothing shall come of it." And waving a menacing finger, he arranged his hood, and stalked off.

The Count, at once cursing and chuckling at this unexpected intrusion, lingered on in the garden. He turned his gaze back to the cucumber patch, but the girl was no longer there. Looking around, he caught a fleeting glimpse of her white dress and pink ribbons in the manor window. He saw the path she'd cut through the beds. For a brief moment the leaves, spurned by her nimble foot, tossed and trembled then fell still like a body of water grazed by a swallow's wing. On the spot where the girl had been standing only her basket remained, bobbing downside up on a sea of leaves, its cargo of fruit gone to the bottom.

Moments later, all was quiet and solitude. The Count, all ears, fixed his gaze on the house and mused on while his riders remained motionless behind him. At last, as when the swarm returns to the empty hive, the deserted house began to buzz with sounds—murmurs at first, then audible talk, then boisterous shouts. Clearly, the hunt was back, and the servants were bestirring themselves with breakfast.

Great was the bustle throughout the house. Servants carried out plates, platters of viands, bottles, and silverware. The hunters, dressed as they'd come, in their green shooting coats, sauntered from room to room. Plate and wine cup in hand, they ate and drank. Others lounged against the window casements, talking of guns, hares and hounds. The Judge sat at the table with the Chamberlain and his wife. The young women chatted quietly in the corner. Clearly, there was no standing on ceremony here as at luncheon or dinner. A novel custom in an old-fashioned Polish household. Far from approving of this want of order, the Judge put up with it for breakfast.

The table lay spread with an array of dishes suited to men's and women's tastes. Trays bearing a complete coffee service came whisking out, enormous trays, handsomely painted with floral motifs. Each came with its own fragrantly steaming coffeepot of beaten tin, a set of gilded cups of Saxon porcelain, and a dainty cream-jug.

No country serves a better cup of coffee than Poland! Ancient custom requires every proper household to engage a maid expressly charged with the brewing of the coffee. She has beans of the finest quality brought in from the city, or procures them directly from the trading wherries.[16] The preparation requires special knowledge; only the coffeemaker is privy to its secret, for the brew must be black as coal, clear as amber, fragrant as mocha, and thick as honey. As to the importance of good cream it is common knowledge; cream is easy to come by in the country. First thing in the morning, the maid sets the coffee pots on the stove to steep, then repairs to the dairy. After skimming off the topmost layer of cream with her own hands, she apportions it into the little pitchers, one per setting, sufficient to crown each cup with its own coat of skin.

The older women, having risen earlier and taken their coffee had had another brew prepared: a bowl of mulled ale, whitened with cream and swirling with cheese curds, finely chopped. For the men there was a wide choice of cold meats: tender goose-breast, sliced ham and ox-tongue, all of exquisite quality, home-cured and smoked in juniper. Last of all, they brought in the main course—beef stew and gravy. Such was the hearty refection served at the Judge's house.

Two separate companies stood gathered in adjoining rooms. The elders sat around a small table, discussing the latest farming methods and the Tsar's increasingly stern edicts. The Chamberlain appraised the current rumors of war and reflected on the political outcome; meanwhile, the Steward's daughter, donning a pair of blue spectacles, amused the Chamberlain's wife with a deck of tarot cards.

The youth congregated in the adjacent room. Here talk ran on the morning's hare course but without the usual strife and rowdiness. The Notary and the Assessor, mighty orators both, foremost connoisseurs in the hunting-craft and first-rate marksmen, sat sullenly silent opposite each other. Apparently, both had slipped their leashes correctly. Both were certain their hounds would bring the quarry to book, when, on a level stretch, the hunt happened upon a peasant's parcel of uncut grain; the hare nipped right in. Scut and Peregrine were about to seize it when the Judge checked the horsemen at the boundary mark. The hunters vigorously protested but had no choice but to obey; the hounds emerged quarryless, and no one knew for certain if the hare had given them the slip or been chopped by Scut, by Peregrine, or both. Opinions diverged, and the contest raged on.

Meanwhile, the old Steward, gazing absentmindedly from side to side, strolled through the adjoining rooms. He took no interest in the general talk; his mind was on other matters. Leather flapper in hand, he halted here and there, ruminated for an instant, then plastered a fly to the wall.

Tadeusz and Telimena stood alone in the connecting doorway. They spoke softly, as the two groups of guests were not far apart. Only now did Tadeusz learn that his Auntie Telimena was a woman of substance and that they were not so closely related as to be separated by the canons of the Church. Indeed, there was no certainty that Telimena was any blood relation of her nephew at all, even though his uncle called her "sister" (mutual kin of theirs used to refer to them as siblings, despite their disparity in years). In addition, Tadeusz learned that while living in Saint Petersburg, Telimena had rendered his uncle a number of invaluable services. For this reason, he held her in high regard and was given in society—perhaps out of false ambition—to refer to himself as her brother, to which for friendship's sake Telimena raised no objection. All these revelations came as a relief to Tadeusz. A great many other confidential things passed between them, and all this took place in one short moment.

Meanwhile, in the room to the right, the Notary was baiting the Assessor. "I told you the hunt would draw a blank," he said off-handedly. "Too early yet with grain still in the ear and so many peasants' plots standing unharvested. It explains why the Count refused to join the course despite the invitation. The Count knows all about hunting and holds strong opinions on when and where to hunt. Having spent the better part of his life abroad, he takes a dim view of our barbarous hunting habits. We flout the laws and government regulations, show scant respect for landmarks and boundaries, and ride roughshod over a peasant's parcel of land without his knowledge. Spring or summer, we course the fields and forests. Sometimes, we punish the fox in molting season and allow our hounds to run down—nay, torment!—a laden doe in the winter grain, and in so doing, we wreak great harm on our game. Hence the Count's painful admission that Muscovy enjoys more culture than we, for in Russia at least you have the Tsar's hunting edicts, police surveillance, and penalties to fit the crime."

Telimena was facing the room to the left, fanning her shoulders with a cotton batiste handkerchief. "So help me," she said, "the Count is right. I know Russia well. You doubt me when I insist that Russia's stern vigilance is laudable in its way, but I have been to Saint Petersburg, and not just once. O sweet memories! Charming bygone times! What a city! Have you never been to Pieter? I'll show you a plan if you like. I always keep one in my escritoire.

"Every summer, Petersburg society deserts the city for the *dacha*, a summer villa—*dacha* is their word for country house. I lived in one such house. It stood on a man-made knoll overlooking the Neva at an ideal distance from town. Ah, what a place! I still have a plan in my escritoire. Anyhow, to my great misfortune, a little *chinovnik*, a minor police functionary, leased the house next door. He kept a number of wolfhounds. You've no idea what a torment it is having a petty clerk and his dogs live next door. I'd no sooner step out into the garden with my book to enjoy the moon and evening air than one of these ferocious hounds would fly up, ears pricked up, tail swishing. I often took fright at the sight. In my heart I knew grief would come from those dogs, and that's exactly what happened.

"I'd just stepped out one morning when, at my very feet, one of these hounds choked the life out of my dear darling *bolonka*.[17] Ah, what a sweet little doggie she was!—the gift of Prince Sukin[18] himself. Clever little thing! Quick as a squirrel! I'd show you a picture, only it would mean a trip to my escritoire. The shock of seeing her lifeless before me brought on fainting spells, muscular spasms, and heart palpitations.

"My health might have taken still worse a turn if the Master of the Imperial Hunt, Kirilo Gavrilich Kozodushin,[19] hadn't popped in for a visit. On learning the cause of my dudgeon, he had the clerk dragged in by the ear. There he stood, the hapless wretch, pale and trembling, out of all possession. 'You dare'—thundered Kirilo Gavrilich—'to stalk a laden hind in the spring, and under the Tsar's very nose!' In vain the stupefied clerk swore he hadn't been out stalking, and if it pleased His Excellency, the quarry was a dog not a doe. 'Blackguard!' roared Kirilo Gavrilich. 'You presume to know more about venery and wild game than I, Kozodushin, the Tsar's *Jaegermeister*?[20] Let the Chief of Police judge between us.' They summoned the police chief and launched an official inquiry. 'I'—stated Kozodushin—'swear he was stalking a doe. This dolt here claims it was a lapdog. Now you judge between us. Who's better in the know?' The Chief of Police knew his duty. Aghast at the clerk's sauciness, he took him aside and urged him in brotherly fashion to make a clean breast of the matter. Thus appeased, Kirilo Gavrilich agreed to put in a word and have the wretch's sentence lightened. And that was that. The hounds were strung up, and the clerk spent a month in the clink. The little incident kept us in stitches the entire evening. By the next day it was the talk of the town. The Jaegermeister had interposed on behalf of my lapdog. And I know for a fact the incident drew a hearty guffaw from the Emperor himself."

Laughter rang out in both rooms. All this time, the Judge had been engaged in a round of matrimony with the Bernardine. When Telimena began her anecdote, he was on the point of making an important play, spades being trumps, and the Monk was barely breathing from excitement. Listening intently, chin upraised, hand poised for the casting, the Judge heard out the tale while the Bernardine sat waiting in the direst suspense. Finally, the story told, he cast his queen of spades, laughed, and spoke forth:

"If people wish to praise the Teuton for his high culture and the Muscovite for his law and order, let them! If Greater Poland[21] wants to learn from the Swabian how to litigate over a fox or have a hound arrested for trespassing on somebody's spinney, by all means, say I. But thank heaven we in Lithuania stand on our old ways. We've plenty of game to go around. You'll never see us launching police inquiries over such trifles! Here we have no shortage of grain; no one starves if a hound goes coursing through the spring wheat or rye. All the same, I draw the line at the peasant's balk."

"Small wonder, sir," piped up the Bailiff from the other room. "You pay through the nose for such game. Our rustics rub their hands on seeing your hounds tear through their standing crop. A dozen shaken ears of rye and you compensate them with a haycock. Even then it's not quits. Often, they receive a bonus of a thaler. Depend on it, sir, our peasantry's getting cheeky. If only . . ."

The Judge never heard the rest of the Bailiff's remarks. Their discourse had sparked a dozen more exchanges, anecdotes, tales, and even disputes.

Entirely forgotten in the fray, Tadeusz and Telimena had eyes only for each other. Telimena was delighted to see Tadeusz so amused by her anecdote; the youth, in turn, plied her with compliments. Telimena's speech grew slower and softer. With all the noise around them, Tadeusz feigned not to hear, and replied in whispers. By now he'd drawn so close to her that he could feel the pleasant warmth of her brow on his face. He held his breath, caught her sighs with his lips, his eye seized on every sparkle of her glance—when, suddenly, there flashed by between them a fly! followed directly by the swish of the Steward's swatter.

Lithuania swarms with flies. Among them thrives a species of blowfly known as the noble. Except for his broader thorax and larger abdomen, he resembles any other fly in color and shape. When flying, he drones and bombinates intolerably, and he is strong enough to perforate a spider's web. Should he find himself snagged in the toils, he will buzz there for three days on end, as he is perfectly capable of fending off the spider. All this the Steward had had occasion to observe. More than this: he claimed it was from these very flies that the lesser folk sprang. The noble was to the common fly what the queen bee was to the swarm; his extinction meant the end of the entire strain. Needless to say, holding to other views on the genesis of the fly, neither the housekeeper nor the village priest gave the Steward's hypothesis the time of day, but the Steward held fast to tradition. No sooner would he spot such a fly than off he'd go after it.

Precisely one of these nobles had droned past his ear. Twice he flailed and— heavens!—missed. He swung a third time and all but took out the window. Addled by this commotion, the fly spotted two figures blocking its retreat through the doorway. In desperation, it hurled itself right between their noses. Even there the Steward's arm went after it. So lusty was the stroke that the two heads started back like the two halves of a thunder-cloven tree. Both heads struck a bruising blow against the doorposts.

Fortunately, no one observed the incident, as what had passed in the far room for polite if loud and lively conversation was building up to an explosive crescendo. When foxhunters deployed in an extended line enter the forest, you hear the occasional cracking of tree limbs, random gunshots, and the babble of the hounds. But when one of the hunters chances to rouse a wild boar, he sets in motion a general hue and cry so tumultuous that all the trees of the forest give tongue. So it is with conversation: Talk moves along at a leisurely pace until it lights upon an engaging topic, like a wild boar. The boar on this occasion was the Notary's and the Assessor's fierce contest over their prize hounds. The dispute was of short duration, but much ground was covered in a moment's compass.

In one breath they fired off such a volley of words and invectives as to exhaust the usual three-fourths of a quarrel—taunts, anger and challenge—and now they were on the point of exchanging blows.

Starting to their feet, the guests in the adjacent room surged through the doorway, sweeping aside the couple presiding there like bi-fronted Janus of the threshold.

Even before Tadeusz and Telimena had time to smooth their ruffled hair, the menacing noises died down. Murmurs and laughter rippled through the crowd. A truce brokered by Robak stood declared. Despite his age, the Monk was a burly fellow of broad-shouldered build. No sooner had the Assessor closed with the Notary and the two were squaring for battle than he seized them both by the back of the collar, cracked their heads together like two Easter eggs, and spreading his arms like a fingerpost flung them to opposite corners of the room. For a while he stood there, arms spread wide, repeating, "*Pax, pax, pax vobiscum!* Peace be with you!"

The two factions stood thunderstruck. Some laughed out loud. Their deference to a man of the cloth checked any impulse to rebuke him, and after such a show of strength no one felt disposed to lift an arm against him. But now that the Bernardine had restored peace to the gathering it was clear he had no interest in proving his prowess. Without further threat to the brawlers, without so much as a snort of anger, he arranged his hood, and thrusting his hands under his belt quietly took his leave.

Meanwhile, the Judge and the Chamberlain interposed themselves between the two factions. The Steward, roused as from a deep meditation, stepped forward and eyed the throng fiercely. Wherever a murmur arose, he silenced it with a priest-like flourish of his leather sprinkler;[22] at last, raising the fly-fap solemnly like a marshal's mace, he called them to order.

"Becalm yourselves!" he repeated. "Give thought, you big guns of our district, to the scandalous effects of your contention. Have you any idea! Behold our youth, the hope of our country, the ones we count on to bring fame to our forests and groves. Alas, as it is, our youth shirk the hunt, and now they may have fresh cause to despise it. See? The very ones to set them an example bring home nothing but tumult and brawls! You might also show regard for my silver hairs, for I knew greater hunters than you. Often was I called to arbitrate between them. Who in Lithuania's forests measured up to Tadeusz Rejtan? Who, when it came to deploying beaters or closing with wild game, stood equal to our Białopiotrowicz? Show me a shooter today of the caliber of noble Żegota; he'd pick off a sprinting jackrabbit with a pistol-shot. I knew Terajewicz; a stout pike was all he needed to hunt wild boar. And Budrewicz!—why, he'd wrestle bruin down with his bare hands! Such were the men our forests once knew. And when it came to disputes, they knew how to settle the matter. They called on an arbiter and laid their stakes. Ogiński forfeited two thousand hectares of woodland over a wolf! A badger once cost Niesiołowski several villages! So, gentlemen, take after your elders and settle your score. Only place more modest stakes, for words are an idle wind. Shouting matches come to nothing. Why waste breath over a hare? Choose your arbiter and yield in good faith to his verdict. For my part, I shall entreat the Judge to impose no limits on the master of the hounds, even if it means leading the course through a cornfield. I trust he will grant us this boon."

So saying the Steward squeezed the Judge's knee.

"My horse!" cried the Notary. "I'll stake my horse and harness. More than that: I'll swear an affidavit before the district court and pledge this ring to our referee as payment."

"And I—said the Assessor—shall wager my gold-ringed dog collars lined with shagreen and my exquisitely wrought velvet leash with its glittering precious stone of matching craft. I'd intended to leave these articles to my future children in the event I should marry. They were Prince Dominic's gift to me when he, Marshal Sanguszko, General Mejen[23] and I went on a hunt together, and I set my hounds against theirs. There, unprecedented in the annals of hunting, I bagged three brace of hare with one bitch. We were hunting on the Kupisko Common. The Prince, unable to restrain himself, leapt from his horse, clasped my famous Kite by the neck, and after kissing her three times on the head and patting her thrice on the snout declared, 'Now shall you be called Queen of Kupisko!' Just so Napoleon makes of his generals princes of the site of their signal victory."

But Telimena was growing weary of this strife. She longed for a breath of air outside and sought a companion.

"Gentlemen," she said, lifting a basket off the peg. "I see you mean to stay cooped up inside, but I have a mind for mushrooming. Who cares to may follow me."

With that she wrapped her head in a red cashmere shawl, seized the Chamberlain's youngest girl by the hand, and gathering up her skirts above the ankles took her leave. Without a word Tadeusz hastened after her.

The proposal of an outing delighted the Judge. Here was a way of clearing the air. "Gentlemen," he announced. "To the woods, for mushrooms! Who graces our table with the finest milkcap shall sit by the loveliest young lady. I shall appoint her myself, and should a lady so grace the board, the pick of our boys shall be hers."

NOTES

1. "On your feet, boy!" (Latin)
2. Franciscan friars had three knots on their rope cinctures, symbolizing their threefold vow of poverty, chastity and obedience.
3. The quixotic count is evidently an anglophile.
4. The "Tweedledum" to "Tweedledee" Protase Brzechalski—the Court Usher. The humorous choice of given names derives from the Roman saints' names Gervasius and Protasius.
5. Pronounce: *Rem-by-lo*. Gervase's Lithuanian-sounding surname is derived from the Polish verb *rąbać*, meaning "to hew." His facetious style *Mopanek*, here rendered as "Old Boy," is a diminutive form of *Mości Pan*, a familiar address of the time.
6. For a detailed description of the ancient Lithuanian battle club (*nasieka*), see note 10 to Book IX.
7. The Polish tri-cameral Parliament was made up of the King, an Upper House (the Senate) formed by bishops, voivodes, castellans, and ministers, and a Lower House (or *Sejm*) made up of deputies who were elected by the regional diets or dietines (*sejmiki*). From 1573, Parliament convened regularly every two years for six weeks, except in case of emergency when more frequent sessions were held for two-week periods. Convocations of Parliament took place in Warsaw (regular sessions), Grodno (every third parliament) and Kraków (coronation parliaments).
8. [*Author's note*] An organ was ordinarily set in the choir of the old castles.
9. The primate of Poland, the archbishop of Gniezno, was the highest dignitary in Poland after the king. He officiated at coronations and reigned during the *interregna*.
10. Pronounce: *Yah-tsek*.
11. Known as *czarna polewka, czernina, czarnina*, or even *barszcz szary* ("gray borscht"), the black soup was made of duck, goose, or pig blood and a clear poultry broth. When served at table to a suitor, as Mickiewicz explains in his notes, it signified the family's refusal of his courtship.
12. The Four-Year Parliament (also known as the Constitutional Parliament), in session from 1788 to 1792, adopted the celebrated May Third Constitution in 1791. By the terms of the constitution, the burghers were granted full equality before the law, the peasantry were placed under the protection of the government, and the notorious *liberum veto* was abolished.
13. A *hajduk* was a Polish nobleman's servant dressed in Hungarian livery.
14. A *muzhik* is a Russian peasant.
15. The mace (*buława*) symbolized the authority of the hetman, the commander-in-chief of the Polish Army.
16. [*Author's note*] Wherries (*wiciny*) are large boats on the Niemen with which the Lithuanians conduct trade with the Prussians, freighting grain down the river and receiving colonial wares in return for it.
17. A little white dog similar to the French Bolognese of today (the Polish name *bonończyk* derives from Bononia, the Latin name for Bologna). Through the connection between the Russian and French aristocracy in the eighteenth and nineteenth centuries, the breed was brought to Tsarist Russia and became known as the *French bolonka*. These lively toy dogs were favorites of the fashionable ladies of the period.
18. Not an entirely uncommon Russian surname, but with the "doggie" connection here it cannot help but bring *сукин сын* to mind (i.e. Prince Sonovabich).

19. To achieve his comical effect in Polish, Mickiewicz polonizes the Russian surname to *Kozodusin*, i.e. goat-strangler—from *koza* (goat) and *dusić* (choke or strangle). The Russian cognate of *dusić* is *душить* (*dushít'*). Hence the more natural Russian name would have been *Козодушин* (*Kozodushin*). But, transliterated into Polish, this would have yielded *Kozoduszyn*, and the desired association would have been obscured. Interestingly, a Russian statesman with a name of parallel etymology actually existed: namely, Kozodavlev—from *давить* (*davít'*), also meaning "to choke." Osip Petrovich Kozodavlev served as the Tsar's Minister of the Interior from 1810 to 1819. The poet would doubtless have heard of him during his period of exile in Russia.

20. Master of the Hunt [*Jägermeister*] (German)

21. Greater Poland refers to the northwestern part of the old Polish kingdom, which fell under Prussian rule.

22. The reference is to the *asperges*, the rite of sprinkling the faithful with holy water at the start of High Mass in the Roman Catholic Latin Rite. In Poland, the instrument, still used for this purpose, resembles a small whiskbroom, called *kropidlo* in Polish.

23. [*Author's note*] Prince Dominik Radziwiłł (1786-1813), a great lover of hunting, emigrated to the Grand Duchy of Warsaw and at his own expense equipped a regiment of cavalry, which he commanded in person. He died in France. With him became extinct the male line of the Princes of Ołyka and Nieśwież, the most powerful lords in Poland and in all probability in Europe. General Jan Jakub Mejen distinguished himself in the national war under Kościuszko. Mejen's ramparts still exist near Wilno. [C. Z.: Exactly which Marshal Sanguszko the poet had in mind is uncertain; the Sanguszkos were a powerful family of Lithuanian princes.]

BOOK III

Romantic Pursuits

Argument

The Count's sally into the garden. A mysterious nymph tends the geese. The mushroom hunters. A comparison with the wandering shades of Elysium. Varieties of wild mushroom. Telimena at her Temple of Musings. Consultations touching Tadeusz's future. The Count as landscape painter. Tadeusz's fanciful depictions of trees and clouds. The Count's musings on art. The bell. A note. A bear, my lordship!

The Count was making for home, yet he kept drawing rein and turning his head back toward the garden. Once more he imagined he caught a glimpse of the mysterious white dress in the manor window. A weightless object seemed to float down from it, cross the garden in a flicker of an eyelid, and shine clear among the green cucumbers. So steals a sunbeam through a cloud and falls upon a slab of flint in the field or on a sheet of water in the grassy meadow.

Alighting from his horse, the Count dismissed his servants and made stealthily for the garden. In no time he gained the fence, found an opening and slipped through like a wolf into the sheepfold. By mischance he brushed against a row of dry gooseberry canes. The little gardener glanced around, as if alarmed by the rustling, but she saw nothing untoward. Still, she ran to the other side of the garden. Meanwhile, slipping sideways through the great leaves of wild rhubarb and yellow dock, the Count dropped down on all fours, and hopping frog-fashion through the grass crept noiselessly up to within a few yards of the girl. He raised his head. A marvelous prospect burst upon his gaze.

Here, amid a scattering of cherry trees, stood a grain patch purposely sown with a wide assortment of crops: wheat, maize, broad bean, English pea, bearded barley, millet, and even the odd flower and shrub. The housekeeper, a famous mistress surnamed Banty *née* Cockalorum,[1] had thought up this little garden for the domestic fowl. Her brainchild signaled an epoch in the annals of poultry farming. Today it is common knowledge, but then it was a novelty known only to the few initiates. In time, it made its way into the pages of the almanac under

the title, *Remedies for Hawks and Kites: A New Method of Raising Barnyard Fowl.*
Here was that garden.

The rooster, strutting his watch, had only to halt, poise his beak, cock his comb sideways (the better to sweep the clouds with his eye), spot a hovering hawk, and sound the alarm; at once the hens would scurry into the grain patch. The geese and peafowl also sought refuge there, and even the startled doves when balked of the safety of the gables.

For the moment no enemy hovered in sight. The fierce summer sun blazed alone in the sky. The birds sought out the shade of the covert; some basked in the grass, others wallowed in the sand.

Rising above the heads of the birds stood a clutch of little human folk, bare-headed, with close-cropped, tow-white hair and necks bared to the shoulders. Among them, taller by a head and with longer hair, stood a young maiden, and directly behind the tots sat a peacock with its hoop of iridescent tail feathers fully expanded. Relieved as in a painting against the tail-feathers' deep-blue background, the white heads took on a vivid radiance—the more vivid for the eyespots that orbed them with starry crowns. There, as through a transparent screen, they shone among the golden maize-stalks, the silver-veined ribbon grass, the blushful love-lies-bleeding and green-leaved mallow. Tone and shape blended together to suggest a trelliswork of silver and gold that swayed in the breeze like a diaphanous veil.

Floating like a baldachin over this polychrome of flowers and grains hung a radiant mist of mayflies[2]—or "dames," as they are commonly called. Almost viewless, they danced on four gauze-like wings, clear as glass, and though they emitted a faint humming sound, they seemed scarcely to stir. The girl swept the air with a gray tassel-like object resembling a tuft of ostrich feathers; clearly, she was driving the golden rain of insects from the little tots' heads. In her other hand was a bright horn-like object—some feeding vessel or other, as she was lowering it by turns to each of the urchins' mouths. The Count took the object for Amalthea's golden horn.

Even while so engaged, the girl, still mindful of the disturbance among the gooseberry canes, kept glancing backward, little realizing that her prowler had crept up from the opposite side and was even now worming his way across the garden beds. Suddenly, he leapt out from the burdocks. Looking up, she saw him bowing low before her just four beds away. Like a startled roller she turned, threw up her arms and prepared to take flight. Her light feet were already skimming the leaves when the little tots, alarmed by the Count's intrusion and the flight of their mistress, raised a piteous wail. Hearing their cries, the girl had second thoughts. Was it seemly to abandon little children in their fright? She stopped, turned, took a step forward, then wavered. But she had to return! Like a reluctant sprite recalled by a warlock's spell, she ran back to attend to the shrillest of her tots. Crouching down, she clasped the child to her breast and soothed the others with tender words and caresses until, huddled around her knees, heads nestled in her bosom, they settled down like little chicks under a brood hen's wing.

"Come," she chided them, "is it nice to be crying so? Is it polite? Why, you'll frighten the gentleman! He had no wish to startle you. This is no nasty old tramp but a visiting guest—a kind young gentleman. See how handsome he is." And she looked for herself.

The Count, clearly delighting in these flatteries, smiled at her sweetly, but the girl, suddenly remembering herself, fell silent, and mantling deeply like a rose lowered her eyes. He was indeed a comely youth: tall of stature, oval-faced, with gentle eyes of cornflower blue, cheeks pale yet fresh-complexioned, locks long and fair. Tufts of grass and leaves gleaned from his passage across the beds clung to his temples like an unraveling wreath of bays.[3]

"You!" he burst forth. "By what name shall I pay you homage?[4] Deity! Nymph! Shadow! Apparition! Speak! Do you walk this earth of your own free will, or does another's hold you captive here? Ah, methinks I know! I'll wager a spurned lover, a great lord or jealous guardian keeps you as one ensorcelled in this castle park. For beauty such as yours, knights-errant fought in the lists. From such as you sprang heroines of melancholy romances! Unfold, my beauty, the secret of your cruel misfortune! You shall find your preserver; even now he hangs upon your beck. As you reign in my bosom, so do you reign over this arm!" And he stretched forth his arm.

Blushing girlishly, yet beaming with joy, she listened to him speak. As a child rejoices in a book of gaudy pictures or takes pleasure in a handful of glittering game counters even before knowing their value, so she, without grasping the substance, delighted in the sonorities of his speech.

"Sir, where have you come from?" she said at last. "What do you seek here among the flowerbeds?"

The Count's eyes rounded with bewilderment and surprise. For a moment he stood speechless; then adopting a less exalted tone, he pursued:

"Please forgive me, miss. I seem to have spoiled your amusement. Forgive me! I was hurrying to the house for breakfast. It is running late, and I hoped to arrive there on time. As you know, the road takes a roundabout route. If I'm not mistaken, the way across the garden is shorter?"

"There is your way, sir," she said. "Only do mind the beds. You will find a path in the grass yonder."

"Right or left?"

The girl raised her eyes and seemed to study him narrowly. The house stood in plain view not a thousand paces from where they were standing, yet here he was asking the way.

"Do you live here, miss?" pursued the Count, eager to draw her into a conversation. "Close to the garden? In the village then? How is it I've never seen you in the house? Have you been here long? Visiting perhaps?"

The little gardener shook her head.

"Forgive me, but isn't that your room by the window yonder?"

Meanwhile, his thoughts ran this way: "True, not your heroine of melancholy romances, but she is undeniably young and pretty. How oft it chances that a noble mind or soul blooms unseen like a rose in the woods. Yet bring such a flower into the world, expose her to the full light of day and she blazes forth with a thousand splendors!"

Without a word, the little gardener rose to her feet. Scooping up the tot that clung to her arm, she seized another by the hand, and driving the rest like a flock of geese before her went forth into the orchard.

"If you please, sir," she said with a backward glance, "be so kind as to drive my scattered birds into the grain patch?"

"What! I?" cried the astonished Count. "Drive your birds!"

But by now she'd fled into the shadow of the next aisle of trees. For an instant he imagined he saw a pair of eyes flash through the foliage.

The Count lingered in the garden. As the earth grows cool after sunset, so his soul began to shed her ardor and take on darker tones. He lapsed into a reverie, but he drew small comfort from his dreams. On coming to himself, he felt vexed; why, he couldn't say. Alas, how little had come of it! His hopes had run too high. With a burning brow and leaping heart he'd crept over the beds toward this shepherdess. All those graces he'd ascribed to the mysterious nymph, all those qualities divined, all those conjectures made—and in the event so wide of the mark! True, her face was pretty, her figure svelte, yet how lacking in poise! And those ample cheeks! Their ruddy hue painted a picture of simple, superabundant bliss, a sign, surely, that her mind and heart lay as yet dormant, inactive. And then her replies! How coarse! How rustic!

"Why delude myself?" he cried out. "My nymph's a common gooseherd."

With the disappearance of the nymph, the whole magical transparency had changed. The veined ribbonry, the charming trellis of silver and gold—alas! was it all merely straw? He stared in anguish at the little bentgrass broom in her hand. So much for the ostrich plumes! And the golden vessel suggesting Amalthea's horn?—a raw carrot! Even now one of the village tots was bolting down the last of it. So it was farewell to the charm! The spell! The wonder! Just so, an urchin spying a clump of chicory flowers[5] is drawn to stroke the soft lavender blue petals. He draws near—he blows—and with the puff the whole inflorescence flies away like down on the wind, leaving behind in the hand of the fastidious observer a naked pedicel of grayish-green hue.[6]

The Count rammed his hat over his eyes, spun on his heel, and returned whence he'd come, only he shortened the way by striding across the flowers, vegetables and gooseberry canes. At last, after vaulting the fence, he breathed freely again. But then he recalled that he'd spoken to the girl of breakfast. Perhaps word of their meeting so close to the house had already got out? What if they'd dispatched servants to fetch him, only to learn he'd run off? No telling what they'd think. Yes, it behooved him to go back.

Keeping low along the fences, he skirted the boundary strips and islands of weeds. At last, to his great relief, after taking a thousand detours, he emerged on the road that made straight for the manor courtyard. He followed the fence without glancing at the garden. Even so the grain pilferer, betraying no sign of his deed or intent, averts his gaze from the granary—such was the Count's circumspection, though no one was about to observe his movements. On he walked, his head turned away from the garden, eyes to the right.

Yonder stood a birch grove, clean of undergrowth and richly swarded. Roaming over that green broadloom, flitting among the white trunks under an awning of low-hung leafy sprays, was a host of shadowy figures. Bizarrely clad, executing strange dance-like motions, they floated like wraiths in the moonlight. Some stood sheathed in black, others wore long, flowing robes as pale as the snow. One had on a broad-brimmed hat, wide as a cooper's hoop, another went bareheaded, still others walked as if wrapped in vapors, headgear trailing in the breeze like a comet's tress. Each figure struck a different pose. One stood rooted to the forest floor; only its lowered eyeballs moved. Another stared straight ahead, moving like a somnambulist, swerving neither to the right nor left, as if treading a line. All continually bent down to the ground in random directions as if making deep bows. Upon approaching one another or crossing paths, they exchanged neither word nor nod, so absorbed were they in their task, so deep was their distraction. The shadowy figures put the Count in mind of the Elysian shades, which, bereft of pain and cares, roam the blessed fields in quiet yet mournful tranquility.

Who would have recognized in these silent folk, so frugal of movement, our friends, the Judge's companions! Having concluded their stormy breakfast, they had gone outdoors to observe the solemn rite of mushrooming. These were sensible folk after all; they knew how to temper their speech, their gestures, and suit them in every circumstance to the place and moment. And so, before following the Judge out into the woods, they'd assumed a new demeanor and a change of dress: loose linen sarafans thrown over their robes, straw hats for their heads—hence their pale aspect reminiscent of purgatorial souls. The youth, too, had changed; only Telimena and a few others were still in their French attire.

The unrusticated Count could make nothing of it. Intrigued to no end, he struck out with all speed for the birch grove.

The forest teemed with wild mushrooms.[7] The lads picked the rosy-cheeked *chanterelle*, an object of high praise in Lithuanian lore. The song calls this mushroom an emblem of maidenhood. Worms never gnaw at it, nor, strange to say, do insects alight on its cap. The maidens sought after the handsome *bolete*, which the ditty calls the "colonel of mushrooms."[8] All hunted for the smaller *saffron milk-cap*. Less exalted in song, these were tastiest of all, as you could eat them fresh or salted, in autumn or winter. Meanwhile, the Steward sought out his *fly agaric*.

Other common varieties of fungi were shunned for their inferior taste or injurious effects. Yet even these were not without their use. They provided the fauna with nourishment, the insect with a nesting place, and the glade with garniture. Like a table service they stood ranged on the meadow's linen: the round-edged *brittlegills*, silvery, yellowish or ruby-red, like goblets a-brim with various vintages; the *birch boletes*, their caps dimpled like the bottoms of upturned cups; the delicate *funnels*, resembling champagne flutes; the *fleecy milkcap*, round and white, broad and smooth like cream-filled teacups of Dresden porcelain; and the spherical *puffballs*, squat as pepper-pots, replete with their black, powdery spore mass.

The rest had names found only in the tongues of the hare and the wolf; human folk had not yet christened these, though they grew in profusion. No one touched these brute varieties. If a gatherer mistakenly reached down for one, he'd snap off the cap in anger or trample it underfoot, though in so sullying the sward he behaved quite unwisely.

Telimena picked neither the brute nor human varieties. Bored and distracted, her head thrown back, she cast her gaze around her. The Notary testily observed she was hunting for mushrooms in the trees. More spitefully, the Assessor likened her to a broody bird spying out a place to build her nest.

But Telimena appeared to be seeking a place of quiet and solitude. Slowly she drew away from her companions. Straying deeper into the forest, she ascended a gently sloping knoll well shaded by the trees growing thickly there. A grayish rock crowned the knoll; from beneath it sprang a little stream. Out it gushed and fled away, as if seeking shade, to water the tall grasses thereabout. Swaddled in the herbage, covered over with leaves, unseen, untroubled and motionless, the frisky little mischief purled. So a querulous child lies tucked in its crib while the mother, bestrewing the pillow with poppy petals, laces up the bright green drapes. Truly a lovely purlieu! Telimena often sought refuge here; she called it her Temple of Musings.

Stopping by the rill, she slipped her carnelian-red shawl from her shoulders and let it float to the ground. As a bathing damsel bends down to the water, bracing for the plunge, so Telimena dropped to her knees, sank slowly to one side, and flouncing down as if seized by a coral tide stretched herself at full length on the grass. There she lay, her elbow planted in the grass, temple resting on the palm of her hand, head canted to one side, eyes poring over the gleaming vellum of a French novel; and as she read, her black ringlets and rose-colored ribbons danced over the alabaster leaves.

Seeing her lying on her crimson shawl, sheathed in her long coral-hued gown, her frame set off at either end by her black hair and slipper, and, laterally, by the shimmering white line of her stocking, handkerchief, arm, and cheek—seeing her lying thus in the luxuriant emerald-green grass, a distant onlooker might easily have taken her for a gaudy caterpillar sprawled on a maple leaf.

Alas, no connoisseur was near to admire the charms and merits of this scene! None of the gatherers paid it any heed, so absorbed were they in their pursuit of mushrooms. But Tadeusz paid heed! Casting sideward glances at Telimena, yet loath to approach her directly, he edged his way up the slope toward her. As when the bird-shooter concealed behind his wheel-mounted blind advances on the bustard, or the snipe hunter, keeping to the blind side of his horse holds his gun steady on the saddle or leveled under the horse's neck, and, like a farmer dragging his harrow along the edge of the balk, draws ever closer to his quarry's covert—even so Tadeusz made his stealthy ascent.

But the Judge foiled his ambuscade. Cutting in before his nephew, he strode briskly up toward the stream. The breeze sported with the white tails of his sarafan and the ample handkerchief knotted around his belt; his straw hat, secured by a string against the rush of air, waved like a burdock leaf, beating now over his shoulders, now over his eyes. So, his stout walking stick gripped in hand, he guided his steps upward. After squatting down to wash his hands, he seated himself on a large rock opposite Telimena, and leaning forward on the ivory ball of his prodigious cane opened his conversation thus:

"You see, my dear, that ever since young Tadeusz has been our guest, I have been sorely distressed. I am childless and getting on in years. The dear lad's my one solace in the world, the future heir to my fortune. God willing, I shall leave him a decent inheritance befitting a nobleman. It's time also to be thinking of his marital prospects and station in life. Now consider, my dear, the difficulty I find myself in. You know that my brother Jacek, Tadeusz's father, is a strange fellow.

His intentions are hard to read. He refuses to come home. God knows where he's hiding now. He forbids us to inform his son that he is alive, and yet he continually gives us directions in his regard. First he wanted to send Tadeusz to the legions; that caused me no little distress. Then he agreed he should stay home and take a wife. That could be easily arranged. I have a match picked out for him. None of our citizens boast a better name or set of relations than the Chamberlain. His elder daughter Anna is eligible, she is comely and suitably dowered. I had a mind to launch the proceedings."

Telimena turned suddenly pale. Closing her book, she rose to her knees then settled back on her haunches. "So help me, dear brother!" she said. "Are you serious? Are you a God-fearing man? Make of him a sower of groats! Is that what you call looking after the boy's interests? Why, you will close the world to him! Depend on it, he will end up cursing you one day. To think of burying such talent in the woods and kitchen gardens! Why, even from what I know of Tadeusz, I can see he is a capable lad, worthy of refinement in high society. You'd do well, dear brother, to send him to the capital—to Warsaw, for instance, or, if you really want to know my opinion, why not Petersburg? I expect to be returning there this winter on business. Together we shall decide the boy's future. I am acquainted with a good many people there and have influence—no better way of making a man! With my help, he will gain admittance into the finest houses, and once he comes to know to people of consequence, he'll secure a rank, win a decoration. Then, if he so chooses, he can resign his post and come home. But then he will be somebody and know the ways of the world. What say you to this, dear brother?"

"True enough," said the Judge, "a change of air and scene in one's early years, a chance to see the world and rub shoulders with society can profit a man. In my own youth I saw a good bit of the world. I have been to Piotrków and Dubno,[9] now following the Tribunal as a barrister, now attending to my own affairs. I've even been to Warsaw! Aye, there's much to be gained by it. I, too, should like to send my nephew out into the world, but as a traveler rather, or an apprentice rounding off his term, that he might learn something of the affairs of men. Not for the sake of ranks or decorations! You'll pardon me, my dear, but a rank in the Muscovite hierarchy, a decoration, what sort of distinction are they? Who among our ancient lords—in truth, who of any prominence in our district today cares for such trifles? Here we esteem a man for his gentle birth, his good name or office, by which I mean an office won by an honest vote of the local citizenry—not through somebody's good influences!"

"If that is your view," said Telimena, "then all the better. By all means, send your nephew out as a traveler."

"You see, dear sister," said the Judge, scratching his head ruefully, "I'd like nothing more, but there's a fresh complication. Jacek refuses to yield oversight of his son, and now he has burdened me with that monk Robak, his companion from across the Vistula whom he has taken into his confidence. Together they have decided the lad's future. They want Tadeusz to wed, to take your ward Sophy as wife. In addition to my own small fortune, the couple shall receive a dowry in ready money from Jacek. As you know, dear, my brother has capital. It is thanks to him that I own the greater part of the domain, and he has every right to take charge in this matter. So, my dear, think how best to smooth the way. They must become acquainted; true, they are very young, Sophy especially, but that's neither here nor there. Anyhow, it's high time she came out of confinement as, by all accounts, she's growing out of childhood."

Telimena, aghast, almost in a panic, raised herself on her knees. A compliant listener at first, she was now signaling disagreement, waving her hand vigorously over her ear, as if to drive the swarm of unwelcome words back into the speaker's mouth.

"What is this? What's this I hear?" she retorted hotly. "Sir, whether that is good or ill for Tadeusz, you may decide for yourself. The boy means nothing to me. Plan for him yourselves! Make him a bailiff, or put him in a tavern! Let him serve drinks or fetch game from the forest. Do as you please with him! But Sophy, what concern is she of yours? Whom she weds is for me to decide. Me alone! Just because Jacek pays for her rearing, affords her a modest yearly allowance, and promises to give more, does not make her his chattels. Besides, it is still widely known that your generosity toward her is not entirely without self-interest. You Soplicas know full well you bear the Horeszko family a heavy debt."

The Judge listened to this part of her discourse with incomprehensible dismay, grief, and visible revulsion. As if dreading to hear what she might say next, he bowed his head and waved assent, flushing deeply.

"I have stood her in the stead of mother," pursued Telimena, closing her argument. "I am Sophy's kin, her only guardian. No one but I shall provide for her happiness."

"And if she should find happiness in this match?" ventured the Judge, raising his eyes. "If she should take a fancy to Tadeusz?"

"Fancy? Fig on a thistle! Much I care for fancies! True, Sophy will not be a wealthy match, but she is no village wench or smallholder's daughter. She comes from a noble line. Her father was a governor, her mother a Horeszko. She *shall* find a husband! Such pains we've taken with her education—why, she'd run wild in this place!"

The Judge listened intently, still looking into her eyes. He seemed to soften, as his reply was cheerful enough.

"Well, my dear," he said. "Nothing more to be said. Lord knows I've done my best to bring the matter forward. Only do not be angry, my dear. If you don't agree, you're quite within your rights. Sad it is, but there's no use in being angry. I urged the suit for my brother's sake only. No one's forcing the match. Since you see fit to refuse Tadeusz's suit, I shall inform Jacek in writing that notwithstanding my best efforts, a betrothal between Tadeusz and Sophy cannot come to pass. Now I can take my own counsel. Most likely, the Chamberlain and I will launch the process and have the whole matter settled—"

But Telimena's anger had begun to subside. "Not so fast, dear brother," she broke in. "I refuse nothing. You said yourself it was too soon, that they were young. Let's not rush into anything. We shall consider the matter; no harm in that. We'll allow the young people to become acquainted and keep an eye on them, for the happiness of others cannot be left to chance. But I must caution you, dear brother, to refrain from putting ideas into Tadeusz's head. No forcing of his attentions on Sophy! The heart is no slave. Love brooks no master, no chains shall constrain it."

With that the Judge rose and walked away, deep in thought. Meanwhile, drawn by an imaginary trail of mushrooms, Tadeusz was approaching from the other side; at the same time, the Count was advancing slowly up from another direction.

All this time, the Count had been watching the Judge and Telimena from his point of espial behind the trees. Deeply stirred by the scene, he drew paper and pencil from his pocket (he never went anywhere without his drawing materials), leaned over a stump, and spreading the sheet before him busied himself with sketching studies.

"Arranged as by design," he muttered to himself. "He on the rock, she on the sward. A picturesque ensemble! Distinctive heads, contrasting lines."

Drawing closer, he checked himself to wipe his lorgnette and eyes with his handkerchief, then continued to gaze.

"Must this lovely, enchanting tableau vanish or be transformed upon nicer inspection?" he mused. "Shall that velvet sward resolve itself into a patch of poppies and beet-tops? Shall I, in yonder nymph, discover a bailiff's mistress?"

Though the Count had often seen Telimena at the manor (he was a frequent caller there), he had never paid her much attention. What was his amazement now when he recognized the model of his sketches! The beauty of the natural setting, the grace of his subject's posture, and the elegance of her attire had transformed her almost beyond recognition. Anger still smoldered in her eyes.

Enlivened by the breeze, by the recent quarrel with the Judge, and now by the sudden approach of the two youths,[10] her face flushed with tones all the more vivid and intense.

"Please forgive the bold intrusion, ma'am," said the Count. "But I come bearing both apologies and words of gratitude: apologies for stealing upon your footsteps, gratitude for the honor of witnessing your musings. A grave offense committed, a heavy debt incurred, for I intrude upon a moment of your meditations and stand obliged for several more of inspiration. Felicitous moments! Now censure the man, but the artist awaits your grace. Having risked much, I shall risk more. Be my judge!"

And kneeling down beside her, he handed her his landscapes.

Telimena appraised his studies courteously yet as one knowledgeable in matters of art; while slow to praise, she was quick to encourage.

"Bravo!" she exclaimed. "I congratulate you. There is no small talent here, only see you do not neglect it. Above all, seek out lovely, natural settings. Italy's sunlit skies. Rome's imperial rose gardens. Tiber's classic cataracts. Posilipo's awesome caverns. There, my dear Count, is your land for painters. Here? Lord have mercy! A child of the Muses suckled at Soplica Manor would starve to death. My dear Count, I shall have your sketches framed or place them in my album together with several other drawings I've picked up along the way. By now I've no mean store in my escritoire."

They began to talk of azure skies, murmuring seas, redolent breezes, and craggy peaks. Here and there in the manner of many a traveler they dropped scornful remarks and poked fun at their native land.

Yet all around them, in all its imposing splendor, stretched Lithuania's ancient woodland! All around stood the bird cherry with her festoonery of wild hop; the rowan, fresh and mantling like a shepherdess's cheek; the maenad hazel with her verdant thyrsi wreathed in a grape-like garniture of pearly nuts. Beneath them stood the forest children, the guelder rose in the clasp of an alder, the black-lipped bramble entwined around a raspberry bush. Leafy-fingered trees and shrubs stood in a circle, hands joined, like village lads and their maids poised to tread a measure around the newlyweds; and, in their midst, surpassing the rest of the forest party in grace of form and charm of hue, stood the happy couple—a silver birch, the beloved, and her groom, a hornbeam. Farther back, like elder-folk gazing silently down at their children and grandchildren, reared the hoary beeches, the matronly poplars, and a solitary, moss-bearded oak. Bent under the weight of five centuries, he leaned on the petrified trunks of his grandsires, which towered from the forest floor like the blasted columns of an ancient mausoleum.

Tadeusz fidgeted and squirmed, bored to no end by this long discourse in which he had no share. When the Count and Telimena began to sing the praises of exotic groves and rhyme off every species of tree—the orange, cypress, olive, almond, cactus, aloe, mahogany, sandal, lemon, ivy, walnut, even the fig—and then enlarge upon their shape, blossoms and texture of bark, he could only bridle and pout. At last, he could stand it no longer. Though a simple youth, he knew how to delight in natural beauty. His imagination set ablaze by the sight of his native forest, he began to speak his mind.

"I have been to the botanical gardens in Wilno, seen the celebrated trees that grow in the Orient or down south in that fair Italy of yours. Which of them compares with our own native trees? The aloe whose twigs stick up like lightning conductors? The lemon?—that dwarf of a tree with her gilded knobs and lacquered leaves, short and squat like a rich but ugly old lady. Your vaunted cypress?—that meager tree which seems to express boredom rather than sorrow! People say the cypress looks so mournful beside a grave. I say the thing's more like a German flunkey in court mourning; motionless he stands for fear of offending against funeral etiquette!

"Is not our honest-hearted birch comelier? Picture her as a village woman, a mother grieving for her son, or a widow her spouse. She wrings her hands, her hair, fetched out over her shoulders, cascades to the ground. Mute with grief she stands, and yet in her posture how expressively she weeps. If painting's your passion, sir, you ought to be painting the trees whose shade you now enjoy? Truly, sir, you shall be the laughingstock of the district if, biding in Lithuania's fertile plains, you paint only craggy peaks and desert wastes."

"My friend," replied the Count, "natural beauty is but the form, the backdrop, the raw material, so to speak; the soul of art is inspiration. Art ranges on the pinions of invention; taste must polish it, sound principles ground it. Nature is not enough, neither is fervor, for the artist must lift himself into the realm of the Ideal! Not every species of beauty lends itself to the painter's brush. All this you shall learn in good time in the course of your reading. As to painting, know that a picture requires a point of vantage, grouping, arrangement, and a sky—an Italian sky! So it is with the art of landscape. That is why Italy has always been the birthplace of painters and why, apart from Bruegel[11]—not Van der Helle, mind, but the landscapist (there are two Bruegels)—why, apart from Bruegel, and Ruysdael too, we in the northern latitudes boast of so few genre painters of the highest order. Skies! Skies are what we need!"

"Take our painter Orłowski,"[12] broke in Telimena. "Now *there* was one with Soplica taste! (You should know that this is a disease among the Soplicas; they have but one abiding passion—their native land.) I speak of Orłowski, the famous artist who spent his years in Petersburg. I keep one or two of his sketches in my escritoire. He lived next door to the Emperor's court—a veritable painter's paradise! Yet, my dear Count, you wouldn't believe how he pined for his land. He loved nothing better than to reminisce on his youth and sing the praises of all things Polish—the fields, the skies, the forests . . ."

"And rightly so!" rejoined Tadeusz hotly. "From what I hear, those clear blue Italian skies of yours are like water frozen over! Are not gales and inclement weather a hundred times lovelier? Here you've only to look up. No end to the sights! How many pictures and scenes unfold from the play of the clouds alone. Each cloud is unique. Take the lazy autumn cloud: tortoise-wise it creeps along, great with showers, lowering long streamers like unbound tresses to the earth. Those are streams of rain! And the hail cloud: like a ball it scuds before the wind, dark-blue and round, with a glint of yellow in its core, and all around a mighty roar! Take even your regular white clouds like those up yonder. See how changeable they are! Like a flock of swans or wild geese they drive along. The falcon-wind swoops down from behind, bunches them up; they mass together, swell, thicken, and lo, sprouting curved necks, manes and legs, they gallop across Heaven's steppeland like a herd of silvery-white ponies. Yet another shifting! The ponies' necks sprout masts, the manes billow into broad sails and the herd reshapes itself into a proud schooner. Serene and leisurely, she navigates the blue plain of the sky."

Telimena and the Count sat gazing up at the cloud. Tadeusz was pointing to it with his hand while gently squeezing Telimena's with the other. Several minutes of quiet contemplation elapsed. The Count spread a sheet of foolscap over his hat and reached for a pencil. Just then the mournful sound of the manor bell broke upon their ears. Instantly, the quiet forest broke out into a tumult of shouts and halloos.

"So, with the tolling of the bell," lamented the Count, shaking his head, "does Destiny put a period to the things of this world: the reckonings of great minds, the inventions of ranging fancy, the tender diversions, the delights of friendship, the outpourings of gentle hearts. When the bronze roars from afar, all falls into confusion, chaos and turmoil, and vanishes away." And gazing tenderly at Telimena, he said, "What remains?"

"Memories!" she replied; and to sweeten his sadness, she tendered him a fresh-culled forget-me-not. The Count touched it to his lips then pinned it to his bosom. Meanwhile, on the side opposite, Tadeusz was parting the leaves of a shrub. A white object was threading its way through the leafage toward him—a lily-white hand! Seizing it up, he buried his lips silently into the open palm, like a bee in a lily cup. Something cold touched his lips—a key with a screw of white paper inserted through the bow; it was a little card. He snatched it up and thrust it into his pocket. What the key signified he had no idea, but, doubtless, the card would shed light on it.

The bell continued to clank. From deep within the silent wood, scores of shouts and cries answered back like echoes; it was the sound of men and women seeking one another out, hailing and hallooing, a sign that the day's mushrooming had come to a close. Yet these echoes were scarcely funereal, as it seemed to the Count; if anything, there was a prandial ring to them. Every day at noon the bell rang out from under the manor gable summoning the guests and servants to luncheon. Many of the older domains observed this custom. Soplica Manor held fast to it.

And so, carrying chip punnets, wicker baskets, and tied-up handkerchiefs, all bulging and brimming with wild mushrooms, the party issued forth from the grove. Every young lass held a magnificent bolete like a folded fan in one hand and a bundle of *honey mushrooms* and *brittlegills* of various hue in the other—all neatly tied with a string like a nosegay of field flowers. Next came the Steward clutching his precious *fly agaric*, Telimena followed empty-handed, and the youth brought up the rear.

The party entered the great hall in orderly fashion and drew up in a circle around the table. The post of honor rightfully belonged to the Chamberlain; it was the privilege of his office and senior years. Bowing in turn to the ladies, elders and youth, he advanced toward the table; the Bernardine quester stationed himself beside him, the Judge next to the Bernardine. The Monk recited a brief benison in the Latin tongue, the men took vodka, whereupon they sat down one and all, and tucked silently into the beet-leaf soup, chilled Lithuanian-style.

The noon meal passed more quietly than usual. Despite the host's entreaties, no one was in the humor for talk. The two factions embroiled in the great strife over the two greyhounds had tomorrow's contest and wager on their minds. (Great thoughts will constrain lips to silence.) Though Telimena talked constantly to Tadeusz, she felt obliged to turn now and then to the Count and even vouchsafe the Assessor an occasional glance: so keeps the fowler his eye on several gin traps at once, one for snaring the goldfinch, another for the sparrow. Both Tadeusz and the Count felt pleased with themselves, both were happy and hopeful, and neither of them had a list to talk. The Count proudly eyed his forget-me-not. Tadeusz cast furtive glances into his pocket to ensure that the key hadn't slipped away; he even reached in his hand to finger the card, as he'd not yet had time to read it. Meanwhile, the Judge waited attentively on the Chamberlain, offering him champagne and Hungarian wine and squeezing his knee. Yet even he lacked zest for talk; clearly, he was burdened by private cares of his own.

The plates and dishes came and went in silence. Suddenly, an unexpected guest broke the tedious flow of the meal. It was the forest ranger. Heedless of his intrusion on the lunch hour, he strode hurriedly up to the Judge. You could tell by his mien and the set of his shoulders that he bore tidings of great and unusual import. All eyes turned on him. "A bear, your lordship!" he gasped out, after catching his breath.

The rest they could surmise for themselves. The bear had forsaken his lair in the old forest and was striking out for the woods across the Niemen. They must stalk it without a moment's delay—all realized this, neither counsel nor reflection was needed. That they were of one mind was clear from the ensuing welter of clipped words, lively gestures, and brusque commands, which, while flowing tumultuously from so many pairs of lips at once, all tended toward the same purpose.

"To the village!" cried the Judge. "Ho there! To horse! Summon the foreman! Have a troop of beaters ready at daybreak! Volunteers, mind! Whoever shows up with a spear gets off two days' roadwork and five days' field service!"[13]

"Bustle about!" barked the Chamberlain. "Saddle my gray, ride post-haste to the house and fetch my two bulldogs[14]—aye, the pair the whole neighborhood talks about. The male answers to the name Constable, the bitch Procureuse.[15] Muzzle 'em, throw 'em in a sack, and bring 'em here on the double, on horseback, so as not to waste time."

"Vanka!" cried the Assessor to his servant boy in Ruthenian. "Run my Sanguszko hunting knife over the whetting stone. Aye, the one I received as a gift from the Prince. Then fill my cartridge belt; and see that every round is armed!"

"Guns!" cried one and all. "Get the guns ready!"

"Lead, fetch me lead!" the Assessor kept yelling. "You'll find a bullet mold in my bag."

"Tell the parish priest" cried the Judge, "that Holy Mass will be said for the hunters in the forest chapel at daybreak tomorrow. Aye, Saint Hubert's Mass[16]—the one with the short office."

Their orders issued, the guests relapsed into thoughtful silence. They began to sweep the room with their eyes as if searching out one among them. Slowly, the venerable face of the Chief Steward began to draw upon itself and unite their gaze; clearly, they were looking for someone upon whom to confer the huntmaster's mace, and their choice had fallen on the Steward. Rising to acknowledge the will of his comrades, the Steward struck the table a solemn blow, then plunging his hand deep into his bosom drew out by its gold fob a pocketwatch the size of a large pear.

"Tomorrow," he declared, "at half past four in the morning, our brother hunters and our troop of beaters shall present themselves before the forest chapel!"

With that he withdrew from the table, the forest ranger following close on his heels. The two now had a hunt to plan and arrange. Just so withdraw the commanding officers after announcing the hour of the imminent battle: in the camp, the rank and file clean their arms, chew on their rations, or, setting their cares aside, sleep on their saddles and greatcoats; meanwhile, the general and his staff ponder their plans in the quiet of the tent.

There was no more thought of eating. The rest of the day was spent in shoeing horses, feeding the hounds, collecting and cleaning guns. Scarcely anyone bothered to attend the evening meal. Even Scut and Peregrine's champions ceased to concern themselves with the great contest; the Notary and the Assessor were now arm in crook, scouring the premises for lead.

Worn out by the day's events, the rest of the company retired early so as to be up at the crack of dawn on the morrow.

NOTES

1. The Polish text gives the humorous appellations *Kokosznicka* and the run-on *Jendykowi-/Czówna*.

2. In the eastern borderland region of the poet's birth, these dancing insects were called *babki*, probably under the influence of the Russian *babochka* (butterfly). In standard Polish *babka* means "dame" or "granny."

3. Compare this description with that of the shipwrecked Odysseus suddenly appearing before Nausicaä's maidens "in his defilement with the sea-wrack" (*The Odyssey*, VI, 149, tr. T.E. Lawrence).

4. This manner of launching an address is common to heroes of classical literature from Homer onward. The fragment bears a resemblance to the *Odyssey*, where Odysseus addresses Nausicaä: "O Queen: yet am I in doubt whether you are divine or mortal. If a goddess from high heaven. . ." (VI 164 inf.). Compare also Aeneas' greeting of his mother Venus in *The Aeneid*, I, 327-329: *O – quam te memorem, virgo? Namque haud tibi vultus / mortalis, nec vox humanum sonat; o dea certe! / An Phoebi soror? an Nympharum sanguinis una?* And just as Sophy addresses her little tots, so Homer's Nausicaä calls to her startled maidens: "*Rally to me, women. Why run because you see a man? You cannot think him an enemy . . .*" (218 inf.). Similar affinities have been noted with Polish neo-classical works, notably the humorous *Ode to a Bullwhip* ascribed to Adam Naruszewicz. According to Pigoń, Mickiewicz knew this ode well and evidently used it here for mock-heroic effect: "His contemporaries, knowing this verse, would have sensed the playfulness of applying it to a young girl. Though the count has a "romantic cast of mind" and a fondness for romantic curiosities, he expresses himself in a manner typical of Polish poets of the eighteenth century. The entire phraseology of this fragment is reminiscent of Naruszewicz, Trembecki and Koźmian, who frequently began their odes with the apostrophe, "O thou!"

5. This extended simile has long perplexed the botanically minded reader. Is the poet refer-
ring to the chicory flower (*cichorium intybus*) with its fluffy clump of volitant light-blue seeds
(hence the Polish word "bławaty"—literally, "blue petals"). Or is he referring to the common
dandelion, as K. Łapczyński posited in his monograph on the flora of *Pan Tadeusz*, suggest-
ing that *cykoria* was a regional designation for the *brodawnik mleczowy* or *mniszek*? In either
case, the simile would seem infelicitous, though, interestingly enough, "blue dandelion" is
among the many English names for the common chicory flower. Both flowers belong to the
Asteraceae family. See K. Łapczyński, *Flora Litwy w "Panu Tadeuszu"* (Kraków, 1894), 28.

6. This is the first adumbration of the "theme of disenchantment," which runs like a *leitmotif*
throughout Mickiewicz's entire work. See also note 28 to Book XII.

7. The popular and scientific names of the mushrooms mentioned by the poet are as follows:
chanterelle (*lisica*), *Cantharelus cibarius*; cep or king bolete (*borowik szlachetny*), *Boletus edulis*;
saffron milkcap (*rydz*), *Lactarius deliciosus*; fly agaric (*muchomór*), *Amanita muscaria*; brittlegill
(*surojadka*), varieties of the *russula* spp.; birch bolete (*koźlak*), varieties of the *leccinum* spp.;
funnel (*lejek*), varieties of the *clitocybe* spp.; fleecy milkcap (*bielak*), *Agaricus* vellereus; puffball
(*purchawka*), varieties of the *bovista* spp.; honey mushroom (*opieńka*), *Armillaria mellea*.

8. In his notes the poet mentions the "folksong" (*pieśń gminna*) that tells of the regiment of
mushrooms marching off to war under the lead of the king bolete. The song, existing in
Belorussian and Polish versions, describes the properties of edible mushrooms.

9. The poet is deliberately poking fun at the judge's parochialism and limited horizons. Neither
town falls outside the borders of the old Polish-Lithuanian Commonwealth. Piotrków
was the seat of the Royal Tribunal, the highest court of Poland in 1578-1793. Dubno (in
Volhynia) was the site of a famous annual fair.

10. In the ensuing verbal contest between Tadeusz and the count, the poet once again harks
back to the stock conventions of classical literature—this time to the idylls of Theocritus
and Virgil in which two swains typically vie for the attentions of a nymph or shepherdess in a
pastoral setting.

11. The Bruegels were a famous family of Dutch painters in the sixteenth and early seventeenth
centuries. The count has in mind the brothers Pieter (1564-1638), known as "the Bruegel
from Hell" (*van der Helle*) because of his fondness for infernal scenes, and Jan (1568-1625),
a master landscape painter. Jacob van Ruysdael (1628-1682) was another noted Dutch land-
scape painter, especially of pristine forests unspoiled by man. He was highly regarded by the
Romantics.

12. Aleksander Orłowski (1777-1832), student of Norblin and Bacciarelli. In 1802 he settled in
Saint Petersburg as Archduke Constantine's court painter. Residing near the Imperial court at
the Marble Palace, he lovingly depicted Polish historical figures and themes (among them the
Massacre of Praga). He was also fond of painting horses. As Mickiewicz observes in his notes,
Orłowski was actually a genre painter. His landscapes are less well known. While staying in
Petersburg in 1828 and 1829, the poet met the artist who painted his portrait. Telimena's use
of the past tense is inapposite, since in 1811 Orłowski was still living and painting.

13. That is, *corvée* labor (pol. *pańszczyzna*), or unpaid field labor owed by a peasant to his feudal
lord.

14. [*Author's note*] The breed of small strong English dogs that we call *pijawki* [literally: leeches]
is used for hunting big game, especially bear.

15. The Polish names of the chamberlain's bulldogs (*Sprawnik* and *Strapczyna*) derive from the
Russian titles of two officials who, as the poet adds in his notes, having "frequent opportuni-
ties for abusing their authority" [were] "held in great loathing by the people." These were the

ispravnik, the chief of the Tsarist rural police, and the *strapchiy*, a sort of government procurator. *Strapczyna* would be the feminine variant of *strapchiy* or refer to his wife or widow. There is an intriguing Shakespearean connection here, namely with Malvolio's "Lady of the Strachy" of *Twelfth Night* (TN 2.5.37). Dyce's *Glossary to the Works of William Shakespeare* observes that "the term 'strachy' is now only preserved in the Russian language; but it was probably taken by Shakespeare from some novel or play, upon which he may have founded the comic incidents of this drama. Corroboration can [...] be derived from the list of all the Crown servants of Russia, sent every year to the State Secretary of the Home Department at St. Petersburg; in which, for 1825 and 1826, Procureur Botwinko was reported to be imprisoned at Vilna for [corruption], and that the Strapchy of Oszmiana was acting in his stead as Procureur *pro tem*." (*op.cit.*, London, Bickers & Son, 1880, p. 420). Nikolai Novosiltsev, Tsar Alexander I's commissar of the Council of State of the Kingdom of Poland, had Mickiewicz similarly imprisoned at the Basilian Monastery in Wilno in late 1823 or early 1824.

16. Hubert was the patron saint of hunters. According to the judge, the Mass in the saint's honor had a short office (*officium parvum*).

BOOK IV

Diplomacy and the Hunt

Argument

An apparition in curl papers wakes Tadeusz. A mistake discovered too late. The tavern. The emissary. The deft use of a snuffbox steers a discussion back on the right course. The Lairs. The bear. Tadeusz and the Count in peril. Three gunshots. Sagalas vs. Sanguszko. The dispute decided in favor of a Horeszko single barrel. Hunter's stew. The Steward's tale of the duel between Dowejko and Domejko interrupted by a hare course. Dowejko and Domejko concluded.

Coevals of Lithuania's Grand Dukes! You trees of Białowieża, Świteź, Ponary, and Kuszelewo![1] Your shade once fell on the crowned heads of the dread lord Witenes, mighty Mindowe, and Giedymin, when sprawled on a bearskin by the hunters' fire, he listened to the croonings of his sage Lizdejko.[2] Gazing down from the Ponary heights, lulled to sleep by the sight of the Wilia and the brawl of the Wilenka,[3] he dreamed of an iron wolf, then roused to the task at the clear behest of the gods founded the city of Wilno that broods in the forest like the wolf among the bison, bear, and wild boar. As Rome sprang from the she-wolf, so from Wilno sprang Kiejstut, Olgierd, and the entire Olgierd line—intrepid knights and hunters all, equally unswerving in the charge and the chase. And so our future stands revealed in a hunter's dream: timber and iron—of these Lithuania shall always have need.

You ancient woodlands! The last of *them* came hunting your game, last of our princes to sport Witold's kalpak. Last of Jagiełło's line of blithe warriors! Lithuania's last monarch of the chase![4]

O my native trees! My old friends! If Heaven grants that I should see you again, shall I find you yet? Do you still live?—you, at whose feet I used to crawl as a babe. Does mighty Baublis[5] live? Reamed out by the ages, his hollow chamber could comfortably seat a dozen guests around a table. Does Mendog's grove still blossom by the parish church?[6] And yonder, in the Ukrainian borderlands, does the ancient linden still stand before the Hołowiński[7] house on the banks of the Ros? A hundred youths and a hundred maids found ample room to dance beneath her spreading shade!

Our monuments! How many of you toppled each year by the timber merchant and Muscovy's axe! Scarce a haunt remains for the woodland songster, or the bard who holds your bowers equally as dear! Did Jan's[8] beloved linden not hang upon his every word? Did she not prompt him with rhymes by the score? And that prattling oak! No end to the marvels he croons in our Cossack poet's ear![9]

And I! How much *I* stand in your debt, my native forests! What thoughts didn't I, a trifling hunter, pursue in your quiet solitudes after fleeing my comrades' taunts over a quarry missed. Deep in the old forest, the hunt long out of mind, I'd sit me down on a small knoll. Around me glint patches of silver-bearded moss shot through with the crimson of crushed bilberries. Yonder mantles the rolling heath, festooned with mountain cranberry as with chaplets of coral. Darkness embosoms me! A canopy of interlacing branches hangs low over my head like an overcast of dense green cloud, and high above that motionless vault, the wind soughs and moans, whistles, wails and booms. A strange, heady din! You'd swear a boisterous sea hung suspended there.

Below sprawls a conurbation of ruins! An overthrown oak towers up like a vast pile of building; on either side of it lean half-rotted trunks and bristling stumps resembling shattered columns and fragments of wall; tall grasses hedge it round. Prying eyes beware! Behind that palisade dwell the lords of the waste—the wild boar, the bear, the wolf. Half-gnawed bones of unwary guests bestrew the entranceway! Now and anon, a pair of antlers springs out of the undergrowth like two water-jets. Away streaks the stag!—a tawny blur passing through the trees like a fugitive sunbeam.

Silence returns below. A woodpecker taps lightly at a spruce then flies off and vanishes from sight, yet he goes on tapping like a concealed child beckoning to its seekers. A squirrel sits on his haunches gnawing at a nut; his brush overhangs his brow like a hussar's helmet plume, yet nothing escapes those darting eyes. A stranger intrudes! Away flies our dancer of the woods! Like a levin-flash he leaps from tree to tree, to slip at last into a hidden cleft, like a wood sprite returning to his native tree. Silence again.

A rowan-tree stirs. A clustering branch draws back, and a face ruddier than a rowanberry pokes through the opening. A village maiden out foraging for fruit and nuts! Her rude birch-bark basket brims with cranberries for the taking, fresh and red as her lips. At her side walks her swain; he reaches down a hazel spray while she grasps for the flashing cobs.

Suddenly—horn blasts! Hound music! A hunt draws near. Alarmed, the pair fly into the leafy thicket, melting from sight like woodland deities.

Soplica Manor was all astir. Yet neither the noise of the hounds, nor the neighing of the horses, nor the creaking of the carts, nor yet the blare of the horns announcing the start of the hunt roused Tadeusz from his slumbers. Sound as a marmot he slept, still in the clothes he'd worn on dropping into bed that night. None of the youths thought to look for him in the house; all were about their affairs, anxious to be at their posts. Their sleeping companion passed entirely unnoticed.

On he snored. Through a heart-shaped opening cut out of the window shutter, a fiery shaft of sunlight streamed into the darkness, falling full on the sleeping lad's brow. He would have dozed on, but even as he turned from the glare, an urgent tapping sound awoke him. Happy awakening! He felt blithe as a bird and he breathed softly. He felt glad, he smiled—and in full memory of last night's assignation,[10] he blushed; and he sighed, and his heart began to race!

He glanced up at the window. Ye gods! Shining in the sunlit aperture, enclosed within that heart were two bright eyes, opened wide, as one would expect of eyes peering into the darkness from the broad daylight. He saw a small hand raised fan-wise to the temple to shield the eyes from the glare. The rosy light made transparencies of the delicate fingers, suffusing them with a ruby hue. He made out a pair of curious lips, slightly parted, a gleaming row of little teeth like pearls in the coral, and cheeks that, even without the roseate hand shading them, mantled red as a rose all over.

Tadeusz lay on his back by the window. Unseen in the darkness, he marveled at the apparition hovering directly above him almost touching his face. Was he awake, he wondered, or simply imagining one of those radiant little faces that haunt the dreams of our innocent youth?

The face peered down at him. Trembling with awe and delight, Tadeusz gazed hard upon it, and only then—to his indescribable chagrin!—recognized the short, pale-gold tresses wrapped in snow-white curl papers, the same silvery pod-like objects he'd seen flaming in the sun like a saintly glory.

He sat up with a jerk. The vision vanished, startled by the movement. In vain he waited for it to reappear. Presently, he heard three more taps and an urgent voice, saying, "Sir, it is time to get up for the hunt. You have overslept yourself!"

Tadeusz sprang from his couch and dashed back both shutters with such violence that the hinges rattled, and the leaves, flying open, crashed against the wall on either side. Landing on the ground outside, he looked about him in surprise and bewilderment. Not a soul in sight! Hard by the window ran the garden fence overgrown with flowers and leafy bine. The leafage still trembled, as if a light hand or a breath of wind had brushed over it. Long he stared at the leaves, but he was loath to venture into the garden; instead, he leaned against the fence, raised his eyes, and pressing his finger to his lips enjoined himself to silence, lest by a hasty utterance he should break his train of thought. Several times he tapped his forehead as if stirring memories that had long lain dormant there. At last, gnawing at his fingers, he drew blood.

"Serve a man right! Serve him right!" he cried at the top of his compass.

The courtyard, alive with shouts just moments earlier, stood hushed and deserted like a cemetery. The entire hunting party had ridden out. Hollowing his hands, Tadeusz raised them like trumpets to his ears and listened intently. Presently, the sound of bugles and hunters' cries in the forest came floating on the wind toward him. Finding his saddled horse waiting for him in the stable, he seized his gun, vaulted astride and sped off like a madman toward the two taverns by the chapel, where the hunt had agreed to meet at dawn.

The two inns, leaning inward from either side of the highway, peered menacingly into each other's windows like mortal enemies. The older one belonged to the castle owner by right of deed, the new one to Judge Soplica, who'd built it as an act of spite against the castle. Gervase lorded it over the one as over his own inheritance, Protase held the post of honor in the other.

While the new inn looked perfectly ordinary, the old one hewed to an ancient model conceived by the carpenters of Tyre, which the Jews later brought with them into the world. The architectural style is foreign to builders abroad—we inherit it from the Jews. From the front, the inn resembled an ark, from the rear a temple. The ark was a veritable Noah's ark, a quadrangular box-like structure known to us now by the prosaic name of stable. Stalled inside were farm animals of every kind, horses, cows, oxen, bearded goats; in the rafters thronged every species of bird and reptile (a pair of each at least—a male and its mate) and swarms of insects. The rear portion of the inn resembled a marvelous temple recalling that great edifice of Solomon's which Hiram's builders skilled in the joiner's craft first erected on Mount Sion; the Jews imitate it even now in their synagogues, and the same plan informs their stables and inns. The roof, made of thatching and roughly cut boards, tapered upward into a peak like a tattered Jewish hat. From the gable wall jutted a covered gallery supported by a row of close-set wooden columns—architectural wonders in their bearing strength, as they were rotted half through and out of the perpendicular like Pisa's tower. Over these columns ran semicircular arches, hewn also of wood in imitation of Gothic art (no capitals or plinths here, as with columns of the Greek order) and the upper surface of the shafts stood adorned with intricate motifs, all crooked of line like the branches of a Sabbath menorah, hewn out not with a burin or chisel but by dint of deft strokes of the carpenter's adze. From the top of each column hung small button-like knobs suggesting the tassels of the prayer shawl that the Hebrew throws over his head and calls *tzitzis* in his tongue. Seen from afar, the whole tottering, lopsided hostelry brought to mind a Jew nodding his head in prayer, the roof suggesting his hat, the ragged thatch his beard, the grimy, smoke-smeared walls his black coat, and the relief carvings the *tzitziot* hanging from his brow.[11]

The interior of the tavern was divided in two equal halves like a Jewish schoolhouse. One part consisted of a number of narrow rectangular rooms reserved for gentlemen travelers and their ladies, the other housed an ample hall. Narrow, many-legged wooden tables ran the length of its walls, and alongside each table ran short-limbed benches resembling their sires, the tables, in every respect, only smaller.

Ranged even now on these encircling benches sat men and women of the village and members of the minor nobility. Shoulder to shoulder they sat; only the Bailiff sat by himself. After morning Mass at the chapel—the day being Sunday—they'd dropped in at Jankiel's for a tipple and a spot of good cheer. A tumbler of home-brew liquor stood frothing before each guest; above them hovered the barmaid, bottle in hand, and in the center of the hall stood the innkeeper Jankiel in a black floor-length coat fastened with silver clasps. With one hand tucked under his satin sash, the other solemnly stroking his gray beard, he cast his gaze about, issuing orders here, greeting new arrivals there, striking up conversations with the seated, settling quarrels, but serving no one—he being merely the proprietor making the rounds.

Jankiel was an old Jew respected everywhere for his probity. In all the years he'd kept the inn, no rustic or nobleman ever lodged a complaint at the Manor—nor was there cause, for his drinks were always neat and choice. He kept a strict account and cheated no one. Boisterous spirits he tolerated, but he drew the line at drunken behavior. Fond of parties, he threw open his house for every wedding and christening, and, on Sundays, he invited over the village band with their array of musical instruments, including a bull fiddle and doodle sack.[12]

Jankiel knew music; indeed, he was famous for his musicianship. Now and then he made tours of the country houses with the cymbalon,[13] the instrument of his people, amazing all with his playing and songs, which he delivered in a voice that was trained and true. Though a Jew, he spoke Polish with a clean accent. He had a special fondness for Polish folksongs. Of these, after each excursion across the Niemen, he brought back a good many—mazurkas from Warsaw, *kolomyjkas*[14] from Galicia. Rumor had it (of uncertain reliability to be sure) that he was the first to bring home and popularize the song now famous around the world, the one our legions' bugles first pealed forth to the Lombard on the Ausonian fields. The art of singing pays handsomely in Lithuania; it wins people's affection, makes one famous and rich—Jankiel made a fortune. In time, having had his fill of fame and profit, he hung up his nine-stringed dulcimer, and settling into the inn with his children turned to ply his trade as a spirits vendor. (He also served as an under-rabbi in the neighboring town.) Wherever he went, he was received as a welcome guest and trusted advisor, for he knew the trading wherries and the grain business—indispensable items of knowledge in the country; in short, people esteemed Jankiel as an honorable Pole.[15]

It was Jankiel who put an end to the bloody brawls that often broke out between the two taverns; he leased the pair of them. Respected alike by the old Horeszko partisans and the Judge's serving-men, he alone knew how to hold the grim Warden and fractious Court Usher in check. In Jankiel's presence both men bridled their grudges: Gervase curbed his formidable arm, Protase his formidable tongue.

Today, Gervase was absent, having left with the hunting party. Loath to let the raw young Count venture alone on so perilous an expedition, he'd set out with him for counsel as well as protection.

The Bernardine sat in Gervase's seat between two benches in the corner farthest from the door where those of the Orthodox faith hang their holy icons. Jankiel himself had seated him there. The Jew evidently held him in the highest regard, for whenever he saw the Monk's mead-pot run low, he had it promptly replenished. By all accounts, they'd befriended each other in their youth while traveling abroad. Robak often visited the tavern under the cover of night to confer with the Jew on various important matters. Word went around that the Monk trafficked in contraband, but this malicious rumor warranted no credence.

Robak sat hunched over the table, holding forth in a low voice. Our squirearchy crowded attentively about him, noses bent over his snuffbox. Helping themselves to a pinch, they fired off a salvo of sneezes, loud as mortar-shots.

"*Reverendissime!*" snorted Skołuba. "Now there's snuff that goes straight to your head. In all the days I've lugged this hooter of mine. (Here he stroked his long nose.) I've never sniffed the like. (He sneezed again.) Genuine Bernardine! From Kowno[16] no doubt—a city famous for her snuff and mead. I was there once. When was it now—?"

"Good health!" broke in Robak. "Good health to all you, gentlemen! As to the snuff, well, it hails from a good deal farther than Mr. Skołuba supposes. Jasna Góra! Our Holy Hill! Aye, the Pauline Fathers grind this snuff in Częstochowa, home of the wonder-working image of the Blessed Virgin, Queen of the Polish Realm. Even now she goes by her other title of Grand Duchess of Lithuania; even now she holds the royal office, and yet schism reigns over the Duchy!"[17]

"Częstochowa, you say?" struck up Wilbik. "I made my confession there once, when I went on pilgrimage thirty years ago. Is it true the French bide there now and mean to tear down the church and seize the treasury?—because it's all written up here in *The Lithuanian Courier*."

"Not true!" countered the Bernardine. "His Imperial Highness Napoleon is an exemplary son of the Church. The Pope himself anointed him; they see eye to eye, and together they revive the faith of France, which, admittedly, has seen better days. Aye, Częstochowa pours ample silver into the national coffers for the good of the Fatherland—for Poland! God himself enjoins it! His altar tables have always fed the nation's coffers. A hundred thousand patriots—perhaps soon even more—stand under arms in the Duchy of Warsaw. Who's to pay for it? Is it not up to you, Lithuanian Poles? Why, it's coppers you drop into Moscow's chest."

"Devil take it!" cried Wilbik. "They seize it by force."

"Reverend Father," piped up a meek little rustic bobbing and scratching his head. "The nobility suffer, aye, but not 'alf as bad as us. Why, they fleece us to the bone!"

"Bumpkin!" yelled Skołuba. "Fool! It's easier for you yokels. You're used to being skinned like eels, but we born-and-bred gentlefolk are accustomed to our golden liberty. Aye, my brothers, in the old days 'The gentleman on his grange—'"

"Yes, yes, we know," they cried one and all, "The gentleman on his grange stands equal to the Governor!"[18]

"Aye," Skołuba resumed, "but now they question our pedigree and send us rummaging for our letters patent."

"Oh, spare me!" yelled Juracha. "Your sires were but ennobled peasants, whereas I spring from princes. To ask *me* for my letters! Why, God only knows when I got my title! Let the Muscovite ask the oak who gave him the patent to stand taller than the shrubs."

"Beguile others with your tales, O Prince," said Żagiel. "You'll find more than one house here with a coronet."

"You have a cross on your coat of arms," cried Podhajski, "an allusion to a converted Jew gracing your line."

"Lies!" broke in Birbasz. "I spring from Crimean counts, yet I have crosses over the galley charging my shield."

"A Rose Argent, with a coronet, done on a field *d'or*," shouted Mickiewicz. "Now there's a princely blazon! You've only to consult Stryjkowski.[19] His armorial makes frequent mention of it."

A great murmur broke out in the inn. Robak fled to his snuffbox and offered them each a pinch; at once, the noise subsided as they politely inhaled a few grains and fired off another salvo. Profiting from the pause, the Bernardine resumed:

"Great men have sneezed on taking this snuff. Would you believe it if I told you Dąbrowski took four snorts from this box?

"Not *the* Dąbrowski?" they said.

"The very one, the General. I was in his camp the day he took Gdańsk from the Germans.[20] He had a letter to write. Afraid of nodding off, he took a snort, sneezed, and clapped me twice on the shoulder. 'Father Robak,' said he, 'if all goes well, we shall meet in Lithuania before the year is out. Be sure her sons greet me there with snuff. This Częstochowa snuff, mind! I'll take no other.'"

Robak's words aroused so much wonder, such transports of joy in the boisterous throng that for a moment they fell silent. Soon half-audible whispers made themselves heard: "Snuff? From Poland? Częstochowa? General Dąbrowski? From Italy?" And all at once, as if thought had fused with thought and word with word, the entire assembly cried out in unison, "Dąbrowski!" And joined in that single roar, they fell into a common clasp: rustic embraced Crimean Count; Coronet embraced the Cross; Roses Argent—Galley and Griffin. All cares went by the board, even the Bernardine sat forgotten. They sang out the Dąbrowski mazurka, all the while shouting, "Vodka! Mead! Wine!"

Father Robak suffered them to sing on, but at last it was time to intervene. Seizing the snuffbox in both hands, he broke up their singing with a sneeze; before they could start up again, he hastened to speak.

"You find my snuff praiseworthy. Is it not so, esteemed gentlemen? But take a closer look at the box and see what's depicted there."

And wiping the soiled base of the box with his handkerchief he revealed to their gaze a miniature portraying a tiny, swarm-like army. In its midst stood a mounted rider, big as a beetle, clearly the commander of the host. With one hand on the rein, the other raised to his nose, he was rearing his horse, as though urging it into the heavens.

"Now," said Robak, "look well on this awesome figure. Guess who?" Intrigued to no end, they examined it closely.

"He's a great man," added Robak. "An emperor, but not Russia's. Tsars never snort snuff."

"A great man wearing a gray capote?" said Cydzik. "I thought all great men went about in gold. Even the lowest-ranking general among the Muscovites drips with gold like a saffron-dusted pike."

"Not true!" chimed in Rymsza. "As a lad, once, I saw Kościuszko, our Commander-in-Chief. Now there was a man! He went about in a peasant's caftan, a *czamara*, that is."

"*Czamara* my eye, sir!" snorted Wilbik. "You mean a *taratatka*."[21]

"A *czamara* has braids," countered Mickiewicz. "A *taratatka*'s smooth all over." Contention broke out over the various cuts of frock and coat. Seeing the talk go astray, the artful Robak brought it back to a focus—to his snuffbox; again, he proffered it. They sneezed and drank each other's health. The Monk resumed:

"When Emperor Napoleon in an engagement sniffs pinch after pinch of snuff, it is a sure sign he is winning. Take Austerlitz, for example. The French stand beside their guns like so. A host of Muscovites bears down on them and the Emperor watches in silence. Each French salvo cuts a wide swathe through the Muscovite regiments. Regiment after regiment come charging up and tumble from the saddle, and whenever a regiment falls, the Emperor takes a snort. Finally, Tsar Alexander, his brother Constantine, and the German Prince Franz flee the field, and Bonaparte, seeing the battle won, breaks out into a laugh and dusts the snuff from his fingers. So keep this in mind, should any of you gentlemen present here come to serve in the Emperor's army."

"Ah, dear Father," cried Skołuba, "when will that be? The year drags on from feast day to feast day, and each time they announce the arrival of the French. We strain our eyes, we stare and stare until we blink, and still the Muscovite has us gripped by the neck. Why, by the time it dawns, the dewfall will have dimmed our eyes!"

"Come, sir," rejoined the Monk. "Grousing's for grannies! It is the Jewish thing to stand idle till a traveler comes knocking at the tavern door. With Napoleon on our side, it's no trick to beat the Muscovite. Three times he's tanned the Swabian's hide! Has he not drubbed the dreaded Prussian? Flung the English back across the sea? The Muscovite will get his due, never you mind. But what'll come of it, sir, if our nobility take to horse and sword when there's no one left to fight? Having done it all himself, Napoleon's sure to say, 'I shall manage without you, sirs. Who are you?' It's not enough to stand waiting for a guest, or even to invite him in. A good host summons his servants and sets the tables. Before the feast he must clean the house of dirt. Clean the house, I say. I repeat, clean the house, my sons!"

There fell a moment of silence. Soon voices in the crowd piped up.

"Clean house? But how?" What does Father mean by that? We'll do all you say. We stand ready for anything. Only please, Father, do make your meaning clear."

But the Priest suddenly waved silence; something outside had arrested his attention. He drew his head back from the window and rose to his feet.

"No time now," he said. "We shall have occasion to discuss this at greater length later. Tomorrow I have errands to run in the district town. On my way back I'll be looking in on you, sirs, for alms."

"Then be sure to spend the night with us in Niehrymów!" called out the Bailiff. "The Ensign will be glad to see you. Why, it's an old maxim in Lithuania, 'Happy as an alms collector in Niehrymów!'"

"And look in on us, if you would," said Zubkowski. "Father can rely on us for a bolt of linen, a tub of butter, a fatted calf or sheep. Remember these words, 'In Zubkowo the almsman lacks for nothing!'"

"And don't forget us!" cried Skołuba.

"Nor us!" yelled Terajewicz. 'No alms quester left Pucewicze feeling peckish!'"

Such were the entreaties and pledges with which the nobility plied the Monk, but by now he was well out the tavern door.

It was a pale, sullen-faced Tadeusz he had just seen burning up the highroad past the window. The sight of the lad hunched low in the saddle, bareheaded, belaboring his horse with crop and spur, caused him great consternation. Striking a brisk pace, the Monk set out after the youth. The road took him in the direction of the great forest, which brooded low on the horizon as far as the eye could see.

Who has searched the depths of Lithuania's wilds, probed their innermost recesses, their deepest vitals? The fisherman on the shore scarcely sounds the Deep. The hunter stalks but the fringes of Lithuania's forests, he knows but their outward form and features; their heart, their *penetralia*, lie beyond his ken. Only legend and fable have knowledge of the happenings there. Strike but deep enough into those ancient woodlands and shaggy forests and you run up against a great barricade of tree stumps, logs, and roots fortified by quaking bogs, a myriad streams, foot-enmeshing grasses, ant-heaps, wasps' and hornets' nests, and coiling snakes. Those who by superhuman effort brave these obstacles and strike deeper, encounter still greater perils. Small lakes, half overgrown with grass and deep beyond imagining, lie in wait at every turn like wolves' lairs; in all likelihood, demons inhabit them. Their waters, flecked with flakes of blood-hued rust, give off a subdued light, and from deep within rises a foul-smelling fume, a pestilence that strips the environing trees of leaf and bark. Drooping limbs—bare, stunted, worm-eaten, sickly, and matted with moss—and bearded boles, humped by grotesquely misshapen fungi, press up to these meres like a coven of witches huddled around a cauldron cooking a corpse.

Beyond these plumbless pools, man's eye and foot probe in vain. All lies covered by a thick cloud of vapors that rises eternally from the quaking bogs. Yet beyond the farthest reach of these mists (so runs the common lore) stretches a fertile region of unparalleled beauty, the capital city of the animal and plant kingdom. There lie in store the seeds of every tree and herb whence spring all the generations of plants that populate the world. There, too, as in Noah's ark, enjoy refuge at least a pair of every kind of beast—a male and his mate. In the very heart of the city (so our people say) stand the palaces of the forest emperors, the ancient Auroch, the Bison, the Bear; in the surrounding trees lodge their watchful ministers of state, the glutton Wolverine and the keen-eyed Lynx. Farther out dwell their feudatories—the Wild Boar, the Gray Wolf, the Beamed Elk; and high overhead soar the Falcons and wild Eagles—free riders living off the boards of their liege lords. Hidden in this kernel of the wilderness, unseen by man, these archetypal pairs of beasts dispatch their young to inhabit the world beyond the forest, while they themselves remain in the capital and enjoy their repose. Neither steel nor shot ends their lives; reaching the full span of their years, they die a natural death. They even have their own graveyard, where nearing death the bird lays down its feathers and the four-legged beast its pelt. When the bear wears down his teeth and can no longer chew his fare; when the grizzled roebuck's limbs grow stiff; when the hoary hare feels his blood thicken in his veins; when the raven's quills turn silvery-gray, the falcon's eye grows dim, and the eagle's ancient beak grows so bent as to close tight and provide no nourishment for his throat[22]—then all these beasts repair to the cemetery. Even the lesser creatures, sickening or suffering an injury, seek to die in the land of their sires, and so no trace of animal bones is ever found in the places known to and frequented by men.[23]

The beasts of this metropolis are said to enjoy gentle manners, for they govern themselves. Unspoiled by human civilization, they know no rights of property that embroil the world of men. Nor have they any knowledge of duels and the art of war. Just as their grandsires lived in Paradise, so their descendants, wild and tame alike, thrive today in a spirit of love and amity. They neither butt nor bite, and were an unarmed man to fall in among them, he'd pass safely through their midst. The beasts would train on him that same look of awe with which, on that last, sixth day of creation, their forbears in the Garden gazed upon Adam before sin set God's creatures at strife. Happily, Man does not enter these repairs. Toil and Terror and Death bar his way.

Yet rash bloodhounds, hard on the quarry's traces, have been known to blunder into those sloughy, mossy, gully-riven regions. Horrified by the sights that greet them there, they fly with wild looks and appalling whines; and long afterwards, they stand trembling at their master's feet, frozen in terror, uncomforted by his soothing hand. These hidden precincts unknown to man our hunters call "The Lairs."[24]

Foolish bear! Had you but kept to your haunts, the Steward would never have found you out. The scent of beehives? A hankering after ripe oats? Whatever the enticement, you ventured away to where the trees grew thinner, and the ranger happened upon your tracks. At once he dispatches his beaters, clever spies, to reconnoiter your lying and grazing grounds; and now, extending their lines between you and the Lairs, the Steward and his beaters have blocked your path of retreat!

By the time Tadeusz arrived on the scene, the hounds were probing the deepest repairs of the forest.

A profound silence! In vain the hunters strain their ears; in vain they hearken to the silence that speaks to them in the most eloquent of tongues. For an age they stand motionless, listening, yet catching only the distant music of the wilderness. The bloodhounds sweep the waste like dippers probing the deep. The shooters train their guns on the forest, their gaze on the Steward.

The Steward dropped to his knees and put an inquiring ear to the ground. As an ailing man's friends strive to read the verdict of life or death in the physician's face, so the hunters, trusting in the Steward's skill, fix on him their gaze of anxious hope. "He's here! . . . He's here!" he muttered half-audibly, and he sprang to his feet. He'd heard it! The others listen on. At last they hear it too. A hound speaks, now two, now twenty! Now the entire scattered pack noses the scent and gives mouth. The baying grows louder, more frenzied. They own the line! No longer the music of hounds carrying the scent of a fox, hare or hind, but prolonged bursts of short, sharp, staccato cries—the full cry of a pack hunting by sight! The cry breaks off. They hold him! Fresh howls and roars! The bear fights back, evidently inflicting wounds; more and more howls of mortally stricken dogs rise above the din.

Guns primed, bodies tensed like strung bows, the shooters face the forest and hang fire. At last, they can stand it no longer: one after another they abandon their posts and make for the woods, all craving to be the first to close with the quarry. Bootless the Steward's warnings! In vain he circles their positions on horseback; in vain he threatens to lay his crop on the back of the next yokel or nobleman to quit his post! The shooters dash heedless into the forest. Three muskets discharge at once, a wild cannonade ensues! At last, over the detonations of the guns, the bawl of the bear breaks forth, filling the woods with its echoes. A dreadful roar of pain, fury and despair! Instantly, the forest erupts in a thunderous din of crying hounds, shouts, and horn blasts! Some of the hunters strike deeper into the woods, others cock their pieces, all wrought to the highest pitch of elation. The Steward alone despairs of his hunt. "They shoot abroad!" he groans. The hunters and beaters run one way, across the bear's tracks, heading him from his lying grounds in the old forest; meanwhile, alarmed by the throng of dogs and men, the beast doubles back to terrain less narrowly guarded—to the forest's edge, which the gunners have all but deserted, and where, of the once strong ring, only the Steward, Tadeusz, the Count, and a handful of beaters remain.

Here the forest stands thinner. A loud roar and the crack of snapping tree limbs sound from within. Suddenly, like a bolt from a thunderhead, the bear bursts out of the thicket. Dogs assail him from every quarter, tearing at his flanks, startling him. Fending them off with his roars, he rears on his hind legs and surveys the ground. With his forepaws he wrenches up roots, sunken rocks and charred stumps and heaves them at the dogs and the hunters; then felling a tree and swinging the trunk from side to side like a club he makes a rush straight at the ring of beaters and its two remaining guardians, Tadeusz and the Count. The two youths stand their ground, guns leveled at the quarry like a pair of lightning rods thrust into the heart of a thundercloud. In the same instant—oh, the inexperience of youth!—they pull their triggers. Both guns discharge—and miss! The beast springs forward. Two pairs of hands scramble for the hunting spear planted in the ground. Grappling for the weapon, the youths glance up to see, towering above them, a pair of gaping red jaws flashing two tiers of fangs; even now a clawed paw comes sweeping down on their heads. Paling with terror, they recoil and bolt for the sparse brush. Hard on their heels, the bear rears up and takes a swipe with his paw. He swings wide! Again he charges, rears and takes aim at the Count's yellow hair. That swarthy paw would have dashed off his scalp like a hat were it not for the Notary and the Assessor, who come leaping out from either side; and running directly toward the bear some hundred paces behind come Gervase and the weaponless Monk. Three muskets fire as one, as if on command. Like a hare beset by hounds, the beast vaults into the air then crashes headlong down, rolls heels over head, and rams the bloody mass of its body sheer under the Count, striking him clean off his feet. Still roaring, the bear struggles to rise, but at that moment the Chamberlain's bulldogs, the enraged Constable and ferocious Procureuse, pounce and hold him down.

The Steward reached for the horn strapped across his shoulder—a buffalo horn, long and speckled and snaked like a boa's coils. Pressing it to his lips with both hands, he blew out his cheeks like balloons; blood started to his eyes. Half-closing his lids, he drew in his belly to the utmost and transferred to his lungs all the reserves of air stored within; and he wound the horn! With the irresistible force of a mighty whirlwind, the horn sent its music into the wilderness then repeated it with its echoes. The shooters fell silent, the baiters stopped in their tracks, all mesmerized by the strength, the purity and wondrous harmony of the notes. Once more the old master regaled the ears of the hunt with all the artistry that made him famous in the forests of bygone years. Instantly, he filled and enlivened the woods and groves as though he'd released into them a whole pack of hounds and set the hunt in motion, for his playing encapsulated the history of the chase: first, a brisk flourish of vibrating notes—the morning call; then a series of whining moans—the cry of the hounds; then an occasional harsher tone like thunder—the crack of a hunting piece!

He broke off, but the horn remained at his lips. All imagined he was still blowing, but it was only the echoes answering.

Again he blew. The horn seemed to reshape itself at his lips, growing now thicker, now thinner as it mimicked the wild beasts' calls. Now, stretching like a wolf's neck, it broke into a long, baleful howl, now like a bear's throat it swelled and roared, now it rent the air with a bison's bawl.

He broke off, but the horn remained at his lips. All imagined he was still blowing, but it was only the echoes answering. The trees, catching the magisterial horn piece, passed it on—oak to oak repeated it, beech to beech!

Again the Steward blew; now the horn contained a hundred horns! You heard, all playing off against one another, the shouts of the baiters, the shooters' yells of rage and alarm, the cry of the pack, the roar of the beasts; and raising the horn, the Steward smote the clouds with his triumphant paean.

He broke off. Still the horn remained at his lips. All imagined he was blowing, but it was only the echoes answering. As many winding horns as there stood trees in the forest! From tree to tree, as from choir to choir, the music carried. Ever farther, ever wider it ranged, ever softer, ever more pure and sublime it grew until, reaching Heaven's gates, it vanished clean away.

The Chief Steward withdrew both hands and spread wide his arms; the horn fell free and swung loose by its strap. Like a man inspired, face flown and radiant with high emotion, he stood gazing up, listening to the last fading notes of the horn. A thunderous ovation rang out, a thousand cheers and good wishes issuing from as many pairs of mouths!

Gradually, the noise subsided. The eyes of the hunt turned to the fresh carcass of the bear. Riddled with shot and drenched in blood, the beast lay face down, forelegs flung wide, its chest buried deep in the thick matted grass. It still breathed; blood jetted from its nostrils, and though its eyes remained open, its head lay motionless. The Chamberlain's bulldogs clung fast to its neck below the ears, Procureuse on the left, Constable on the right, sucking on the gore, gorging his throat.

At the Steward's command the hunters thrust iron bars into the dogs' jaws, prized them open, and rolled the great carcass over with their musket stocks. Three more rousing cheers smote the clouds!

"So," said the Assessor, twirling his gun by the barrel. "So, my shooting iron, it's bully for us. Aye, little iron! A simple fowling gun,[25] yet some account she gave of herself, eh? No surprise to her, mind. She's never been known to muff a shot. See? The gift of Prince Sanguszko himself!"

He showed them his gun, an exquisitely crafted piece, to be sure, though somewhat on the small side; he was rhyming off its virtues when the Notary, wiping the sweat from his brow, broke in:

"I was right on the bear's heels when the Steward calls out, 'Hold hard!' But how could I stand there? The bear was making for the open field. Every second he was forging ahead; meantime, I was running out of puff and falling behind, no hope of catching up. Then I look to my right and see him lolloping through the thinning brush. I put a bead on him, 'Freeze, Bruin!' says I to myself, and basta!—dead as a doornail he lies. Noble firearm! Genuine Sagalas! Here, take a look at the inscription, *Sagalas London a Bałabanówka*. A famous Polish gunsmith lived there crafting Polish guns but adorned them in the English style."[26]

"A hundred thousand bears!" snorted the Assessor. "What! *You* killed him? Enough of your ravings."

"Listen, you!" retorted the Notary. "This isn't a police inquiry; it's a hunt, and I take everybody here for a witness."

A fierce contest arose among the hunters as one side took the Notary's part and the other the Assessor's. None gave Gervase a thought; with everyone running up from both sides, they failed to see what was unfolding before them.

"At least now we have grounds," declared the Steward, "for, this, gentlemen, is no jackrabbit. Here we have a bear! Here we needn't scruple to seek satisfaction. Saber, pistol and ball—take your pleasure! Your quarrel's hard to settle, and so according to our ancient custom we'll allow you to fight a duel. I recall two neighbors in my day, worthy gentlemen of ancient lineage. They lived on either side of the Wilenka—one was named Domejko, the other Dowejko.[27] Both fired simultaneously on a bear. Who killed her was hard to tell. They got into a terrible row and swore to shoot at each other across the length of the bearskin. Now there's nobility for you!—all but muzzle to muzzle! The duel set the whole neighborhood astir. Songs were sung about it in my day. I was their second. How it happened, I shall tell you from beginning to end."

But before the Steward could begin his tale, Gervase settled the matter. After cautiously circling and inspecting the bear, he drew out his hunting knife and cut the snout asunder. Slicing open the lobes at the back of the skull, he found and extracted the ball, wiped it on his frock coat, measured the gauge and fitted the ball to his flintlock.

"Gentlemen," he said, holding out the lead on the flat of his hand. "Neither one of you fired this ball. It sped from this Horeszko single. (He raised his antique piece, all wrapped in cord.) But it was not I that fired it. Oh, no, that took nerve!

I shudder to recall it. Terror dimmed my eyes. Both lads were running straight toward me, the bear right on their heels, almost on top of the Count—aye, last of the Horeszkos, albeit on the spindle side. *'Jesu Maria!'* I cried. And the angels sent the Bernardine to my aid. He's put us all to the blush. Brave priest! As I stood there trembling, finger frozen on the trigger, he seized the gun from my hands, aimed, and fired. To shoot between two heads! At a hundred paces! And to hit the mark! In the very center of the jaws—aye, that's how to knock out a tooth! Gentlemen, in all my born years I have seen but one man capable of such marksmanship, a man once famous among us for the many duels he fought, a man capable of shooting the heel from out under a lady's buskin. That knave of knave, renowned in memorable times—Jacek *vulgo*[28] Whiskers! I'll not utter his surname. Anyhow, his hunting days are done. I'll warrant the ruffian sits roasting in hell, right up to his moustaches. Glory to the Monk! Two men's lives he saved, perhaps three. Gervase will not boast, but had the last child of Horeszko blood fallen to the jaws of the beast, his warden would no longer be among the living. Even now would Bruin be gnawing on his brittle bones! Come, Father, let us drink your health!"

But Robak was nowhere to be found. All they could ascertain from witnesses was that the Monk had remained briefly on the scene after the shooting; that on running up to the youths and finding them both safe and sound, he'd raised his eyes to heaven, muttered a quick prayer and made off across the open field like a hunted hind.

Meanwhile, on the Steward's command, the men heaped up logs and armfuls of heather and dry brushwood. A blaze burst forth, a gray pine of smoke rose aloft, spreading out like a canopy over their heads. In no time they erected a trestlework of pikes over the flames, hung broad-bellied copper kettles from the shafts, and emptied the wagons of their store of vegetables, meal, roasted meat, and bread.

The Judge opened a huge packing case filled with rows of upright whitenecked bottles. Of these he picked out the largest, a crystal flask he'd received as a gift from Father Robak; it contained Gdańsk vodka, the cherished spirits of the Poles.

"Long live Gdańsk!" he cried, raising the flask. "The city, once ours, shall soon be ours again." And he poured the silver liquor by turns until the gold leaf dripped out and sparkled in the sun.[29]

The stew was on the boil. Not easy to express in verse the extraordinary taste, the hue and delectable aroma of our hunter's goulash! The urban stomach hears only the sound of the words, the iteration of the rhymes; never shall it divine their substance! To do justice to Lithuania's fare and songs one needs good health, rustic living, and to be homeward bound from a hunt. Even without these seasonings our *bigos*[30] is no ordinary dish, for it consists in an ingenious blending of the finest vegetables, cabbage being the chief ingredient, finely cut and cured and so tasty that, as the saying goes, it finds its own way into your mouth. Cooked in a boiler, embosoming the best portions of the choicest meats, the kraut simmers for hours until every drop of goodness is drawn out, and the steam, hissing from the rim of the vessel, gives off its exquisite odors.

The stew was ready! Armed with spoons, the hunters raised three cheers and attacked the kettles with lunges and prods. The clank of the copper! Clouds of steam! The stew fled away, evaporating like camphor, leaving only the steam to billow forth, like volcanic vapors, from the jaws of the kettles.

At last, having eaten and drunk their fill, the hunters hoisted their game on a cart and mounted up. All were in hearty, voluble spirits—all except the Notary and the Assessor who were now more on the outs than ever. They argued over the merits of their guns, the one his Sanguszko, the other his *Sagalas a Bałabanówka*. Equally dispirited were Tadeusz and the Count. They burned with shame over muffing their shots and shying from the bear. Lithuania sets an enduring black mark against the hunter who allows his quarry to escape the ring; not easy to erase it. The Count insisted that he'd been the first to reach the spear; that Tadeusz had thwarted him from closing with the bear. Tadeusz maintained he'd meant to help him, he being the stronger of the two and the more adept at wielding the heavy weapon; and so, amid the boisterous shouts of their comrades, Tadeusz and the Count continued to trade taunts.

The Steward rode in their midst, more jubilant and talkative than ever. Seeking to amuse and bring the quarrelers to terms, he resumed his anecdote of Domejko and Dowejko.

"Mr. Assessor, if I urged you to a duel with the Notary here, do not suppose I am set on seeing spilt blood. God forbid! Diversion was my purpose. I had in mind a species of comedy—to revive a conceit of mine of forty years ago, a truly remarkable one. You, being young, would scarce remember it, but, in my day, it caused quite a stir from here clear to the Pripet Marshes![31]

"Dowejko and Domejko's strife[32] arose, strangely enough, from the awkward similarity of their names. When Dowejko's champions sought backers during the regional diets, someone would whisper to a nobleman, 'Vote for Dowejko!' and he, not hearing aright, would cast his ballot for Domejko. When Marshal Rupejko raised his banquet toast, 'Long live Dowejko!' some would chorus, 'Domejko!' while those in the middle could never quite make it out, the more so, as dinner talk is always less than articulate.

"It got still worse. In Wilno, once, a drunken nobleman received two cuts in a brawl with Domejko. Quite by chance, while ferrying home from the city, this nobleman ran into Dowejko. So there they were, riding the same raft down-stream. 'Who's that?' the nobleman asks a traveling companion. 'Dowejko,' says he. And without further ado the nobleman whips his rapier from under his mantle. Slash! Slash! A pair of whiskers drops to the deck. Whose? Domejko's naturally! By deputy!

"To crown all, a similar muddle took place on the hunt. Standing next to each other, our two near-namesakes fired simultaneously on a bear. True, the sow dropped dead on the spot, but her belly had already been riddled with a dozen rounds, and seeing as several others carried guns of the same gauge, well, you try and sort it out!

"'Enough!' they cried. 'Time to settle the matter once and for all. God or Satan joined us, so let us put us asunder. Two suns, one planet—one sun too many.'

"They draw their sabers and take their positions. Worthy knights these! The more we try to pacify them, the more furiously they let fly at each other. From sabers they pass to pistols and resume their positions. 'Much too close!' we yell. To spite us all, they vow to shoot with only the thickness of the bearskin separating them. Certain death! Point-blank—and both were dead shots!

"'Steward, be our second!' they yell. 'Very well,' say I. 'But tell the sacristan to dig a grave, for an encounter of this kind can have but one outcome. And have it out like noblemen, I say, not butchers. No coming closer! That you are brave lads I can see, but surely you won't shoot with your muzzles pressed into each other's numbles? No, I'll not allow it! I agree to pistols, but you shall observe a distance neither greater than nor less than the full length of the bearskin. As your referee, I shall spread the hide on the field of honor and position you myself. You, sir, shall take your ground at one end, at the point of the snout, and you, sir, at the tip of the tail.'

"'Agreed!' they yell. Time? Tomorrow. Place? Usza Tavern. They ride off. Meanwhile, I turn to my Virgil—"

Just then a cry of "see-ho" cut the Steward off. A hare broke covert directly under the hunters' mounts. Like a shot Peregrine and Scut went after it. Their owners had brought them along on the good chance that, returning home through the fields, the hunt would start a hare. Even before the hunters had time to cry, "sic 'em!" the two greyhounds, who happened then to be walking off leash beside their masters' horses, tore off in pursuit. The Notary and the Assessor would have followed, but the Steward checked them.

"Hold hard!" he cried. "Stand and watch! No one's to move! We can all see perfectly well from here. See? She's making for the field."

Indeed, alive to the hunters and dogs behind it, the hare was pelting into the field, ears erect like a young buck's horns. Across the glebe in a long gray blur it streaked, legs projecting like four rods beneath it. Those limbs seemed scarcely to stir, to be merely tapping the ground, even as a swallow on the wing kisses the surface of the water. Behind the hare trailed a cloud of dust, and behind the dust coursed the hounds. Seen from afar, hare, dust and hounds seemed to merge into a single body and slither across the field like an outlandish serpent—the hare its head, the dust its bluish neck, and the two dogs its sinuous double tail. The Notary and the Assessor watched open-mouthed and held their breath. Suddenly, the Notary turned white as a handkerchief; the Assessor blenched. The course was going horribly wrong! The farther the serpent slithered, the longer it stretched; now it had broken in half, and the neck of dust was melting away. The head was just yards from the forest, the tail a good stretch behind. Next moment, the head vanished into the thicket. A white tassel-like object flashed for an instant before the forest engulfed it too, and the straggling tail sheered away.

Baffled, the poor hounds cast up and down the edge of the thicket. For a while they seemed to confer with each other and trade accusations; then turning they limped back across the furrows. Eyes downcast, ears drooping, tails cleaving to their bellies, they rejoined the hunt, but, in their shame, instead of returning to heel, they halted well short of their masters.

The Notary's head sank to his chest; the Assessor cast gloomy looks around. They began to plead their case. The hounds were unused to walking off leash; the quarry had started without warning; a plowed field made for a poor course— indeed, booties would have been in order with all those rocks and jagged stones about. Strong was their case, for they were both experienced huntsmen. Their audience might have picked up a number of pointers, but no one paid much attention. Some started to whistle, others laughed out loud, the rest, the bear hunt still fresh on their minds, talked of precious little else.

The Steward scarcely gave the hare a glance. Seeing the quarry make its escape, he turned as if nothing had happened and closed his tale.

"Now, where was I? Right! I'd secured both men's word that they'd shoot across the full length of the bearskin. Our nobility were up in arms. 'Certain death!' they cried. 'All but nozzle to nozzle.' But I only laughed. I'd learned from my old friend Maro[33] that an animal's hide was no ordinary yardstick.[34] Gentlemen! You all know how Queen Dido arrived on the Libyan coast and how, after a great deal of haggling, she managed to procure there a patch of land such as could be covered by an ox's hide. On that patch of land arose the great city of Carthage! So that night I turn the matter over in my mind.

"The day had scarcely dawned when Dowejko comes riding up in a dog-cart from one side, Domejko on horseback from the other. What do they see?

A shaggy bridge thrown across the river—a belt of bearskin cut into thin strips! I station Dowejko at the tip of the tail on one bank and Domejko opposite him on the other. 'Now pop away to your hearts' content!' I yell. 'But until you come to terms, you stay put right there.'

"Oh, they fumed all right. Our nobility went into convulsions with laughter. The parish priest and I held forth aloud, drawing object lessons from the Gospels and the Book of Statutes. There was no help for it, so the two burst out laughing and make their peace. The quarrel eventually led to a life-long friendship. Dowejko wedded Domejko's sister. Domejko married his brother-in-law's sister, Mistress Dowejko. They divvied up their property in two equal parts, and on the spot where this unlikely incident took place, they built a tavern and named it 'The Little Bear.'"

NOTES

1. The Białowieża Primeval Forest straddles the border between Poland and what is now Belarus. Świteź (Svitez) is a small forest-enclosed lake in the vicinity of Nowogródek (Novogrudak). Ponary (Paneriai), now a neighborhood of Vilnius, is located on a range of low, wooded hills. The ancient Kuszelewo Forest stands in the southwestern part of the old Nowogródek district.

2. Witenes (Vytenis) was Grand Duke of Lithuania around 1300 A.D. Mendog or Mindowe (Mindaugas, d. 1263) ruled as Grand Duke in the mid-thirteenth century. He was converted to Christianity by the Teutonic Knights in 1251 and crowned king in 1253 by Pope Innocent IV. His residence was in Nowogródek. Giedymin (Gediminas), the father of Kiejstut (Keistutas) and Olgierd (Algirdas), ruled as Grand Duke from 1316 to 1341. He founded the city of Vilnius and was chiefly responsible for the development of the powerful medieval Lithuanian state. In his notes the poet refers to the tradition according to which "Grand Duke Giedymin had a dream on Ponary's heights of an iron wolf and acting on the counsel of his bard Lizdejko founded the city of Wilno."

3. Wilno (Vilnius) stands at the confluence of the rivers Neris and Vilnia (or Vilnele). The poet refers to these rivers by their Polish variant names *Wilia* (or *Wilija*) and *Wilenka* (or *Wilijka*) respectively. The latter is a shallow river with shoals and cataracts; hence the "brawl" (*szum*). In Mickiewicz's day it was navigable by means of shallow-draft "ferries" (*promy*) or river rafts (*tratwy*).

4. The reference is to King Sigismund August (1548-1572), the last lineal representative of the Jagiellonians, who ruled over the Polish-Lithuanian state from 1385 until 1572. Jagiełło (Jogaila), son of Olgierd (Algirdas) and the dynasty's progenitor, was crowned King Władysław IV after the conclusion of the Treaty of Krevo (1385). He was victor of the great medieval battle at Tannenberg (1410). The poet notes that Sigismund August, an avid hunter, was "raised to the throne of the Grand Duchy of Lithuania according to the ancient rites; he girt on him the sword and crowned himself with the soft fur hat (*kołpak*)." Witold (Vytautas), elected Grand Duke of Lithuania in 1392, was Jagiełło's brother.

5. [*Author's note*] In the district of Rosienny on the estate of Rural Secretary [Dionizy] Paszkiewicz [c. 1765-1830] there stood an oak called *Baublys*, which in pagan times was

honored as a sacred tree. In the interior of this decayed giant, Paszkiewicz founded a cabinet of Lithuanian antiquities.

6. The ancient limes that once grew near the parish church of Nowogródek. The poet notes that many of these were felled about the year 1812.

7. The family of Herman Hołowiński resided at Steblów (Stebliv) on the River Ros, a right-bank tributary of the Dnieper. The poet visited the estate in February of 1825 on his way to Odessa. A remnant of the old lime-tree survived until the end of the nineteenth century.

8. The reference is to Jan Kochanowski (1530-1584), Poland's greatest poet to the time of Adam Mickiewicz. In a number of poems Kochanowski describes the beauty of his hereditary estate Czarnolas and its lindens.

9. The reference is to the Romantic poet Seweryn Goszczyński (1801-1876), especially his poem *Zamek Kaniowski* (The Castle of Kaniów), published in 1828.

10. The passage alluding to Tadeusz's secret tryst with Telimena appeared at the close of an earlier variant of Book Three but was dropped in the final draft, leaving the reader to surmise that a tryst had taken place.

11. Pigoń comments here that the poet may have confused two different things: *tefillin* and *tzitziot*. The *tefillin* are the phylacteries, the two small black boxes that the pious Jew straps to his forehead and arm for weekday morning prayer and on special feasts. The *tzitziot* (singular: *tzitzit* or *tzitzis*, *cyces* in Polish), on the other hand, are the specially knotted "fringes" or "tassels" attached to the observant Jew's prayer shawl (*tallit katan*). To liken the phylacteries to "button-like knobs" would indeed be infelicitous. The confusion seems to arise from the poet's regional use of the word *leb* in the neutral, non-pejorative sense of "brow" or "forehead" (cf. *lob* in Russian and Belorussian). Yet the confusion would vanish if we saw this in light of the poet's fondness for synecdoche, by which the "brow" is *pars pro toto* for the head.

12. A kind of bagpipe or musette [cf. *Dudelsack* (ger.) and *dudy* (pol.)]. The poet uses the word *kozica* deriving from *koza* (goat), the bag being made of goatskin.

13. The hammer dulcimer; a musical instrument of various shapes. Jankiel's is the nine-stringed "gypsy dulcimer" (*cymbały cygańskie*), a trapezoidal box tuned to as many as four octaves with taut metal strings. The player strikes the strings with leather-bound hammers. Jews often made a living with these instruments by going the rounds of the manors and towns.

14. The *kolomyjka* is a lively Ukrainian song and dance. Galicia took its name from Halych, the former capital of Red Ruthenia (*Czerwona Ruś*), now western Ukraine. The name referred to the southeastern portion of the old Polish-Lithuanian Commonwealth, which fell under Austrian rule.

15. [H.B. Segel] Although the majority of the Jews in Poland lived apart from the Christian community and faithfully preserved their traditions, customs and language, they could identify themselves with Poland's struggle for independence. History has recorded the heroism of Jews who appeared alongside their fellow countrymen on the field of battle. As a good Jew and a patriotic Pole, Jankiel stands as a symbol of the mutual understanding and respect that Mickiewicz hoped one day would exist in Poland among all her citizens.

16. Kowno (now Kaunas) is Lithuania's second largest city.

17. That is, the Grand Duchy of Lithuania. The "schism" is a reference to the Eastern Orthodox Church and Russia's domination over Catholic Lithuania. Częstochowa was in the Duchy of Warsaw. Father Robak envisages the reunion of Lithuania and the old Kingdom of Poland.

18. An old jingle (*szlachcic na zagrodzie równy wojewodzie*) expressing the equality before the law of all members of the Polish nobility.

19. Maciej Stryjkowski (1547-1582), author of a chronicle of Lithuania, and one of the important sources for the early history of that country. Mickiewicz enjoyed reading Stryjkowski and drew on his chronicle for his own narrative poems about medieval Lithuania, *Grażyna* and *Konrad Wallenrod*.

20. As the head of the newly created Polish Army of the Duchy of Warsaw, General Dąbrowski took part in the siege and capture of Gdańsk (Danzig) in 1807.

21. *Pan Tadeusz* makes frequent mention of the national Polish dress, which began to be superseded by modern European apparel in the late eighteenth century. The *taratatka* was a kind of long coat extending to the knees, with embroidery work and loops for fastening. The *czamara* was a long dark-colored frock coat, braided on the back and chest like a hussar's uniform, with tight sleeves and a buttoned-up collar. By wearing a peasant's caftan (*sukmana*), Kościuszko demonstrated his solidarity with the common people whose cause he made his own. Polish noblemen traditionally wore the *kontusz*, a long vividly colored robe with loose slit sleeves (*wyloty*) and girded by a massive brocaded fabric belt (*pas kontuszowy*). The *kontusz* was worn over the *żupan*, a light narrow-sleeved tunic with a low, open, rounded collar and ornate buttons down the front. Polish Jews traditionally wore a long black gown also called a *żupan*. Mickiewicz gives an accurate description of the garment when introducing Jankiel in Book Four, though he refers to it there as a *szarafan*. The present translation renders *kontusz* and *żupan* as "robe" and "tunic" (or "coat") respectively.

22. [*Author's note*] The beaks of large birds of prey become more and more curved with advancing age; eventually, the upper part grows so crooked that it closes the bill and the bird dies of hunger. This popular belief has been accepted by some ornithologists.

23. [*Author's note*] It is a fact that there is no instance of an animal's skeletal remains ever being found.

24. The Polish term *matecznik* has no precise counterpart in English. It refers to the wildest and most inaccessible parts of the primeval forest.

25. [*Author's note*] A fowling piece (*ptaszynka*) is a gun of small caliber used with a small bullet. With such a gun a good marksman can hit a bird on the wing.

26. The Notary is only partly right as to the provenance of his gun. In the period depicted in *Pan Tadeusz* hunting arms were imported. In this instance, the English firm "Sagallas a London," which then enjoyed wide renown, found a worthy imitator in the Ukrainian village of Balabanovka. The local black- and locksmith by the name of Ivas' became a kind of compositor of hunting arms. Using procured locks and barrels, he fashioned his own stock and forestock, assembled the parts and produced his own line of firearms which bore the inscription "SAGALAS LONDON a Bałabanówka." If we are to believe the Notary, the product enjoyed a modest renown of its own. See: *Słownik tematyczny języka poematu Adama Mickiewicza "Pan Tadeusz."* http://nevmenandr.net/tadeusz.

27. Pronounce: *Do-may-ko* and *Do-vay-ko*. Dowejko (*lith. Doveikos*) was a common Lithuanian surname. The rhyming "Domejko" is a humorous reminiscence of the poet's friend and schoolmate, Ignacy Domejko, a professor of geology who went on to become rector of the University of Santiago in Chile. During the writing of *Pan Tadeusz*, Mickiewicz and Domejko shared the same living quarters.

28. commonly called (Latin)

29. [*Author's note*] Bottles of Gdańsk vodka contain a sediment of gold leaf.

30. The *bigos* was not prepared on the spot. It was cooked beforehand, stored in casks, brought to the hunt, and then reheated.

31. That is, Polesia; one of Europe's largest marshy areas located in the southwestern part of the East-European Plain, now straddling Belarus, Ukraine, Poland, and Russia.
32. To savor the full humor of the Steward's anecdote about Domejko and Dowejko one really needs to hear it read in the poet's rhymed alexandrines.
33. That is, Publius Virgilius Maro, author of *The Aeneid*.
34. [*Author's note*] Queen Dido had a bull's hide cut into strips, and thus enclosed within the compass of the hide a considerable piece of territory, where she later built the city of Carthage. The steward did not read the description of this event in the *Aeneid* but in all probability in the scholiasts' commentaries.

BOOK V

The Brawl

Argument

Telimena's hunting plans. The little gardener prepares to enter fashionable society and listens to her guardian's precepts. The return of the hunters. Tadeusz experiences a great shock. A second encounter at the Shrine of Musings. A reconciliation mediated by a colony of ants. The case of the hunt is argued at table. The Steward's tale of Rejtan and the Prince de Nassau interrupted. A shadowy figure with a key. The ensuing brawl. Gervase and the Count hold a council of war.

His hunt crowned with success, the Steward was riding home from the forest; meanwhile, deep in the solitude of the house, Telimena was just beginning her hunt. True, she was sitting motionless with her arms folded over her bosom, but in her thoughts she was pursuing two beasts of her own. She was thinking up a way of cornering and bagging the two at once—Tadeusz and the Count. The Count was a well-situated youth, heir to a noble house, comely, attractive; indeed, he was half smitten already. But what of it? His feelings might change. And was his love true? Would he consider marriage? With a woman several years his senior? And less well to do! Would his kinsmen allow it? What would society say?

Absorbed in these thoughts, Telimena got up from the sofa and raised herself on the tips of her toes. Aye, that gave her another two inches! Baring her bust to greater advantage, she leaned over sideways, surveyed herself keenly, then once more sought the advice of the mirror. A moment later, she dropped her gaze, sighed, and resumed her seat on the sofa.

The Count was a titled gentleman. The rich had fickle tastes. The Count was a blond, and blonds were not overly passionate. But Tadeusz? Now *there* was a simple heart! An honest lad! Scarcely more than a child! He was only beginning to discover the delights of love. Suitably watched, he was not likely to break off his first romantic attachment; besides, was he not now under certain obligations to Telimena? Young men may be given to sudden changes of mind, but unlike their grandfathers, having tenderer consciences, they hold fast to their affections. Long does the pure and single heart of a youth cherish the sweets of a first love; it greets those delights even as it parts with them, with joy, like the simple meal we share with a friend. Only the gray-bearded drunkard with an inflamed liver recoils from the liquor he drinks to excess. All this Telimena understood perfectly well, as she was wise and fully conversant with the ways of the world.

But what would society say? True, they could always seclude themselves from sight by removing to another part of the district and live out of the way. Better still, they could depart from the district altogether, make a trip to the city, for instance. There, she could acquaint the lad with high society, shape his path, assist him, advise him, instruct his heart, have in him a companion—a brother!—in short, enjoy the world while the years allowed.

Cheered and emboldened by these thoughts, Telimena paced the room briskly several times only to drop her gaze again. Still, it would be well to give thought to the Count! Sophy might not be rich, but she was his equal in rank. She came from a senatorial family. She was a dignitary's daughter. Were a union between them to come to pass, Telimena would be assured of a harborage in her later years. As Sophy's kin and the couple's matchmaker, she'd be like a mother to them both. And after this final consultation with herself, Telimena went to the window and called out to her niece.

Sophy was amusing herself in the garden. Bareheaded, clad in her morning chemise, she was holding a sieve in her outstretched hand while birds flew toward her from every quarter. Here, like rolling balls of yarn, ran a flock of plumped-up hens; there, spurred feet splayed, shaking their purple helms and thrusting their wings like sculls, ruff-necked cockerels came leaping over furrow and shrub. Behind them strode the stately turkey tom, puffing his feathers and clucking at his giddy helpmate's strident yelps. From the meadow yonder long-sterned peafowl glided up like a fleet of river rafts, and here and yon a silver-plumed dove descended like a fluffy clump of snow. All converged on the raised circular grass-plat on which Sophy was standing—a raucous, roiling crush of domestic fowl compassed by a narrow white band of doves. The inner circle comprised a motley of stars, streaks and stripes. Amber beaks here, coral crests there—all rose from that mass of plumage like fish in the sea. Up thrust their necks, continually swaying with gentle movements like water lilies. A myriad flashing eyes stared up at Sophy.

High above them, all white in her long chemise, she whirled round like a fountain playing in a flowerbed. Scooping up the pearled barley in her pearly white hand, she scattered the provender generously over the welter of wings and heads.

That grain was fit for lordly tables. It was the staple of Lithuania's broths. The girl had pilfered it from the housekeeper's cupboard; to feed her birds, she inflicted material loss on the manor.

"Sophy!" she heard her name called. That was Auntie's voice! The playful girl tossed the rest of the dainties to the birds, then twirling and beating the sieve in time skipped her way like a tambor dancer through the press of hens, peacocks, and doves. The startled fowl fluttered up in a throng. Sophy seemed to soar the highest, her feet scarcely touching the ground. Like Venus in her dove-drawn car she flew, a flush of silver pigeons leading the way.

Bursting in through the bedroom window, she gave out a gleeful shout and dropped breathless into her auntie's lap. Telimena, kissed her, stroked her chin and with joy in her heart studied the pretty child's lively features; truly, she loved her young ward! Then resuming her grave expression, she rose to her feet and began once more to pace the room.

"Really, Sophy dear," she said, holding her finger over her lips. "You forget both your station and your age. Why, just today you turned fourteen! Time you dropped your turkeys and hens. Fie on you! Are they fitting amusements for a dignitary's daughter? As for those grimy peasant children, you've cosseted them quite long enough. Ah, Sophy! The very sight of you makes me want to weep. How dreadfully swarthy you are! What a gypsy you've become! You move and gesture like a parish wench. All this I shall have to address; indeed, I shall begin this very day. I've decided to bring you out. Yes, you shall accompany me into the drawing room to meet the guests of whom we have a large number today. Now see you don't put me to shame."

Sophy sprang up, clapped her hands, and flung her arms around her aunt. "Oh, Auntie," she said, at once laughing and crying with joy. "It's been ages since I last saw a guest. In all the time I've been living here with the turkeys and hens, I've had but one caller, and that was a mourning dove. I find it so dull being cooped up like this in this room. Even the Judge says it's bad for my health."

"The Judge!" snorted her aunt. "He never stops pestering me to bring you out. 'She has come of age,' he keeps muttering. Of course, never having rubbed elbows with high society, the old man has no idea what he's talking about. I know better how long it takes to train a young lady and how best to present her. Understand, Sophy, that no matter how pretty and clever the girl, if she grows up under society's constant gaze, she creates no impression, for people will have grown used to seeing her from childhood. But let a mature and refined demoiselle appear glittering before the world from no one knows where, and everyone crowds eagerly around her. They study her every glance and gesture, attend to her words and repeat them to others, and once she comes into fashion, everyone is bound to praise her. I expect you to give a good account of yourself. Remember, you grew up in the capital. Though you've lived in these parts for two years, you cannot have completely forgotten Petersburg. So, Sophy, attend to your toilet. You'll find everything arranged on my dressing table. Come, do get along! The hunt will be back any minute."

She summoned the chambermaid and the serving girl. They emptied a water-ewer into a silver basin. Like a sparrow Sophy splashed in the water. With the maid's assistance, she washed her hands, face and neck. Meanwhile, broaching her Petersburg stores, her aunt drew out bottles of perfume and jars of pomade. She proceeded to sprinkle Sophy with an exquisite scent, which filled the room, and apply the gum arabic to her hair. Sophy put on white openwork stockings and a matching pair of satin shoes procured in Warsaw. After lacing the bodice, the maid spread a dust-wrap over her bosom and began removing the curl papers. Since Sophy's hair was short, they braided it into two plaits, leaving a smooth fringe over the brow and temples. The maid wove a garland of fresh-culled cornflowers and passed it to Telimena, who pinned it deftly to Sophy's head from right to left. Even as in the cornfield the flowers accented her pale tresses. Finally, the wrap came off, and her toilet was complete. Tossing a white frock over her head and folding a white batiste handkerchief in her hand, Sophy presented herself for inspection—the very picture of a white lily. A few more nice adjustments to her hair and dress, and she was made to parade up and down the room. Telimena followed her ward's movements with a drill sergeant's eye, frowning and growing increasingly cross. At last, brought to despair by Sophy's curtsy, she could contain herself no longer.

"Alas the day, Sophy! See what happens from living with gooseherds and ganders. Why, you stride along like a boy! Your eye roves from right to left like a divorcée's. Now drop me a curtsy. Mercy me, how awkward you are!"

"Oh, Auntie!" pleaded poor Sophia. "It isn't my fault. You've kept me locked up, and I've had no one to dance with. It's only from boredom that I tend the poultry and nanny the children. But just wait, Auntie, give me a little time to mingle with people and you'll see how I improve."

"Of the two evils, poultry's decidedly the lesser," stated her aunt. "I'd sooner have you consorting with the barn fowl than with the riffraff we've been receiving so far. You've only to recall our recent visitors: the parish priest mumbling his orisons or poring over the checkerboard, the barristers puffing on their tobacco pipes. There's suitors for you! Fine manners you'd learn from them. Now at least you have someone to whom to show yourself, for we have distinguished company visiting. Mark well, my dear, the Count is here, a true gentleman, young and well-bred—a kinsman of the Governor. Be sure to mind your manners with him."

The sound of men and horses fell upon their ears. Why, here was the hunt at the gate! Hooking her arm through Sophy's, Telimena hastened to the drawing room. None of the hunters had yet entered. Loath to join the ladies in their hunting tunics, they'd retired to their rooms to change. The first to appear, having dressed in great haste, were the two youths—Tadeusz and the Count. Telimena discharged the duties of hostess, greeting and seating the guests as they entered, diverting them with small talk and presenting her niece to each in turn. As the girl's near of kin, Tadeusz enjoyed the first honor. Sophy bobbed him a polite curtsy; Tadeusz answered with a low bow. He was about to speak when, staring into her eyes, he was suddenly seized by a state of panic. He fell dumbstruck, blushing and blanching by turns. What lay upon his heart he could scarcely guess, but he felt quite wretched. He recognized Sophy, recognized her by her stature, her fair hair, her voice! Here was the same little head and torso he'd seen on the fence. Only this morning this charming voice had roused him for the hunt.

Fortunately, the Steward relieved Tadeusz of his embarrassment. Seeing the lad grow suddenly pale and sway on his feet, he urged him to retire to his room and seek rest. Tadeusz withdrew in silence to the corner, where, leaning against the mantelpiece, he cast wild wide-eyed glances now at the aunt, now at her niece. Telimena could scarcely fail to notice the strong impression wrought on him by Sophy's glance, but, being busy with the guests, she could not surmise all. Still, her eyes never left the youth. At last, seizing a favorable moment, she ran over to him. Was he not well? she asked. Why so downcast? She pressed her questions, alluded to Sophy, and even tried to jest with him, but Tadeusz, leaning motionless on his elbow, only frowned and grimaced in blank silence. This only further confused and astonished Telimena. Instantly her face and tone of voice hardened. Rising in anger, she let loose a stream of harsh words, taunts and reproaches. Tadeusz, stung to the quick, started up, frowned and spat on the floor, then kicking aside the chair stormed wordlessly out of the room, slamming the door behind him. Fortunately, the scene went unnoticed by the rest of the guests.

He fled out of the gate and made straight for the fields. As when the jackfish, feeling the leister pierce its breast, thrashes about in the water then plunges deep, trying to break free, yet never parts with that dart and line, so Tadeusz carried within him the hurt that refused to let go. Crossing ditches and leaping fences, he wandered aimlessly, without direction. At last, on entering the woods, he arrived—by chance or by design—at the knoll that only yesterday had been the scene of his joy, the place where he'd received the little note in an earnest of love—the spot already known to us as the Shrine of Musings.

Whom should he see there, on looking around, but *her*—Telimena, alone and lost in her thoughts. Nothing about her garb and posture recalled the nymph of the previous day. She was dressed in white, sitting motionless on a rock, as if carved out of stone. Her face lay buried in her open hands, and though you could not hear the sobs, you knew that the tears were falling fast.

Tadeusz fought a losing battle with his heart. He felt an anguish of pity and compassion. Long he watched in silence from his point of espial behind a tree. At last, heaving a sigh, he began to reproach himself. "What a fool I am!" he thought. "Why should I blame her for my mistake?" He peered cautiously out from behind the tree, but at that moment Telimena started up from the rock and began thrashing about to the left and the right. Fording the stream at a jump, she threw up her arms and pelted, pale as a ghost, through the forest, her hair streaming wildly behind her. She leapt in the air, fell to her knees, then cast herself to the ground. Unable to rise, she lay writhing on the turf, clearly in the throes of terrible torments, tearing at her breast, her neck, her ankles and knees. Tadeusz sprang up, thinking some unclean spirit or terrible malady had taken possession of her, but this was not the cause of her convulsions. The nearby birch wood was home to a mighty colony of ants. These resourceful, nimble black insects were given to roaming freely over the grass thereabouts. Whether out of need or mere fancy, they found a particular attraction in the Shrine of Musings. From their citadel on the hill they had beaten a path down to the edge of the rill, and along this path they regularly marched their rank and file. Alas, Telimena sat right athwart it. Lured by the luster of her white stockings, the ants swarmed under her dress and set busily to work, tickling and biting. Telimena was forced to flee and shake them off. Finally, she seated herself on the sward and began plucking them off with her fingers.

Tadeusz could scarcely refuse to come to her aid. He brushed off her frock, working his way down to her feet; his lips strayed close to her temples. So, in this friendly attitude, without saying a word, the two put their morning spat behind them. Who knows how long their silent discourse might have lasted if they hadn't been roused by the tolling of the manor bell?

The summons to dinner! Time to return home, the more so, as they heard the cracking of brushwood close by. Were there people out looking for them? As it wouldn't do to be seen walking from the forest together, the pair took their separate ways: Telimena to the right, toward the orchard; Tadeusz to the left, toward the high road. Yet in so retiring, neither was spared cause for alarm. Telimena could have sworn she caught a glimpse of Robak's gaunt hooded face in the bushes, and more than once Tadeusz spied a tall white shadow to his left. Who it was, he could not unerringly say, but he had a strong suspicion it was the Count in his long English riding coat.

Dinner was served at the castle. Despite the Judge's prohibition, the willful Usher had once again, in the absence of the company, stormed the castle with what he called an *intromissio*[1] of the tableware. The party entered the great hall in orderly fashion and drew up in a circle around the table. The post of honor rightfully belonged to the Chamberlain; it was the privilege of his office and senior years. Bowing in turn to the ladies, elders and youth, he advanced toward the table. As the Bernardine was absent tonight, the Chamberlain's wife stationed herself at the Chamberlain's right elbow. After some reassignment of seats, the Judge blessed the table in the Latin tongue, the men took vodka, whereupon they sat down one and all, and tucked silently into the beet-leaf soup, chilled Lithuanian-style.

After the soup came crayfish, chicken and asparagus washed down with Hungarian and Malaga wines. The guests ate and drank in stony silence. Never had these castle walls, which had so lavishly fêted so many sons of the nobility and resounded with so many hearty hurrahs—never, since the day they were built, had these walls witnessed such a feast of gloom! But for the popping of corks and the rattle of plates one would have sworn the great hall was deserted or that an evil spirit had sealed the banqueters' lips.

Many were the reasons for this silence. True, the men had returned from the hunt in a boisterous frame of mind. But when their elation abated and they began to think over the hunt, they realized they hadn't come out of it with any great glory. Had it required a monk's hood appearing out of nowhere 'like Philip out of the hemp'[2] to expose the shooters of the district? O shame! What would they make of this in Oszmiana and Lida districts, their long-time rivals for supremacy in the hunting-craft? Such were the thoughts that ran through their minds.

As to the Notary and the Assessor, in addition to their old animosities they had the disgrace of their hounds still fresh on their minds. An arch hare sped before their eyes. Legs outthrust, it loped, taunting them from the edge of the thicket with an insolent flick of its scut. Like a lash that tail cut across their hearts! So, staring down at their plates, they sat. And now the Assessor had even more pressing cause for chagrin: the sight of his two rivals seated around Telimena.

Telimena sat half-turned away from Tadeusz. In her confusion she scarcely dared glance at him. She sought instead to amuse the Count, to draw him into a conversation and restore his humor, for he'd returned from his walk (or *ambuscade*, as Tadeusz was inclined to think) in a strangely sullen frame of mind. But on hearing her address him, the Count only raised his head haughtily, frowned, and stared at her with an expression bordering on contempt. He shifted away from her in his seat and turned his attentions to Sophy: he poured her wine, passed her plates, and plied her with a thousand gallantries, bowing and smiling constantly;

now and again he rolled his eyes and sighed deeply. Despite the clever ruse, it was clear his flirtations had no other object than to spite Telimena, as every time he turned to her, seemingly unconsciously, he glared at her with a glowering eye. Unable to make sense of it, Telimena shrugged her shoulders and put it down to his eccentric ways. And so, not entirely displeased with the addresses the Count was paying to Sophy, she turned to her other partner at table.

Tadeusz sat equally sullen. Eating nothing, scarcely drinking, eyes never straying from his plate, he pretended to listen to the talk around him. Telimena topped up his wine cup. He balked at the imposition! Asked about his health, he merely yawned. He no longer took kindly to her precipitate advances—so much had he changed over the course of one evening. The immodestly low cut of her dress scandalized him. But what was his astonishment when he raised his eyes! The shock almost threw him into a panic. His eyesight had grown suddenly keener. No sooner did he glance at Telimena's glowing cheeks than he discovered a terrible secret. Ye gods! The woman was rouged!

Was the blush of inferior quality? Had Telimena smudged it inadvertently with her hand? The rouge lay unevenly spread, revealing patches of coarse-complexioned skin. Perhaps, on drawing too close to her at the Shrine of Musings, Tadeusz himself had smeared the carmine that overlay the whiting like the fine dust on a butterfly's wing. Whatever the reason, after her hasty return from the forest Telimena hadn't had time to touch up her face, and now there were freckles showing through, especially around the mouth. Suddenly, like a pair of crafty spies, having found one treason out, Tadeusz's eyes began to examine the rest of her charms only to unmask a host of additional little perfidies: two missing teeth, wrinkles along the brow, crow's feet around the eyes and a thousand more creases concealed under the chin.

Alas! thought Tadeusz. The vanity of holding up a thing of beauty to minute scrutiny! The shame of playing the spy on one's beloved! O fickle taste! O fickle heart! But who of us is master of his heart? In vain he charged his conscience to square his deficit of love, to warm his heart anew with the rays of her eyes, but now her gaze, like the moon's, bright yet throwing no heat, glanced off the carapace of his soul—a soul grown chill to the core; and with such regrets and self-reproaches, Tadeusz bent silently over his plate and gnawed at his lip.

Meanwhile, an evil spirit lured him with a fresh temptation: to eavesdrop on Sophy and the Count. Charmed by the latter's gallantries, the girl had blushed at first and dropped her gaze, but soon the pair were laughing together. Their talk turned to a certain encounter in the garden, to a certain sally into the burdock and flowerbeds. Straining his utmost to listen, Tadeusz swallowed the bitter words, digesting them in his heart. A terrible feast! As the fork-tongued adder sucks on a poisonous herb then coils up on the garden path, imperiling the unwary foot, so Tadeusz, bloated with jealousy's venom, feigned indifference while bursting with malice.

Let but a few sit sullen at the merriest of gatherings and their gloom quickly spreads to the rest of the company. The hunters had long since fallen silent, and now, infected by Tadeusz's spleen, the far end of the table fell silent too. Even the Chamberlain seemed out of sorts. Seeing his comely, well-dowered daughters in the prime of life—the finest matches in the district in everyone's estimation—sitting mute and ignored by the silent youth, he too showed little zest for talk. The cordial Judge was also upset, and the Steward, remarking at the general silence, called it a feast of wolves, unfit for Polish folk.

Now the Steward's ears were peculiarly averse to silence. Garrulous by nature, he was inordinately fond of chatterers. Small wonder! He'd spent his entire life in the company of the nobility, attending dinner banquets, hunts, assemblies, and the regional diets. He was accustomed to the presence of noise around him even when he himself was silent or prowling the rooms with his fly-flap, or merely dozing in his chair with his eyes shut. By day he constantly sought out conversation; at night, he insisted on having someone close by to tell the beads with, or spin him a yarn. He considered the tobacco pipe his mortal foe thought up by the German to depolonize the Pole. "A Germanized Poland is a Poland bereft of her tongue," he was wont to say.[3] Having prattled all through his life, the old master now thrived on prattle for his repose. Silence awoke him from his sleep. Just so the drone of the wheels lulls the miller to sleep. But let them grind to a halt and he starts to his feet and cries out, "The Word was made flesh!"[4]

Bowing to the Chamberlain, then signaling to the Judge with a light touch of his hand to his lips, the Steward made known his wish to address the guests. Both men replied to his mute gesture with a nod, as if to say, "By all means."

The Steward struck up: "I make bold to prevail on our youth to make merry at the banquet table as we did in olden times, and not to chew in silence! What, are we Capuchin monks? The nobleman idling his tongue is like the hunter that lets the shot rust in his gun. I laud the loquacity of our ancestors. After a hunt they gathered round the table not only to partake of the victuals but also to share their thoughts. Whatever lay on their hearts, be it reproach or praise for the hunter, the beater, the hounds, the shots—all was brought out into the open, producing a noise as sweet to the sportsman's ear as a second hunt. I know, I know what ails you. This cloud of somber cares wafts from the Bernardine's hood! You feel ashamed your shots went abroad. But do not burn with shame. I knew hunters whose aim was better than yours, and yet missed. To hit, to miss, to learn from one's mistakes, that is the life of a hunter! I, too, have shot wide on occasion, though I've hunted with a gun since I was a boy.

"The great sportsman Tułoszczyk was known to miss. Even Rejtan, rest his soul, didn't always hit the mark. More on him anon. As for letting the bear escape the ring and our two young gentlemen shying away, though they had a spear at hand, well, no one shall praise or condemn it. To beat a retreat with a loaded gun has always been regarded as the height of cowardice. And shooting blindly, as many do, not closing with the quarry or taking proper aim, that is a shameful thing. But he who aims well, who allows the quarry to approach, and misses, may fall back without disgrace. Then again, he may resort to the spear, but only as he sees fit, for he is under no obligation; the spear is there strictly for self-defense. So it has always been. So take my words to heart, dear Tadeusz and my dear Count. Let not your retreat upset you unduly. Henceforth, as often as you recall today's incident, remember this piece of advice from your old Steward. Never stand in another's way, and never should a pair of hunters fire simultaneously on the same game."

No sooner did the Steward utter the word "game" than the Assessor fired back with a half- audible "dame." "Bravo!" cried the youth. Murmurs and laughter began to ripple through the hall as the Steward's advice made the round of the guests, some insisting on "game," others laughingly repeating "dame." "*Coquette!*" muttered Bolesta under his breath, upon which the Assessor, glaring daggers at Telimena, reposted, "*Grisette!*"[5]

The Steward hadn't meant to poke fun at anyone, nor was he aware of what was being whispered around him. Delighted to have brought mirth to the youth and the women, he now sought to bring cheer to the hunters. Charging his cup, he struck up again.

"I look in vain for our almsman. I should like to relate to him a curious incident not unlike the one that occurred during the hunt today. The Warden said he knew of but one man capable of shooting as true and at so great a range as our Monk. I knew another! Two men he saved with an equally well-aimed shot. I saw it myself the time the Deputy Rejtan and the Prince de Nassau came up to Naliboka Forest. They did not envy that nobleman his glory; indeed, they were the first to pledge his health. Past telling the gifts they heaped upon him in addition to the slain boar's pelt. As one who was there and saw it, I shall tell you of that boar and that shot, for the event was very much like the one that took place this morning, and it happened to the finest shooter of my day, the Deputy Rejtan and the Prince de Nassau—"

But here, replenishing the Steward's cup, the Judge broke in: "I pledge Robak's health! Steward, raise your beaker! If we cannot enrich the Bernardine with a gift, then at least we shall endeavor to repay him for the spent powder.

The bear slain in the forest today shall keep his cloister's kitchen amply supplied with meat for two years—this we solemnly promise. But the hide I shan't give up. Either I shall take it by force or the Monk will yield it to me as an exercise in humility. Then again, I may purchase it, though it cost me the pelts of a dozen sables. At any rate, we shall dispose of the hide as we think fit. The first crown and glory has already been taken by our servant of God. Now His Excellency the Chamberlain will award the bearskin to the one that earned the second prize."

The Chamberlain rubbed his forehead and lowered his eyes; meanwhile, the hunters began murmuring among themselves. Each laid his own claim to the prize, one for rousing the bear, another for wounding it, another for setting on the hounds, still another for heading the beast from the river. Once more the Assessor and the Notary fell out, the former adamantly extolling the merits of his Sanguszko fowling piece, the latter his Sagalas *a Bałabanówka*.

"My dear Judge and neighbor," spoke up the Chamberlain at last, "The first prize rightfully belongs to our servant of God. As to the second prize, that is not easy to decide. All seem to have acquitted themselves with distinction, all showed equal address, skill and courage. But fate placed two among us in special peril. Two came closest to the bear's claws—the Count and Tadeusz. Both have claim to the pelt, but Tadeusz, as the younger, and as the kinsman of our host, will be happy, I am sure, to forgo the prize. Therefore, dear Count, the *spolia opima*[6] fall to you. May the bearskin adorn your trophy room! May it serve you as a reminder of today's sport, a talisman of good fortune in the chase, a spur to future glory!"

He fell silent, blithely thinking he'd cheered the Count. He could not have known how painful a thrust he'd dealt him. At the mention of 'trophy room,' the Count instinctively looked up and around him. He saw the stag frontlets, the branching antlers lining the walls like a stand of bay laurels sown by the hands of the fathers to bind the brows of their sons. He saw the row of portraits adorning the pillars, the ancient half-goat emblazoning the vault. Everything spoke to him with the voice of the past. The Count roused himself. He recalled where and whose guest he was—a scion of the House of Horeszko, a guest under his own roof feasting with the Soplicas, his ancestral foes. And now the jealousy he felt toward Tadeusz only further provoked him against the Soplica clan.

"My house is too small," he said with a bitter smile. "It has no room worthy of so superb a trophy. Better the skin remain here with these antlered trophies until the Judge decides to return it to me along with the castle."

Seeing where things were tending, the Chamberlain rapped on his gold snuffbox and begged the floor.

"My dear Count and neighbor!" he said. "You are to be commended for minding your interests even at the dinner table, unlike so many fashionable young gentlemen of your age who live thoughtlessly from day to day, without foresight. That my court shall bring about an agreeable settlement is my earnest hope and wish. One obstacle remains, the question of the manorial farm. What I propose is an award of land in exchange for the farm on the following terms . . ."

And he launched, as always, into an orderly exposition of his plan. He was halfway through his speech when an unexpected disturbance arose at the far end of the table. A number of the guests were suddenly pointing at something that had drawn their attention, and others were staring in the same direction, until finally, like ears of grain bowed by a contrary wind, every head was turned away from the Chamberlain and facing the corner.

From a tiny doorway concealed among the pillars where hung a portrait of the last of the Horeszko Pantlers, a shadowy figure emerged. It was Gervase, instantly recognizable by his demeanor, tall stature, and the silver half-goats embroidering his yellowed coat. Straight as a ramrod he walked, silent and grim; in his hand flashed a dagger-like key. Opening a cabinet, he began to perform a number of manual rotations.

By a pillar at each of two corners of the hall stood a musical clock enclosed in a wooden cabinet. Quaint old fellows these! Long at odds with the sun, they often struck the noon hour at dusk. Gervase never undertook to repair the works, but he wouldn't dream of allowing the timepieces to go unwound. Every night he tormented them punctually with his key, and now was the hour for winding the clocks.

As the Chamberlain held the attention of those who cared to listen, the Warden pulled on the weights. The rusty sprockets began to grate and grind. The Chamberlain shuddered and stopped in mid-phrase.

"I say, dear brother," he said, "attend to that urgent task of yours some other time."

And he resumed the exposition of his plan. But the arch Warden yanked the other weight with even greater violence, whereupon the bullfinch perched atop the clock began to flap its wings and chirp out the chimes of the hour. The bird was well crafted. Pity it was out of repair! It whizzed and it quavered, and the longer it chirped, the worse it sounded. The guests gave out a roar of laughter. Again the Chamberlain was forced to interrupt his speech.

"Warden," he cried, "or should I say, screech owl? If you value your beak, you'll put a stop to that racket."

But Gervase, uncowed by the threat, placed his right hand solemnly on the clock, rested his left on his hip, and thus buttressed rejoined:

"My dear little Chamberlain, a great lord is free to jest. A sparrow is smaller than an owl, and yet domiciled in his own nest of shavings he is braver than the owl that squats under another's roof. A Warden is no screech owl. He that steals into another's garret by night is the owl. And I mean to flush him out!"

"Show him the door!" roared the Chamberlain.

"Count!" cried the Warden to the Count. "Do you see what passes here? Is your honor not yet sufficiently tainted by eating and drinking with these Soplicas? Must now I, Gervase Rębajłło, keeper of the Horeszko keys, be reviled under the roof of my lords? And you put up with it?"

Thereupon Protase called out three times:

"Silence, clear the hall! I, Protase Balthazar Brzechalski,[7] bearer of two titles, formerly Sergeant-at-Arms, *vulgo* Court Usher, hereby render my *obductio*[8]— calling as witnesses every born gentleman present here, and charging the Assessor in attendance to launch a formal inquiry in behalf of His Honor Judge Soplica as to an *incursio*, that is to say, an unwarrantable intrusion upon another party's premises, to wit, the castle, which the Judge holds by right of law; to which I adduce the plain fact that he is dining here tonight—"

"Why, you squawking magpie!" bellowed Gervase. "I'll show you!"

And yanking his iron keys from his belt, he whirled them over his head and shied them with all his might at Protase. Like a stone from a sling hurtled that mass of iron. It would have smashed the Usher's skull into little bits had he not ducked in the nick of time.

The guests started from their seats. For a moment there was a dead silence; then the Judge cried out, "Confine that mischief-raiser in the stocks! Ho there, boys!"—and briskly ran the servants along the narrow corridor between the wall and bench; but the Count barred their way with a chair.

"Stand back!" he cried, placing his foot on the frail barricade. "Judge, none shall lay a hand on my servant in my house! If anyone has a complaint against the old man, let him lodge it with me."

The Chamberlain regarded the Count out of the corner of his eye. "Sir," he said, "I need no help from you to chide this insolent old fellow. Besides, you anticipate the court's decision. You are not the lord here, nor, sir, are you the host. Sit you still as before, and if you honor not my gray hairs, then defer at least to the district's highest office."

"What is that to me?" fired back the Count. "Enough of this prattle. Weary others with your office and favors! I was fool enough to join in your drinking bouts that end in coarse brawls. You shall answer for this slight to my honor. Until we meet again, sober of mind! Come, Gervase, follow me!"

Not in his wildest imaginings did the Chamberlain expect such a reply. He was just filling his winecup when the Count's insolent words burst upon him like a thunderbolt. Dumbfounded he sat, bottle sloped over his glass, his head canted to one side, ears pricked up, eyes rounded, lips partly open, but he squeezed the glass so hard that it burst with a ping and sent the wine spraying into his eyes. You would have sworn fire poured into his soul with the wine, so flushed was his face, so inflamed was his eye. He sprang up to speak. The first word he mashed indistinctly in his mouth before finally expelling it through his teeth:

"M-m-mountebank! you cub of a count, I'll . . . Thomas, my saber! I'll teach you *mores.* Fool! Damn you! So my office and favors weary that delicate little ear, eh? Why, I'll slice his lobe off—earring and all! Outside with you, sir, and draw your steel. Thomas, my saber!"

The Chamberlain's friends hastened to his aid.

"Hold sir!" cried the Judge, seizing him by the arm. "This is our affair. I was challenged first. Protase, my sword! I'll make him dance like a bear on a pole."

"Uncle! Excellency! spoke up Tadeusz, restraining the Judge. "Does it befit your high degree to have to do with this fop? Are there no young men about? Entrust me with the task! I'll see he is duly chastised. And you Hotspur, who call out our elders, we'll see what a grim knight you are. Tomorrow we decide on the place and arms, and settle the matter. Now go while you have breath to draw!"

It was timely advice, for Gervase and the Count were in serious straits. A great hue and cry had gone up from the upper end of the table, and from the lower end there were bottles flying about the Count's head. The terrified women pleaded and wept. "Alas the day!" wailed Telimena, and raising her eyeballs went off in a dead faint. She slumped over the Count's shoulder, pressing her swansdown bosom against his chest. The Count choked back his rage and began to revive her, rubbing color into her cheeks.

Meanwhile, Gervase was reeling under the barrage of bottles and stools. Even now a throng of bare-knuckled servants was bearing down on him from either side. Fortunately, Sophy saw the assault. Moved to pity, she leapt up and shielded the old man with her outspread arms. The servants stopped in their tracks while Gervase slunk back and vanished from sight. They were still look-ing for him under the table when he sprang out from the other side, hoisted a bench in his powerful arms, and swinging it round cleared half the hall. He seized the Count, and with the bench serving them as a shield, the two men backed away to the door. On reaching the threshold, Gervase stopped and eyed his foe again. For a moment he hesitated, at pains to decide if he should beat an orderly retreat or avail himself of his new weapon and seek fresh fortunes of war. He chose the latter course. Raising the bench to use as a battering ram, he swung it back, lowered his head, and thrusting out his chest and lifting his foot made ready to charge, but then suddenly catching sight of the Steward he fell aghast.

The Chief Steward had been sitting quietly with half-shut eyes, as if lost in thought. Only when the Count began to quarrel with the Chamberlain and threaten the Judge did he begin to pay attention. Twice he took a pinch of snuff and wiped his eyes. He was only distantly related to the Judge, but, having long enjoyed the hospitality of the latter's house, he'd grown highly solicitous of his companion's welfare, so it was with growing alarm that he watched the unfolding brawl. Placing his fingers lightly on the table and cupping a knife in the hollow of his hand, the helve running the length of his index finger, blade turned up toward his elbow, he raised his arm and drawing it back twirled the knife about in his fist as if toying with it—but his eye never left the Count.

Now the art of knife throwing, so terrible a part of hand-to-hand combat, had long since fallen into disuse in Lithuania. Only a few old timers were acquainted with it. Gervase would sometimes resort to it during a brawl in the tavern, and the Steward was an old hand at it. You could tell by the backward stroke of his arm that the blow would be hard, and the direction of his gaze left no doubt as to the intended target: the Count himself—last male representative of the Horeszkos, albeit in the female line. The less attentive youngsters failed to grasp the old man's gesture, but Gervase paled at the sight. He swung the bench in front of the Count and drew back to the doorway.

"Catch 'em!" roared the throng.

Caught unawares over his kill, a wolf turns blindly on a pack of hounds that surprises him at his feast. He lunges at them, ready to tear them to pieces. Suddenly, amid the clamor of the dogs, he hears the faint click of a gun hammer. He knows the sound. Looking around, he sees the hunter at the rear of the pack. Stooped on one knee, the hunter stares down his barrel at him, finger on the trigger. Instantly the wolf flattens his ears and scuttles off, tail cleaving to his belly. Howling in triumph, the pack goes after him, tearing at his shaggy flanks. Now and again the beast turns, confronts them and snaps his jaws; the merest rasp of his white fangs sends them into a whimpering panic. Such was Gervase's grim mien. Just so he held back his assailants with his stern eye and upraised bench until, reaching the doorway, he and the Count vanished deep into the shadowy opening.

"Catch 'em!" roared the throng again.

Their triumph was short-lived. Without warning, the Warden reappeared by the old organ in the gallery. With an appalling crash he set to tearing out the tin-lead pipes. Great might have been the havoc he wrought from above, but by this time the guests were legging it helter-skelter out of the hall. Loath to be left behind, the terrified servants seized armfuls of dishes and decamped on the heels of their lords. What remained of the tableware they abandoned to the victors.

And who, braving threats and blows, was the last to quit the scene of battle? The Court Usher—Protase Brzechalski! Standing motionless behind the Judge's chair, he continued calmly to intone his formal *obductio*. Not until he'd fully discharged his usher's office did he retire from the deserted field—a field now bestrewn with the dead, the maimed, and the detritus of battle. True, there were no human casualties, but every bench had its legs put out, and the banquet table, unlimbed of a leg and bereft of its cloth, lay slumped over piles of wine-spattered plates like a slain knight stretched on ensanguined shields. All around lay the bodies of capons and turkeys, a carving fork stuck into every breast.

Within minutes total calm was restored to the solitary Horeszko castle. Night closed in. The remains of the splendid lordly banquet lay on the floor like the nocturnal repasts of Forefathers' Eve[9] at which the enchanted spirits of the dead are said to gather. Thrice from the gable the lych-owls screeched like warlocks, as if greeting the rising moon. Projected through the casement, her pale tremulous image danced like a purgatorial soul on the table. From holes in the cellars below hellish rats leapt up to gnaw and drink. Ever and anon, a forlorn champagne bottle popped a toast to the presiding spirits.

On the second floor, in the mirrorless room formerly known as the hall of mirrors, the Count stood cooling himself in the air by the door to the gallery which overlooked the terrace and castle gate. He wore his frock coat with one arm through the sleeve and the tails and the other sleeve wrapped about his throat so that the garment draped his chest like a cloak. Meanwhile, Gervase paced the hall with giant strides. Both men were deep in thought, muttering to themselves.

"Pistols!" said the Count. "Then again, broadswords, if they so wish." "The castle and the village," said the Warden, "both ours!"

"Uncle, nephew . . . I'll call out the whole tribe!" exclaimed the Count.

"I say seize the castle, the village *and* the land!" said the Warden, and turning to the Count resumed: "If it's peace you want, seize it all. Why bother with lawsuits, old boy? The thing's as clear as day. For four centuries the Horeszkos have owned this castle. After Targowica, they seized a part of the land and awarded it, as you well know, to the Soplicas. Don't settle for a part. You must take it all as recompense for your legal fees and the pillaging of the castle. Haven't I always urged you to forgo the courts? Haven't I always urged you to mount up and raid 'em? That's how we did it! Whoever seizes the land is the rightful heir. Who wins on the field wins in court. As to settling our older scores with the Soplicas, we have my

Jackknife here, wieldier than any court of law, and if Matthias should lend a hand with his Birch, why, the pair of us shall cut the Soplicas into thin strips!"

"Bravo!" replied the Count. "Your plan smacks of the Sarmatian and Gothic. Your idea is more to my liking than all this legal wrangling. You know what we shall do? We'll mount a raid such as hasn't been seen in Lithuania for years—and a high time we'll have of it! Two years have I bided here, and all the action I've seen are boundary scuffles with the local rustics. But our expedition promises bloodshed! I took part in one such raid during my travels abroad. I was biding with a prince in Sicily when a band of robbers abducted his son-in-law. They took him into the mountains and brazenly demanded a ransom from his kin. In short order we raised our men and vassals and mounted an attack. Two of the brigands I ran through myself. I was the first to storm the camp and free the captive. Ah, dear Gervase, what a splendid triumphal progress we made upon our return—in true knightly-feudal style! The populace hailed us with flowers. The prince's daughter, grateful to the deliverer, fell on my neck and wept. When I returned to Palermo, it was in all the papers. Women pointed me out. The incident even became the theme of a romance entitled *The Count, or the Mystery of Rocca Birbante Castle*—and it mentioned me by name. Tell me, are there any dungeons in this castle?"

"We have ample wine-vaults," replied the Warden, "but they're empty now. The Soplicas drained them dry."

"My jockeys!" said the Count. "We must arm my jockeys and raise our vassals in the hamlets!"

"*Lackeys?* God forbid, sir," broke in Gervase, not hearing right. "Are forays acts of villainy? Whoever heard of mounting a foray with yokels and lackeys? I can see your lordship knows nothing about forays. And *wassails*, you say?—that's different.[10] We could do with a few wild revelers, but you don't raise them in the hamlets. For that we go to the noble villages—Dobrzyn, Rzezików, Ciętycze, and Rąbanki![11] Nobility there since time out of mind! The flower of our knighthood!—all friendly to Horeszko and sworn foes of Soplica. There shall we raise some three hundred of your noble wassailers, but that is a task for me to discharge. Meantime, you, sir, return to your hall and sleep the sleep of the just. A heavy task awaits us on the morrow. You are fond of sleep, old boy, and the hour is late. Hark! A second cock crows. I shall remain here and guard the castle until daybreak. Come sunrise, I shall be darkening the doorways of Dobrzyn."

The Count quitted the gallery, but before taking leave of the castle he took a peep through one of the embrasures. He saw the manor house ablaze with lights.

"Blaze away," he murmured. "By this time tomorrow, we'll have lights in the castle, while you languish in darkness!"

Gervase sat down on the floor, leaned back against the wall and lowered his heavy brow. The moonlight fell on the polished dome of his skull upon which he could be seen tracing designs with his finger, evidently plotting strategies for future raids. His eyelids grew heavy, his head began to nod uncontrollably. Feeling the onset of sleep, he muttered his night prayers. Somewhere between the paternoster and the ave, a host of strange shadows rose up and passed before his eyes. The Warden saw his former masters, the Horeszkos, some bearing sabers, others maces.[12] Each flashed a fell eye, curled a moustache, and struck his pose with his saber, or brandished his mace. Behind them glided a somber-faced wraith with a splash of blood on its breast. Gervase shuddered. He recognized the Pantler! He blessed himself all round, and so as the better to drive away these horrid apparitions, he recited the Litany of the Poor Souls.

Once more his eyelids began to close tight. A noise rang in his ears. A mounted troop of the nobility, sabers scintillant, thundered before him. An armed foray! The raid on Korelicze, Rymsza riding headmost and Gervase among them. Full tilt astride his gray he rode, his terrible sword upraised, his tunic unbuttoned, skirts snapping in the wind, his red-plumed confederate's cap sliding over his left ear. Onward he sped, striking down the standing and mounted, and now he was setting a burning brand to Soplica's barn . . .

And weighed down by these dreams, his head sank to his chest. So drifted off to sleep the last of the Horeszko wardens.

NOTES

1. As court usher, Protase habitually interlards his speech with Latinate legalese. The Polish term *intromisyja* signifies the seizing of goods adjudged to the plaintiff.
2. [Author's note] "Once in Parliament, a deputy called Philip from the village of Konopie [literally: hemp], having obtained the floor, strayed so far from the subject that he raised general laughter in the Chamber. Hence arose the saying, 'to pop up like Philip out the hemp.'"
3. An untranslatable quibble on the Polish word for "German" (*niemiec*), which derives from the word *niemy*, meaning "dumb" or "mute."
4. A line from the *Angelus*, a prayer to the Blessed Virgin, traditionally said at noon. Interestingly, in his novel *War and Peace* Leo Tolstoy uses the same extended simile in describing Gerneral Kutuzov at the war council prior to the Battle of Austerlitz : "When the monotonous sound of [General] Weyrother's voice ceased, Kutuzov opened his eye, *as a miller wakes up when the soporific drone of the mill wheel is interrupted.*" The fact that the scene takes place in a "nobleman's castle" (albeit, recalling Judge Soplica's manor house, "of modest dimensions") coupled with the detail of Count Langeron playing with "a gold snuff-box on which was a portrait," and the additional presence of the Polish Prince Ignacy Przybyszewski would further suggest that Tolstoy was well acquainted with Mickiewicz's poem. (See also note 33 to Book I).
5. The Polish text gives *kobieta* (woman) and *kokieta* (coquette) respectively.

6. Spoils of honor (Latin)
7. One of several of Mickiewicz's suggestive names; it derives from the hunting expression *sroka brzecha* (the magpie squawks). In discharging his office, a court usher was more than often required to raise his voice.
8. The Polish legal term *obdukcja* signifies an oral summary of the existing state of affairs.
9. An ancient Byelorussian folk rite in which the spirits of the dead are invoked. The poet made it the subject of his drama *Dziady* (Forefathers' Eve).
10. The humor of the ensuing passage rests on an untranslatable word play. Gervase, apparently hard of hearing, or simply ignorant of the count's Anglo-Gallicisms *jockey* and *vassal*, confuses them with the Polish words *lokaj* (lackey) and *wąsal* (whiskered one), large bushy moustaches being hallmarks of the Polish nobility of the time. Given Napoleon's admiration of the Polish uhlan's bravery in combat, whence the origin of the French saying *saoul comme un Polonais*, my metonymical substitution of the Anglo-Saxon "wassailers" for Poland's whiskered nobility would not seem too egregious a liberty. See https://fr.wiktionary.org/wiki/saoul comme un Polonais.
11. The fictional names suggest the inhabitants' prowess with the sword in carving (*rzezać*), cutting (*ciąć*), and hewing (*rąbać*) respectively.
12. A special kind of mace (*buzdygan*—from the Turkish). It was the staff of office of the higher military command in the Polish Army, just as the *buława* was that of the hetman or general. Each was a short rod topped with a knob, but the knob on the *buzdygan* was round and adorned with precious stones, while the one on the *buława* was pear-shaped and fluted.

BOOK VI

The Noble Village

Argument

First intimations of the armed foray. Protase's errand. Robak and the Judge hold counsel on the commonweal. Protase's fruitless errand continued. A digression on hemp. The noble village of Dobrzyn.[1] A description of Matthias Dobrzyński[2] and his household.

A pallid dawn crept imperceptibly out of the raw murk. Behind her slunk the morning with a lightless eye. Day had long since broken, but you would scarcely know it. A heavy mist overhung the earth like the straw thatch of a Lithuanian hovel. By the spread intensity of whiteness in the eastern sky, you knew that the sun had risen and from which quarter he would appear, but clearly, his march was joyless, and he slumbered along the way.

Taking its cue from the heavens, life on earth was running behindhand. The cattle, driven belatedly to pasture, surprised the hare at their tardy breakfast. Normally, they would have been back in the woods by dawn. Today, in the gloom of the mist, they crunched on the chickweed, or, bunching in pairs, made scrapes in the sand, intent on enjoying the open air; but with the arrival of the cattle they scampered back to the forest.

Even the forests stood silent. A bird awoke, but it tuned no note. Shaking the dew from its plumage, it huddled up to the tree, tucked its head into its shoulders, and shutting its eyes sat waiting for the sun. A stork rattled its bill by the edge of a pool; on the hayricks sodden crows sat plying their raucous prattle—irksome sounds to the farmer's ear, like portents of dirty weather.

The field folk had long been astir. The reaper women struck up their wonted song, dull, plaintive and dreary as a rainy day, the more dismal as the fog muffled its strains. The reaphooks clinked, the meadow clinked back. A line of mowers swished through the rowen, whistling their tune. At the close of each stave they halted to hone their blades, beating their hammers in time. The fog hid them all.

All you could hear were the rasp of the sickles and scythes and the strains of the reapers' songs—a symphony of invisible voices.

The Bailiff sat on a grain sheaf among the harvesters. Weary of watching their labors, he kept glancing down at the crossroads where extraordinary goings-on had drawn his attention. Since daybreak the highway and the lesser-traveled roads had been the scene of unusual traffic. A peasant's creaking cart flew past like a post-chaise. A nobleman's caleche rattled by at a full gallop. Another passed it coming the other way, then another. From the left an errand-bound rider sped by; a dozen more riders thundered up from the right and headed off in separate directions. What could all this mean? The Bailiff rose to his feet. He'd take a closer look and find out. Long he stood by the roadside, but he only ended up shouting himself hoarse; no one stopped. No one was recognizable in the fog, the riders flitted by like wraiths. Now and again, the thud of iron hoofs and, stranger still, the clank of sabers fell upon his ears. All this both gladdened and alarmed the Bailiff. Though Lithuania was still at peace, dull rumors of war had long been circulating—rumors about the French, Dąbrowski and Napoleon. Could these riders and their arms be omens of war? The Bailiff hurried off to report all to the Judge, hoping also that he'd learn something himself.

After last night's brawl, the inmates and guests of the house had risen in dejected spirits. Bootless the Steward's daughter's attempts to interest the women in the tarot cards! On deaf ears fell her suggestion of the men engaging in a round of *marriage*—no one was in the mood for games or amusement. All brooded quietly in their corners. The men pulled at their pipes, the women plied their knitting needles; even the houseflies drowsed.

Oppressed by the silence, the Steward threw down his fly swatter and sought out the servants in the kitchen where the shouts of the housekeeper, the threats and buffetings of the cook and the cries of the kitchen boys better satisfied his craving for noise. Gradually, the steady roll of the roasting spits lulled him into a pleasant state of drowsiness.

Since early morning the Judge had remained enshrined in his study drafting a writ of summons while Protase waited patiently under the window on the turf bench that fronted the house; at last, the Judge called him inside. He read aloud his complaint: against the Count for the insults and slights to his honor, and against Gervase for the mischief and mayhem he'd wrought; both men he cited before the magistrates' court for their proud boasts and the cost of the legal process. The summons was to be served this very day—by word of mouth, in the presence of the parties, before the sun went down.

As soon the Usher caught sight of the writ, his ears and hand went up. His mien was solemn, his bearing grave, but he would have gladly leapt for joy.

The very thought of forensic action set his blood astir. He recalled the old days when on the promise of a generous retainer he'd brave bruises to serve a summons. Just so, after a lifetime of fighting wars, a legless old campaigner languishes in his hospital bed. But let the sound of a bugle or a distant drumbeat fall on his ear, and starting up he cries out with a sleepy yell, "Thrash the Muscovites!" and peg-legs it out of the ward so fast that a youth is hard put to keep up with him.

Protase hastened to put on the court usher's costume. No nobleman's robe or white tunic today, as these were reserved for solemn sessions of the court. For field errands he donned a different garb: loose riding breeches, a coat with skirts that could be buttoned up or lowered to the knees, and a cap with folding earflaps tied over the head by a string and worn up in good and down in dirty weather. Thus appareled, he seized a cane and set out on foot. Court ushers serving a summons are like scouts spying out the field for battle; they must assume various guises and costumes.

It was just as well he'd hurried off, for he would have taken brief comfort in serving the writ. Even now a fresh strategy was being plotted in the manor. An anxious-looking Robak suddenly broke in on the Judge.

"Judge," he said, "this mistress aunt of ours, this giddy-brained flirt, Telimena, spells trouble. When Jacek confided our poor Sophy to her care, it was with the understanding that she was a worthy matron who knew the ways of the world. But all she does is muddy the waters and engage in intrigues. She makes eyes at Tadeusz—I've seen this myself, having kept a close watch on her. Perhaps she has designs on the Count as well. We must consider how best to remove her. Her actions may give rise to gossip, bad example, and strife among our young people, which may hamper your talks."

"Talks!?" cried the Judge with unwonted passion. "I've done with talks! Finished with them, broken them off."

"What's this?" exclaimed Robak. "Where's your head? Where's your sense? What are you saying? Not another quarrel?"

"No fault of mine, as you'll see come out in court," said the Judge. "That peacock and fool started it, the Count, and that scoundrel of his, Gervase . . . but that's for the court to decide. Pity you didn't dine with us at the castle. You'd have witnessed the gross affront he dealt me."

"But whatever drove you to those ruins!" cried Robak. "You know full well I cannot abide the castle. I swear now no foot of mine shall cross its threshold again. Another quarrel! Merciful God! Quick, tell me what happened! The matter will have to be put right. Enough of this silliness! I've more serious worries than reconciling litigious parties, but once again I'll bring you to terms—"

"Terms? What do you mean, terms?" broke in the Judge, stamping his foot. "Why, you and your terms can go to the devil! The nerve of the monk! Treat him nicely and the fellow thinks he can lead you around by the nose. Understand, sir, Soplicas don't take kindly to terms. They sue to win! Many a time they sat out a lawsuit in their name only to win it after six generations. I was foolish enough to follow your counsel and file a third appeal with the boundary court. No more talks! No more, I say. No, sir! No, sir! No, sir! (And pacing the room, he pounded the floorboards with his feet.) Besides, after last night's outrages, the Count must either beg my forgiveness or grant me satisfaction!"

"But, my dear Judge, what if Jacek hears of this? Why, he'll be driven to despair! Have the Soplicas not caused enough grief at the castle? Dear brother, I've no wish to recall that terrible incident, but you know yourself how the Targowica[3] confederates seized part of the domain from the castle holder and awarded it to the Soplicas, and how Jacek, repenting of his sin, pledged upon constraint of absolution to make good those lands; so he took the poor Horeszko heiress Sophy into his care and spared no expense on her rearing. His abiding aim has been to wed her to his son Tadeusz and thus unite the disaffected houses, restoring honorably to the heiress what had been plundered from her."

"What has that to do with me?" said the Judge hotly. "I never knew Jacek or so much as laid eyes on him. I heard almost nothing of his riotous life, as I was still a schoolboy then, studying rhetoric in the Jesuit college. After that I served as the Governor's page. They awarded me the estate, and I took it. Jacek asked me to take in Sophy. I took her in, cared for her, and now fret over her future. And now, as if this woman's business weren't tiresome enough, the Count has to poke his nose in here—and with what claim to the castle? Why, you know yourself, my friend, there's barely a drop of Horeszko blood in his veins.[4] And he's to insult me? And I'm to talk terms with him!"

"Come now, brother," rejoined the Monk, "there are compelling reasons. Do you recall how Jacek wanted the lad to go for a soldier but then kept him back in Lithuania? Why? Because he decided Tadeusz would better serve our country at home. You must have heard the spreading rumors of which I've been the principal instigator. Well, now is the time to make it all plain. The hour has come! Momentous things, dear brother. War's upon us! The war for Poland, dear brother! We shall be Poles again! War is unavoidable. When I set out on my secret errand here, the Army's advance guard had already reached the Niemen. At this very moment Bonaparte's mustering the largest array the world has seen, or history recorded. The entire Polish Army is marching with the French—our Poniatowski,[5] our Dąbrowski, our white eagle standards! Even now they're on the move; at the first sign from Napoleon, they'll cross the Niemen, and our Fatherland, dear brother, rises out of the ashes!"

The Judge removed his glasses in silence, folded them and stared at the Monk. Tears welled to his eyes, and heaving a sigh he flung himself on the Bernardine's neck.

"My good Robak!" he cried. "Can this be true? My good Robak! Can it really be true? All those dashed hopes! Do you not remember? 'Bonaparte's on the march!' they'd tell us, and we'd wait for him. 'He's reached the Kingdom!' they'd say. 'He's beaten the Prussian. He's on his way to us!' Then what does he do? Sign the Treaty of Tilsit![6] So can it really be true? Are you not imagining it?"

"As God is in heaven, it's true."

"Then blest be the lips that bear these tidings!" said the Judge, raising his arms. "You shan't regret your errand, Robak. I'll begrudge your convent nothing. Two hundred choice muttons I hand over to your cloister. Yesterday you took a shine to my chestnut mare and praised my bay. This very day they shall stand tied to your alms wagon. Ask your will of me, I'll refuse nothing. Only please, touching this whole affair with the Count, say no more. He slighted my honor. I've served him a writ. It wouldn't do to back out now."

The astonished Monk wrung his hands and stared at the Judge.

"So," he said, shrugging his shoulders, "while Napoleon brings freedom to Lithuania, and the world trembles in its boots, you still have lawsuits on your mind? After all I've told you, you're going to sit idly by, when it's action that's called for?"

"Action?" queried the Judge. "What action?"

"Have you not read it in my eyes? Still no promptings in your heart? Oh, dear brother, if you have a drop of Soplica blood in your veins, consider but this. The French strike from the front? Well, suppose we stir up a popular insurrection in the rear. What say you to that? Let Lithuania's heraldic charger snort again! The Bear of Samogitia[7] roar once more! Oh, were but a thousand men—even half that many!—to strike at the Muscovite from the rear, a rising would spread through Lithuania like wildfire. What if we seized Moscow's guns and standards and went as victors to meet our country's deliverers? We'd march up, and Bonaparte, seeing our lances, would ask, 'Whose troops are these?'—'Insurrectionists, Your Imperial Highness! Lithuania's militia!' we'd shout back—'Who leads you?' he'd ask. 'Judge Soplica!' we'd say. Oh, who then would breathe a word of Targowica? Aye, for as long as the Ponary Hills stand overlooking the city of Wilno and Niemen runs his course, the people of Lithuania shall revere the bearer of the Soplica name. To her grandsons and great-grandsons Jagiello's city will point him out and say, 'There goes Soplica of those noble Soplicas who fathered the Uprising!'"

"Never mind what people will say," said the Judge. "I've never cared for worldly praise. God's my witness, I'm innocent of my brother's sins. I was never one to meddle in politics, I carry out my official duties and tend my acre of ground. But I am a born gentleman and I should be glad to clear my family's name. As a loyal Pole, I should be glad to be of service to my country, aye, lay down my very life for her! Swordplay's never been my strong point, though I've dealt a few cuts in my time. Everyone knows how during Poland's last muster of the diets I challenged and wounded the two Buzwik brothers, who . . . but let that pass. So what say you? Do we take the field? Mustering riflemen will be no trouble. We've no shortage of powder. Our parish priest keeps a small field-piece in the rectory. I also recall Jankiel saying he has lance-heads in store at the tavern and we were welcome to use them in time of need. Whole crate-loads he smuggled in from Konigsberg! We'll fetch 'em and whittle shafts at once. Of swords we have plenty. Our nobility will mount up, and with my nephew and me leading the van—well, we shall do our best."

"O noble Polish blood!" cried the Monk, deeply moved, throwing his arms around the Judge's shoulders. "True child of the Soplicas! God charges you with the task of wiping clean your prodigal brother's sins. I have always held you in high esteem, but now I love you like a born brother. We shall make every preparation, aye, but now's not the time to take up arms. I shall inform you of the hour and place. This I know: the Tsar has sent emissaries to Napoleon to sue for peace. War has not yet been declared, but Prince Joseph heard from Monsieur Bignon,[8] a member of Napoleon's Imperial Council, that nothing will come of these talks, and that war is certain. The Prince dispatched me here as a spy with instructions that upon Napoleon's arrival Lithuania should stand ready to be reunited with her sister the Crown, and thus reinstate the old Commonwealth.

"In the meantime, dear brother, you must make peace with the Count. I know he's a crank, somewhat whimsical in his views, but he's a good, honest young Pole. We stand in need of such men. Cranks, I know from experience, can be very useful in revolutionary times. Even fools can be useful so long as they're honest and led by men of prudence. The Count is a magnate and wields influence among the nobility. If he joins the revolt, the whole district will rise with him. Knowing his vast fortune, every nobleman will say, 'It must be a sure thing, as even our magnates are in it. Where do I sign up?'"

"Let him come to me first!" rejoined the Judge. "Let him come here. Let him beg my forgiveness. I'm his senior in years and hold an office. As to the lawsuit, the court of arbitration—"

The Monk slammed the door behind him.

"Pleasant journey!" called out the Judge.

Robak leapt into his wagon, cracked his whip, stung the horses' haunches with the traces; the wagon jolted forward and vanished into the fog. Ever and anon, a gray cowl could be seen above the mist like a vulture riding the clouds.

Meanwhile, the Court Usher had reached the Count's hall. Lured by the smell of pork fat, a wily fox makes for the bait, yet, aware of the hunter's ruses, he halts every few steps, sits up, raises his brush in the air and fans it to his nostrils to ensure the bait hasn't been tainted. Just so, having swung off the road into the adjacent hayfield, Protase circled the house, twirling his cane, halting now and then, as if he'd spotted a cow in distress. Thus maneuvering, he fetched up at last in the garden; and there, stooping down, he made a sudden dash forward (a bystander would have sworn he was after a corncrake), cleared the fence, and plunged into the hemp.

Both man and beast find a measure of safety in this odorous patch of vegetation encircling the house. Not seldom, the wild hare, sprung from the cabbage patch, darts into the hemp where he finds safer cover than in the underbrush. Once embowered in this pungent herbage, he need fear neither gaze- nor scent-hound. Here, too, the house servant, escaping the lash or the fist, lies low until the master simmers down. Even peasants fleeing the military draft will sojourn in the hemp while the government officials comb the neighboring forest. Hence, during a battle, foray or requisition drive, both sides take great pains to occupy the hemp ground, which stretches forward to the walls of the house and often backward as far as the hop fields, and thus covers their attack or retreat from the enemy.

Brave soul though he was, Protase was not wholly without trepidation. The very scent of the leaves wafted back memories of previous expeditions when the hemp patch had borne witness to his pains. He recalled the incident with the nobleman from Telsze whom he'd summoned to court. Putting a pistol to his breast, Dzindolet (that was his name) made him crawl under the table and bark out a retraction of the summons like a dog. That was one time Protase had to leg it into the hemp. Then there was the incident with the proud and insolent Wołodkowicz.[9] Seizing the writ from the Usher's hand and ripping it to shreds, that scourge of the dietines and disrupter of court sessions stationed a pair of cudgel-bearing Haiduks at the door, and poising his naked rapier over Protase's head snarled, 'Either you eat these scraps or I run you through!' Being the prudent soul he was, Protase went through the motions of chewing, inched his way to the window, and took a header into the hemp.

True, greeting a summons with a sword or a whip was no longer common practice in Lithuania, and in truth, only rarely had the Court Usher met with such abuse for his pains. But Protase could not have known of this change of custom, for he hadn't served a writ in years. Though he was ever eager to go and constantly pressed the Judge to send him, he was always refused on account of his advanced years. Today, the matter being especially urgent, the Judge accepted his offer to serve the summons.

Protase looked around and listened. Not a sound! Thrusting his hands cautiously into the hemp, he parted the forest of stalks and plunged through the vegetation like a diver breasting the deep. He raised his head. Not a sound. He crept up to the windows. Not a peep anywhere. He peered into the house. Not a soul in sight. Heart a-flutter, he stepped onto the veranda and pushed open the door. The house stood deserted—a veritable enchanted castle! Seizing the moment, the Usher whipped out the summons and began reading the contents aloud. A footfall fell upon his ear. His heart leapt to his mouth; he was all set to make a dash for the hemp when, to his great relief, the familiar figure of Robak appeared in the doorway. Both men stood there greatly surprised.

Evidently the Count and his entire retinue had left the house, and in a great hurry, as the door was left open; clearly, they'd been busy arming themselves. The floor lay strewn with double-barrels and sporting pieces along with ramrods, gun-cocks, locksmiths' tools and all the necessaries for mending firearms; there was even powder and paper for manufacturing cartridges. Had the Count and all his train gone on a hunting expedition? But why the side arms? Here lay a rusty hiltless saber, there a sword bereft of its knot; evidently, the Count had been drawing weapons and even ransacked his store of obsolete arms. After carefully examining the guns and swords, Robak went scouting about the farm in search of a servant that might know of the Count's whereabouts. Eventually, running into two old peasant women in the deserted yard, he learned that the master and his entire household had set out as an armed body for Dobrzyn.

Now the village of Dobrzyn was famous throughout all of Lithuania for the courage of its noblemen and the comeliness of its women. Once it had been a populous and thriving place. When King Jan Sobieski mustered the general militia,[10] the ensign of the Province supplied His Majesty with six-hundred fully armed knights from Dobrzyn alone. But now the clan had grown small and poor. In former days they found an easy living in the courts of magnates, serving in the army, mounting forays, and taking part in the regional diets. Now they were forced to shift for themselves, toiling like mere peasants, only, instead of the peasant's caftan, they wore a long white coat with black stripes, and on Sundays, the loose-sleeved nobleman's robe. The same was true of the gentlewomen of the village. Even the poorest of them dressed differently from their rustic neighbors. Eschewing the peasant women's homespun vest, they went about in drill or percale. When grazing their cattle, they wore leather rather than baste shoes, and when reaping and even spinning, they always wore gloves.

The people of Dobrzyn differed from their Lithuanian brethren in their language, stature and physiognomy. Pure Polish blood ran in their veins. All had jet-black hair, high foreheads and aquiline noses. The clan originally hailed from Dobrzyń in Mazovia,[11] and though they had struck roots in Lithuania four centuries earlier, they still preserved their Mazovian manners and speech. When christening their young, they invariably chose the name of one of the Crown's patron saints, Bartholomew or Matthias.[12] Matthias baptized his son Bartholomew; Bartholomew—Matthias. The women invariably took the names Catherine or Maryna. To avoid any confusion, men and women took various nicknames deriving from some personal quirk or attribute.[13] Sometimes, as a token of his fellows' scorn or esteem, a nobleman received more than one nickname. The same gentleman might go by one in Dobrzyn and by another in the neighboring village. Other noble families of the district would take after the Dobrzyński and resort to nicknames as well—only they called them 'ekenames.' Nowadays almost every family resorts to nicknames. Few are aware that the custom originated in Dobrzyn, but there the usage served a purpose, while in the rest of the country it arose out of foolish imitation. The family's patriarch Matthias Dobrzyński had first been nicknamed "Weathercock." Later, during the rising of 1794, he became known as "Hipsmiter." Among his own folk, he went by the appellation "King Rabbit,"[14] while among the Lithuanian folk he was known as "Matthias of Matthiases."

As Matthias ruled over the people of Dobrzyn, so his house, standing as it did between the tavern and the church, dominated the village. To all appearances, it was rarely visited and inhabited by the very poorest of folk. The posts marking the entrance stood gateless, and the garden was neither fenced nor sown. Birch trees had grown up in the vegetable beds. Yet this old farmhouse appeared to be the village capitol. Compared to the other cottages, it was better constructed and more spacious, and its right wing which housed the parlor was built of brick. Nearby stood the lumber house, granary, barn, byre, and stable—all clustered together in the manner typical of our minor nobility's homesteads. Everything about the little grange had an aspect of extreme decrepitude and decay. The house roof shone green, as if sheeted with tin; in fact, it was overgrown with moss and grasses as rank as prairie herbage. The thatched roofs of the granaries resembled hanging gardens, rich in plant life— stinging nettle, red crocus, yellow mullein, and the gaudy-plumed amaranth. All kinds of birds nested there. There were dovecotes in the lofts, swallows' nests in the windows. White rabbits frisked by the front door and burrowed in the untrodden turf; in a word, the rambling farmhouse resembled a cage or rabbit hutch.

Yet the place had known sieges! Reminders of frequent, fiercely fought battles were everywhere visible. An old cannonball the size of a child's head lay rusting in the grass by the gate; this relic of the Swedish Wars had substituted for a rock to keep the gate open. In the yard, on unconsecrated ground overrun with weeds and wormwood, stood the moldering stumps of a dozen or more crosses—signs that a sudden unexpected death had visited those buried there. Anyone observing the house, lumber house, and granary with a keener eye would see that the walls stood dappled from top to bottom with small round spots, as if a swarm of black insects had alighted there; in the centre of each of these spots lodged a musket-ball like a bumble-bee in its earthy burrow.

Every door had its knobs, studs and hooks shorn off or gouged by a sword-stroke; clearly, the temper of Sigismund steel had been tested here, steel so hard you could easily smite off the head of a nail or slice through a hook without nicking the blade. Above the door lintel, partly hidden by shelves of cheeses and plastered up with swallows' nests, stood the Dobrzyn device.

The house, stable and coach-house stood cluttered like ancient armories with accoutrements of every description. From the roof of the coach-house hung four huge helms, formerly adornments of martial brows, now home to Venus' birds, the doves; here, the purring pigeon fed his unfledged squabs. Over the manger in the stable swung an enormous open hauberk and ring-mail corselet—a makeshift fodder rack from which the stable boy forked down clover to the colts. Several rapiers lay about in the kitchen, their temper spoiled in the hearth by the impious maid who used them as roasting spits. A horsetail,[15] booty plundered from the Turk at Vienna, served as a duster for the grain mill. In a word, Mars had ceded the field to frugal Ceres. Along with Pomona, Flora and Vortumnus, she presided over Matthias' house, stable and granary. Alas! These deities must yield sway again. Mars had returned.

In the early gray of the morning a dispatch bearer rode into Dobrzyn. Going from house to house, he roused the residents like a bailiff recruiting feudal labor. The noble brethren scrambled from their beds and spilled out into the streets. The tavern rang with shouts, the rectory window blazed with candlelight. People ran to and fro. "What's happening?" they asked. The elders held council, the young men saddled their horses, while the mothers restrained their squirming boys, who rared to go and fight without a notion of whom they were to fight or why. Alas, stay home they must! A meeting raged in the crowded rectory. At last, failing to come to an agreement, they decided to refer the matter to their old patriarch Matthias.

Matthias was seventy-two years old, a sprightly old master of small stature and a former Bar Confederate.[16] Friend and foe alike knew him by his prodigious saber of damascene steel (facetiously dubbed *The Birch*), with which he was wont to chop up pikes and bayonets like chaff. He quit the Confederacy, and siding with the Crown stood with Tyzenhaus,[17] Lithuania's Under-Treasurer. But when the King took Targowica's part, he deserted the royal cause. These changing allegiances gave rise to the nickname Weathercock, as he seemed to turn his standard to the wind like a weather vane.[18] There was no understanding his shifting alliances. Perhaps he was over fond of war. Defeated on one side, he sought his fortunes on the other. Or perhaps he was merely a shrewd observer of the spirit of the times, crossing to whichever side he saw as tending to the advantage of his country. Who knew! One thing was certain. He was never swayed by a desire for personal glory or paltry gain. Nor did he ever side with the Tsarist cause. The very sight of a Muscovite made him foam and froth at the mouth. After the last partition of his country, he kept indoors, out of sight, like a cave-bound bear sucking on his paw.

His last action was with Ogiński[19] in Wilno where both men served under Jasiński. There he and his Birch performed wondrous feats of valor. Legendary was his leap from Praga's ramparts in a single-handed attempt to rescue Pociej, who had been left languishing on the battlefield with twenty-three wounds. All Lithuania gave them up for lost, but, even though their bodies were riddled through like sieves, the pair made it back to safety. After the war, Pociej, an upright man, sought to reward Dobrzyński handsomely. He offered him a homestead with five buildings for life along with an annuity of a thousand *złotys* in gold. But Matthias wrote back to him, saying, "Let Pociej be Matthias' debtor, not Matthias Pociej's!"[20] He refused the homestead, declined the gold, and returned home to toil by the sweat of his brow. There he framed beehives, compounded remedies for the cattle, snared partridge for the county fair, and hunted wild game.

Dobrzyn was home to several wise elders, men versed in Latin who'd practiced at the bar from their youth on. There were also richer men. Yet of the entire clan it was the poor and simple Matthias who enjoyed the highest repute, not only as the celebrated wielder of The Birch but as a man of good sense and solid views. Conversant with the history of his nation and the traditions of his family, he was practiced in law, skilled in husbandry, and expert in the hunter's and apothecary's crafts. People even ascribed to him knowledge of extraordinary and preternatural events, though this the parish priest sternly disclaimed. At the very least, he was keenly attuned to atmospheric changes and able to predict the weather more accurately than any farmer's almanac. Small wonder, then, that when it came to matters like deciding when to sow the crops, or dispatch the wherries, or harvest the corn, or yet when to launch a court action and when to seek terms, none of these things was undertaken in Dobrzyn without first seeking Matthias' advice. Not that he actively sought out such standing; indeed, he'd dearly be rid of it. He huffed at his clients. Often he said nothing at all and pushed them out the door. Seldom did he impart advice and then not just to anyone. Only when it came to settling the most pressing disputes and disagreements would he offer his opinion when consulted, and even then, only in the tersest of terms.

Today, everyone counted on Matthias to take the matter in hand. None doubted that he'd place himself at the head of an armed foray, for ever since his youth he'd loved a good fight; besides, he was a sworn foe of the Muscovite race.

Matthias was strolling through his deserted yard, humming snatches of *When Early Breaks the Dawn*.[21] He was glad it was clearing. The mist, not lifting in the usual manner and forming clouds, sank steadily earthward. The breeze unfurled her fingers and stroked it, smoothing and spreading it over the fields; meanwhile, the sun broke through with a thousand rays, limning the mist with tints of vermilion, silver and gold. So a pair of weavers craft the gold-fibered belts of Słuck. A maid sits under the web threading silk on the loom, smoothing the surface with her hand while the master lowers down strands of purple, silver and gold, creating brilliant flower motifs—even so the breeze wove its web of vapors over the earth while the sun embroidered it.

Matthias sat warming himself in the sun. He'd said his prayers and was addressing himself to his domestic chores. Gathering up a handful of grain and leaves, he seated himself in front of his cottage, and whistled. A host of rabbits started from their burrows. Their long white ears poked up from the grass like instantly sprouting daffodils; below the ears winked their bright little eyes, gleaming like blood-red rubies thickly sown in the velvety sward. Up they sat, all eyes and ears, then lured by the cabbage leaves, the entire little flock of snowballs made for Matthias. Hopping and skipping, they scampered up to his feet and leapt onto his lap and shoulders. White as a rabbit himself, the old master loved having them gather around him. He stroked their warm furry bodies with one hand, scooped millet seed from his hat with the other and scattered it on the grass for the sparrows. A noisy throng dropped from the roof.

Suddenly, as Matthias sat delighting in their banquet, the rabbits bolted for their holes. With a flutter of wings the sparrows returned to the eaves. A party of new guests was quickly approaching the yard. The deputation from the rectory had arrived to seek Matthias' counsel.

"Praised be the Lord Jesus Christ," they greeted him from a distance with low bows. "Now and evermore,"[22] replied Matthias.

On learning of the party's pressing business, he ushered them into his house. They filed inside and seated themselves on the bench. The leading delegate stood up and began to lay the matter before him; meanwhile, more and more of the nobility arrived. Most of these were Dobrzyn folk, but there were also a good many neighbors from the surrounding noble villages. Some were armed, some not. Some arrived in britzkas, some in dogcarts. Others came mounted, still others on foot. They drew up their rigs, hitched them to the young birch trees, and burning with curiosity over the progress of the talks began to swarm through the house. The parlor being now filled, they crowded into the hallway. Others, thrusting their heads through the open window, listened intently.

NOTES

1. [H.B. Segel] The "noble village" (*zaścianek*) was inhabited by families of the most impoverished of the minor nobility who, despite their distinctive manners, lived on the level of the peasantry. The poet notes that "the term *okolica* or *zaścianek* in Lithuania is given to a village of the minor nobility, to distinguish them from true villages, which are settlements of peasants." In point of fact, *okolica* and *zaścianek* were not the same thing. An *okolica* arose as the result of nobility of different backgrounds (and hence of different names) settling in one locality. A *zaścianek* on the other hand, arose as a result of the growth of a single family and the subdividing of the common ancestor's original domain into several farms. Thus, all the nobility inhabiting a *zaścianek* carried the same family name and were related.

2. Pronounce the surname: *Dob-zheen-ski.*

3. The Confederacy of Targowica formed in 1792 by Polish nobles who opposed the liberal Constitution of May Third, 1791. Their appeal for Russian assistance provided Catherine II with a pretext for invading Poland. The country was partitioned for the second time and the Constitution abolished.

4. The literal translation of the Polish line is: "To the Horeszkos he is merely the tenth water on the *kisiel.*" In explanation, the poet adds the following note: "*Kisiel* is a Lithuanian dish, a sort of jelly made of oaten yeast, which is washed with water until all the mealy parts are separated from it; hence the proverb."

5. Prince Józef Antoni Poniatowski (1763-1813), a nephew of King Stanisław August and commander-in-chief of the army of the Duchy of Warsaw. He was a brilliant soldier and a staunch supporter of Napoleon to the end of the campaigns. He was named a Marshal of France shortly before he perished in the battle of Leipzig.

6. The Peace of Tilsit, concluded by Napoleon with the Prussians on July 7, 1807. By the terms of the treaty, a rump state known as the Grand Duchy of Warsaw (*Księstwo Warszawskie*) was carved out from the territories acquired by Prussia in the second and third partitions. Gdańsk (Danzig), however, was kept as a free city and was not included. The Duchy was ruled by the House of Saxony in the person of Frederick August I under the protection of Napoleon. After the fall of Napoleon, it ceased to exist in 1815 by decision of the Congress of Vienna.

7. The coat of arms of Lithuania (*Pogoń*) depicts a knight on a white charger in full career. The Bear (*Niedźwiedź*) is the coat of arms of Żmudź (Samogitia), a Baltic region of Lithuania.
8. Baron Louis-Pierre-Edouard Bignon (1771-1841), a French diplomat; from February 1811 to 1812 Napoleon's representative in Warsaw.
9. [*Author's note*] After various brawls, this man was seized at Minsk and shot in accordance with a court decree.
10. Jan III Sobieski, the "deliverer of Vienna" (1683), reigned over Poland from 1674 to 1696. The poet notes that when the king was to assemble the general militia, "he had a pole set up in each parish with a broom or bundle of twigs tied to the top symbolizing his authority to inflict punishment. This was called 'sending out the twigs' (*rozdać wici*). Every adult man of the knightly order was obliged, under pain of the loss of the privileges of gentle birth, to rally at once to the royal governor's standard."
11. Mazovia (*Mazowsze*) is a province in central Poland; its capital is Warsaw.
12. Matthias is *Matjasz* in Polish, its variant form being *Maciej* (dim. *Maciek*). Bartholomew is *Bartłomiej* (dim. *Bartek*). The present translation eschews these variants and diminutives.
13. The poet inaccurately equates the *przydomek* (byname) with the sobriquet or nickname (*imionisko*). *Przezwisko* (also best translated as nickname) would be a better equivalent. The gentry took their *przydomek* from their estates, title, etc. The *przezwisko* originated in individual physical or behavioral characteristics and could not be passed from father to son, unlike the *przydomek*. [H.D. Segel]
14. The Polish word *królik* means both "little king" and "rabbit."
15. The horsetail (*buńczuk*) was a staff topped with a crescent and a knot of horsehair; it served as an ensign for Turkish regiments. The article was also used in the Polish Army as a symbol of the hetman's authority. After the numerous military victories over the Turks, it was a piece of booty commonly found in knightly homes and estates.
16. The Confederacy of Bar (named after the Podolian town where it was formed) was organized on February 19, 1768 by Polish patriots who sought to free Poland from Russian political domination. Their four-year struggle ended in defeat and the first partition of Poland, 1772. The Bar Confederacy was the subject of a play in French by Mickiewicz—*Les Confédérés de Bar*.
17. Antoni Tyzenhaus (1733-1785), First Grand Secretary, later Under Court Treasurer of Lithuania, a long-time unswerving partisan of King Stanisław August Poniatowski.
18. During the Bar Confederacy, Matthias had opposed the king because of his subservience to Russia but rallied to his support when Stanisław August attempted to continue the process of national renewal after the first partition in 1772. Twenty years after, Matthias found himself again in opposition to the throne during the Targowica Confederacy when Stanisław August abandoned resistance to the Confederacy, submitted to it, and paved the way for the second partition. Although he is called *The Weathercock*, Matthias' behavior was consistently patriotic. He opposed whatever he considered harmful to his country's best interests.
19. Michał Kleofas Ogiński (1765-1833), the composer and prominent statesman; he took part in the insurrection of 1794 and was a member of the Provisional Government. The poet met him in Italy in 1830.
20. [*Author's note*] On his return to Lithuania after the war, Alexander Count Pociej assisted those of his fellow countrymen who were emigrating abroad and sent considerable sums to the treasury of the Legions.
21. The opening line of the popular hymn (*Kiedy ranne wstają zorze*) by Franciszek Karpiński (1741-1825).
22. A common pious greeting and reply in Catholic countries; it is used by the Poles even today.

BOOK VII

The Council

___

Argument

The salutary advice of Bartholomew called the Prussian. The martial views of Matthias christened Baptizer. *The political views of Mr. Buchman. Jankiel's conciliatory plea cut short by Jackknife. Gervase's speech demonstrates the power of parliamentary oratory. Old Matthias' protestations. The sudden appearance of armed reinforcements breaks up the deliberations. Harrow! Hang Soplica!*

It was the turn of the delegate Bartholomew Dobrzyński to say his piece, the one who regularly plied the waterways to Konigsberg. His kinsmen jokingly called him "The Prussian" because he loathed the Prussians yet could not resist talking about them. He was well advanced in years and had seen much of the world in his travels. An avid reader of the newspapers and a canny politician besides, he was able to shed a good deal of light on the subject under discussion.

"So, Matthias, brother, revered father of us all," he summed up, "their aid is not to be sneezed at. In wartime I'd rely on the French as on four aces in the hand. Valiant folk the French. Not since Tadeusz Kościuszko's day has the world seen such a military genius as the great Emperor Bonaparte.

"I remember when the French crossed the River Warta in the year of grace 1806. I was biding abroad then, busy with trading ventures in Gdańsk. Having several kinsmen in Poznań Province, I'd gone up there for a visit. So there I was shooting small game with Joseph Grabowski[1]—he's colonel of a regiment now, but then he was still living on his estate near Objezierze. Greater Poland was at peace as is Lithuania now. Then came word of a terrible battle. A courier from Mr. Todwen came rushing up to us. 'Jena! Jena!'[2] yelled Grabowski on reading the letter. 'They beat the Prussians! We've won.' Down I leapt from my horse, fell on my knees and offered thanksgiving to God.

"We rode into the city pretending we had business there and were none the wiser. What do we see? Every hofrath, landrath, commissar and other like varlet bowing and scraping before us, all pale and trembling like cockroaches³ doused in boiling water. We laugh and rub our hands. Then all cap-in-hand-like we ask for news. 'So what's the word from—Jena?' You should have seen them start! They were amazed we already knew about it. *'Ach, Herri Got! O vey!'*⁴ they cried; and hanging their heads in shame, they ran into their houses then helter-skelter out into the street again. Oh, it was bedlam, I tell you, every highway and byway in Greater Poland crowded with fleeing Germans. Like columns of ants they crawled along, dragging their conveyances behind them ('vagens' and 'fornagels' they call them there), men and women with teapots and tobacco pipes, lugging wooden chests and featherbeds, all decamping as best they could.

"Meanwhile, we quietly take council together. Harrow! To horse! Snarl up Fritz's retreat! Now we give it to the landraths, make schnitzel of the hofraths, grab the *herr offiziers* by their queues! General Dąbrowski enters Poznań and proclaims the Emperor's command. 'Poles, rise up!' Within a week our people have beaten the Germans and driven them out. Not a blessed Prussian as far as the eye can see.

"Now suppose we in Lithuania went it with the same verve and panache and gave the Muscovites a similar drubbing? Eh? What say you to that, Matthias? If Moscow decides to have it out with Bonaparte, it'll be no ordinary fight. Napoleon's the world's number one hero—commands troops past telling. Eh? What say you, Matthias, our father King?"

He had had his say. All eyes turned to Matthias, but Matthias neither moved his head nor raised his eyes; instead, he kept slapping his hip as if groping for a sword. (Since the partition of his country, he'd sworn off carrying a blade, but the very mention of Moscow brought back his old habit of slapping his left side; clearly, he was feeling for his Birch, whence his other nickname "Hipsmiter.") At last he raised his head. A deep hush fell over the room, but he disappointed the general expectation; he frowned and dropped his head to his chest again. At long last, he spoke out, slowly and emphatically, punctuating each phrase with a nod of his head.

"Silence!" he said. "Whence this intelligence? How close are the French? Who leads them? Have they declared war on Moscow? If so, where and why? Who knows their line of march? What is their strength? What foot? What horse? Who'll answer these questions? Speak!"

The nobility eyed one another in silence.

"I say we wait for Father Robak," ventured Bartholomew the Prussian. "It was he that brought us the news; meantime, we should dispatch trusty spies to the border and quietly arm the district. But now we must proceed with all due caution and not betray our plans to the Muscovite."

"What!? Wait? Prate? Delay?" broke in another Matthias christened Baptizer after his prodigious battle club, dubbed *The Sprinkler*. He'd brought the weapon with him and was standing behind it, his hands resting on the ball, his chin on his hands.

"Wait? Prate? Debate?" he bellowed. "Hem, haw—then scram, is it? I've never been to Prussia. Konigsberg logic may suit the Prussians, but I rely on our Polish nobleman's sense. This I know: you mean to fight, grab your sprinkler; you mean to croak, call a priest—basta! As for me, I aim to live and fight. What use is the Monk? Are we schoolboys? Eh? What's Robak to me? It's we who'll be the maggots gnawing at Moscow.[6] Spies, reconnoitering—shillyshally! You know what that means. Why, that you're gaffers and dodderers! Eh, brothers? The pointer's business is to sniff and point. The almsman's to quest for alms. Mine's to soak and douse. Soak 'em! Douse 'em! Basta!"

Here he patted his club, and the entire assembly repeated after him, "Soak 'em! Douse 'em!"

Another Bartholomew took Baptizer's part, the one nicknamed Razor after his razor-thin rapier, and another Matthias styled "Watering Can" after the blunderbuss he carried; it had a muzzle so wide that buckshot poured out of it like water from a watering can. "Long live Baptist and his Sprinkler!" they cried. The Prussian tried to speak out but could barely make himself heard over the noise and laughter.

"Down with the cowardly Prussians!" they cried. "Let the poltroons among us hide under a monk's habit!"

Once again old Matthias raised his head; the noise subsided.

"Do not make fun of Robak," he said. "I know him—a padre, aye, but a crafty one! This maggot has gnawed tougher nuts than you. I met him only once and was on to his little game the moment I laid eyes on him. He turned his gaze from me, afraid I'd ask him for his confession. But that's not my business, though I could say a lot on that score. Anyhow, he'll not come here. No use calling the Bernardine. If all this news comes from him, then who knows to what purpose? Robak's one devil of a priest. If this is all you know, then why come to me? What do you want?"

"It's war we want!" they yelled.

"What war?" he asked.

"War on Moscow!" they roared. "A fight! Thrash the Muscovites!"

The Prussian kept shouting, raising his voice higher and higher until thanks partly to his polite bows and partly to his shrill, piercing tones, he gained their hearing.

"I, too, want to fight," he cried, thumping his chest. "I may not wield Baptizer's Sprinkler, but I did give a proper christening to four Prussians with a barge pole the day I had a few too many, and they tried to drown me in the Pregel."

"That's the spirit, Bartholomew!" roared Baptizer. "Douse 'em, I say!"

"But for the love of Jesus," Bartholomew went on. "First we must know whom we are fighting, and why. The world needs to know; how else will the people follow us? Where will they go if even we have no idea when or where to go? Fellow noblemen! Brothers! All this requires careful consideration. Brothers! Here we need order and organization. If it's war we want, then let's form a confederacy[7] and think the matter through: where to raise our banner, under whose staff to ride. That's the way it's done in Greater Poland. We see the Prussians in full retreat. What do we do? We hold a secret council, arm the peasants and nobility, and wait for Dąbrowski's order. Then harrow! we take to horse and rise up as one man."

"I beg the floor!" spoke up the estate manager from Kleck, a comely young man dressed in the German fashion. Though his name was Buchman, he was of pure Polish stock, born in Poland proper. No one knew if he were of gentle birth, nor did anyone care to ask. All esteemed him for the fact that he served a great magnate, loved his country, and had a great deal of learning. He'd taught himself the science of husbandry from foreign books and ran his estate in an orderly manner. On politics, too, he'd formed wise opinions. He wrote a flawless hand and expressed himself elegantly; and so when he began to speak, everyone stopped to listen.

"I beg the floor," he repeated, twice clearing his throat; and making a bow he addressed the conclave in a sonorous voice.

"Our foregoing eloquent speakers have touched on all the salient, essential points. They have raised the discussion to a higher plane. All that remains is to bring into focus the pertinent thoughts and considerations thus far presented; this way I propose to reconcile the contrary views. Our discussion runs, I note, along two distinct lines. Since the lines have been drawn, I shall pursue them accordingly. First, why undertake an insurrection and in what spirit? That is first vital question. The second touches the matter of revolutionary power. The lines have been aptly drawn, only I propose to reverse the order. Begin first with the question of authority; when once we have grasped what that constitutes, we may proceed to deduce the essence, spirit and aims of the insurrection. So let us start with the question of authority.

"When we survey the history of humankind, what do we see? Man scattered throughout the forests in his savage state, musters, bands together, unites for the purpose of common defense and considers the matter; that is the first consultation. Next, he agrees to lay aside a part of his liberty for the common good; that is the first sovereign act from which all subsequent laws flow as from a wellspring. We can see, then, that government is created by an act of the general will, not God's, as some mistakenly claim. Thus, since government rests on a social contract, the division of power is but its necessary consequence—"

"So there you are at contracts!"[8] broke in old Mathias. "Which? Kiev's or Minsk's? There you have it, Mr. Buchman—Babin government![9] Whether it be God or the devil who foisted the Tsar upon us, I've no wish to argue, but pray tell us how best to be rid of him."

"Aye, there's the nub of it," bellowed Baptizer. "If I could just mount his throne and anoint him with my Sprinkler here, he'd never be back—not for any shady transaction in Kiev or Minsk or any of Buchman's contracts; and no archpriest, nor yet the great Arch-Fiend himself could raise him back to life. Give me sprinkling any day! Mr. Buchman, silver-tongued you may be, but talking's so much hem and haw. Sprinkling's the thing!"

"That's it! That's it!" squeaked Bartholomew Razor, rubbing his hands and darting between Baptizer and Matthias like a weaver's shuttle. "If you, Matthias of the Birch, and you, Matthias of the Club, would only agree on it, so help me, we'd make mincemeat of the Muscovites. Razor here marches under Birch's orders—"

"Orders are for parade drills," broke in Baptizer. "Our old Kowno brigade had but one standing order—short, with knobs on. Strike terror and never flinch! Into the fray and never give ground! Wade in often and lay 'em on thick. Slam-bang!"

"Now you're talking!" squealed Razor. "There's orders for me! What good are treaties? Why waste ink drawing up acts of confederation? Have we need of a confederacy? Is that what the fuss is about? Let Matthias be our marshal—*The Birch* his staff of office!"

"Long live Weathercock!" roared Baptizer. "Long live the Sprinklers!" roared the nobility.

But now murmurs vigorously suppressed inside the room could be heard from the corners; evidently, the council was breaking up into two factions.

"I deplore agreements!" cried Buchman. "That is my philosophy."

"*Veto!*"[10] cried another, "I say 'nay!'" Others chimed in from the corners.

Suddenly, the deep voice of the newly arrived Skołuba burst upon their ears.

"Gentlemen of Dobrzyn!" he began. "What is all this? Some pretty mischief in the wind? How about us? Shall we be deprived of our rights? When the invitation came to our village (it was the Old Boy, Rębajło, who invited us), they said great events were at hand, events touching not just Dobrzyn folk but the whole district, the entire nobility. Robak hinted as much, though he could never quite finish what he had to say, always stammering and expressing himself obscurely. Anyhow, after dispatching runners to all our neighbors, here we are at last. You are not alone, men of Dobrzyn! Ten score men we've mustered from the other villages. So let us all consult together. If we need a marshal, then we shall all vote together. One man, one vote! Long live equality!"

Taking Skołuba's side, both Terajewiczes, the three Mickiewicz brothers, and the four Stypułkowski yelled, "Long live equality!"

Meanwhile, Buchman kept interjecting, "Agreement will be the ruin of us!"

"Then we'll get by without you!" cried Baptizer. "Long live our marshal, Matthias of Matthiases! Come on, brothers, rally to his staff!"

"Throw in with us!" yelled the Dobrzyn gentry.

"*Veto!*" cried others.

The assembly broke into two opposing parties. Shaking their heads in contrary directions, one side shouted, "We say nay!", the other, "yea!"

Matthias sat silent between them, the one steady head in the room. Opposite him stood Baptizer, his arms draped over his club, his head swinging from one side to the other like a gourd balanced on a tall stake. "Douse 'em! Douse 'em!" he roared tirelessly. Razor darted nimbly back and forth between Baptizer's and Matthias' benches, while Watering Can paced slowly to and fro between the Dobrzyński and the rest of the nobility, as if to unite them.

"Shave 'em!" yelled Razor. "Soak 'em!" cried Watering Can.

Matthias held his peace, but it was clear he was losing his patience. For a full quarter of an hour the uproar raged on. Suddenly, a shaft shot up above the heads of the raucous throng—a rapier, a fathom long, a handspan wide, double-edged—clearly, a Teutonic blade cast of Nuremberg steel. They gazed at the arm in silent awe. Its bearer stood hidden by the throng, but they guessed at once who he was.

"It's Jackknife! *Vivat* Jackknife!" they roared. "Long live *Jackknife*, emblem of Rębajłło village! Long live Rębajłło! The Old Boy! Scarpate! Half-Goat!"

Pushing his way through the ruck into the center of the room, Gervase (for it was indeed he) flourished his gleaming Jackknife, then lowering the point before Matthias as a sign of greeting, he spoke forth:

"Jackknife salutes The Birch. Fellow noblemen from Dobrzyn! I shall give no advice. None at all. I shall only tell you why I called this muster. What to do and how to do it, you may decide for yourselves. No doubt you are aware of the rumors going about the noble villages. Great events are at hand. Father Robak has talked about it, so you must know what I'm talking about, right?"

"We know!" they roared.

"Right then!" he went on, eyeing them sharply. "Now a clever head needs but few words to the wise, right?"

"Right!" they answered.

"Right then," continued the Warden. "When the French emperor moves east and the Russian tsar west, it's war, see? Tsar against emperor, king against king. They'll go at it head to head. That's what monarchs do. Meantime, shall we stand idly by? When the bigwigs go for each other's throats, how say we go for the small fry, each his own man? A brawl from above and from below, great against great, small against small. We'll start such a swinging match that this entire piece of roguery will come crashing down, and so happiness and the Commonwealth shall flourish again. Am I not right?"

"Right!" they roared. "He puts it to a nicety."

"You said it, brother!" roared Baptizer. "It's whack! thwack! Basta!"

"My tonsorium's always open for business!" echoed Razor.

"But first, dear Baptizer and Matthias, you must agree on who's to lead us," said Watering Can politely.

"Agreement's for fools!" broke in Buchman. "Debate never harms matters of the common weal. Be silent, gentlemen! We're listening, and we stand to gain by it. The Warden considers the matter from a fresh point of view."

"Not at all," said Gervase. "Nothing new in my approach. Great matters are for the great to decide. For that we have emperors, kings, senates, and parliaments. Such things are done in Cracow or Warsaw, old boy, not here in the village of Dobrzyn. Acts of confederation are not written on a chimney in chalk, or aboard a trading wherry, but on parchment scrolls. No writs for us. For that we have our clerks of the Crown and Lithuania. My business is to slash with my Jackknife."

"And mine to splash with my Sprinkler!" roared Baptizer.

"And mine to pierce with my Awl!" added Bartholomew nicknamed Bodkin, drawing his small rapier.

"I take you all as witnesses," said Gervase, getting to the heart of the matter. "Did Robak not tell us to clean house before inviting Bonaparte in? You all heard him. But did you take his meaning? Who's the scum of our district? Who's the traitor that slew the worthiest Pole among us? Who robbed him and looted his castle and even now would seize what's left from his rightful heir? Who, I say? Need I tell you?"

"Why, Soplica! He's the rascal," cried Watering Can.

"Aye, the tyrant!" squealed Razor.

"Then douse 'im!" roared Baptizer.

"If he's a traitor, then to the gallows with him!" shouted Buchman. "Harrow!" thundered the throng. "Harrow! Hang Soplica!"

But the Prussian rose in the Judge's defense.

"Gentlemen!" he called out to his brethren, raising his hands. "Dear oh dear! God help us! What is it now? Warden, have you gone mad? Is this what we're talking about? So a man has a crazy outlaw brother—what of it? Shall we punish him on account of his brother? Is that the Christian way? I think the Count has a hand in this. The Judge hard on the nobility? Not true! In Heaven's name! Why, you're the ones suing him in court, while he would make terms with you. He waives his rights and even covers the costs. So he takes the Count to court! What of it? They are both rich. Let lord have it out with lord. What is that to us?

"The Judge a tyrant?" he went on. "But he was the first among us to forbid the peasantry to bow before him. A sin, he said it was. Numbers of times have I seen a company of rustics seated at table with him. He pays the village taxes. You won't see that in Kleck, Mr. Buchman, though you run things there after the German fashion. The Judge a traitor? Why, I've known him since we were schoolboys. He was honest then, and so he is now. Our Poland's dearer to him than anything in the world. He preserves the Polish ways, brooks no Muscovite inroads. Whenever I return from Prussia and need to wash myself of German contamination, I visit Soplica Manor, as though it were the very heart of Poland. There a man can breathe, imbibe his native country!

"Men of Dobrzyn," he pursued. "I am your brother, but so help me I'll see no harm done to the Judge. Nothing good will come of it. This is not the way they did it in Greater Poland, my brothers. What spirit we had! What harmony! The very thought of it warms my heart. No one there would dream of troubling a council with such trifles."

"It's no trifle to gibbet a knave!" roared back the Warden.

The murmurs grew louder. Then Jankiel sought audience. He leapt on a bench and drew himself up, his waist-length beard hanging over the throng like a truss of straw. Removing his fur hat with one hand and righting his skullcap with the other, he thrust his left hand under his belt, bowed low, and flourishing his hat with his right addressed the throng.

"Now, gentlemen of Dobrzyn, I am but a poor Jew. The Judge is neither kith nor kin to me. I respect the Soplicas as my good lords and squires. But I also respect you Matthiases and Bartholomews as my good neighbors and patrons. Here is what I think. If you mean to do harm to the Judge, that is not a good thing. You'll come to blows, and blood will be spilt, men will die. And don't forget the assessors! The constable! The dungeons! A horde of soldiery stands billeted in the village—yagers every one! The Assessor bides in the manor. He has only to whistle, and the whole troop will come marching up as ordered.

Then see what happens! And if you're counting on the French, they still have a fair stretch to come.

"I am a Jew," he went on. "War's not in my line, but I have been to Bielica and talked to my fellow Jews on the border. They tell me the French stand massed on the banks of the Łososna, and if war breaks out, it won't be until after winter. So I say wait. Soplica Manor is not a market booth you can take apart and cart off as you please; it will still be there in the spring. As to the Judge, he is not a tenant publican. He won't run away. You'll still find him come spring. But now pray disperse! No more carrying on aloud about what's past, as that's idle talk. Come, my noble sirs, who'll do me the honor? My Sarah has just given birth to a little Jankiel. Today I shall stand you all to a round of drinks. We'll make loud music together! I'll bring in a couple of fiddlers, a doodle sack, and a bass viol. My friend Matthias here is fond of old linden mead and new mazurkas. I have new mazurkas! Are not my brats fine little singers, eh? I taught 'em myself."

Jankiel's words went straight to their hearts, so dearly did they love him. Joyous shouts and applause broke out. A murmur of assent was already spreading beyond the confines of the house when Gervase suddenly pointed his Jackknife at Jankiel. The Jew leapt down and melted into the crowd.

"Begone, Jew!" roared the Warden. "Keep your nose out of this. It doesn't concern you. And you, old boy," he said, turning to the Prussian, "so now that you run a pair of paltry barges for the Judge, you think you can speak for him? Have you forgotten your father sailed *twenty* Horeszko wherries down to Prussia? That is how he and his family came into their fortune. Nor was he the only one! All of you living in Dobrzyn stand in his debt. You oldsters remember and you youngsters will have heard that the Pantler was a father and benefactor to you all. Whom did he send to Pinsk to run his estate? A Dobrzyński! Who kept his books? The Dobrzyński! Who were his stewards? Whom did he trust to the charge of his pantry? None but the Dobrzyński—his household was full of them! It was he that pressed your cases in court and secured pensions for you from the King. It was your children he boarded by droves in the Piarist schools,[11] paying out of his own pocket for their clothes, meals and lodgings, and later securing their preferments—also at his own charges. And why did he do this? Because he was your neighbor. And now the Judge's boundaries encroach on your land. What good has he ever done you?"

"Not a blessed thing!" piped up Watering Can. "That's because he's nothing but a jumped-up smallholder.[12] When he huffs, it's all pshaw! pshaw! nose in the air. Remember the time I invited him to my daughter's wedding? I poured him a drink. He refused it, saying, 'I do not drink like you Dobrzyn folk. You, brothers, swill like bitterns.' Now there's a nob for you! A mollycoddle kneaded from

Marymont flour![13] Wouldn't drink with us. So we pour one down his throat. 'Outrage!' he cried. Just wait! I'll pour him an outrage."

"The fraud!" roared Baptizer. "I too have a reason to soak him one. My son used to have his wits about him. Now he's grown so daft they call him Sack,[14] and all on account of Soplica. 'What drives you to the manor?' I ask the boy. 'God help you if I catch you there!' Then like a shot he's back at Sophy's again. Finding him skulking in the hemp, I grab him by the ear and anoint him one. He blubbers and bawls like a peasant's babe. 'Father, beat me if you will, but I must go there,' he sobs. 'What's the matter with you, son?' I ask him. He's in love with Sophy! Wants to steal a glance at her! I feel sorry for the lad. So I say to Soplica, 'Judge, let Sophy wed my Sack!' 'She's too young,' says he. 'Wait another three years or so, then she can decide for herself.' The knave! He lied. Even now he's lining up another match for her, or so I hear. Now see if I don't invite myself to the wedding and anoint their nuptial bed with my Sprinkler!"

"So, is such a knave to lord it over us?" cried the Warden. "Is he to ruin our ancient lords, men far worthier than he? Meanwhile, the Horeszko name and its memory perish? Oh, where is there gratitude in the world? Clearly, none in Dobrzyn! Brothers, you wish to do battle with the Russian Tsar, yet you're afraid to make war on Soplica Manor? Afraid of the dungeons, is that it? Do I summon you to brigandage? God forbid! Fellow noblemen, I stand on my rights. The Count has won the case. Several awards of court have been made in his favor. All that remains is to have them executed. That's how we did it in the old days! The court issued its decree, our knighthood carried it out. Who precisely? Why, you, the Dobrzyński! That is how your name became famous throughout Lithuania. Aye, it was the Dobrzyński who fought the Muscovites in the foray against Mysz.[15] The Russian general Voinilovich[16] led them, he and that scoundrel friend of his, Mr. Wołk[17] of Ługomowicze. Remember how we took Wołk captive and were about to string him up from the barn rafters for tyrannizing over the peasantry and aiding the Muscovites? But then our stupid peasants had to take pity on him. Oh, one of these days I'll roast him alive on my Jackknife! I'll not mention the many other great raids we took part in. Always we came away with booty, general acclaim and glory, as befitted noble knights. But why bother to recall it! Today the Count, your neighbor, has to waste his time with lawsuits and winning decrees. No one will come to the poor waif's aid. The heir to the same Pantler who put bread on your tables now finds himself friendless— except for me, his Warden, and my trusty Jackknife!"

"And *my Sprinkler!*" chimed in Baptizer. "Where you go, dear Gervase, there I go too. So long as I have an arm to swing, I'll make it go splish, splash! Two makes a pair, by heaven! You have your sword, Gervase, and I my Sprinkler.

So help me, you'll slash and I'll splash, and between the two of us, we'll clobber 'em. Splish! Splash! Let the others prattle."

"You'll not exclude Bartholomew, eh, brothers?" squeaked Razor. "You just provide the suds and I'll do the shaving!"

"I'll ride with you, too," cried Watering Can, "since we seem unable to settle on a marshal. Voting and ballots mean nothing to me. I've another sort of ballot—lead! (And taking a fistful of shot from his pocket he rattled it in his hand.) Here's my kind of ballot. Each of these has the Judge's name on it!"

"We'll join with you!" cried Skołuba.

"Where you go, there we go too!" yelled the nobility. "Long live Horeszko! Long live Half-Goat! *Vivat* Warden Rębajło! Harrow! Hang Soplica!"

Even so did the eloquent Gervase twist his audience around his little finger. Everyone had his own grievance against the Judge, as neighbors often do, some over damages done, others over timber encroachments, still others over a boundary dispute. Anger goaded some, jealousy of the Judge's wealth others, hatred united them all; and raising their sabers and clubs they pressed up to the Warden.

At last the dour and silent Matthias rose from his bench. Stepping slowly into the center of the room, he clapped his hands to his hips, stared his audience in the eye and spoke forth, shaking his head. Each word he uttered with deliberation, between emphatic pauses.

"You stupid, stupid fools! You fools! Pay the piper, face the music. So when the restoration of Poland and the Commonwealth is in question, you—fools!— are all at loggerheads. You cannot hold a proper debate—fools!—or bring it to order, or even—stupid fools!—settle on a man to lead you. You fools! But the moment someone raises a private grievance, you—stupid fools!—are all in agreement. Begone from my sight! As sure as my name's Matthias, I'll see you all to hell. And may a hundred million drays of hogsheads and devils go with you!"

They fell silent, as though struck by a lightning bolt; but just then a loud cry went up outside the house.

"Long live the Count!"

The Count, gallantly accoutered, rode into Matthias' yard with a troop of ten armed jockeys. He was suited in black; investing his shoulders was a great sleeveless walnut-hued cloak of Italian cut fastened at the throat by a silver clasp. He sported a round hat with a plume and held a rapier in his hand. Wheeling his horse, he saluted the throng with a flourish of his blade.

"Long live the Count!" they cried. "With him we live and die!"

The nobility ran to the cottage window then pressing on the Warden's heels made for the door. Gervase dashed out; the throng tumbled through the doorway behind him. Matthias drove out the stragglers, slammed the door and threw the bolt; then opening the window he stuck out his head and yelled "Stupid fools!" one last time.

Meanwhile, the nobility swarmed around the Count. They repaired to the village tavern. There, observing the old custom, Gervase called for three noblemen's belts and had three casks hoisted from the cellar—one contained vodka, another honey mead, the third ale. He drew the stoppers. Three streams, one silvery white, the second amber red, the third tawny yellow, gushed out with a hiss and cascaded like a tri-colored rainbow into a hundred resonant goblets and cups.

The nobility milled about the yard, now drinking heartily, now pledging the Count a hundred years. "Harrow!" they yelled. "Hang Soplica!"

Jankiel quietly mounted an unsaddled horse and galloped off. The Prussian, ignored though still protesting eloquently, also tried to slip away. "Traitor!" yelled the nobility, going after him. Meanwhile, Mickiewicz stood off at a distance. He hadn't joined in the clamor, nor had he offered his counsel, but they guessed from his demeanor he was up to no good. They drew their swords. Up and at him! He broke away and fell back; now he was bleeding, his back pressed to the wall. Fortunately, his friend Zan and three Czeczots[18] arrived in the nick of time. The nobility gave way, but in the skirmish two men received cuts to their hands, another to the ear; the rest were already mounting their horses.

The Count and Gervase marshaled the men, handed out arms and orders, and the entire host started at a gallop down the long village street.

"Harrow!" they shouted. "Hang Soplica!"

NOTES

1. Józef Grabowski (1791-1881) was in fact a second lieutenant, an adjutant to Sokolnicki, head of Marshal Murat's army. Grabowski retired from the army with the rank of lieutenant colonel and as a knight of the Legion of Honor. In 1831, he entertained the poet and his brother Franciszek on his estate of Łukowo, near Objezierze in Greater Poland.
2. Napoleon's decisive victory over the Prussians at Jena took place in October 1806. After Jena, the emperor summoned the Poles to his standards.
3. The Polish word for the common cockroach is *karaluch*, but Bartholomew the Prussian is here referring to the smaller German Cockroach (*blattella germanica*) called *prusak* in Polish.
4. The Polish text gives *Achary Herri Got! O Wej*. Bartholomew's corruption of the German *Ach, Herr Gott! O Wej!* (O Lord! O woe!).
5. The Polish word is *kropidło*, the instrument with which the priest sprinkles the baptizand with holy water. The Polish verb *kropić* (to sprinkle) can also mean "to thump" or "wallop." See also note 22 to Book II.
6. The Polish word *robak* means "worm" or "maggot."

7. Confederacies, which date as far back as the thirteenth century, were extra-parliamentary citizens' organizations formed for the purpose of attaining specific goals, often by the use of armed force. Once the goals were realized, they ceased to exist. Some confederacies came into existence to maintain peace during *interregna*; others were used to circumvent the limitations of the *liberum veto* in Parliament (in a confederacy, unlike Parliament, majority vote ruled). The most famous confederacies in Polish history were those of Bar and Targowica.

8. The contracts of Kiev and Minsk were famous fairs, held annually. As these are the only contracts Matthias has heard of, the word, as used by Buchman with reference to Rousseau's *Contrat Social*, naturally puzzles him.

9. The Republic of Babin (*Rzeczpospolita babińska*) was a comic society founded in 1568 by Stanisław Pszonka (d. 1580) on his estate, Babin, near Lublin. With sixteenth century French and Italian parodic academies and societies as its model, the Babin Republic became principally a liars' society (*omnis homo mendax* was its motto) conferring titles, offices, and rewards on notorious braggarts and liars.

10. A reference to the notorious *liberum veto*, by which a single vote could effectively render null and void the entire body of legislation enacted to date at a session of Parliament. It was abolished by the Four-Year Parliament (1788-92).

11. The Piarists, a Catholic teaching order, improved the education of the noble youth, especially, since the introduction of modernizing reforms by Father Stanisław Konarski in 1740.

12. The Polish term *szlachciura* refers to a rough, impoverished nobleman. The term describes the actual circumstances of the judge's brother, Jacek, before his being awarded the greater part of the pantler's domain after the events unfolding from the Targowica confederacy.

13. Marymont, a village near Warsaw; famous for the delicate flour produced by its mills. It was named after Maria Kazimiera d'Arquien (1641-1716), the French-born queen consort to King Jan III Sobieski from 1674 to 1696.

14. The Polish word *sak* denotes a kind of duffel bag. Used figuratively, it means "fool."

15 The Polish attributive *myski* makes it unclear as to whether the reference is to Mysz or Myssa. Mysz was a small Nowogródek district town belonging at the time to Józef Count Niesiołowski. An armed foray took place there, albeit in 1771, when Niesiołowski seized possession of his wife's dowry. However, no skirmish with the Russian Army is recorded and the considerably younger Wojniłowicz and Wołk (noted subsequently) could not have taken part in it. Myssa, on the other hand, was a village in Oszmiana district belonging to the Bukaty family. Wołk lived in the Oszmiana area, but the details of that foray remain unknown.

16. The reference appears to be to Florian Wojniłowicz (d. *circa* 1820), a general in the Tsar's service, owner of Mańkow estate in Nowogródek district.

17. Samuel Wołk Łaniewski (d. *circa* 1850), owner of Łogumowicze, a village situated north of Nowogródek in the western corner of Oszmiana district between the Niemen and Berezina rivers. Under Wołk's ownership, Łogumowicze became the center of a vast fortune, which allegedly owed its beginnings to the provisioning of the Russian Army with grain through shady deals worked out by Wołk and the officers. The incident subsequently described in *Pan Tadeusz* is authentic, only the time was altered.

18. Close friends and university colleagues of Mickiewicz, whose names the author chooses to immortalize in his epic poem.

BOOK VIII

The Foray

———

Argument

The Steward's astronomy. The Chamberlain's view of comets. A mysterious scene in the Judge's room. Tadeusz's skillful attempts at self-extrication land him in hot water. A new Dido. The foray. The last protest of the Court Usher. The Count takes Soplica Manor. Storm and butchery. Gervase as cellarer. The feast.

There is a moment of brooding calm before the storm when the rapidly advancing thundercloud halts over men's heads and with a louring look checks the breath of the winds. In silence it probes the earth with lightning glances, marking out the places where it will shortly rain down its bolts. Precisely such a calm brooded over the Soplica house. It was as if a foreboding of stupendous events had sealed up the lips of its inmates and borne their spirits into the realm of dreams.

After dinner, the Judge and his guests repaired outdoors to take the evening air. Seating themselves on the turf embankment fronting the house, the entire party gazed up at the heavens in an attitude of gloomy silence. The sky seemed to be sinking, contracting, pressing ever closer to the earth until, like a pair of lovers draped in darkness, the two substances began their intimate colloquy, confiding their feelings through stifled sighs, murmurs, whispers, and half-uttered words. All this comprised the peculiar music of the evening.

The screech owl moaned from the gable, launching the concert. Bats rustled their delicate wings, flitting about by the house where the lattices and peoples' faces shone. Closer still, drawn in great numbers by the women's white dresses, whirred the bats' tiny sisters, the moths. They picked on Sophy in the worst way, beating about her face and sparkling eyes, which they took for a pair of candles. A great swarm of insects whirled round and round in the air, humming like musical glasses. Among the myriad sounds, Sophy's ear distinguished the midges' harmonies, the gnats' jarring semitones.

Meanwhile, in the field below, the evening concert had barely begun. The musicians had just finished tuning their instruments. The corncrake, first fiddle of the meadow, rasped out three times. From the slough yonder, the bittern's booming bass replied. Snipe rose whirling in the air, repeating their drum-like cadences. Then, like the enchanted tarns of high Caucasia that drowse by day and croon by night, two meres picked up the chatter of the birds and insects and broke forth in a two-part chorus. One of these meres had pellucid depths verged with sand; a soft and solemn moan issued from its deep-blue breast. The other had a miry bed and mud-choked waters; it answered back with a cry both sad and passionate. In both reservoirs warbled frogs without number. Each choir stood tuned to a mighty chord, one sang *fortissimo*, the other *sotto voce*. One seemed to complain mournfully, the other heaved sighs. So, like a pair of Aeolian harps murmuring by turns, the two bodies of water conversed across the fields.

The shades of twilight deepened. Only the eyes of prowling wolves flashed like taper-flames among the thickets and withy beds bordering the brook. Yonder, shepherds' watchfires could be seen glimmering on the shrinking horizon. At last, the moon kindled her silver lamp, swung clear of the forest and lit up both heaven and earth. Side by side like a happily married couple they slept, partially covered by the gloom, earth's silvery bosom wrapped in heaven's chaste embrace. Opposite the moon, a star winked, then another, then a thousand, then a million! Prominent among them were the twin stars Castor and Pollux, which the ancient Slavs called *Lel* and *Polel*,[1] but which the people had now renamed *Lithuania* and *The Crown*.

Farther out glittered the two pans of the celestial Scales. Upon these, on the morning of Creation (so the old folk tell), God weighed the Earth and all the planets in turn before setting them in the chasms of space; later, he suspended these golden pans from the firmament as a prototype for the balance scales of men.

To the northward shone the circle of the starry Sieve.[2] Through it, God was said to have sifted the grains of corn when scattering it from heaven for our forefather Adam whom he had banished from Eden for his sin.

Somewhat higher in the heavens, ready for mounting, stood David's Chariot,[3] its long shaft turned toward the North Star. The old Lithuanians knew better; they insisted the people erred in calling it David's, for it was the Angel's Chariot. Lucifer rode it eons ago when, challenging God to combat, he bore down on the heavenly gates along the Milky Way until Michael smote him and drove the chariot off the road. There among the stars it lies ruined; no one may repair it—the Archangel Michael has laid a ban on it.

The old Lithuanians also knew—this reportedly from the rabbis—that the great Dragon of the Zodiac, which wound its starry coils around the heavens, was not a serpent as astronomers mistakenly claimed, but a great fish—Leviathan by name. For eons it inhabited the deeps, but after the Great Flood, it perished for want of water. Then the angels attached its bones to the celestial dome as both a curiosity and a remembrance for the world. Just so the parish priest of Mir adorned the walls of his church with the excavated ribs and femurs of giants.[4]

With such stories, all culled from books or passed down by oral tradition, the old Steward entertained the guests. Though he had feeble vision by night and could distinguish nothing in the skies even with the aid of spectacles, he knew the name and shape of every constellation by heart. With his finger he pointed them out along with the trajectories they described.

This evening the guests paid him scant attention. No one took the slightest interest in the Sieve, or the Dragon, or even the Scales. Today, all eyes and thoughts stood riveted on the new guest that had recently risen to their ken—a comet of great size and power.[5] The celestial body had appeared in the west and was bearing northward. With its bloody eye sideways intent upon Lucifer's chariot, it dragged its great tress like a haul-net behind it, sweeping a third of the heavens and gathering up a vast multitude of stars; meanwhile, its head bore higher to the northward, bound straight for the Polar Star.

Each night, with a sense of nameless foreboding, the Lithuanian folk gazed at the heavenly sign, reading dark meanings into it. They noted other signs as well. Not seldom were ill-omened birds seen gathering in vast flocks in the bare fields. Cawing balefully, they sharpened their bills, as if relishing the prospect of carrion flesh. Not seldom were dogs seen scratching the ground, howling in terror, as if the smell of death, famine or war were in the air. The forest rangers claimed to have seen the Maid of Plagues[6] stalking the churchyard. Towering over the tallest trees she strode, waving a blood-soaked kerchief in her hand.

The Overseer drew all manner of inferences from these signs; he'd come to report on the day's labors and was standing by the fence, holding forth quietly with the accountant. But the Chamberlain, who was seated on the turf embankment fronting the house, cut short the guests' talk. All knew he was about to speak. His great snuffbox flashed in the moonlight.

The article was wrought of gold and set with diamonds around a glass-covered miniature of King Stanislas. Tapping on it with his fingers, the Chamberlain took a pinch and spoke forth:

"My dear Steward, all your talk about the stars is but an echo of what you learned at school. But when it comes to portents I'd sooner listen to our common folk. I also studied the stars—for two years in Wilno. Madame Puzinina, a rich and learned lady, endowed the university with a village of two hundred souls for the purchase of various lenses and telescopes. Our famous Father Poczobut,[7] then rector of the Academy, was a watcher of the skies; eventually, he gave up his chair and telescopes and retired to his quiet cell in the abbey where he died an exemplary death. I am also acquainted with Śniadecki,[8] a highly learned man, though a layman. Now, as I see it, our astronomers observe planets and comets much as our townsfolk do a traveling coach. They are quite able to tell you if someone is drawing up before the Royal Castle or departing abroad through the city turnpike; but who rides in it and why, what the ambassador discussed with the King, and whether His Majesty replied with a declaration of peace or war—this they never ask. I recall the time Branicki left for Jassy[9] in his carriage. That vile car had a whole host of Targowica partisans in tow, like a comet's tail. Our common folk who took no part in the public deliberations guessed right away that the tail foretokened treachery. I hear they called the comet a besom that would end up sweeping millions away."

"It is true, Your Excellency," replied the Steward with a bow. "I remember well what I heard as a child. Though I was not yet ten, I recall seeing the late lamented Sapieha[10] at our house. He was still a lieutenant in the dragoons then; later he became Marshal of the Royal Court and died Grand Chancellor of Lithuania at the ripe old age of a hundred and ten. He served under Hetman Jabłonowski's banner when Sobieski raised the siege of Vienna. The Chancellor described the moment King Jan mounted his horse for the great battle. The papal nuncio had just blessed him, and the Austrian ambassador Count Wilczek was kissing his foot and passing him the stirrup, when the King exclaimed, 'See what passes in the heavens!' Looking up, they saw a comet streaking from east to west along the path taken by Mohammed's host. Later, Father Bartochowski would compose a panegyric titled *Orientis Fulmen*[11] for the triumphal progress through Cracow. He made much of that comet. I also read about it in a work entitled *The Janina*,[12] which describes the late king's entire campaign. The book contains aquatints of Mohammed's mighty standard and shows just such a comet as we see today."

"Amen to that," said the Judge. "I take your omen to signal the advent of another Jan the Third. Today we have a new champion in the West. God willing, the comet will bring him hither to us."

The Steward nodded gloomily. "Aye," he said. "Comets may foretoken wars, or simply quarrels. That this one should appear above Soplica Manor does not bode well. Perhaps it portends some domestic misfortune. Yesterday we had contention and disputes enough during the hunt and banquet. The Notary and the Assessor argued all morning, and in the evening Tadeusz challenged the Count to a duel—all over the bearskin. If the Judge hadn't interrupted me,

I might have reconciled the parties at the table, for I meant to tell them about a curious hunting incident not unlike the one that occurred yesterday. It happened to the finest pair of shooters of my day, the Honorable Deputy Tadeusz Rejtan and the Prince de Nassau; and it fell like this:

"The General Starosta of Podolia, Prince Czartoryski,[13] was traveling from Volhynia to his Polish domains, or if I remember rightly to attend Parliament in Warsaw. On his way he paid visits to the local nobility, partly for amusement and partly to build up his popularity. He called on Tadeusz Rejtan of sainted memory, who was later our deputy from Nowogródek and in whose house I grew up from childhood. So, in honor of the Prince's visit, Rejtan arranged a reception. The nobility came out in large numbers. They staged a play. The Prince loves the theater! Kaszyc (the one who lives in Jatra) supplied the fireworks, Tyzenhaus sent over a troupe of dancers, and Ogiński and Sołtan (the one from Zdzięciół) provided the orchestra; in a word, the entertainment of the house was lavish beyond compare, and in the forest they held a splendid hunt. Now it is well known to you gentlemen that almost all the Czartoryski in living memory, though they trace their origins to the Jagiełłos, have never much taken to hunting, not from laziness, mind, but from their foreign tastes. The Prince would sooner glance into a book than a kennel, sooner peer into a lady's bower than a forest thicket.

"Accompanying him was the German Prince de Nassau[14] of whom it was related that as a guest in the Libyan country he had joined a hunting expedition with the Moorish kings and there slain a tiger with a spear in close combat; he was much given to boasting about it. Now on this particular occasion we were hunting wild boar. Rejtan brought down a huge sow at great risk to his life; he'd fired his gun at close range. We were amazed and commended him warmly for his feat of marksmanship. Only de Nassau stood unimpressed. He strutted about, mumbling under his breath that a good aim proved but a bold eye, while cold steel proved a bold arm; and he began holding forth again on his Libyan hunting expedition, his Moorish kings, and the tiger he'd speared. Rejtan listened to him sullenly. Always a fiery-tempered fellow, he slapped his saber and cried out, 'Your Highness, who looks boldly, fights boldly! Wild boars are equal to tigers, sabers to spears!' There followed a heated exchange of words.

"Fortunately, Czartoryski intervened and appeased them in French. What he said I've no idea, but it was like ashes over live coals, for Rejtan had taken the matter to heart. He bided his time, swearing to play a trick on the German. That prank nearly cost him his life, and he played it the very next day. Just how, I'll tell you in a moment."

Here the Steward paused, and raising his right hand beckoned for the Chamberlain's snuffbox. He took the snuff slowly, as if deliberately holding his audience in the keenest state of suspense. At last he resumed, but once again the tale which compelled such rapt attention was broken off. A servant entered with word that a caller awaited the Judge on a matter of urgent business. The Judge bade them all a good night and took his leave. The company dispersed at once, some to their sleeping quarters in the manor, others to the hayloft in the barn. The Judge went indoors to give audience to the caller.

While the rest of the household slept, Tadeusz lingered in the hallway pacing like a watchman outside his uncle's door. He wished to consult with him on an important matter, and it had to be now, before going to bed. He dared not knock on the door, as the Judge had locked it; evidently, a private conference was in progress. Tadeusz waited, straining his ears. He heard sobbing within. Taking care not to touch the doorknob, he peered through the keyhole. A strange sight greeted his gaze. The Judge and Robak were on their knees, in a tight embrace. Both were weeping and shedding tender tears. Robak held the Judge's hand to his lips while the Judge, wracked by sobs, clung to the Bernardine's neck. At last, after a pause lasting a quarter of an hour, Robak spoke in barely audible tones:

"Dear brother, as heaven's my witness, I have never until now divulged these secrets to which I bound myself in the confessional as penance for my sins. God knows I've lived and wished to die a Bernardine monk, devoting myself entirely to Him and my country, renouncing pride and earthly glory, concealing my name not only from the world but also from you and my own son. But now the Superior General has given me leave *in articulo mortis*[15] to make the disclosure. Who knows if I shall return alive or what they're up to in Dobrzyn! Oh, dear brother, what an utter, utter shambles! The French have still far to come. We must wait until spring, but I hear there's no restraining our nobility. Perhaps I was overzealous in stirring up the uprising. Apparently, they misunderstood me. The Warden has snarled everything up, and now this crazy Count of ours, I hear, has rushed off to Dobrzyn. I couldn't prevent him, and this for a good reason: old Matthias knows who I am. Were he to give me away, I should have to forfeit my head to Jackknife. Nothing will stop the Warden. My life is of no account, but the discovery could spell doom for our plans.

"Still, I must go there and see what they're about, though I die in the attempt. Without me the nobility are sure to run amok. Keep well, dear brother, keep well! I must hurry. If I die, you alone will sigh for my soul. If war breaks out, the whole secret being known to you, finish what I began. Above all, remember you are a Soplica!"

With that the Monk wiped his tears, straightened his habit, drew up his hood, and quietly opening the shutter at the rear of the study leapt out into the garden. The Judge remained in his chair and wept.

Tadeusz waited a moment before rattling the doorknob; the Judge admitted him. Entering quietly, he made a low bow.

"Dear Uncle," he said. "I have been here only a few short days and barely had time to enjoy my stay with you. But I must leave this evening, tomorrow at the latest. As you know, we demanded satisfaction from the Count. Fighting him is my affair, and I have issued my challenge. Since dueling is forbidden in Lithuania, I intend to cross the border to the Duchy.[16]

The Count is a braggart, I know, but he is not lacking in pluck. I have no doubt he will appear at the appointed place. We shall have it out. God willing, I shall give him his due then swim the Łososna to join the ranks of my fellows who stand waiting on the other side. I understand my father's last will and testament provides for my going for a soldier. Who gainsaid it, I do not know."

"My dear Tadeusz," replied his uncle. "Has someone scalded you with boiling water, or are you jinking like a hunted fox that waves his brush one way and runs another? True, we have called out the Count and cannot back down, but to leave now! What's got into you? It's customary to dispatch a second before a duel and set terms. The Count may yet offer an apology and retract his insult. So wait a while, there's plenty of time. Or perhaps there's some other burr under your saddle, eh? Come, speak plainly. What is it about? I'm your uncle. I may be getting on in years, but I know what goes on in a young man's heart. (Here he chucked his nephew's chin.) I have been a father to you. A little bird tells me you've been intriguing with the ladies. By jiminy, our youth waste no time in taking to the fairer sex! Come, Tadeusz, be honest with me. Speak plainly."

"Yes, Uncle, you are right," mumbled Tadeusz. "There are other reasons, and perhaps I am at fault. A mistake! What can I say? A misfortune! Hard to remedy. No, Uncle, I can stay no longer. A youthful error. Please, ask me no more questions! I must leave the Manor without delay."

"There, I knew it!" exclaimed his uncle. "A lover's quarrel! Last night I noticed you biting your lip and frowning at a certain young lady. I saw the sour look on her face too. I know all about these trifles. When a pair of children fall in love, there's no end to these little mishaps. Happy one minute, sad and fretful the next. Now they snap at each other over God knows what, now they sulk silently in the corner—sometimes they even bolt for the fields! If such a fit has taken hold of you, be patient, for there is a remedy. I shall undertake to reconcile you shortly. I know all about these trifles. I, too, was young once. Now tell me all, for I've something to say as well. This way we shall take each other into mutual confidence."

"Uncle," said Tadeusz, kissing his hand and blushing. "I shall tell you the truth. I've grown very fond of the young lady Sophy, your ward, even though

I have seen her on but two occasions. They tell me you plan to wed me to the Chamberlain's daughter, a handsome girl—a rich man's daughter. But I could never marry Mistress Rose, as I am in love with Sophy. The heart must be true to itself, and it would be dishonest to marry while loving another. Perhaps time will heal the wound. I am leaving, and for a good while—"

"Tadeusz, my boy," his uncle broke in. "It strikes me as a strange way of loving. Fleeing the object of your love. I'm glad you are frank with me, but don't you see how silly it would be if you left now? What would you say if I arranged to wed you to Sophy? Eh? What? Not jumping for joy?"

"Your kindness astonishes me, sir," said Tadeusz after a moment's pause. "But it's futile. Your favor would be in vain. Alas, a fool's hope! Mistress Telimena will never allow it."

"We shall ask her," said the Judge.

"She'll never agree," said Tadeusz brusquely. "No, Uncle, I cannot wait. I must leave now, at sunrise, Only please give me your blessing. I have everything in readiness. I ride for the Kingdom without delay."

The Judge curled his whiskers and glowered angrily at the boy. "You call this plain speaking?" he said. "Is this how you confide in me, first the duel, and now this romantic attachment and sudden departure of yours? Oh, some intrigue's afoot, I'll warrant. People have talked! I have had you followed. You, sir, are a philanderer and a scapegrace! You, sir, tell lies. And what were you up to the other night, sniffing about the house like a pointer? Oh, Tadeusz, could it be that you've seduced Sophy and now intend to fly the coop? Well, young cock, you shan't wriggle out of this so easily. Love or no love, you shall wed Sophy, or bear the lash! Tomorrow you shall stand at the altar. And he talks of feelings and a constant heart! You, sir, are a lying rascal! Faugh! I'll look into this, Tadeusz. I'll make your ears smart yet. I've had trouble enough today till my head fairly aches with it, and now he'd deny me a good night's rest! Off to bed with you, sir!"

With that he flung open the door and summoned the Court Usher to help him disrobe.

Tadeusz left quietly, drooping his head, the bitter exchange heavy on his mind. Never in his life had he been scolded with such asperity. He felt the justice of his uncle's charges and crimsoned at his conduct. What now? What if Sophy should find out? Should he ask for her hand? But what would Telimena say? No! He could stay no longer. Engrossed in these thoughts, he'd barely taken a few steps when something swept into his path. Looking up, he saw a white wraith-like figure advancing toward him. Tall, meager and haggard, it glided along, the moonlight hanging tremulously on its garments.

"You ingrate," groaned the wraith, stopping before him. "You sought out my looks and now you shun them. You sought out my words and now you stop up your ears, as if my words and glances were poison. Serves me right! Now I see what you are—a man! Not given to coquetry, I was loath to torment you. I sought to make you happy. And this is how you repay me. Conquest of my tender heart has hardened yours. After winning my heart with immoderate speed, you're as quick to scorn it. Oh, it serves me right! But depend upon it, this cruel lesson has taught me to despise myself with a scorn far greater than yours!"

"Telimena!" he said. "Please believe me, it is not that I am unfeeling, nor do I shun you out of scorn. But consider the matter yourself. People have been watching, spying on us. Can we go on like this, in the open? What will people say? Why, it isn't proper. My God, it's a sin!"

"A sin, is it?" she said with a bitter smile. "O babe in the woods! You lambkin! If I, a woman under the power of love care not if the whole world should discover me and blacken my name, why should you, a man, who can blithely own to having a dozen lovers? Tell me the truth. You mean to desert me."

And she burst into tears.

"But Telimena!" said the youth. "What would people say on seeing an able-bodied man of my age settling down in the country for a life of love when so many young men, so many married men are leaving their wives and children and flying abroad to march under our nation's colors? Even if I cared to stay, does it depend on me? My father declared in his will that I should be a soldier in the Polish Army, and now my uncle commands it too. I leave tomorrow. I've made my decision, and by God, I'll not go back on it."

"Far be it from me to stand in the way of your fame and happiness," said Telimena. "You are a man. You shall find a lover worthier of your heart—wealthy and fairer-looking. Only before we part, grant me this one solace. Tell me that your affections sprang from the heart; that this was no idle dalliance, no wanton fling, but an instance of true love. Tell me my darling Tadeusz loves me. Let me hear once more from his own lips the words, 'I love you.' Let me sear them deep into my soul, engrave them in my mind so that, knowing how you loved me once, I may the more easily forgive you."

Again she burst into sobs.

Seeing her weep and entreat him so tenderly for a trifle, Tadeusz felt an anguish of pity. Honest compassion welled up within him. Had he then searched the recesses of his heart, he would have been at pains to tell if he loved her or not.

"Telimena!" he said with feeling. "Heaven strike me if it be untrue that I was fond of—yes, even loved—you. Brief as were our moments together, they passed so sweetly and tenderly they shall long remain in my heart. So help me God, I'll never forget you."

Telimena leapt up and flung her arms around his neck.

"There! I knew it," she said. "You do love me. So I live again! Today I was on the point of taking my life. But now that you say you love me, my darling, can you really think of deserting me? My heart and all that I have are yours. I shall follow you wherever you go. With you every nook in this earth shall be dear to me. Depend on it, our love shall turn the barrenest of wastes into a garden of delights."

"What!?" said Tadeusz, tearing himself free. "Have you taken leave of your senses? Where? What for? Follow me? A simple soldier? You, a camp follower!"

"Then we shall be married," she said.

"No, never!" cried Tadeusz. "I've no intention of marrying at this time, nor will I be anyone's lover. Trifles! Enough of this! I beg you, my sweet, come to your senses. Compose yourself! I'm grateful to you, but marriage is out of the question. Let us love each other, but at a distance. I cannot stay any longer. No, no, I must go. Keep well, my Telimena. I depart tomorrow."

So saying he put on his hat and turned to leave, but Telimena's medusan gaze froze him in his tracks. Against his will he remained, staring in terror at the pale figure standing motionless, devoid of life and breath, before him.

"Hah!" she exclaimed, stretching forth her arm and pointing a sword-like finger straight at his eyes. "Just what I wanted to hear. Worm tongue! Lizard's heart! That because of you I should scorn the addresses of the Count, the Notary, and the Assessor—that you should seduce then cast me away like an orphan—that is of no account. You are a man, and I know your knavery. That you, like others of your sex, should break faith with me is no surprise, but I had no idea you were capable of such base lying. I listened in at your uncle's door! So, it's the child, Sophy, is it? Fond of her, eh? Treacherous designs! No sooner do you beguile one hapless soul than under her very nose you seek out a fresh victim. Fly, if you wish, but my curse shall hound your footsteps. Remain, and the whole world shall know of your perfidy. No more shall your arts deceive others as they duped me. Out of my sight! I scorn you, sir! You are a liar, a base scoundrel!"

Tadeusz shuddered under the force of her invective. These were mortal insults to a nobleman's ear; no Soplica had ever been so rebuked. He turned deathly pale, stamped his foot, and pursing his lips muttered "Stupid fool!"

He stalked off. But the word 'scoundrel' kept ringing in his heart. He cringed in anguish. Deep down he knew he deserved the rebuke, that he'd treated Telimena with great unfairness. Her rebuke was just, his conscience told him, and yet her reproaches made him despise her all the more. Oh, Sophy! But he dared not think of her for shame. So! Uncle intended to wed them all along. Dear, sweet Sophy! She might have been his bride. But Satan had so ensnared him in web upon web of sin and lies, and now, with a sneer, left him rebuked and despised by all. A few brief days and his prospects lay in ashes; and he felt the full justice of his requital. Suddenly, the thought of the duel flashed like an anchor of repose in the turmoil of his brain.

"Kill the Count! The scoundrel!" he cried out in anger. "Avenge myself or die!" But what exactly for, he didn't know; the rage subsided as quickly as it arose. Once more he was seized by an anguish of sorrow. What if there was an understanding between the Count and Sophy? Perhaps the Count was truly in love with Sophy. Perhaps Sophy reciprocated his love and wished to take him for her husband. What right had he to sunder their union? Who was he, hapless one, to ruin the felicity of others?

He fell into a desperate funk. He saw no way out for himself except in immediate flight. Flight to where? His grave! no doubt. And with his fist pressed to his heavy brow, he made for the two ponds at the bottom of the field. Stopping by the miry mere, he plunged his gaze into the greenish depths and drew the muddy scent lustily into his lungs. Like every wild extravagance, self-violence has its fanciful aspect. In the mad turmoil of his thoughts, Tadeusz felt an inexpressible desire to drown himself in the turbid waters.

But Telimena, guessing the youth's despair from his wild aspect and seeing him make for the meres, took fright on his account. Though still burning with righteous anger, she was at heart a caring soul. True, it pained her that Tadeusz had presumed to love another, and for this she had a mind to punish him, but never would she wish him dead! With outstretched arms she ran after him, crying, "Stop! No matter! Love, wed, leave as you please, but for God's sake, stop!" But he'd forged on ahead at a run and was even now standing on the marges of the mere.

Now by a strange quirk of fate the Count was at this very moment riding along this very bank at the head of his troop of jockeys. Entranced by the serenity of the night and the marvelous music of the aquatic orchestra (those same choirs that sang like Aeolian harps; no creatures sing as sweetly as our Polish frogs!), he drew rein. Forgetting the raid, he turned his ear to the pond and listened intently. His gaze swept the fields, the immensity of the sky—clearly, he was composing a nocturnal landscape in his mind.

It was indeed a picturesque spot. The two ponds leaned inward upon each other like a pair of lovers. The waters of the pond on the right were smooth and clear like a maiden's cheek. The one on the left had a duskier surface like the cheeks of a youth sprouting a manly down. The first pond was verged with golden sand as with locks of shining hair, the brow of the other bristled with osiers and tufts of willows; both meres stood draped in green herbage. From each of these reservoirs there flowed a small brook. Like two arms they met and joined as one. Farther down, the brooklet tumbled into a gloomy ravine and fled away— away, but not out of sight, for the stream bore the moon-luster along. The water cascaded in sheets. Upon each lucent layer sparkled a bouquet of moonbeams. Inside the ravine the light broke into shivers, which the brook then snatched up and bore away even as fresh bundles of moonbeams came showering down. You fancied the Naiad of Świteź[17] were seated there, decanting a spring from a bottomless ewer while dipping into her apron pocket and bestrewing the surface of the water with enchanted gold.

Once through the ravine, the brooklet flowed out on a level plain. There, slowing to a leisurely meander, it fell silent. Yet still you saw it move as the moonbeams continued to glint along the shimmering stream. So stirs Samogitia's lovely snake, the one the Lithuanian folk call *givoytos*.[18] Though it seems to slumber in the heather, yet it constantly moves, for its enameled skin, ever changeful, turns now gold, now silver, until it vanishes from sight among the mosses and fern. So lapsed away the meandering brook among the alder-trees whose feathery forms loomed on the far horizon like phantom spirits half seen, half wreathed in mist.

A watermill stood hidden in the ravine between the two meres. As when a grumbling old guardian eavesdropping on a pair of lovers shakes his head, sways, waves his arms, and belabors his charges with stern admonitions, so the mill suddenly shook its moss-encrusted brow and set its bladed fist in whirling motion. No sooner did the mill come to life and begin to grind its mandibles than it drowned out the love talk of the meres and woke the Count from his reverie.

Astonished to see Tadeusz standing so close to his armed party, the Count cried out, "To arms! Seize him!" The jockeys leapt from their horses and before Tadeusz had time to react, they'd taken him captive, then galloping on to the manor house, the party quickly overran the courtyard. The house awoke. The dogs made noise. Watchmen cried alarm. The Judge ran out, half-dressed. At first he took the armed troop for brigands, but then he recognized the Count.

"What is the meaning of this?" he cried.

The Count flashed his sword over his head, but seeing that the Judge was unarmed he checked himself, suppressing his anger.

"Soplica!" he said. "Ancestral foe of my clan! This day I redress your wrongs, both recent and old. This day, before I avenge the insult to my honor, you shall render me an account for the seizure of my domain."

"In the name of the Father and the Son!" cried the Judge, crossing himself. "Faugh! Are you a brigand, sir? Heavens! Does this befit a man of your birth, your high degree, your breeding? I'll brook no harm done here."

Meanwhile, the manor servants bearing cudgels and muskets ran out to join their master. The Steward hastened after them, his eyes fixed on the Count, knife thrust up his sleeve. They would have set to on the spot if the Judge hadn't stopped them. Plainly, resistance was futile; even now a new foe approached. A light flashed among the alders followed instantly by the discharge of a harque-bus. Even now a troop of horsemen came thundering over the bridge.

"Harrow! Hang Soplica!" roared a thousand voices. The Judge recognized Gervase's battle cry and shuddered.

"This is nothing yet," the Count assured him. "Soon there'll be more of us. Judge, lay down your arms! These are my allies."

Just then the Assessor ran up. "I arrest you in the name of His Imperial Highness!" he cried. "Surrender your sword, sir, or I shall call out the army. You know the penalty for mounting a raid at night. Ukase twelve hundred states—"

The Count struck him in the face with the flat of his blade. The Assessor fell without a sound and crawled into the nettles. All thought him dead or injured.

"So there *is* banditry afoot!" cried the Judge.

A collective groan went up, overtopped by Sophy's shriek. Flinging her arms around the Judge, she squealed like a child undergoing a bloodletting. Meanwhile, Telimena leapt in among the horses, her clasped hands extended toward the Count. "Upon your honor!" she cried out in a piercing voice, head thrown back, hair spread wildly across her shoulders. "By all that's holy, we entreat you upon our knees. Do you dare refuse us, my lord Count? Harsh man! You must slay us women first." And she went off in a dead faint.

Surprised and unnerved by this scene, the Count leapt to her aid.

"Mistresses Sophia and Telimena!" he cried. "Never shall I imbrue this sword in the blood of defenseless souls. People of Soplica Manor! You are my prison-ers. So did I once in Italy, on the crag the Sicilians call Birbante Rocca, when I took a robber's camp. The armed men I slew; those relieved of their weapons I seized and had bound. They walked behind my horsemen—a splendid train enhancing my triumphal march! Later, we hanged them at Etna's foot."

It was a stroke of singular good luck for the Soplicas that the Count had swifter horses than the nobility. In his zeal to be the first to engage the enemy, he'd outstripped the main body of horsemen by at least a mile. Well-disciplined and orderly, his jockeys comprised a regular army of sorts, unlike the rest of the nobility who, as is often the case with insurgents, were unruly and all too quick at hanging.

Now that his ardor and rage had cooled, the Count considered how he might end the raid without bloodshed. He ordered his men to confine the Soplica family in the manor and station guards at the doors. With a "Harrow! Hang Soplica!" the nobility rushed on in a body, encircled the yard and took it by storm—all the more readily, as their captain had been taken and the garrison had fled the field. But the victors' blood was up; they sought out the enemy. Barred from the house, they ran to the farmyard and burst into the kitchen. The sight of the pots and pans and the hearth not yet grown cold, the smell of recent cooking and the sound of dogs crunching on the scraps of the evening meal—all this went straight to their hearts and set their thoughts on a different course. While cooling their wrath, it inflamed their desire for food. Worn out by their march and the whole day spent in deliberations, they thrice roared in unison, "Meat! Meat!" "Drink! Drink!" followed the refrain. The nobility broke into two choirs, one calling for meat, the other for drink. Their cries echoed throughout the Manor; wherever they were heard, mouths watered, bellies growled. And so, at a signal from the kitchen, the entire host dispersed to forage for victuals.

Meanwhile, repulsed from the Judge's rooms, Gervase was forced to defer to the Count's guards. Unable to avenge himself upon his enemy, he turned his mind to his second main objective. Being practiced and skilled in the law, he was eager to establish the Count's legal title to his new inheritance, and so he set out in search of the Court Usher. After a lengthy search, they found Protase skulking behind the stove. Gervase seized him by the collar and dragged him out into the yard.

"Mr. Usher!" said he, prodding his breast with his Jackknife. "The Count makes bold to bid your honor proclaim before our noble brethren my lord's formal *intromissio* of the castle, the manor, the village, and fields both sowed and fallow—in a word, *cum grovesibus, forestis, et borderibus, villeinsibus, bailiffsibus et omnibus rebus; et quibusdam aliis.*[19] You know how it goes. So out with it. Let's hear you bark. And leave nothing out!"

"Now hold on a moment, Warden," said Protase uncowed, thrusting his hands under his belt. "I'm quite ready to do the bidding of either party, but I warn you, a decree proclaimed under the threat of violence and in the dark of night carries no weight."

"Threat! What threat?" said the Warden. "There's no violence here. Why, I'm asking you nicely, sir. If you find it dark, old Jackknife here shall oblige and strike you a light so bright that seven churches could scarce outshine it!"

"Come now, Gervase, old fellow," Protase replied. "Why so testy? I'm only the court usher. Not for me to examine the merits of a case. Everyone knows it is the plaintiff that summons the usher. He tells him what to say and the usher proclaims it. Court ushers are but emissaries of the law and not subject to punishment, so I cannot imagine why you're keeping me under guard. I shall pen a writ at once. Bid someone fetch me a lamp! Meanwhile, I'll make the announcement. Brothers, come to order!"

So as to be better heard, he climbed the large pile of logs seasoning by the garden fence. Directly he got to the top of it, he vanished from sight as if a gust of wind had swept him away. They heard him land with a thump in the cabbage patch below. They saw his confederate's cap streak like a white dove through the dark hemp. Watering Can took a pot-shot at it. Missed! They heard the snapping of poles. Protase had reached the hop thicket. "I protest!" he yelled, now sure of his escape; behind him were the withy bed and the brook's miry ground.

Protase's cry of demurral was like the last cannon shot upon the taking of a redoubt. All resistance ceased at Soplica Manor. The ravenous nobility fell to rapine and pillaging at will. The Baptist took his stand in the cowshed where he dispatched an ox and two calves with single blows to the head. Razor slit open their throats with his thin blade. With equal expedition Bodkin stuck the sucklings and porkers between the shoulder blades; and now slaughter threatened the poultry. The watchful geese, ancient Rome's preservers, honked in vain for help. Alas! no Manlius stood by to repel the treacherous Gaul.[20] Matthias Watering Can broke into the pen. He wrung the necks of some, others he took alive, lashing them to his belt by their necks. In vain the geese gurgled and writhed! In vain the ganders hissed and nipped at their assailant! Covered in sparks of goose down and borne on by the wheel-like flapping motion of the wings, Matthias made straight for the kitchen. You'd swear he was *Chochlik!*[21]— the winged evil sprite.

But the most appalling if quietest butchery took place in the hen-roost. Young Sack burst inside. Using a halter, he yanked the ruffled hens and crested capons from their perches. One after the other, he wrung their necks and piled them on the floor. Beautiful birds! Fattened on pearls of barley. Foolish Sack, what fit of folly took you? Now, you shall never appease Sophy's wrath!

Recalling the old days, Gervase appealed to the nobility for their ceremonial belts. They lowered them into the Soplica cellars and drew up casks of home-brew vodka, oak-seasoned mead and ale. Some of these they broached at once; the rest they seized lustily and rolled toward the Count's headquarters in the castle where, swarming like ants, the entire host was gathering to spend the night.

Laying a hundred bonfires, they began to boil, broil and grill. Tables groaned with meat, rivers of spirits flowed; the nobility meant to eat, drink and sing the night out. Gradually, they began to drowse and yawn. Eye after eye drooped shut. The head of every man began to nod. All dozed off where they sat, one over his bowl, another over his cup, still another over his joint of beef. Sleep, Death's brother, had vanquished the victors.

NOTES

1. Lel and Polel or *Lelum* and *Polelum*: Castor and Pollux in pagan Slavic mythology. The Polish Romantic poet and dramatist Juliusz Słowacki introduced them in his drama *Lilla Weneda*.
2. The constellation is also known as the Northern Crown; it resembles a broken ring of stars.
3. [*Author's note*] The constellation known to astronomers as *Ursa Major*.
4. [*Author's note*] It was customary to adorn the walls of churches with any fossil bones that might be discovered. The people regard them as bones of giants.
5. [*Author's note*] The memorable comet of the year 1811.
6. [Mickiewicz, *Konrad Wallenrod*] "When the plague is about to strike Lithuania, the eye of the seer divines its coming, for, if one may believe the bards, the Maid of Pestilence often appears in the desolate graveyards and meadows. She wears a white garment and has a fiery crown on her head. Her brow towers over the trees of Białowieża, and in her hand she waves a bloody kerchief."
7. Marcin Poczobut Odlanicki, an ex-Jesuit, was rector of the University of Wilno in the years 1780-1799 and founder of the Wilno Observatory. "Father Poczobut [notes Mickiewicz], published a work on the Zodiac of Denderah and by his observations aided Joseph Jérôme Lalande [1732-1807] in calculating the motions of the moon. See the biography by Jan Śniadecki."
8. Jan Śniadecki (1756-1830), a distinguished Polish mathematician, astronomer, and philosopher. In the poet's student years he was professor (and later rector) at the University of Wilno. His hostility to romanticism in Polish literature was attacked by Mickiewicz in his poem *Romantyczność*.
9. At Jassy, in Romania, peace was concluded in 1792 between Russia and Turkey. The poet presents Franciszek Ksawery Branicki (d. 1819), one of the founders of the Targowica Confederacy, as the first to rush to Potemkin's camp at Jassy where negotiations with the Turks were in progress. In fact, he arrived after Szczęsny Potocki, Rzewuski, and other opponents of the Constitution of the Third of May 1791.
10. Scholars are in doubt as to which Sapieha, if any, is meant, ascribing the reference to the Steward's fertile imagination.
11. A prose panegyric in honor of King Jan III Sobieski by the Jesuit Wojciech Bartochowski (1640-1708). It was published in Kalisz in 1684. Its full title is *Fulmen Orientis Joannes II, rex Poloniarum ter maximus*.
12. The reference is to Jakub Kazimierz Rubinkowski's *Janina zwycięskich triumfów Jana III* (The Victorious Triumphs of the Janina), published in Poznań in 1739. The *Janina* is the coat of arms of the Sobieski family.
13. Adam Kazimierz Czartoryski (1734-1823), a cousin of King Stanisław Poniatowski, director of the Warsaw Military Academy and one of the leading men of his time in Poland and Russia.
14. [*Author's note*] Properly, Prince de Nassau-Siegen (1745-1808), a famous warrior and adventurer of those times. He was a Muscovite admiral and [in 1788] defeated the Turks in the [Dnieper] bay near Ochakov; later, he was himself defeated by the Swedes. He spent some time in Poland, where he was granted the *indygenat* [full rights of citizenship extended to

a foreigner—C. Z.]. The combat of the Prince de Nassau with the tiger was noised abroad at the time by all the newspapers of Europe.

15. At the point of death (Latin).

16. I.e., the Grand Duchy of Warsaw.

17. The *świtezianka*, an undine or water sprite inhabiting Świteź, a forest-enclosed lake in the vicinity of Nowogródek. Apparently, an invention of Mickiewicz and not an authentic folk belief as the poet suggests.

18. The poet refers to this half-mythical snake of ancient Lithuania in the text and notes of his narrative poem *Grażyna*. According to ethnographers Jan Łasicki and Maciej Stryjkowski, whom the poet cites, the reptile was said to enter a peasant's hut and breathe over the sleeping inmates, thereby fortifying them with the life of the earth, imparting health, strength, etc.

19. The macaronisms reveal the limits of Gervase's command of Latin.

20. Manlius Marcus, called *Capitolinus*. Commander of the garrison during the siege of the Roman Capitol by the Gauls in 390 B.C. Awakened by the cries of the geese, he repelled a surprise night assault by the enemy and saved Rome.

21. According to popular belief, notes Mickiewicz, *Chochlik* was an arch sprite who led wayfarers astray by appearing as a will-of-the-wisp (*ignis fatus*). He appears as a character in Juliusz Słowacki's tragedy *Balladyna* (1834).

BOOK IX

The Battle

Argument

On the perils consequent upon disorderly encampment. Unexpected succor. The sorry plight of the nobility. The almsman's visit, a portent of rescue. Major Plut's excessive gallantry brings down a storm on his head. A pistol shot, the signal for battle. The Baptizer's exploits, Matthias' exploits and perils. Watering Can's ambush saves the manor. Cavalry reinforcements, assault on the infantry. Tadeusz's feats of valor. The leaders' duel cut short by an act of treachery. The Steward tips the balance of the battle by a decisive maneuver. Gervase's bloody exploits. The Chamberlain, a magnanimous victor.

So soundly did the nobility sleep that neither the flickering glow of the lanterns nor the irruption of several dozen men roused them from their slumbers. The intruders fell upon them even as the wall spider known as the harvestman[1] alights on a drowsy fly. Scarcely has his victim time to emit a sound when the grim assassin enfolds it in his long legs and throttles the life out of it. The nobility slumbered sounder than any fly, not a peep out of anyone; all lay as dead, though strong hands seized and turned them bodily like sheaves for the binding. Only Matthias Watering Can, who held his liquor better than any reveler in the district, who was capable of draining half a hogshead of linden mead[2] before growing unsteady on his legs or slurring his speech, only Matthias, though he'd feasted long and slept soundly, showed any sign of life. He opened one eye. Horrors! What a sight! Two wraith-like mustachioed faces bent directly above him. He felt their breath on his cheeks, their whiskers brushing his lips; two pairs of hands whirred like wings over his body. Terrified, he tried to bless himself, but he found his arm pinned to his side. He tried to move his left arm. Alas! The wraiths had swathed him up tighter than a new-born babe. More appalled than ever, he shut his eyes and lay motionless. His blood ran cold. You would have sworn he was dead.

But Baptizer struggled to defend himself. Too late! they'd constrained him with his own belt. Undeterred, he curled himself into a ball and flipped forward onto his feet with such *élan* that he landed prone on the chests of his sleeping companions. Rolling clear of their heads, he began to toss about like a jackfish on a sandy shore and roar like a bear, for he had a lusty pair of lungs. "Treachery!" he bellowed. Instantly the roused nobility picked up the chorus, "Treachery! Murder! Treachery!"

Their cries echoed all the way up to the hall of mirrors where the Warden, the Count and his jockeys were sleeping. Awakened by the noise, Gervase struggled to rise only to find himself stretched and bound on his rapier. Looking up, he saw a body of armed men in short black shakos and green tunics standing by the window. One of them was girt with a sash and directing his underlings with the point of his sword. "Bind them! Bind them!" he whispered. At his feet lay the jockeys, all trussed up like sheep for the shearing. The Count was in a sitting posture, unbound but disarmed; two riflemen stood guarding him with naked bayonets. Gervase recognized them at once: Muscovites!

Now the Warden had often found himself in such straits. Not seldom had he been bound hand and foot and yet always he'd managed to set himself free. Being uncommonly strong and full of resource, he had ways of bursting his bonds. The situation requiring craft, he closed his eyes and feigned to sleep on. Straightening his limbs by degrees, he took a deep breath, and shrinking his belly to the utmost began to hunch up and stretch and arch his body. As the molting snake draws its head and tail into its coils, so Gervase the long grew short and stout. The cords stretched, creaked, even, but they refused to snap. Ashamed and dismayed, Gervase rolled over, buried his face angrily in the ground, and shutting his eyes lay still as a stone.

A battery of snare drums suddenly broke out into a slow roll that grew steadily faster and louder; at this given signal, the Muscovite officer gave orders for the Count and his jockeys to be confined under guard in the castle hall, and the nobility escorted back to the manor where the other company of yagers was stationed. In vain Baptizer fumed and tossed.

The staff officers waited for them in the yard. With them stood a large number of armed noblemen, the Podhajski, the Birbaszes, the Hreczechas and Biergels, all friends and kinsmen of the Judge. On hearing of the raid, they had hastened to his relief, all the more eagerly, as they'd long been at loggerheads with the Dobrzyński.

Who had summoned the Muscovite battalion from the villages? Who so quickly mustered the nobility from the neighboring settlements? Was it the Assessor? The innkeeper Jankiel? All kinds of rumors made the rounds, but no one knew with certainty, either then or later.

By now it was growing light. The sun, blood-red, dull-edged and beamless, glowed half visible among the inky clouds like a horseshoe embedded in the forge's coals. A keen wind sprang up from the east, driving the scud along like jagged lumps of ice; each passing streamer sprinkled a chilly drizzle. No sooner did the wind dry the rain than another moisture-laden rack came driving up, and so by turns the day was wet and cold.

Meanwhile, the Major ordered his men to haul down logs from the woodpile by the house. This done, he had them hew out semicircular notches at regular intervals along the length of each log, thrust the prisoners' legs into the notches, lower another log on top, and nail the ends together so that the two beams fastened around the ankles like a bulldog's jaws. Still tighter were the captives' hands bound behind their backs; and to add to their torment, Plut had their caps struck off, their cloaks, robes, tunics and *taratatkas* torn from their backs. So ranged and confined in the stocks they sat, teeth chattering in the growing cold and wet. In vain Baptizer fumed and tossed.

Bootless the Judge's appeals on the nobility's behalf! Bootless Sophy's tears and Telimena's pleas that the prisoners be more humanely treated. Doubtless the Captain would have allowed himself to be swayed, for deep down, though a Muscovite, Nikita Rykov was a decent sort. But what could he do? Major Plut was a man to be obeyed.

The Major, a Pole by birth, hailed from the village of Dzierowicze.[3] Common report had it that his real name was Płutowicz and that after converting to the Orthodox faith he'd russified it to Plut. A scoundrel he most certainly was,[4] as is so often the case when a Pole turns renegade in the service of the Tsar. Arms akimbo, pipe in mouth, he stood facing his troops, cocking his nose at the petitioners as they came bowing and begging before him; at last, replying with a surly plume of smoke, he stalked off toward the house.

Meanwhile, the Judge worked on appeasing Rykov. Taking the Assessor aside as well, he sought their advice on how they might end the affair out of court, and, above all without alerting the authorities.

"Sir!" said Rykov, approaching Major Plut. "What use are all these prisoners? Shall we drag them before the court? Think of the grief it will inflict on the nobility, and there's not a kopeck in it for us. Know what I think, Major? Better settle the matter amicably. Let the Judge repay us for our trouble, and we'll say we dropped in for a visit. This way the goat will be safe and the wolf satisfied. Remember the Russian proverb, 'All's possible that's prudently done.' Or this one: 'Broil your portion on the Emperor's skewer.' Or this one: 'Harmony's better than discord.' Come, sir, tie a good knot and stick the ends in the water. We'll make no report and no one will be the wiser. 'God made hands to be greased.' Now there's a Russian saw!"

Hearing this, Plut rose to his feet and snorted indignantly: "Rykov, are you mad? This is the Tsar's service! Service isn't chumship, you know. Stupid old Rykov! Have you taken leave of your senses? Release these troublemakers? In times of war like these? Hah, you Polish lordlings! I'll teach you rebellion! Hah, you rascal Dobrzyński nobles! I know you! Let the scum enjoy a good soaking! (And looking out the window he gave out a roar of laughter.) Why, that same Dobrzyński sitting over there with his coat on … Hey, you there, tear his coat off! … that same Dobrzyński over there picked a quarrel with me at last year's masquerade ball. Who started it? Why, him of course, not me! 'Show the thief the door!' he yelled while I was engaged in a dance. Being then under suspicion of having my hand in the regimental till, I was greatly put out. Anyhow, what business was it of his? There I was dancing the mazurka and he shouts 'Thief!' behind my back, and the nobility chorus 'Hear! Hear!' after him. Insulted me, see? Now I have the rascal in my clutches. 'Hey, Dobrzyński!' I say to him. 'So the goat comes to the cart, eh? Now you'll see what's what, eh Dobrzyński? You're in for the switch.'"

And leaning over he whispered into the Judge's ear: "So, Your Honor, if you want to get off lightly, it'll run you a cool thousand rubles per head, in cash. A thousand rubles. That's my final word."

The Judge tried to bargain with him, but the Major remained adamant. Once again he began to strut up and down the room, trailing thick clouds of smoke like a rocket or lighted squib. In vain the women ran begging and weeping after him.

"Major," said the Judge, "so you take the matter to court. What's the good of it? No battle was fought, no blood spilt. So they helped themselves to some chicken and smoked goose. Very well then, they shall make recompense according to the law. But I'll not lodge a complaint against the Count. A neighborly squabble, that's all it was."

"Ever read the Yellow Book?"[5] said the Major. "What yellow book?"

"Better than your Book of Statutes," said Plut. "Full of words like, 'Siberia,' 'gallows,' 'noose,' and 'knout'—aye, the book of martial law that stands proclaimed throughout all of Lithuania. Your courts are worthless now. According to the wartime decrees, your prank will earn you a stint of hard labor in Siberia at least."

"I'll appeal to the Governor," said the Judge.

"Appeal to the Emperor, if it pleases you," said Plut. "You know full well that when the Tsar consents to ratify a sentence, he's as likely to double the penalty. So, by all means, Judge, launch an appeal. If need be, I'll find something to pin on you too. That spy Jankiel whose movements the authorities have long been watching is a tenant of yours. Bides his time in his tavern, eh? If I cared to, I could arrest the lot of you on the spot."

"Arrest me?" exclaimed the Judge. "You'd dare? Without orders?"

Just as their exchange was turning into a fierce contest, a new guest drove into the courtyard. A bizarre, tumultuous cortege! Gamboling ahead of it like a ceremonial runner came a huge black wether, its head bristling with four horns, one pair decked with bells and arched around the ears, the other branching sideways with small brass globes dangling from the tips. A herd of bullocks followed, then a flock of sheep, then goats, and behind the livestock rolled four heavy-laden ox-wagons.

No one could mistake the arrival of the Bernardine almsman. The Monk, face half-hidden by his hood, drove the first wagon. They recognized him at once when, riding past the prisoners, he turned and signed to them with his finger. Nor did the driver of the second wagon escape recognition. It was old Matthias Birch, dressed in rural weeds. The moment he came into view, a loud cheer went up from the nobility. "Stupid fools!" he growled back at them before silencing them with a peremptory wave of his hand. The Prussian, clad in a threadbare capote, drove the third wagon, while Zan and Mickiewicz brought up the rear in the fourth.

Meanwhile, observing the sorry plight of their Dobrzyn brethren, the Podhajski, the Isajewiczes, the Kotwiczes, Birbaszes, Biergels and Wilbiks felt their old animosities cool. For, the Polish nobility, though prone to ructions and easily provoked to combat, are not vindictive. Seeking counsel, they ran in a body to Matthias; he, in turn, marshaled them around the wagons and bade them wait.

The Bernardine entered the parlor. He was wearing his usual monk's habit, but they scarcely recognized him. Normally solemn and preoccupied of mien, he now held his head erect, face beaming like a jovial friar's. Before addressing the inmates, he gave out a long hearty laugh:

"Ha! Ha! Ha! Ha! Greetings! Greetings! Ha! Ha! Ha! Splendid! Well done! Most sportsmen stalk by day, but you, my dear officers, stalk by night. Excellent hunting!—I've seen your game. Oh, pluck 'em, pluck 'em, I say. Skin 'em. Rein 'em in, as our nobility's a restive steed. Major, I congratulate you on bagging our young Count. Lots of meat on him. Moneybags! A sire of ancient lineage! Have him cough up three hundred ducats for his release, and while you're about it, spare three groats for me and my convent, for I'm always praying for your soul. We Bernardines give serious thought to the state of the soul. Does death not snatch even staff-officers by the ear? As Baka wrote,[6] *'Death rends the purple by the yard, / Plants heavy blows on broadcloth too, / With equal zest he scissors linen, / And army serge, and cowls, and curls.'* Aye, Baka puts it well: *'Death's an onion, fetcher of tears, / Takes all to his bosom, spares none, / Nor sleeping tot, nor boozing sot.'* Aye, Major, now we drink, anon we rot! Ours but what we eat and sup today. Apropos, dear Judge, is it not time we broke fast? I take my seat at the table and bid you all join me. Major, what say you to beef stew and gravy? Lieutenant, what is your fancy? A bowl of punch?"

"Indeed, Father," agreed the two officers, "high time we ate and pledged the Judge's health."

The household gaped in amazement at the Monk. Whence came this new manner and jovial air! The Judge ordered the cook to bring in the punch bowl, sugar, bottles, and beef. Plut and Rykov fell to with such keen dispatch that in the space of a half-hour they'd downed two dozen beef collops and drained several quart vessels of punch.

At last, Plut, replete and in genial spirits, leaned back in his chair. He took out his pipe, lit it with a banknote, and wiping his lips with the tip of a napkin turned his mirthful eyes to the womenfolk.

"Now, pretty ladies," he said, "you shall be my dessert. By my major's epaulets, after a breakfast of stewed beef there's no better relish than a chat with pretty ladies such as yourselves. Eh, pretty ladies? A round of cards? *Elb Zvelb*?[7] Whist? Or what say we dance a mazurka? Eh? Three hundred devils strike me dead if I ain't the finest mazurka dancer in the regiment!" And saying this, he leaned over toward the women, spreading compliments and clouds of smoke.

"Yes, let's dance!" cried the Monk. "When in my cups even I, a Bernardine monk, am not averse to hiking up my habit and treading the odd measure. But look you, Major, here we sit drinking while your yagers stand frozen to the bone outside. Now carousing's carousing! Judge, send out a keg of vodka! The Major won't mind. Let our brave yagers enjoy a tipple."

"Indeed, why not?" said the Major. "But I don't insist."

"Make it a keg of pure spirits," whispered Robak to the Judge; and so, while the officers drank merrily in the house, the men outside went on a spree of their own.

Captain Rykov downed his liquor sturdily in silence; meanwhile, the Major caroused and paid court to the women of the house. Finally, itching to dance, he threw down his pipe and seized Telimena by the hand, but she promptly tore herself free. Then turning to Sophy, he bowed unsteadily and begged for the honor of a mazurka.

"Rykov!" he cried. "Stop puffing on your pipe. Put it away! You're handy with the balalaika. See the guitar there? Strike us up a mazurka. As commanding officer, I'll take the top of the dance."

The Captain picked up the guitar and began tuning the strings. Once more the Major sought to entice Telimena to a dance.

"I give you my major's word, dear lady, call me no Russky if I lie. May I be a son of a bitch if I do! Ask around if you doubt me. The officers—indeed, the whole army—will tell you that in the Second Army, Ninth Corps, Second Infantry Division, Fiftieth Yager Regiment, there's no mazurka dancer equal to Major Plut. So, come, little lady, do not be skittish or we shall have to serve you out, officer-style."

With that he sprang to his feet, seized Telimena by the hand and smacked her white shoulder with a loud kiss. Instantly, Tadeusz leapt up from aside and dealt him a resounding slap across the face. Kiss and slap rang out in rapid succession like a brisk repartee.

Thunderstruck, Plut rubbed his eyes. "Rebellion! Rebel!" he roared, pale with rage, and drawing his sword drove furiously at Tadeusz; but the Bernardine pulled a pistol from his sleeve.

"Shoot, boy!" he cried. "Shoot like the blazes."

Tadeusz seized the small-bore from his hand and took aim. The charge exploded. The shot went wide, but it stunned the Major and blackened him with powder. Rykov leapt up, guitar in hand. "Rebellion! Rebellion!" he cried, and made toward Tadeusz, but at that moment, the Steward who sat across from the two officers swung back his arm and let fly. The blade sang through the air between their heads and struck home even before they saw it flash; it smote the guitar box and went clean through. Rykov dodged smartly aside, narrowly escaping with his life, but that brush with death gave him a nasty fright.

"Yagers! Rebellion! By thunder!" he cried out, and drawing his sword backed away toward the vestibule.

Just then a large host of the nobility burst into the house at the far end of the room. In through the windows they swarmed, rapiers drawn, Matthias at their head. Plut and Rykov ran to the door, yelling for help. Three yagers nearest the house answered their summons: three gleaming bayonets poked through the door, three stooping black shakos came gliding in behind. Like a cat lying in wait for a rat Matthias stood by the door, his back to the wall, his Birch upraised. He struck a terrible blow; it would have trimmed all three heads from their necks, but, alas, weak eyesight, or perhaps an excess of dispatch, caused the old master to lunge prematurely. Before the necks could show themselves, he smote on the shakos and swept them off, bringing his sword down on the bayonets with a heavy clang. The Muscovites drew back. Matthias raced into the courtyard after them.

Outside reigned even greater confusion. Soplica's men were frantically tearing at the stocks, vying with one another to be the first to free the captives. The yagers, seizing their muskets, flew at them. Bursting in upon the stocks, a sergeant ran Podhajski through with his bayonet, wounded two others, and fired upon a third. The nobility took to their heels.

All this occurred close to where Baptizer sat confined. His hands now free and ripe for battle, he rose to his feet, doubled his long-fingered fist and brought it down sheer upon the Russian's back. So hard was the blow that it rammed the sergeant's brow into the musket firelock. The hammer clicked, but the blood-soaked powder failed to ignite; the sergeant pitched full length on his weapon at Baptizer's feet. Bending down, Dobrzyński seized the musket by the barrel, gave it a flourish like a sprinkling broom, and whirling it over his head smote two privates across the shoulders. A corporal caught a crashing blow on the head; the rest of the yagers took fright and backed away from the stocks. Just so Baptizer raised a whirling roof over the heads of his brethren.

At last the stocks were broken, the last cords cut. No sooner freed than the nobility made for the Bernardine's wagons, there helping themselves to rapiers, sabers, broadswords, scythes, and muskets. Watering Can found a bag of shot and two blunderbusses. Pouring powder into the muzzle of his own gun and priming the other, he handed it to Baptizer's son Sack.

More yagers appeared. A tight scuffle ensued. Denied elbow-room, the nobility could neither cut nor parry, nor could the yagers fire their muskets. They fought it out at close quarters, exchanging blow for blow. Steel clashed on steel, blades shivered, sword broke on bayonet, scythe on crossguard. Thrust met thrust. Fist met fist.

Rykov and a handful of yagers made a dash for the barn where it backed onto the paddock fence. From his fresh command post there the Captain shouted orders to break off the disorderly combat, as deprived of the use their muskets his yagers were succumbing to the enemy's fists. Infuriated by his inability to open fire—there was no way of telling Pole and Muscovite apart—he cried *"Стройся!"* (which means "fall in!" in Russian), but in the din no one heard the command.

Meanwhile, ill-suited to close-quarters combat, old Matthias fell back. Left and right he flailed, clearing a space for himself: here with the tip of his Birch he sheared bayonet from barrel like a wick from a candle; there, lunging lustily, he cut and jabbed. Even so did wary old Matthias retire to open ground.

He found himself pressed hardest by a seasoned old *Gefreiter*,[8] the regimental instructor and grand champion of bayonet exercise. Gathering his strength and drawing himself up, the Gefreiter tightened his grip around his rifle—right hand over the firelock, left midway up the forestock—and launched into a series of twists and turns, leaps and squats, now dropping his left arm and thrusting his weapon with snake-strike speed with his right, now drawing it back and resting it on his knee.

Taking due note of his opponent's skill, Dobrzyński rammed his spectacles over the bridge of his nose with one hand, and holding Birch close to his chest with the other backed away, warily eying the Gefreiter's every movement. He feigned a drunken lurch. Emboldened by this action, the Gefreiter lunged forward. To reach the retreating Matthias, he was forced to rise and thrust with his weapon to the full extent of his right arm. Such was the weight and momentum of the musket that he lost his balance, and here Matthias rammed his sword-hilt in between the bayonet and barrel, heaved the musket into the air, and bringing Birch down took a slice at the Muscovite's arm; then, swinging lustily again, he split open his jaw. Thus fell the finest *fechtmeister*[9] of all the Russias, knight of three military crosses and four-time medal winner.

Meanwhile, out by the stocks, the nobility's left flank was on the verge of victory. There, conspicuous in the distance, fought Baptizer. Yonder ran Razor, weaving in among the Muscovites, unseaming torsos even as Baptizer bludgeoned skulls. Even as that brainchild of German masters which we call a thresher, though, having both flails and blades, it doubles as a chaff-cutter—even as that fell engine slices through stalks and threshes the grain, so Baptizer and Razor wrought their combined havoc on the enemy, one from above, the other from below.

With victory virtually assured, Baptizer made for the right flank, where a new peril threatened Matthias. A young ensign eager to avenge the Gefreiter's death was harrying the old man with a long spontoon (something between a pike and axe, now obsolete in the infantry though still used in the navy). The ensign weaved nimbly from side to side; each time Dobrzyński knocked aside his weapon and stepped smartly out of reach. Unable to shake him off or cut him, Matthias could only parry his thrusts. Already his opponent had gashed him slightly, and now, raising his pike, the ensign stood poised for the killing blow. Despairing of reaching Matthias in time, Gervase halted in mid-stride, swung his weapon and sent it hurtling with bone-shattering force at the yager's legs. The ensign released his halberd and slumped to the ground. Again Baptizer charged, a body of noblemen followed, but scattered units of yagers from the left flank pursued them, and thus a fresh skirmish began to rage around Baptizer.

In order to save Matthias, Baptizer had sacrificed his weapon. The deed almost cost him his life. Two strapping yagers leapt on him from behind, buried their hands in his hair, and steadying their feet pulled on him like wherrymen on the vessel's halyards. Baptizer lashed back with random punches. No use! he began to keel over. Catching sight of Gervase who was fighting close by, he cried out, "*Jesu Maria!* Jackknife!"

Sensing Baptizer's plight by the urgency of his voice, Gervase whirled round and swung his rapier down hard between Dobrzyński's head and the yagers' arms.

With cries of terror they recoiled, but a severed hand hung ensnarled and ensanguined in the hair. Just so, in its frenzied struggle with a young eagle that seizes it with one set of claws while anchoring itself to a tree with the other, the hare rips the bird apart so that one bloodied set of claws remains fastened to the tree in the forest and the other is borne away into the fields by the fleeing hare.

Free once more, Baptizer cast his eyes about, stretched out his arms, sought for a weapon, *yelled* for a weapon, all the while brandishing his fists and manfully standing his ground at the Warden's side; at last, he caught sight of his son Sack in the melee. The lad was aiming his blunderbuss with one hand and dragging behind him a gnarled, fathom-long tree-trunk with the other. (No one could have lifted it except Baptizer.)[10] Seeing his cherished Sprinkler, Dobrzyński seized it up, pressed it to his lips, then leaping in the air for joy whirled it over his head and promptly imbrued it in blood.

Idle to sing of the wondrous feats he went on to perform! Idle to sing of the carnage he wrought on every hand! No one would believe the Muse. Neither did anyone believe the old woman who, from her point of vantage atop Wilno's Ostra Gate, saw the Russian General Deyov[11] entering the city. Even as they swung open the gate, a townsman surnamed Czarnobacki slew Deyov and put his entire Cossack regiment to rout.

Enough to say things came to pass exactly as Rykov had foreseen. The hampered yagers fell before the stronger foe. Twenty three lay dead in the dust. Another thirty or so lay groaning from various wounds. Many fled into the orchard and hop field; some made for the river, others ran to the house seeking safety among the womenfolk.

Shouting for joy, the jubilant nobility dashed off, some in search of kegs of spirits, others plunder and booty. The Monk alone refused to share in their triumph. He'd refrained from taking part in the fighting (canon law strictly forbids a priest to engage in combat); nevertheless, he had imparted expert advice and made a complete circuit of the battlefield. With a glance here, a hand signal there, he put the fighting men on their mettle and cheered them to the assault; now he was calling on them to join him in a strike on Rykov and press home the advantage. Meanwhile, he dispatched a runner to the Captain informing him that if the yagers laid down their arms, he would spare their lives; if they delayed, he would have them encircled and cut down to a man.

But Captain Rykov was far from begging quarter. Mustering the half-battalion around him, he cried out, "Ready!" With a loud clatter the yagers shouldered their loaded muskets. "Level!" he cried. A long line of barrels flashed upward. "Fire by volley!" he cried. One company after another, they discharged their guns. One fired, another loaded, still another stood at the ready. Musket balls zipped, firelocks crashed, ramrods thudded home. The line put one in mind of a wood louse with its hundred gleaming legs all beating at once. But strong spirits had addled the yagers' brains. Their aim was poor, and they fired wide; few inflicted wounds and scarcely one killed his man. Even so, two Matthiases fell wounded and one Bartholomew went down to the dust. The nobility, replying sparingly with the odd harquebus, were all for flying at the enemy with their sabers, but the older men restrained them; meanwhile, bullets whizzed thickly around them, hitting some, driving others back. Before long the musketry cleared the yard, and now there were balls patting around the manor windows.

All this time Tadeusz had remained indoors on the Judge's orders guarding the womenfolk. On seeing the battle take a turn for the worse, he ran out into the yard. The Chamberlain hastened after him (his valet Thomas having at last fetched him his saber). In short order, he joined the nobility, took his place at their head, and raising his saber led them in a charge. The yagers hung fire, allowed them to approach, then raked the line with a hail of lead. Isajewicz was killed on the spot. Wilbik and Razor fell wounded. Robak and Matthias, who stood at either flank, halted the charge. Unnerved, the nobility began to look around and fall back; and now Captain Rykov decided to mount a final strike, to sweep the courtyard clean and storm the house.

"Prepare to attack!" he cried. "Fix bayonets! Quick march!"

Heads lowered, rifle barrels thrust out like a rack of antlers, the line advanced, gradually quickening its pace. Powerless to stem the onset head-on, the nobility fired from the flanks. By now the yagers had cleared half the courtyard.

"Soplica!" shouted the Captain, pointing his sword at the manor door. "Lay down your arms or I'll burn you out."

"Burn away!" said the Judge. "I'll fry you in the flames."

O Soplica Manor! If your whitewashed walls still stand under the limes,[12] if the nobility still gather there to feast at the generous board of their neighbor Judge Soplica, then surely they must drink the health of Matthias Watering Can, for without him the manor would be no more.

Thus far Matthias had shown little proof of valor. Though he was the first to be freed from the stocks and retrieve his beloved blunderbuss and bag of shot, he was loath to enter into the fray. He always said he could never trust himself on an empty stomach; and so, having first approached a vat of pure spirits standing nearby, he scooped up generous quantities of the liquor with his hands and gulped it down. Only when he'd adequately warmed and refreshed himself did he right his cap, seize his blunderbuss from between his knees, ram home a charge, sprinkle the pan, and take a survey of the field. He saw the wave of gleaming bayonets dashing over and scattering the nobility. Thither he swam, to meet the wave! Head down, he plunged into the long grass in the center of the courtyard where the nettles grew thick; and there, signaling to Sack with his hand, he lay down in ambush.

Sack was standing with his blunderbuss outside the manor house, home of his sweet Sophy whom he still loved dearly and would gladly die for, though she'd spurned his addresses. As the yagers waded into the nettles, Watering Can discharged his gun; a dozen chopped-up bullets poured from the flared muzzle into the Muscovite line. Sack let fly a dozen more from the porch. The yagers fell into a panic. Surprised by the ambush, the extended line huddled up into a ball and drew back, abandoning their wounded to Baptizer who promptly dispatched them with his Sprinkler.

It now being too far to return to the barn, Rykov, fearing a drawn-out retreat, made smartly for the garden fence. Checking his company in their flight, he drew them up again, only this time he changed their formation. From a single line he formed a triangle with its apex projecting forward like a wedge and its two sides extending back to the garden fence. He did well to do this, as just then a body of horsemen came bearing down on them from the castle.

Confined in the castle until the guards panicked and fled, the Count had ordered his men to mount up. Hearing the detonations of the musketry, he urged his riders into the firing line—he at their head, his sword raised aloft.

"Half-battalion, open fire!" roared Rykov.

A fiery thread ran the length of the line of leveled guns as the pans ignited and three hundred whining musket balls sped from the blackened barrels. Three riders fell wounded, another lay lifeless in the dust. The Count's charger took a ball and tumbled, unhorsing its rider. Seeing the yagers train their guns on the last male representative of the Horeszko line (albeit on the spindle side), Gervase gave out a yell and ran to his aid, but Robak, who happened to be nearer, flung himself in front of the Count and took the bullet intended for him. Dragging the Count from under the horse, he led him away, all the while shouting to the nobility to spread out, take better aim, save ammunition, and seek cover behind the fence, well paling, and cowshed. As to the Count and his horsemen, a more favorable occasion was soon to present itself.

Tadeusz understood Robak's plan and executed it to perfection. He took cover behind the well, and being sober and skilled in the use of a double (he could hit a złoty piece tossed in the air), he wrought havoc on the Muscovites, picking off the officers one by one. With his first shot, he struck down the sergeant major, then discharging one barrel after the other felled two more sergeants. Time and again he fired, here at a gold braid, there into the midst of the triangle where the officers stood. Rykov fumed with rage, stamping his foot, gnawing at his sword-knot.

"Major Plut!" he cried. "What's to become of us? At this rate, there'll be no one left to take charge."

In an access of fury Plut called out to Tadeusz: "You! Pole! Shame on you for hiding behind a bit of board. Are you a coward? Come out into the open! Fight with honor as befits a soldier!"

"Major," Tadeusz replied. "If you are so brave a knight, why cower inside a ring of yagers? I do not fear you. Come away from the fence! I dealt you one across the face and stand ready to deal another in close combat. What's the use of this bloodshed? The quarrel's between us. Let sword or pistol settle the matter! Choose your weapon—field-piece, poniard, it's all one to me. Refuse, and I'll pick you off like wolves in their lair!"

So saying he fired off another round with such truth of aim that he felled the lieutenant standing next to Rykov.

"Major," whispered Rykov. "Go and fight this duel! Avenge his earlier slight to your honor. Depend on it, if someone else kills this Polish lord, you'll never wash away the disgrace. You must lure him into the open. Since firearms won't do the job, kill him with the sword. Old Suvorov used to say, 'Rifles are trifles. The trick is to stick 'em.' So, Major, go out, or he'll pick us all off. See? He's taking aim again."

"Rykov, old friend," said the Major. "You're the ace with the blade. Go out yourself, my boy. Or, tell you what, we'll send one of the subalterns. As major here, I cannot desert my soldiers. I command the battalion after all."

Hearing this, Rykov raised his sword, stepped boldly out from behind the fence, and waving a white handkerchief called for a ceasefire. Tadeusz was offered his choice of arms. After discussion, the two agreed on foils. Since Tadeusz did not carry such a blade, they were obliged to find him one, but even as they were engaged in the search, the Count ran up, flourishing his *épée de combat*.

"Mr. Soplica," he said, interrupting the talks. "With all due respect, it was the major you called out, but I have an earlier grievance against the captain here, for it was he who broke into my castle—"

"*Our* castle, you mean!" broke in Protase from behind.

"—at the head of a band of robbers," finished the Count. "It was Rykov who had my jockeys bound. I recognize him. Now shall I punish him as I did those brigands on the crag the Sicilians call Birbante-Rocca."

There fell a deep silence. All shooting ceased as the two armies eagerly watched their champions meet on the field of combat. Facing sideways, the Count and Rykov closed distance, threatening each other with their right arm and eye; then, doffing their hats with the left hand, they bowed courteously (an honorable custom this, the principals exchanging greetings before proceeding to slaughter);

and engaging their blades, they clashed. Front leg thrusting, knee flexing, the contending knights leapt forwards and backwards in rapid succession.

Meanwhile, seeing Tadeusz directly opposite him, Plut conferred quietly with Corporal Gont, reckoned the finest marksman in the company.

"Gont," he whispered. "See that gallows' bird over there? Lodge a bullet under his fifth rib, and I'll see you get four rubles in silver."

Gont drew back the hammer of his musket, put his eye to the sights while his cronies covered him with their cloaks. He took aim, not at Tadeusz's rib, but his head. He fired. The bullet struck home—almost! It went clean through Tadeusz's hat. The youth spun round. Baptizer made for Rykov. The nobility, crying foul, followed him, but Tadeusz threw himself in their path, and Rykov, falling back, regained the safety of his ranks in the nick of time.

Once more the Dobrzyński and Lithuania went on the attack in a spirit of amicable rivalry. Their old differences set aside, they fought like brothers, each exhorting his comrade-in-arms. The Dobrzyński cheered at the sight of Podhajski prancing before the yager line and mowing it down with his scythe. "A Podhajski! A Podhajski!" they cried. "Forward, Lithuanian brothers! Hurrah! Hurrah for Lithuania!" The Skołubas, seeing the valiant Razor, though wounded, charge with sword upraised, yelled in reply, "A Dobrzyński! A Dobrzyński! Long live Mazovia!" So, urging each other on, they sallied forth against the Muscovite. In vain did Robak and Matthias try to restrain them.

Just as the nobility mounted this frontal assault on the yager company, the Steward quitted the battlefield and repaired to the garden. Protase padded warily beside him, paying close heed to his instructions.

In the garden, close to the fence that formed the base of Rykov's triangle, there stood a great old cheese house resembling a cage built of a latticework of beams lashed across one another. Several scores of gleaming white cheeses stood piled within, and all around hung bundles of drying herbs, sage, blessed thistle, wild thyme—in a word, the Steward's daughter's entire stock of herbal medicines. The cage measured four fathoms across, and the entire structure rested like a stork's nest on a great pillar of oak, which, being old and half-rotted, canted at a precarious angle and was in imminent danger of giving out. The Judge had often been urged to dismantle the decaying structure, but he always said he'd sooner repair than take it down, or at least have it erected elsewhere. He put off the business to a more favorable time; in the meantime, he had the old pillar propped up with two supports. Thus buttressed, the unstable structure reared above the fence, overlooking Rykov's triangle.

Armed with stout spear-like poles, the Steward and the Usher advanced stealthily through the hemp toward the cheese house. Behind them came the bailiff mistress and a kitchen boy—a small lad, but strong as they come. On reaching the spot, they thrust their poles deep into the top of the rotted pillar and hanging from the pole-ends began pulling down with all their might. Just so wherrymen thrust out from the river bank with long spars and heave their grounded vessel into deeper waters.

With a loud crack the pillar gave out. The cheese house tottered and crashed down on the Muscovite triangle with its load of beams and cheeses, crushing, killing and maiming at random. Where the yagers had been standing lay a wreckage of timbers, bodies and snow-white cheeses imbrued in blood and brain matter. Rykov's triangle was shattered into bits; and now Sprinkler, Razor and Birch broke inside. Sprinkler thundered! Razor flashed! Birch slashed! More noblemen came running in a body from the manor, and from the courtyard gate the Count set his horsemen on the scattered fugitives.

Eight yagers and their platoon sergeant held on. The Warden made a rush at them. The yagers stood their ground. Nine barrels stood aimed at a point sheer between his eyes. Straight into their sights he ran, brandishing Jackknife. The Monk, seeing Gervase's blind charge, ran across his path, dropped down on all fours and struck him off his feet; both men fell to the ground the instant the platoon fired. Scarcely had the hot lead whistled past over their heads when Gervase was up again, diving into the smoke. In an instant's compass, he'd hacked off two heads. The yagers fled in dismay. Gervase went after them, plying his rapier. They dashed across the yard, the Warden in hot pursuit. They ran into the open barn. Thither, panting on their heels, went Gervase. He vanished into the darkness. Still he did not desist from the fray! Groans, yells and heavy blows echoed from within. Soon all was quiet. Gervase emerged alone from the barn, his blade dripping with blood.

By now the nobility had taken the field and were busy pursuing, cutting down, and spiking the last of the scattered yagers. Only Rykov held out. He fought on, swearing he'd never lay down his arms; but then the Chamberlain, raising his saber, stepped forward and addressed him solemnly:

"Captain, you shall not stain your honor by accepting quarter. Brave, hapless knight! You have proved your valor. Give up this futile struggle. Lay down your arms before we disarm you with our sabers. Your life and honor are safe. You are my prisoner."

Swayed by the Chamberlain's solemn tone, Rykov bowed and surrendered his saber, the blade ensanguined to the hilt.

"My brother Poles," he said. "My misfortune was in not having a single cannon. Old Suvorov put it well. 'Remember, Comrade Rykov,' he used to say. 'Never venture against the Pole without a field-piece.' What can I say? My yagers were drunk.

The Major would have them swill. Ah, Major Plut! He's done enough mischief for one day. He'll answer to the Tsar, for he was in charge. As for me, Chamberlain, I shall be your friend. 'The better the shover, the better the lover' goes a Russian saw. Aye, you Poles! Good at the bottle and good in the battle, but, please, no more pranks on my yagers."

On hearing these words, the Chamberlain raised his saber and ordered the Court Usher to proclaim a general pardon. The wounded were tended, the dead cleared from the field, the remaining yagers disarmed and taken captive. Long they searched for Plut. The Major had plunged deep into the nettles and was playing dead. Eventually, he came out of hiding, but only after the battle was well and truly over. So ended the last armed foray in Lithuania.[13]

NOTES

1. The *Opilones* (syn. *Phalangida*) belong to a relatively numerous order of arachnids (over six thousand species). The most common of these is the "common harvestman." Whether this or any other of these species is quite the "grim assassin" (*mistrz strogi*) described by the poet is a matter of conjecture.

2. The text gives *dwa* (two) *antały*. The old-Polish *antal* was a small cask with a capacity of 18 *garncy*, which converted into today's system of measurements is equal to about 70 liters. Incredibly, Matthias Watering Can was capable of downing 140 liters (over 18 US liquid gallons) before showing the effects.

3. The fictitious name of Plut's birthplace suggests cheating, "skinning" (from *odzierać*).

4. *Plut* means "cheat" or "swindler" in Russian.

5. [*Author's note*] So called from its binding; the barbarous book of Russian martial law. Frequently in time of peace the government proclaims whole provinces as being in a state of war, and on the authority of the Yellow Book confers on the military commander complete power over the estates and lives of citizens. It is a well-known fact that from the year 1812 to the November Insurrection of 1831 all Lithuania was subject to the Yellow Book, of which the executor was the Grand Duke, the Tsarevich Constantine.

6. Józef Baka (1707-80), a Jesuit, the anonymous author of the humorous *Uwagi o śmierci nieuchybnej, wszystkim pospolitej* (Reflections on Inescapable Death, Common to All), published in Wilno, 1766. The collection of doggerel verse was highly popular during the poet's student years.

7. Plut's corruption of the German *Halb Zwölf* (half-twelve). The reference is to the French card game *Onze et demie*.

8. A senior private in the Tsarist Army.

9. Fencing master (German)

10. [*Author's note*] A Lithuanian battle club is made in the following manner: a young oak is selected and slashed from the bottom upwards with an axe, so that the bark and bast are cut through and the wood slightly wounded. Sharp flints are thrust into these notches and in time these grow into the tree to form hard knobs. Clubs in pagan times were the chief weapon of the Lithuanian infantry. They are still occasionally used and are called *nasieki* (gnarled clubs).

11. [*Author's note*] After Jasiński's insurrection when the Lithuanian armies retired toward Warsaw, the Muscovites arrived at the deserted city of Wilno. General Deyov at the head of the staff was entering through the Ostra Gate. The streets were empty; the townsfolk had shut themselves in their houses. One townsman, seeing a cannon abandoned in an alley, aimed it at the gate and fired, raking the thoroughfare with grapeshot. This single shot saved Wilno for a time. General Deyov and several officers perished. The rest, fearing an ambush, retired from the city. I do not know for certain the name of that townsman.

12. A lapse of memory on Mickiewicz's part: Book One states that these were birches and poplars.

13. [*Author's note*] Armed forays occurred even later still. Although not as famous, they were bloody all the same, and much talked of. About the year 1817, a man named U[złowski] in the Nowogródek Province led a successful foray against the garrison of Nowogródek and took its leaders captive.

BOOK X

Emigration • Jacek

Argument

The storm. Deliberations aimed at securing the fortunes of the victors. Talking terms with Rykov. The farewell. An important revelation. Hope.

The wraiths of scud, which since morning had been driving like a flock of black birds, kept massing together, rising ever higher in the sky. Scarcely had the sun gained his meridian when that massing flock swathed half the heavens in a vast band of cloud. Driven ever more swiftly by the wind, the great cloud grew denser, sank lower until, half torn from the sky on one side, it swung earthward, spread out along the horizon, and like a great sail gathering up all the currents of air swept the skies from south to west.

There came a moment of calm. The air fell still, as though stricken with fright. The cornfields stood stirless. A moment earlier they had been surging like seas, bending to the ground then recovering themselves with a toss of their golden spikes; now, stalks erect, they stared up at the sky. So, too, the green willows and poplars ceased bowing by the wayside like women plainers over an open grave. No longer did they thrash their limbs and spread their silver tresses on the wind. Now, as if palsied with grief, they stood lifeless like the rock of Niobe of Sipylos. Only the quaking aspen stirred her grayish leaves.

Normally loath to leave the pasturage, the cattle huddled up and trotted briskly homeward without waiting for the drovers. The bull pawed the ground and plowed it with his horn, bellowing balefully at the frightened herd. The milk cow, her mouth open wide with wonder, gazed large-eyed into the sky, sighing deeply; meanwhile, the laggard hog fretted, gnashed his teeth, and stealing into the grain made off with his plundered store of sheaves.

The birds hid away in the forest, under the thatch-eaves, in the tall grass. Only the crows continued to strut in solemn flocks around the pools. Tongues protruding from dry, distended throats, wings a-droop, they swept the jet clouds with their black eyes and awaited the coming bath; then sensing a storm of unwonted violence, they, too, rose up in a cloud and made for the forest. The fleet-winged swallow still braved the skies. Like an arrow he clove the thunder-head until, finally, he, too, dropped earthward like a spent bullet.

It was just then that the nobility had concluded their grim battle with the Muscovites. Seeking shelter of house and stable, they trooped off, abandoning the field to the elements, which now stood massing for their own battle. In the west, still gilded by the sun, the earth glowed a sullen reddish-yellow. Already the cloud was spreading its shadows like a net, snatching up the remnants of light and going after the sun, as though to enmesh him before he sank below. Whistling squalls sprang up, scattering bright raindrops, large, and round, and grainy like hailstones.

Suddenly, two dust whirls met. Seizing each other by the waist, they grappled, spun round, and whistling and twisting over the pools stirred the waters to their very depths. Down upon the meadows they swooped, shrilling through the grass and withy beds. Willow branches snapped, swathes of mown grass flew up like fistfuls of torn-out hair interwoven with curly locks of grain. The whirlwinds fell howling to the ground, rolled in the dust, plowed up and tore at the clod, spawning another twister that reared up in a column of black earth. Up it rose— a whirling, moving pyramid, its head boring into the ground, its feet kicking sand into the eyes of the stars. With each stride forward, the twister thickened, funneling out at the top until, with a triumphant blast, it blazoned the storm like a giant trumpet; and with all this chaos of water, dust, straw, leaves, branches and torn-up turf, the tempest smote the forest, roaring like a bear in the heart of the wilderness.

Drops came splashing down thick and fast like earth shaken through a sieve. A thunderclap rent the air. The rain coalesced into solid streams; now like taut cords binding earth to sky it fell in long tresses, now in broad sheets it poured, as if tossed bodily from a pail. Heaven and earth vanished under a mantle of dark-ness; the blackness of the night and the storm's inkier gloom blotted them from sight. Now and again the horizon split open from one end clear to the other. Like a colossal sun, the storm-angel flashed his face, then palled in darkness again drew back into the heavens and, with a thunderous peal, slammed shut the clouds behind him. Once more the tempest regained strength. Another thun-derous cascade! The gloom deepened, thickened as to become almost palpable. Again the torrent abated. For a moment the storm seemed to nod off; then again it awoke and rumbled. Once more the flood came down. At last, but for the steady patter of the rain and the soughing of the trees around the house, all grew still again.

Nothing could have been more welcome this day than a torrential downpour. After shrouding the battlefield in darkness, the rainstorm flooded the roads, swept away the bridges, and turned Soplica Manor into an unapproachable fortress. Thus news of the events at the Manor could not get out, and for the nobility it was precisely upon the circumstance of secrecy that the sway of the balance now hung.

Weighty deliberations went on in the Judge's room. The Bernardine lay on the bed, exhausted, pale and blood-stained, yet in full possession of his senses. Complying diligently with his orders, the Judge called in the Chamberlain, summoned the Warden, and bringing in Rykov closed the door. The secret negotiations progressed for an hour; finally, tossing a hefty purse of ducats on the table, Captain Rykov brought the talks to a stand.

"My Polish friends!" he said. "There is a common saying among you that every Muscovite's a scoundrel. Now you can tell anyone who cares to ask that you have met a Muscovite Captain—Nikita Nikitich Rykov by name. He holds eight medals and three crosses. I beg you remember it. See? This one for Ochakov, this for Izmailov, these two for Novi and Preussisch-Eylau,[1] and this here for Korsakov's glorious retreat from Zurich.[2] Be sure, also, to add that Rykov received a gift sword for gallantry, three commendations from the Field Marshal, and four citations along with two honorable mentions from the Tsar himself. And I've papers to prove—"

"Aye, Captain," broke in Robak, "but tell us what will happen to us if you refuse our terms. Did you not promise to hush up the affair?"

"So I did, and I pledge it again," said Rykov. "My hand and seal upon it! Why should I desire your ruin? I am an honest man. I like you Poles! You're a cheerful race, good for a tipple. Brave lads, too, good for a tussle. We have a Russian saying, 'Who rides a cart often finds himself beneath it.' 'Today you ride in front, tomorrow you're in the rear.' 'Today you best 'em, tomorrow you're worsted.' So, what's to be mad about? Such is the soldier's life! Why fret and sulk over a lost battle? Ochakov was a bloody affair. At Zurich, our infantry got soundly thrashed. On the fields of Austerlitz, I lost an entire company. Before that—I was a sergeant then—it was your Kościuszko at Racławice![3] His scythemen cut my platoon to ribbons. But what of it, I say. Later, at Maciejowice,[4] with my own bayonet I slew two of your brave noblemen. One was Mokronowski:[5] there he stood, swinging his scythe at the head of the line; he'd just sliced off the cannoneer's hand, lighted linstock and all. Oh, you Poles! The Fatherland! Rykov knows the meaning of the word. The Tsar gives the order, but I feel for you. What business have we with you, anyhow? Moscow for Muscovites, and Poland for Poles—that's what I say. But, alas, the Tsar won't hear of it."

"Captain," said the Judge. "Those who have provided your billets these many years know you to be an honest man. Do not take this gift amiss, my friend. We meant no offense. We made bold to collect these ducats only because we know you to be a poor man."

"Oh, my yagers!" lamented Rykov. "The whole company cut to ribbons. My company! And all thanks to Plut! He was the commanding officer and he'll answer to the Tsar. Keep those pennies of yours, gentlemen! I have my captain's pay, such as it is. It buys me my punch and tobacco. I like you Poles. With you I can eat and drink, hoot it up, and enjoy a good chat; in short, I can live. Rest assured I shall protect you, and when the inquiry comes round, on my word of honor, I shall testify in your favor. We'll say we dropped by for a visit, downed a few, hoofed the odd measure, and got a bit pie-eyed. Then Plut accidentally gave the order to open fire, a skirmish broke out, and somehow his battalion got the worst of it. Meanwhile, be sure to grease the commission's hand with gold, and all will be well. But I must tell you what I told this fellow with the long rapier here. Plut is in charge. I'm only second in command. Plut's alive. He may pull a fast one and sink you yet, for he's a sly customer. You'll need to stop up his mouth with banknotes. What say you, sir? You with the long rapier! Did you talk to Plut? Come to terms?"

Gervase looked around and stroked his bald pate; he made a vague motion with his hand, as if to signify he'd dealt with the matter.

"Well?" insisted Rykov. "Will Plut keep mum? Did he pledge his word?"

Vexed by Rykov's persistence, the Warden turned his thumb solemnly downward and made a motion with his hand, as if to cut short all further discourse.

"I swear by my Jackknife Plut shall not give us away. His lips are sealed!" he said, and lowering his arm snapped his fingers, as though he were dusting the matter from his hand.

Gervase's dark gesture was understood. His listeners stared at one another in amazement, each trying to guess the other's thoughts. There fell a moment of gloomy silence.

"So the fox pays his skin to the furrier," muttered Rykov at last.

"*Requiescat in pace!*"[6] said the Chamberlain.

"Clearly the hand of God," said the Judge. "But I am innocent of this blood. I knew nothing of it."

The Monk rose from the pillows and sat gloomily silent.

"It is a great sin to kill an unarmed captive," he said at last, eyeing the Warden sternly. "Christ forbids revenge, even on one's enemies. Oh, Warden, you shall answer heavily to God for this! One mitigating factor pertains: if the deed were done not from foolish vengeance but *pro publico bono.*"[7]

The Warden nodded, waved his hand, and blinking his eyes repeated the phrase, "*pro publico bono*."

There was no more talk of Major Plut. In vain they scoured the yard for him the morning after. They posted a reward for his body, but all to no purpose. The Major had vanished without a trace, as though he'd dropped into a well. Several conjectures as to his fate made the rounds, but no one knew with certainty either then or later. In vain they pestered Gervase with questions. No utterance passed his lips except "*pro publico bono*." The Steward was privy to the secret, but he'd pledged his word of honor, and so the old man's lips remained sealed as by a spell.

Having agreed to the terms, Rykov left the room; meanwhile, Robak had the fighting nobility called in.

"My brothers," said the Chamberlain, addressing them gravely. "This day God has smiled upon our arms, but I must be frank with you, gentlemen. Dire consequences shall follow from this untimely battle of ours. We have committed a blunder, and each one of us here is at fault: Father Robak for being overzealous in spreading the news, the Warden and the nobility for mistaking his purpose. The war with Russia will not be waged just yet; meanwhile, those who took a leading part in the battle are no longer safe in Lithuania. So, gentlemen, you must fly to the Duchy. I have in mind Tadeusz, Baptizer, Watering Can, and Razor. These named must fly across the Niemen where our nation's host awaits them. We shall lay the blame squarely on Plut and you fugitives and thus save the rest of your kin. I bid you farewell, but not for long, for there is every reason to hope that our liberty shall break forth this coming spring. Lithuania, which now bids you farewell as exiles, shall see you shortly as her conquering saviors. The Judge will attend to your journey, and I, insofar as I am able, shall help with the funds."

The nobility saw the wisdom of the Chamberlain's words. Well they knew that those who ran afoul of the Tsar never found true peace in this world; a man had either to fight or rot away in the Siberian wastes. And so, exchanging sorrowful glances in silence, they sighed and nodded assent. Though known the world over for their love of their land, which they hold dearer than life, Poles have always been ready to go abroad, faring forth to the ends of the earth, suffering years of privation and want, battling man and fate—enduring all this, so long as there shines through it all the hope of serving their country.

They agreed to depart without delay. The sole dissenting voice was Buchman's. A prudent man, he had stayed away from the battle, but on hearing of the council, he'd hurried over to cast his vote. Though favorable to the plan, he sought to elaborate on it. He pushed for certain amendments and clarifications. A formal committee had to be struck, the aims, ways, and means of emigration duly weighed, and many other things besides. But, alas, time was of the essence, and Buchman's motions were promptly shelved. The nobility bade a hasty farewell and at once set out on their journey.

But the Judge, holding Tadeusz back, turned to the Monk. "It is time I told you what I learned with certainty only yesterday. Our Tadeusz is truly in love with Sophy. Let him ask for her hand before he leaves. I have spoken with Telimena. She no longer opposes the match, and Sophia agrees to the will of her guardians. If we cannot wed the young couple today, then at least, dear brother, we may betroth them before the lad's departure. You know well the many temptations a young heart is subject to abroad. With a ring on his finger a youth has merely to glance at it, recall his betrothal, and the fever of foreign seductions cools at once. Believe me, a wedding ring possesses great power. Thirty years ago I entertained a strong affection of my own for Mistress Martha. I'd won her heart, and we were engaged to be married, but God chose not to bless our union. He left me orphaned after taking into his glory the comely daughter of my friend the Steward Hreczecha. All I have left is the memory of her qualities and charms and this gold wedding ring here. The poor lass appears before my eyes each time I glance at it. And so, by the grace of God, I have kept my plighted faith. I never married and remain a widower, though the Steward has another daughter, very pretty and very like my beloved Martha."

Saying this the Judge gazed tenderly at the ring and wiped a tear with the back of his hand. "Well, my brother," he said in closing, "what say you? Shall we have them betrothed? The boy loves her dearly, and I have the aunt's and the girl's consent."

At this Tadeusz stepped forward and spoke with great animation.

"Dear Uncle, how can I thank you enough for the constant care you take for my happiness. If Sophy were pledged to me today, if I knew she were to be my wife, I should be the happiest of men. But I must tell you frankly that for various reasons the betrothal cannot take place today. Ask me no more questions! If Sophy agrees to wait, she may soon find in me a better and worthier man. Perhaps by my constancy I shall earn her affection. Perhaps I shall adorn my name with a modest sprig of glory. Perhaps I shall soon return to the home of my fathers. Then, dear Uncle, shall I remind you of your promise. Then, on my knees, I shall greet my dear Sophy, and if she should still be free, ask for her hand. But now I must leave Lithuania—perhaps for long. Perhaps, in the meantime, another will gain Sophy's favor. I refuse to bind her. To expect a return of affection, an affection I have not yet earned, would be beneath contempt."

As the lad uttered these earnest words, two glistening teardrops, large as pearly berries, started from his large blue eyes and guttered swiftly down his ruddy cheeks.

All through their secret conversation, Sophy had sat ensconced in the alcove next door, listening and watching intently through a crack in the wall. She overheard Tadeusz's bold and forthright declaration of love, and her heart trembled; she saw the two big teardrops in his eyes, yet she could make little sense of it all! Why had he fallen in love with her? Why was he leaving her now? Where was he bound? The thought of his leaving saddened her. Never before had she heard such a strange and novel thing from the lips of a youth—that she was loved! She ran to the family oratory and took from it a holy picture and small relic box. The image was of Saint Genevieve and the box contained a shred of garment belonging to Saint Joseph the Bridegroom, patron of betrothed couples. Armed with these devotional articles, she entered the Judge's room.

"Are you leaving so soon?" she said to Tadeusz. "I have a little gift for your journey and a word of caution too. Carry this relic and image with you always and remember your Sophy. May God keep you well and happy. May he bring you home to us soon, safe and sound."

She fell silent and sank her head. Scarcely had she closed her dark-blue eyes when tears flowed to profusion from under the lashes, and so, with eyelids closed, she stood silent, spilling tears like diamonds.

Tadeusz accepted the gifts. "My lady Sophia," he said, kissing her hand. "Now I must bid you farewell. Remember me. Vouchsafe me an occasional prayer. Sophia . . . !" But he could say no more.

Meanwhile, the Count, who had entered unbidden into the room with Telimena, found himself moved by the couple's exchange of tender adieus.

"How much beauty," he said, casting a glance at Telimena, "in a simple scene like this! A warrior and his shepherdess fain to diverge their wakes like a frigate and its jolly boat in stormy waters! Indeed, nothing so fires the emotions as the forced separation of two souls in love. Time is a blast of wind. The short wick it quenches, great flames it fans to mightier conflagrations. I, too, am capable of loving more ardently from afar. Mr. Soplica, I took you for a rival. This error was the cause of our unhappy contention, which forced me to take up the sword against you. Now I see where I erred. You sighed for this shepherdess, whilst I'd entrusted my heart to this fair nymph here. Henceforth, let us drown our differences in the blood of our enemies. No longer shall we contend with murderous steel. Let our love rivals' quarrel be settled by other means! Let us see who outmatches the other in strength of affection. Let us leave behind these dear objects of our love and hasten forth against the lance and sword. Let us strive together on the battlefields of constancy, sorrow and suffering, and pursue our country's foes with a manly arm!"

He spoke and glanced at Telimena; but she, aghast at his words, stared back at him blankly.

"But my dear Count," the Judge broke in. "Why do you insist on leaving? Take my advice and remain on your estate where you are safe. The authorities may skin the minor nobility alive, but you, dear Count, are sure to come out all right. You know what sort of government you have to deal with. You are rich. You will buy yourself out of prison with half a year's income."

"Not in my character!" stated the Count. "Since I cannot be a lover, I shall be a hero. Made anxious in love, I shall have Glory for my comfortress. Since I am a beggar of the heart, I shall be rich in arms."

"But what prevents you from loving and being happy?" asked Telimena.

"The power of my destiny! A dark prescience impels me in mysterious fashion toward foreign lands and noble feats of arms. I confess that today in your honor I was ready to light the flame on Hymen's altar. But this youth has set me a wiser example. Of his own free will he stands ready to tear the nuptial crown from his temples and ride off to prove his heart against fortune's reversals and the hazards of bloody war. For me, too, shall this day mark the beginning of a new epoch. Birbante-Rocca once echoed with my arms. May these arms now echo throughout the length and breadth of Poland!"

And he proudly smote the sword-hilt at his side.

"Indeed, it would be hard to rebuke such zeal," said Robak. "Go then, and take your money with you. Perhaps you will see fit to equip a company like the young Potocki,[8] who astounded the French by raising a million francs for the war treasury; and like Prince Dominic Radziwiłł, who pledged his lands and chattels to field two new horse regiments. Go, I say, and take your money with you. We have no shortage of fighting brawn in the Duchy, but we do lack funds. Go then, and God speed!"

"Alas, my knight," said Telimena, gazing sorrowfully at the Count. "Nothing, I see, shall deflect you from your purpose. Therefore, I beg you, when you enter the martial lists, cast a tender glance at this love-gage. (Here she tore a ribbon from her frock, and tying a bow fastened it in the Count's buttonhole.) May this badge guide you against the glinting lance, the flaming cannon and raining brimstone. And when your valorous deeds spread your fame abroad, when the imperishable bay shadows your bloody casque, and victory crowns your lofty helm, then cast your eye again upon this favor and recall whose hand affixed it to your breast!"

She tendered him her hand; the Count knelt down to kiss it. And with her handkerchief raised to one eye, and squinting down with the other, she watched him bid her his soulful adieus. Finally, with a sigh and a shrug of her shoulders, she withdrew her hand.

"My dear Count," said the Judge. "Make haste, it's growing late."

"Enough of this!" growled Father Robak. "Be off with you!"

The Judge and the Monk quickly parted the tender couple and showed them the door.

Meanwhile, after embracing his uncle tearfully, Tadeusz kissed Robak's hand. The Bernardine pressed the lad's brow to his bosom, and crossing his hands over his head gazed heavenward, saying, "God go with you, my son!" And he wept.

"What!" said the Judge, as soon as Tadeusz had quitted the room. "Will you tell him nothing? Not even now? Is the poor lad to know nothing at all? Even at his departure?"

"Aye, nothing," said the Monk, and for a while he wept, burying his face in his hands. "Why should the poor boy know he has a father who hides from the world like a scoundrel—a common murderer! God knows how much I wish to tell him, but I forego this solace in atonement for the sins of my past."

"Then it's time to think of yourself," said the Judge. "Considering your age and state of health, there's no question of your going abroad with the others. You say you know of a place where you can weather the storm. Tell me where it is. You must hurry, a britzka stands waiting. But wouldn't the ranger's lodge serve you better?"

Robak shook his head.

"I have until morning," he said. "Now, my brother, send for the village priest. Tell him to come quickly with the *viaticum*.[9] Dismiss everyone but yourself and the Warden, and close the door."

The Judge carried out his behest and sat down on the bed beside him. Gervase remained standing, his elbow anchored on the pommel of his sword, his head resting on his hand.

Before beginning to speak again, Robak turned his gaze on the Warden and eyed him strangely. As when a surgeon lays his warm hand on the patient's body before applying the knife, so the Bernardine softened the expression of his keen eyes. Long he trained his gaze on Gervase's face; then, as if hazarding a blind thrust, he covered his eyes and spoke out forcefully:

"I am Jacek Soplica."

The Warden paled and lurched forward. Like a rock arrested in mid-fall he stood, bent at the waist, one foot raised off the floor. Wide-eyed he stared, whiskers bristling, mouth agape, his white teeth bared. The rapier slipped from under him, but he caught it up with his knees. Seizing it by the pommel and grasping firm hold of the hilt, he drew it back, the dark blade swaying fitfully behind him.

He brought to mind a wounded lynx ready to spring from a tree at the hunter's face: it puffs itself into a ball, snarling, flashing its bloody eyes, twitching its whiskers, vibrating its tail.

"Gervase," said the Monk. "Man's wrath no longer frightens me. The hand of God is upon me. I adjure you in the name of Him Who saved the world, Who blessed His slayers from the cross and heard the robber's plea. Relent, and hear me out! I have made my disclosure. To ease my conscience, I must obtain or at least beg your forgiveness. Hear my confession then do with me as you please."

And he joined his hands, as if in prayer.

The Warden, drawing back in great astonishment, smacked his brow with his hand and shrugged his shoulders.

The Monk began to relate the story of his past friendship with Horeszko, of his love for the Pantler's daughter and the resulting enmity between the Pantler and himself. He spoke at random, often interspersing his confession with complaints and accusations. Often he broke off his tale as if he had finished, only to resume it again. The Warden, being privy to most of the details, was able to make sense of the desultory tale and supply the missing parts, but the Judge was often left in the dark. With stooped heads both men listened intently to Jacek's tale. Meanwhile, Jacek's speech grew increasingly slower. Often it broke off altogether.

"You remember, Gervase, how the Pantler used to invite me to his banquets and drink my health. Often he'd raise his cup and declare aloud that he had no better friend than Jacek Soplica. How he'd clasp me to his bosom! Those who saw it would have sworn he was ready to share his soul with me. He, my friend? He knew perfectly well what was raging in my heart!

"Meanwhile, the neighbors' tongues already wagged. 'Hi Soplica!'—they called—'you woo in vain. A magnate's doorbell exceeds the reach of a cupbearer's son!' I laughed, affecting to scoff at dignitaries and their daughters. What was high nobility to me! If I paid them visits, it was out of mere friendship. Never would I match above my degree, I assured them. Yet the jests cut me to the quick. I was young, fearless, and enjoyed full access to society in a land where, as you know, minor nobility and magnates could aspire to the crown on an equal footing. Why, Tęczyński[10] once begged the hand of a daughter of a royal house, and the King agreed without any hint of shame. Are not the Soplicas every bit as worthy as the Tęczyński—their blood, their arms, their loyal service to the Commonwealth?

"How easy, upon a single instant, to blight another's happiness so that an entire lifetime cannot set it right. One word from the Pantler and how happy we should have been! Who knows, we might all be living still. He might have lived out his declining years in peace and quiet, close to his beloved daughter, his lovely Eva, and his grateful son-in-law. He might have rocked his grandsons' cradles. But, in the event, he destroyed us both. He . . . and that slaying . . . and all the consequences of that crime . . . all my sorrows and transgressions! . . . but I've no right to lay blame. I am his slayer. I have no right to accuse him. I forgive him with all my heart; and yet he . . .

"Had he but once refused me openly (for he was well aware of our feelings), had he forbidden me to visit, who knows, I might have taken my leave, vented my anger, and eventually left him in peace. But that proud fox devised another stratagem—to behave as if it never occurred to him that I might be seeking such a union. And yet he had need of me. The nobility valued me. I was popular among the manor holders. And so, pretending not to notice my feelings, he continued to receive me as before, insisting even that I should visit more frequently. But every time we were alone, he, seeing the tears start from my eyes and my bosom heave, ready to burst, the old fox would promptly turn to idle talk about lawsuits, the regional assemblies, the hunt . . .

"Oh, the times we sat in company, in our cups, and he, moved to tears, took me into his embrace, assuring me of his friendship (for he was always in need of my sword or my vote in the House), and I politely returned the gesture. Each time fury so seized me that the saliva rushed to my lips and my hand tightened around my sword-hilt, so much did I want to spit on his friendship and draw my sword! But Eva, seeing my face and demeanor, guessed what was raging inside me. How? I do not know. She looked at me imploringly and paled. Ah, what a lovely gentle creature! That look of hers! So compliant! So serene! So angelic! It was beyond my power to frighten her or stir her to anger. I held my peace. And so Lithuania's notorious roisterer, who struck fear into the hearts of the mightiest lords, who scarce let a day pass without provoking some brawl or other, who allowed not even a king much less a pantler to offend him, and went into transports of rage at the slightest dissent—I, drunk and incensed as I was, remained meek as a lamb, as though I were gazing on the Sacred Host!

"How many times I wished to bare my soul and beg on my knees before him! But on looking into his eyes and meeting that icy gaze, I was moved to shame on account of my strong feelings. And so in the coolest manner I'd strike up again on the subject of our court cases and regional diets. I even made jests—all this out of pride, so as not to offend the dignity of the Soplica name or lower myself in the Pantler's eyes by wooing in vain and incurring a repulse. Imagine the canards flying if word got out among the nobility that I, Jacek . . .

"The Horeszkos refusing Soplica the hand of their wench! That I, Jacek, had been served up a bowl of black pottage!

"At last, at my wits' end, I decided to raise a small regiment of the nobility and abandon our district and homeland forever. I'd make for regions in Muscovy or Tartary and wage war there. I went to bid the Pantler farewell in the hope that seeing me, his loyal supporter and old friend—indeed, I was practically a member of his household, having campaigned with him and been his drinking mate all those years—that, seeing me about to leave for a distant land, the old man would be moved to show me at least a scruple of human sentiment. Even as a snail reveals his horns!

"Ah, if but a tiny spark of feeling for a friend resides at the bottom of a man's heart, that spark will reveal itself at their parting like the last flicker of life. Even the coldest eye will shed a tear when it gazes for the last time on the brow of a friend.

"My poor beloved! On hearing of my intended departure, she turned pale and slipped to the floor in a dead faint. She could not speak; a stream of tears started from her eyes, and I knew how dearly she loved me.

"For the first time in my life, I recall, I wept. Wept tears of joy and despair! I forgot myself, went raving mad. Once again I was on the point of falling at her father's feet, ready to coil myself like a snake around his knees and beg, 'Dear father! Take me for your son or kill me on the spot.' But then, sullen and cold as a pillar of salt, he raises, in that polite and distant manner of his, the subject of . . . what, you ask? Why, his daughter's wedding! At such a moment! Gervase! Friend! Judge for yourself. You have a heart of flesh.

"'Mr. Soplica,' the Pantler says to me. 'A marriage broker just paid me a visit on behalf of the Castellan's son. Now you are my friend. What say you to this? You know, of course, that I have a rich and beautiful daughter and that he is but a castellan from Vitebsk and thus carries little weight in the Senate.[11] How should you advise me, dear fellow?'

"I've no recollection of what I said to him. More than likely, I said nothing, mounted my horse, and fled."

"Jacek!" exclaimed the Warden. "Full marks for all this special pleading. But what of it? Your fault stands undiminished. Why, you are not the first in the world to fall in love with the daughter of a rich lord or royal personage; not the first to conspire to snatch her away by force, and so avenge yourself openly. But to devise such a cunning plot! To slay a Polish lord! In Poland! And in league with Muscovy!"

"There was no plot," said Jacek with sadness in his voice. "Snatch her away, you say? Of course I might have done it. Neither bar nor lock would have prevented me. Why, I'd have smashed that castle of his into fine dust! Did Dobrzyn not stand behind me? And four other noble villages besides! Oh, if Eva had been like *their* women, strong and hardy, fearless of flight, pursuit, and the clash of arms. But the poor child! How her parents coddled her—frail, timorous thing that she was. A delicate larva! An April butterfly! To snatch her away thus, to touch her with a bloodied hand would have killed her. No, I simply couldn't.

"To avenge myself openly and storm the castle would have been contemptible. People would say I was taking vengeance for the repulse of my suit. Warden! The inferno of slighted pride is foreign to your upright heart!

"The demon of pride whispered better counsels in my ear. 'Take your revenge in blood and conceal the cause. Stop visiting the castle, root out your love, put Eva out of mind, marry another, and then—only then!—dream up some pretext and take your revenge.

"At first, I thought I'd found peace. The fiction pleased me, and . . . and I married the first poor lass I laid eyes on. I did wrong, I know—and sorely have I been punished since. I had no love for her . . . Tadeusz's poor mother. She was a good-natured soul and utterly devoted to me. But in my heart I was choking back my earlier love and rage. I raved like a maniac. I tried to bury my grief in farm work and other business, but to no avail. The demon of vengeance held me in thrall. Ill-humored and sullen, I found solace nowhere, and so, sinking from sin to sin, I turned to the bottle.

"So it was that in a short space of time my wife died of grief, leaving me with this child. And all the while despair devoured me . . .

"How I must have loved my poor Eva! All these years! Where didn't I travel? Even now I cannot put her out of mind. Her dear image stands as if daubed by a brush before me. No amount of vodka would dull the edge of my memory even for an instant. All those lands I saw and still I could not shake her from my mind. And here I lie in this bed, God's servant in a monk's habit, drenched in blood, still going on about her! To speak of such things at such a time. But God will forgive me. I want you to know the depth of my grief and despair when I committed that . . .

"The deed took place soon after she was betrothed. The whole district buzzed with news of the match. People told me that on receiving the ring from the Governor's hand, Eva fainted away and grew feverish. Already she was showing signs of consumption and she sobbed constantly. She loved another in secret, they surmised. But the Pantler, ever serene and jovial, continued to hold balls at the castle and invite his friends. Me, he no longer invited. Of what use was I to him now? The disorder of my household, my wretched state, and my vile addiction had made me an object of scorn, the laughingstock of the world. I, who once had the entire district wrapped about my finger; I, whom Radziwiłł used to call 'dear fellow'; I, who would ride out of my village with a troop more numerous than a princely retinue—I had only to unsheathe my sword and several thousand blades flashed around me, striking terror into the castles of great lords—here I was now, the butt of village urchins; so suddenly had I, Jacek Soplica! fallen from grace in peoples' eyes. Let him who knows what it is to feel pride . . ."

The Monk, growing increasingly weaker, slumped back into the pillows.

"Great are God's judgments!" said Gervase, deeply stirred. "It is the truth! The truth! So, it has been you all along? Jacek Soplica under a beggar's hood? I knew you when you were hale and hearty, the comely squire whom lords flattered and the ladies raved about. The whiskered champion! It wasn't that long ago, after all. How grief has aged you! How did I fail to recognize the shot when you felled the bear so expertly? Lithuania boasted no finer marksman, and next to Matthias, no abler swordsman. It's true! Our women used to sing ditties about you.

> The twitch of Jacek's whisker makes our gentry quail;
> When Whisker's knot is tied, e'en Rádziwill turns pale.

"Oh, you tied one on my lord.[12] Hapless wretch! But is it really you? Reduced to such a state? Jacek the Whisker—an alms quester? Great are God's judgments! And now, sir . . . hah! You shall not escape your deserts. I swore an oath that anyone that spilled a drop of Horeszko blood would—"

But here Robak raised himself to a sitting posture and resumed his tale.

"I was out riding by the castle. Who could name the legion of devils thronging my mind and heart! The Pantler—why, he was killing his child! Me, he'd already slain . . . destroyed! Satan drew me to the gate. Oh, the revels he held at the castle! A ball every night! Windows ablaze with candlelight. Hallways ringing with music. It was a wonder the place didn't come crashing down on that pate of his! Anyhow, give vengeance a thought and Satan slips you the weapon. The thought no sooner crossed my mind than he sent the Muscovites along. I was standing there and saw it all. You know how they stormed the castle . . .

"Because it's a lie that I was in league with Muscovy . . .

"All manner of thoughts passed through my mind as I stood there. First, I broke out into a silly grin like a child entranced by the flames of a fire. Then, expecting to see the castle burn to the ground, I felt a sort of brigandish joy. At times I felt like charging in and rescuing her—the Pantler too . . .

"As you know, you fought them off bravely and with great skill. I could not believe my eyes! The Muscovites were dropping like flies all around me. The cattle couldn't shoot straight if they tried! The sight of their rout sent me into another towering rage. Was the Pantler to taste victory? Was fortune to smile on all he did? Was he to emerge triumphant from this terrible onslaught? In disgust, I turned to leave. The day was just dawning. Suddenly, I saw him—recognized him! He'd stepped out onto the gallery and was facing the sun. I saw the flash of his diamond broach. There he stood, curling his whiskers, proudly surveying the field. He seemed to be singling me out for special abuse. He recognized me, I thought, and was giving me the arm, like this! Mocking and menacing me! I seized a soldier's musket, shouldered it, barely aimed, and fired.[13] You know the rest . . .

"A curse on firearms! Who fights with a blade must first strike his pose, lunge, parry, break. He may disarm his foe or choose to check his mortal thrust. With a firearm it is enough to seize a gun, cock it . . . a split second, a spark . . .

"Gervase, did I run when you took aim from the gallery? No! I just stared into both barrels of your gun. Despair overtook me! A strange sorrow rooted me to the ground. Why, oh why, Gervase, did you miss your mark that day? You'd have done me a service. But, clearly, it had to be . . . to atone for my sin . . ."

Here again he ran out of breath.

"God knows," replied the Warden, "I did my best to gun you down. How much bloodshed resulted from that single shot of yours! How many disasters have befallen your family since—and the rest of us! All through your fault, Jacek! And yet today when the yagers had their sights trained on the Count, last male representative of the Horeszko line (albeit on the spindle side), you shielded him with your own body. And when the Muscovites fired on me, you knocked me to the ground, thereby saving us both. If consecrated monk you truly be, then your habit stands proof against Jackknife. Keep well! No longer shall I seek to darken your doorway. We are quits. The rest we leave to God."

Jacek offered him his hand, but Gervase shrank back. "I cannot," he said, "without affront to my honor, touch a hand bloodied by such a murder, a murder committed for private vengeance and not *pro publico bono* . . ."

But Jacek, sliding down from the bolstered pillows, turned to the Judge. Growing paler by the minute, he asked anxiously for the village priest then appealed to the Warden:

"I beg you, sir, stay a moment longer. I've barely strength to finish. Warden, I shall die this night."

"What is this, my brother?" cried out the Judge. "But I had a look at it. It's hardly a serious wound. Why the priest? Could it be badly dressed? I'll send for the doctor. He'll be at the druggist's—"

But the Monk cut him off. "No need now, dear brother. I took an earlier bullet in the same spot . . . at Jena . . . wound never healed properly . . . now it's infected . . . gangrene . . . I know about wounds. See? Blood, black as soot . . . what good is a doctor? . . . trifling matter . . . We die but once. Today, tomorrow, we must all yield up our souls. Warden, forgive me, but I must finish my tale.

"When the whole nation brands you a traitor there is special merit in renouncing treason, especially for someone with a pride like mine . . .

"The label 'traitor' stuck to me like a plague. My fellow citizens turned their faces from me. Old friends shunned me. The timid greeted me at a distance and gave me a wide berth. Even the merest yokel or Jew, after bobbing his head, would give me a sidelong sneer. The word 'traitor' rang in my ears, echoed throughout my house and over my fields. From dawn to dusk it danced before me like a spot on a diseased eye. But I was never a traitor to my country . . .

"Muscovy took me perforce as one of her own. The bulk of the Pantler's domain passed to the Soplicas. Later, the Targowica confederates wished to honor me with an office. Had I then consented to turn Muscovite—for Satan counseled it, I was already rich and powerful then—had I then thrown in with Moscow, the wealthiest magnates would have sought out my favor. Even our brother nobles, even the rabble so quick to discredit their own, will forgive those fortunates who serve the Muscovite! All this I knew. And yet I could not . . .

"I fled the country. Where didn't I travel? What didn't I suffer . . .

"At last, God showed me the only remedy. I needed to amend myself, and so far as was possible, right the wrongs that . . .

"They transported the Pantler's daughter and her husband the Governor to Siberia. There, she died young, having left behind her a daughter, little Sophy. I saw to it that she was properly looked after . . .

"Perhaps I slew him more from foolish pride than from thwarted love, and so I needed humbling. I took the monastic habit. I, once so proud of my noble birth, I, the swaggerer, bowed my head and became a mendicant friar, with Robak—Worm!—for a name. Because, like a worm in the dust . . .

"A wicked example to my country, an inducement to treason—these had to be redeemed by good example, by blood and self-sacrifice . . .

"I fought for my country. Where? How? No one need know. Not for earthly glory did I so often expose myself to bullets and steel. I'd sooner forget my loud, valorous deeds and recall the quiet, useful ones, and the sufferings that no one . . .

"Many times I crossed the frontier, bearing orders from our leaders, gathering intelligence, hatching plots. Nowhere did my almsman's hood go unrecognized—not even in Galicia, not even in Greater Poland! For a year I was chained to a wheelbarrow in a Prussian fortress. Three times Muscovy flayed my back with the knout. Once they had me on the road to Siberia. The Austrians buried me deep in Spielberg's vaults as a slave-laborer—*in carcere duro*.[14] Yet, by a miracle, the Lord delivered me, and now He allows me to die among my people, with the Holy Sacraments . . .

"But now, who knows? Perhaps I sinned again. Perhaps I exceeded orders in hastening the uprising? Yet the thought that Soplicas should be the first to rise up, that my kinsmen be the first to plant our heraldic charger on Lithuanian soil . . . the thought . . . surely . . . was noble enough.

"You wanted vengeance, Gervase? Well, you have it! You have been the instrument of God's punishment. With your sword, God destroyed my plans. You have snarled the thread of the plot that had been spun for so many years. My great, all-consuming ambition, my last worldly desire which I nursed and fondled like a beloved child—this, you have slain before the father's eyes. And yet, despite all, I forgive you. You--"

"Even so may God forgive you," broke in Gervase. "Father Jacek, if you must take the housel, then I am no Lutheran or schismatic. He sins who grieves a dying man—this, I know. Now allow me to relate something to you; doubtless, you'll find it a consolation. When my late master fell mortally wounded and I knelt over his breast, smearing my blade with his blood and vowing vengeance, he shook his head at me. He pointed toward the gate where you were standing and traced a cross in the air. He was unable to speak, but it was clear he'd forgiven his slayer. I took his meaning, but so great was my wrath that I never breathed a word of that blessing to anyone."

The dying man's agonies broke off all further talk. A long hour of silence elapsed. They waited for the priest; at last, the clatter of hooves burst upon their ears. There was a rap on the door, and the tavern-keeper, breathless after a hard ride, hurried in with an important dispatch addressed to Jacek Soplica. Jacek had his brother read it aloud. It was from Fiszer,[15] then Chief-of-Staff of the Polish Army under Prince Joseph's command, with news that a state of war had been declared in the Emperor's Privy Council. The Emperor was even now proclaiming it to the world. A General Assembly had been called in Warsaw and the federated Mazovian States were about to issue a solemn declaration of union with Lithuania. On hearing the news, Jacek muttered a silent prayer. Holding a blessed candle to his bosom, he raised his eyes, now ablaze with hope, and lavishly spent his last reserve of tears. "Now, O Lord," he prayed, "let thy servant depart in peace."[16] They knelt down. A bell at the door announced the priest with the Body of Our Lord.

Night was just departing. The first roseate sunbeams shot across the milky sky. Like diamond darts they pierced the lattice panes, and hanging on the dying man's head and pillow wreathed his face and temples in gold, so that he shone like a saint enhaloed with a fiery crown.

NOTES

1. Ochakov, not far from Odessa, captured from the Turks in 1788 by Potemkin; Izmailov (Izmail), a fortress in Bessarabia, captured from the Turks by Suvorov in 1790; Novi, northern Italy, memorable for the victory of the Russians and Austrians over the French in 1799; Preussisch-Eylau, a town in old Ducal Prussia, where, on February 8, 1807, the French suffered heavy losses in combat with Russian and Prussian forces.
2. General Aleksander Rimsky-Korsakov (1753-1840) was dispatched in 1799 to Zürich, Switzerland, in aid of Suvorov; he was beaten on September 25 before joining up with Suvorov and was consequently cashiered for a time.
3. Racławice, a village northeast of Kraków. Here, on April 4, 1794, Kościuszko with an army of 6,000, including 2,000 peasants armed with scythes, defeated a numerically superior Russian force under the command of General Tormasov.
4. The battle at Maciejowice, fought on October 10, 1794, marked the defeat of Kościuszko's insurrection. Kościuszko himself was wounded and taken prisoner by the Russians.
5. The Polish name suggests a runny nose!
6. May he rest in peace (Latin)
7. For the common good (Latin)
8. Włodzimierz Potocki (1789-1812), one of the sons of Targowica confederate Szczęsny Potocki. Wishing to wipe away the disgrace of his family, he joined the army of the Duchy of Warsaw. In 1808, he supplied two artillery batteries at his own expense and fought bravely at the Battle of Sandomierz (1809); he died at the young age of 23.
9. Literally, "food for the journey" (Latin), i.e. the Eucharist, as when given to a person near or in danger of death.
10. Jan Tęczyński (d. 1562), Governor of Bielsko, Polish ambassador to Sweden, fell in love with the daughter of the Swedish king, Gustav I. He was seized by the Danes on his way to marry her and died in prison in Copenhagen. His story has been treated in Polish literature by Jan Kochanowski in the sixteenth century, and by Julian Niemcewicz in the eighteenth.
11. The office of castellan (*kasztelan*) was next in dignity to that of governor (*wojewoda*). Except for some very slight military duties, the post was purely titular, but it was prized because it entitled the holder to a seat in the Senate
12. [*H.B. Segel*] Stroking or curling one's moustache coupled with the action of throwing back the loose sleeves of the *kontusz* was considered to be a signal of readiness for a fight or confrontation. The phrase "knotting one's whisker" (*zawiązać węzełek na wąsie*) has the additional suggestion of making a reminder for oneself, as when one "knots" a handkerchief for the purpose of having something remembered.
13. [*H.B. Segel*] Here the poet states in his notes that the pantler Horeszko "appears" to have been slain around the year 1791, at the time of the first war. There is some confusion in the chronology of the poem. From Book One we learn that Tadeusz was born in the year of Kościuszko's insurrection, 1794. In Book One Tadeusz's age at the time of the action of the poem is given as about twenty. This would be consistent with the poet's original plan to set the action of the poem in 1814. When he shifted the action back to 1811-1812, he upset his chronology. Tadeusz then would have been born around 1791, three years earlier than the outbreak of Kościuszko's war. From Jacek's narrative (Book Ten) it appears that Tadeusz was born before the murder of the pantler. In attempting to restore consistency, the poet entered the above note. The "first war" mentioned in the note could only refer to that which followed

the ratification of the Constitution of the Third of May, 1791. This war did not begin, however, until after the proclamation of the Targowica Confederacy, May 14, 1792.

14. In harsh confinement (Latin)

15. Stanisław Fiszer (1769-1812), a former adjutant of Kościuszko. As Minister of War for the Duchy of Warsaw, he was Prince Józef Poniatowski's chief of staff. He died at the Battle of Borodino.

16. The first line of the *Canticle of Simeon* (Lk 2: 29-32).

BOOK XI

The Year 1812

Argument:

Spring omens. The arrival of the armies. The Mass. Official rehabilitation of the late Jacek Soplica. Eavesdropping on Gervase and Protase from which a quick end to the lawsuit may be inferred. A lancer courts his lass. The dispute over Scut and Peregrine settled at last. The guests gather for the banquet. The betrothed couples presented to the generals.

O memorable year! To have seen you in our land! The people still call you the year of the harvest. Our soldiery calls you the year of war. Ever the subject of old men's yarns! Ever the theme of poets' musings! Long did a great sign in the heavens foretoken your coming.[1] Dull rumors began to spread abroad, and when at last the spring sun dawned, a strange premonition, a joyous, expectant long-ing seized the hearts of our people, as though the world were coming to an end.

When the time came for the cattle to go to grass in early spring, they showed little eagerness to graze on the blades greening the clod. Gaunt and famished, they lay lounging in the fields, drooping their heads, bawling, or chewing phleg-matically on their winter-feed. Nor did the villagers plowing for the spring crop rejoice as usual in the long winter's passing. They crooned no song but toiled list-lessly on, as if seed and harvest time were out of mind; and while harrowing the seed fields, they kept checking their draft animals, gazing anxiously westward, as though some great marvel were shaping there.

With a sense of unease they watched the birds return. Even now the stork came whiffling down upon his ancient pine, spreading his white pinion like Spring's first battle flag. Swift upon his heels came shrill regiments of swallows, muster-ing over the bodies of water, scooping up the frozen mud to build their little homes. Woodcock whirred in the dusky thickets. Flocks of weary geese swept over the forest, dropping clamorously into the glades, seeking rest and refresh-ment; and all the while, the cranes, throbbing high in the darkness overhead, gave out their dismal moan. The watchmen wondered anxiously at this great stir in the bird kingdom. What storm had driven the birds hither so early?

At last, like throngs of finches, plovers and starlings, new flocks appeared. A host of bright plumes and pennons flashed on the hilltops and streamed down into the meadows. Cavalrymen!—strangely arrayed, bearing arms never before seen. Regiment after regiment came riding down. Between the lines of horsemen flowed columns of iron-shod troops like freshets in full spate. Endless files of black shakos and glinting bayonets issued forth from the forest; onward, like countless ants, the infantry marched.

All bearing north! It was as if, on the heels of the birds, men were driven by the same strange, instinctive force to leave the fabled South[2] in a mass migration to our land.

Day and night, horses, men, field guns, and eagles streamed past. Here and yon, an incandescent glow lighted the horizon. The earth shook, thunder rumbled from every quarter. War! War! Not a nook in our land where those rumblings went unheard. Not even the rustic woodsman whose sires and grandsires departed this life without ever venturing beyond the forest's bourn; whose ears knew no sound under heaven but the rush of the wind and the wild beasts' roars; whose only visitors were woodsmen like himself—not even he, in these remotest parts, was spared the sights of war. A lurid glare flashed in the sky—a piercing shriek, and a grenade missent from the battlefield sought a path through the trees, snapping branches, uprooting stumps. Trembling in his mossy lair, the venerable bison bristled his shaggy mane. Half rising on his forefeet, he shook his beard and looked about him, startled by the brilliant shower of sparks in the brushwood. The stray piece of ordnance spun around, spluttered and hissed then exploded like a thunderbolt. For the first time in his life the bison took fright, and scrambling to his feet fled into the deeper repairs of the forest.

"A battle? Where? Which way?" the young men asked, seizing their arms. The women implored heaven with upraised hands. "God is on Bonaparte's side!" cried one and all, their eyes bedewed with tears. Of victory there could be no doubt. Napoleon stood with us!

O Spring! To have seen you in our land! Memorable spring of war! O spring of harvests! To have seen you blowing with grass and corn, glittering with valiant men, rich in events and great with hope! Even now you stand before my eyes like a radiant apparition. Born in chains, enslaved while still in my swaddling bands, I have known but one such spring in all my life!

Soplica Manor stood close to the high road leading up from the Niemen. Two generals, our own Prince Joseph and King Jerome of Westphalia,[3] advanced with their armies along this very road. Having taken the part of Lithuania lying between Grodno and Slonim,[4] the King granted the troops a three-day rest. Despite the rigors of the march, the Poles among them raised a howl of protest, so keen were they to gain on the Muscovites.

The Prince's General Staff put up in the neighboring town. Meanwhile, an army of forty thousand and its staff encamped around Soplica Manor. The staff included Generals Dąbrowski, Kniaziewicz, Małachowski, Giedrojć, and Grabowski.[5] The hour being late, they took up quarters wherever they could find them, some in the castle, others in the manor house. Orders went out. Sentries were posted. The weary leaders retired to their rooms. Silence descended on the entire domain—manor, camp, and fields. Roaming patrols stirred like shades in the night. Campfires flickered. Ever and anon, a watchword rang out from a post.

All slept soundly—the lord of the manor, the generals, the troops. The Steward alone forswore slumber's delights; he'd been charged with preparing a grand banquet for the morrow and he was determined it should bring enduring fame to the Soplica house. He'd throw such a banquet as did honor to Poland's revered guests and the double solemnity of the occasion, tomorrow being both a religious and family feast. Three sets of betrothals were due to take place; and hadn't General Dąbrowski this evening made known his wish to partake of a traditional Polish repast?

Despite the late hour, the Steward quickly assembled five cooks from the neighborhood to serve as his under-chefs. Girding his waist with a white apron, he donned the head chef's hat and rolled up his sleeves to the elbow. Swatter in one hand (any greedy fly seen alighting on a delicacy was swept away in an instant), he donned a pair of well-wiped glasses with the other, then reaching deep into his bosom drew out a book and opened it. Titled *The Compleat Chef*,[6] the tome described in detail every specialty of the Polish board. Count Tęczyński had made good use of it in Italy where he threw such lavish banquets as to arouse the awe of Pope Urban VIII himself. Charles "My-Dear-Fellow" Radziwiłł also consulted it when receiving King Stanislas at Nieśwież; so memorable was the banquet that its fame survives in Lithuania's local lore to this day.

Whatever instruction the Steward could make sense of and convey aloud from the book his able assistants promptly carried out. The kitchen seethed with noise and activity. Fifty knives pounded on wooden slabs. Kitchen boys, black as fiends in hell, bustled about, some lugging firewood, others carrying pails of milk and wine. They filled kettles, pots and pans; billows of steam wafted forth. Two lads squatted by the hearth working the bellows. To help the fire along, the Steward had melted butter poured over the logs—a luxury permitted only in prosperous houses. Several more boys piled up the hearth with dry logs, others skewered enormous roasts on broiling-spits, beef, venison, haunches of wild boar and stag. Still others plucked heaps of fowl, raising clouds of down and feathers. Heath cock, black grouse and chickens lay denuded of their plumage. True, there was a general dearth of chickens. Since the night of the raid when bloodthirsty Sack Dobrzyński assailed the hen-roosts and made a shambles of Sophy's enterprise, the Manor had not yet fully regained its reputation as the district's richest producer of poultry. Still, what with the larder, the butchers' stalls, the forests, and neighbors near and far, they amassed a great supply of meat of every description; indeed, there was enough and more to spare. The generous banquet host requires but two commodities, plenty and art. Soplica Manor was rich in both.

The solemn feast day of Our Blessed Lady of the Flowers[7] was breaking. The weather was sublime, the hour early, the sky cloudless. The heavens stood stretched over the earth like an ocean becalmed, incurvate. Several stars still shone clear in the depths like pearls on the sea-bottom. A lone white cloudlet drifted up and dipped its wing into the azure. So melts the guardian angel's pinion when, after a night of attending the prayers of men, the ministrant spirit hastens to rejoin his fellow celestials.

The last pearls of the stars guttered and winked out in the depths of the sky. Heaven's brow grew pale. While the right temple reposed on a pillow of darkness, retaining its swarthy tone, the left grew rosier by the minute. Suddenly, like a great eyelid, the line of the horizon parted to show at its midpoint first the white of the eye, then the iris, then the pupil. A beam shot forth, arced across the vault of the sky then lodged itself in the white cloud like a golden dart. That beam, the signal of day, unleashed a sheaf of fire and flame. A thousand rockets traversed the heavenly vault, and the eye of the sun rose aloft. Still drowsy, it blinked, fluttering its radiant lashes, coloring sevenfold at once, sapphire blue reddening to ruby, ruby red yellowing to topaz until shining forth, first like a crystal vessel then like a lustrous diamond, the eye burst aflame like a throbbing star, large as the moon. Just so the sun began his solitary march across the bournless sky.

Today, as though in expectation of a fresh miracle, the entire local populace had assembled early at the chapel entrance. Curiosity as well as pious devotion had brought them there. Among those expected to attend the Mass at Soplica Manor were the Army's commanders, the famous captains of our legions, whose names the people knew and revered like those of their patron saints, and whose every peregrination, campaign and battle had become the gospel of our land.

Several senior officers and a host of soldiers had already arrived. Peasant folk thronged around them staring in disbelief at their fellow countrymen, all arrayed in uniforms, all bearing arms, all free and speaking the Polish tongue.

The opening procession began. Scarcely could the small chapel contain such a throng! Kneeling on the green outside, the people bared their heads and peered in through the open doors. The tow-white heads of the Lithuanian folk shone like a field of ripened rye. Here and yon, crowned with fresh flowers and pea-cocks' plumes and trailing loose ribbons from braided tresses, a lovely maiden's head stood out among the men's heads like a cornflower or cockle in the grain. The meadow teemed with gaily-clad worshippers; and at the sound of the bell, as under a breath of wind, all heads bowed like ears of wheat.

This was the day when village girls brought spring's first fruits, fresh bouquets of herbs, to Our Lady's altar. The entire chapel—altar, holy image, bell tower, and gallery—stood adorned with posies and floral wreaths. Fresh breezes stirred up from the east, blowing the garlands down on the heads of the kneeling faith-ful, spreading fragrances as sweet as the fumes that waft from the thurible's bowl.

The Mass said, sermon given, the Chamberlain led the entire assembly from the chapel. Recently elected their confederate marshal by a unanimous vote of the district estates,[8] he wore the ceremonial uniform of the province: a gold-embroidered tunic, a fringed robe of *gros-de-Tours* silk, and a gold brocaded belt. A dress sword with a shagreened hilt hung at his waist, and a large diamond pin sparkled at his throat. His confederate's cap was white and topped with a thick tuft of costly egret crest-feathers (only on grand occasions were such rich headdresses worn—the plumes went for a ducat apiece!) Thus appareled, he mounted a rise in front of the chapel, and with the villagers and soldiers pressing around him addressed his audience.

"Brothers!" he began. "You have just now heard liberty proclaimed from the pulpit. His Imperial Majesty has restored it to the Crown and is even now restor-ing it to the Duchy of Lithuania—to the whole of Poland. You have heard the government edict and proclamation calling for a nation-wide General Assembly. I have but a few brief words to say to this community; they pertain to the Soplica family, the lords of these parts.

"No one in the district will have forgotten the mischief wrought here by the late Jacek Soplica Esquire. But now that his sins are known abroad, it is time the world were apprised of the great services he has rendered. Our generals are present here among us; it is from them that I learned what I am about to relate.

"Jacek did not die in Rome as was reported; instead, he mended his ways, changing his name and state in life. All his offenses against God and his coun-try he has blotted out by his holy life and noble deeds. When almost beaten at Hohenlinde, General Richepanse[9] was on the point of sounding the retreat unaware that Kniaziewicz was marching to his relief, it was he, Jacek *alias* Robak, who braved sword and lance to deliver Kniaziewicz's letters with news that our own lancers were taking the enemy's rear. Then again, in Spain, when our lancers took the fortified ridge at Somosierra,[10] Jacek was twice wounded at Kozietulski's side. Later still, as an envoy entrusted with secret orders, he traversed various quarters of our land, gauging the currents of popular feeling, organizing and forming secret societies. Finally, at Soplica Manor, his ancestral seat, while preparing the ground for an insurrection, he was killed in an armed foray. The news of his death reached Warsaw just as Napoleon in recognition of his earlier heroic deeds had conferred upon him the order of Knight of the Legion of Honor.

"And so, taking all these matters into account, I, representing the province, proclaim with my staff of office that by his loyal service and the Emperor's grace, Jacek Soplica has been cleared of the blot upon his name and so stands restored to honorable rank. Once again he holds his rightful place among true Poles. Therefore, any man recalling to the family of the late Jacek Soplica the crimes for which he has long since atoned, shall as penalty for the delict be liable to the *gravis nota maculae*[11]—this in the words of our Statute, which thus reproves *miles* and *skartabella*[12] alike should they spread calumny against a citizen of the Commonwealth. And since general equality before the law has now been proclaimed, Article Three is likewise binding upon burgher and peasant.[13] This edict of the Marshal, the clerk shall duly set down in the Acts of the Confederation, and the Court Usher shall proclaim it aloud.

"As to the Legion's medal of honor, its late arrival shall in no way derogate from its glory. If it cannot do honor to Jacek's breast, then may it serve as a lasting memorial to him. I hereby drape it over his grave. Let it hang here for three days, then let it be deposited in the chapel as a votive offering to the Blessed Virgin."

With that he removed the order from its case. Tying the red ribbon in a knot, he hung the white star with its gold crown from the humble gravesite cross whence its rays sparkled in the sun like the dying gleams of Jacek's earthly glory. Meanwhile, invoking eternal rest upon the poor sinner, the people knelt and recited the Angelus prayer. The devotions concluded, the Judge circulated among the guests and village folk, inviting all to the manor house for the banquet.

On the turf bench before the house, two old masters with brimming mead-pots on their laps sat gazing out into the flower garden. Standing tall as a sunflower among the painted poppies was a Polish lancer in a glittering cap adorned with gilded metal and a cock's feather.[14] Before him, staring up at him with her pansy-blue eyes, was a girl in a dress as green as the low-lying rue; and behind the young couple stood a group of young women picking flowers, their heads averted, so as not to disturb the sweethearts.

The two gaffers pulled on their mead, took snuff from each other's birch-bark box, and ran on like a pair of millraces.

"Quite so, Protase, old boy," said the Warden Gervase.

"Quite so, Gervase, dear fellow" said the Court Usher Protase.

"Yes, quite right," they repeated several times in unison, beating time with their heads. "The action has come to a strange conclusion—no denying," the Usher pursued. "But there are precedents! I recall lawsuits involving excesses far worse than ours, and yet marriage articles settled the matter. That is how Łopót patched things up with the Borzdobohaty family, as did also Krepsztul with Kupść, Putrament with Pikturna, Mackiewicz with Odyniec, and Turno with Kwilecki.

"But what am I saying? The broils between the Soplicas and Horeszkos pale in comparison to those that once beset Poland and Lithuania; but then our Queen Hedwig[15] brought reason to bear on the matter, and their contention was settled out of court. It is well for both sides to have eligible maids or widows ready at hand; this way a compromise is always there to be made. The most protracted litigations take place among the Catholic clergy or between close kin, where the case cannot be resolved through the expedient of marriage. That is why Poles and Russians are always at each other's throats. Lech and Rus were born brothers, after all. This also explains the number of long-drawn-out lawsuits with the Teutonic Knights in Lithuania, before Jagiełło won on the field. Last, it explains why the Rymszas' famous lawsuit with the Dominicans *pendebat*[16] so long on the court calendar until the priory's legal advocate Father Dymsza finally won the case. Hence the saying, 'The Lord God is greater than Lord Rymsza.' To which, I might add, 'mead is better than a jackknife.'"

And pledging the Warden's health, he emptied his quart pot to the drains.

"True, true," replied Gervase with a show of emotion. "Strange have been the fortunes of our beloved Crown and the Grand Duchy. Why, they are like a married couple! God joins them, Satan puts them asunder. God minds his thing, the Devil his. Ah, dear Protase, that our eyes should be seeing this: our brothers from the Crown greeting us once more. I served with them all those years ago. Brave-hearted confederates! Oh, if my lord Pantler had lived to see this moment. Oh, Jacek! Jacek! But what's the use of moaning? Now that Lithuania stands reunited with the Crown, all is made good and right into the bargain."

"And the marvel of it is," said Protase, "that only a year ago today we had an omen, a sign from on high concerning our Sophy, whose hand in marriage Tadeusz is begging this very moment—"

"We ought to be calling her Mistress Sophia now," broke in Gervase. "She's grown up. She's no longer a girl. Highborn too—the Pantler's grandchild."

"Anyhow, the sign was a clear foreshadowing of the future," Protase went on. "With my own eyes I saw it. Here we were on this same feast day, the servants and I, sitting and pulling on our mead, when, from the eaves above, a pair of old fighting cock sparrows dropped to the ground with a plump. One was slightly younger and had a slate-gray throat; the other had a black throat. Off they went scuffling in the yard, rolling over and over in a cloud of dust. As we sat there watching, the servants said to one another, 'The black one's Horeszko, the gray, Soplica.' So whenever the gray has the upper hand, they raise a cheer, 'Up with the Soplicas, and down with the Horeszko cowards.' And when he falls, it's, 'On your feet, Soplica! What? Yield to a magnate? A nobleman would never live it down!' And so we sit there laughing, hanging on the contest's issue, when, suddenly, Sophy, taking pity on the little jousters, runs up and covers them with her hands. Yet still the down flew as the little scraps battled it out under her hands, such was their fury. Meanwhile, gazing at Sophy, the old wives murmured to one another, 'The girl's destined to reunite two star-crossed families.' I can see now that they foretold rightly, though, in truth, they had the Count in mind at the time, not Tadeusz."

"Aye, the world's a strange place," said Gervase. "Who can fathom it? Now I have something to relate as well—not as marvelous as your omen, yet hard to comprehend all the same. Once upon a time, as you know, I wouldn't spit on a Soplica if he were on fire, yet I always took a great shine to the lad Tadeusz. I noticed that whenever he got into a scrap with the other boys, he would always come out the winner. So every time he'd visit the castle, I dared him to perform a difficult task. He was equal to every challenge. He'd snatch a dove from the turret, pluck a sprig of mistletoe from an oak-tree, rifle a rook's nest in the tallest pine. There was nothing the lad couldn't accomplish handily. He must have been born under a lucky star. Pity he's a Soplica, I thought. Who would have imagined that in him one day I should be greeting the castle heir, the husband of my lady, Mistress Sophia."

They ended their talk and drank on, deep in thought; now and anon, they could be heard saying, "Quite so, dear Gervase" and, "Quite so, dear Protase."

The turf bench on which they were seated ran right past the kitchen. The windows gaped open, belching smoke as if a fire raged inside. Suddenly, out of these billows of smoke there shot forth like a dove a gleaming white hat, and the Chief Steward poked out his head. For a while he stood eavesdropping on the two old masters; then leaning over the sill, he passed them down a saucer of biscuits.

"Here's something to wash down with your mead," he said. "Now let me tell you the curious tale of a quarrel that might easily have ended in a bloody brawl. Once, when we were hunting deep in Naliboka Forest, Rejtan played a prank on the Prince de Nassau; it very nearly cost him his life. I brought them to terms. Let me tell you how it came about—"

But at that moment the under-chefs broke in to inquire who was setting the table. The Steward withdrew his head from the window; meanwhile, Gervase and Protase went on sipping their mead. They gazed pensively into the garden where the handsome lancer stood conversing with his young lady; he was holding her hand with his left hand, his right arm resting in a sling—plainly, he'd been wounded.

"Sophy!" he addressed his lady. "Before we exchange rings, tell me plainly, as I must be sure. What does it matter that last winter you were ready to give me your promise. I wouldn't accept it then, for what good is a forced promise? I'd spent but a short time at the Manor and wouldn't flatter myself that a single glance from me were enough to awaken your love. I am no braggart. I wished to win your favor on the strength of my merits, no matter how long it took; and now you've been so gracious as to repeat your promise. How have I earned such a favor? Perhaps, dear Sophy, you take me not out of love but at the insistence of your aunt and uncle. But marriage is a serious matter, Sophy. Consult your own heart in the matter and yield to no one's sway, either to my uncle's threats or to your aunt's entreaties. If what you feel for me is mere kindness and nothing more, then we can put off this betrothal for a while. I should never presume to bind your will. So, dear Sophy, let us wait! Nothing is pressing us; the more so, as last night I received orders to remain behind as an instructor in the local regiment until my wounds have healed. What say you, dear Sophy?"

Sophy raised her head and gazed demurely into his eyes. "I have only a dim recollection of the past," she replied. "All I know is that everyone kept telling me I should take you for my husband, and I always obey the will of heaven and my elders." She lowered her eyes and added: "Before your departure, if you recall, when Father Robak died on that stormy night, I saw how terribly sad you were to be leaving us. You had tears in your eyes. Those tears, I must tell you truly, went straight to my heart. Since then I have believed that you love me. Whenever I offered up a prayer for you, you always appeared before my eyes with those great shining tears. Later, the Chamberlain's wife took me up to Wilno for the winter. There I pined for the manor and the little room where we first met by the table, and where later you bade me adieu. Somehow my memory of you was like a seedling sown in autumn. All winter long it germinated in my heart so that, as I say, I never stopped pining for that room. Something told me I should find you there again, and so it has happened. With such thoughts I often held your name on my lips. It happened to be carnival time in Wilno. My companions said I was in love. So now, if I love anyone, it must surely be you."

Tadeusz, delighted by this frank avowal of love, took the girl by the hand and squeezed it; and leaving the garden the couple repaired to the lady's room, the same room that Tadeusz had occupied ten years previous.

There they happened to find the jubilant Notary, superbly attired, waiting on his plighted lady, bustling to and fro, fetching her rings, little chains, pots, jars, cosmetic powders, and patches. He gazed triumphantly at his young mistress seated before the mirror, putting the finishes to her toilet and taking counsel of the Graces. The chambermaids hovered about her, some freshening up her ringlets with heated tongs, others, kneeling on the floor, attending to the flounces of her frock.

While the Notary stood thus ministering to his betrothed, a kitchen boy suddenly rapped on the window. "A hare, your honors!" The hare had stolen out of the osier bed, sprinted across the meadow and leapt in among the sprouting vegetables. There it sat even now—an easy matter to rouse it from the cabbage patch and course it after placing the hounds near the narrow gap by which it would be forced make its escape. The Assessor ran up, tugging on Peregrine's collar; the Notary raced after him, shouting for Scut. The Steward stationed the men and their dogs by the fence, then seizing his fly swatter went stamping, whistling and clapping into the garden, terrifying the hapless beast. Smacking their lips softly, the Notary and the Assessor restrained their dogs and pointed to the gap in the fence. The hounds—ears pricked, noses to windward—chafed and quivered like a brace of shafts nocked to a single bowstring.

Suddenly, the Steward cried out, "See-ho!" The hare bolted from under the fence and made its point to the meadow. Like a shot Scut and Peregrine went after it. Unswervingly, they fell on the beast from both sides at once. Like the two wings of a hawk they descended, sinking their fangs, talon-like, into its spine. The hare squealed once, piteously, like a new-born babe. By the time the hunters ran up to the quarry, it lay lifeless, and the hounds were tearing savagely at the white fur of its underbelly.

As the two huntsmen patted their dogs, the Steward drew out the hunting knife strapped to his belt and cut off the quarry's feet.

"This day," he said, "your hounds receive equal dues, for they have won equal glory. Equal was their address and equal their labor. As the palace is worthy of Patz[17] and Patz of his palace, so the hunters are worthy of their hounds and the hounds of the hunters! This brings your long, fierce contest to a close. Now I, whom you appointed your referee, render this final verdict—that you are both winners. I return your stakes. Let each man stand by his word and make peace."

And so, at the old master's bidding, the hunters turned beaming faces on each other and wedded their long-separated palms.

"I once staked my horse and trappings," announced the Notary. "I also swore before the district court to deposit this ring as an honorarium for our referee. A forfeit, once pledged, may not be reclaimed. So, Mr. Steward, accept the ring as a keepsake. Have your name or, if you prefer, the Horeszko device chased on it.

The carnelian is smooth, the gold, eleven carats. My horse our lancers have long since requisitioned, but the harness and saddle are still mine. Experts praise these trappings for their comfort, durability, and pleasing looks. The saddle is narrow in the Turco-Cossack style, the pommel inlaid with precious stones, and the seat padded and lined with heavy silk, so that when you vault astride you settle into the down between the bow and the cantle as comfortably as you would in your own bed; and when you break into a gallop (here, Bolesta, who was known for his great love of gesticulation, spread wide his legs as if bestriding a horse, and feigning a gallop swayed slowly back and forth), when you break into a gallop, the sunlight reflects off the housing as though the horse dripped with gold, for the skirts are heavily sprinkled with gold, and the broad silver stirrups are generously vermeiled. The bit and bridle straps are studded with mother of pearl, and a crescent moon—like the one our heraldry calls Leliwa[18]—hangs from the breastplate. This singular garniture was taken, I'm told, from a great Turkish nobleman at the battle of Podhajce;[19] and so, my dear Assessor, please accept these caparisons as a token of my esteem."

The Assessor, clearly delighted by the gift, replied: "And I staked the gift I'd received from Prince Sanguszko, the gold-ringed dog collars lined with shagreen and the exquisitely wrought velvet leash with its glittering precious stone of matching craft. I intended to leave these articles to my children if I should marry—and children I shall have, for, as you know, this is my betrothal day. Nevertheless, my dear Notary, do me the honor of accepting these articles in exchange for your rich harness. Let them serve as a token of the longstanding quarrel that has come to such an honorable close for us both. May amity thrive evermore between us."

They returned to the manor, there to proclaim at table that the dispute over Scut and Peregrine had been settled.

Now rumor had it that the Steward raised the hare at home and released it secretly into the garden as an easy quarry by which to reconcile the two rivals; so cunning was his ruse that he managed to dupe the entire Manor. Some years later, the kitchen boy, wishing to set the Notary and the Assessor at odds again, leaked word of it, but the aspersions he cast on the hounds were to no purpose; the Steward denied the rumor, and no one believed the boy.

The guests, having assembled in the banquet hall, stood talking by the table, awaiting the repast. At last, the Judge dressed in the Governor's uniform entered, shepherding Tadeusz and Sophy before him. Tadeusz touched his brow with his left hand and saluted his superior officers with a military bow, and Sophia, stooping her gaze and blushing, greeted each guest with a curtsy—a curtsy perfectly executed in accordance with Telimena's instructions. Except for the bridal garland binding her temples, she had on the same costume she'd worn that morning in the chapel when offering her spring sheaf to the Blessed Virgin. For the guests, she'd garnered another little herb bouquet. Balancing the shining sickle on her brow with one hand, she proceeded to portion out the flowers and grasses with the other. On receiving their little posies, the officers kissed her hand, and she, cheeks mantling brightly, curtsied again.

General Kniaziewicz seized the girl by the shoulders, planted a paternal kiss on her brow then whisked her up onto the table. "Bravo!" applauded the onlookers, captivated by the girl's grace and beauty and still more by the rustic Lithuanian dress she was wearing. Upon these famous captains who'd spent so much of their nomadic lives roaming foreign lands, the national costume worked a special charm, recalling to mind their youth and romantic attachments of long ago. With tears in their eyes they gathered round the table and gazed intently at the girl. Some begged her to tilt her head and show her eyes, others, to turn around. The girl swung round bashfully, covering her eyes with her hand; and Tadeusz, looking on, rubbed his hands with joy.

Had someone suggested this costume to Sophy, or had instinct prompted her? For surely it is instinct that tells a girl what best becomes her face. Enough that this morning, for the first time in her life, Sophy had braved Telimena's displeasure by stubbornly refusing to wear a fashionable dress. Moved by Sophy's tears, her aunt had yielded and abandoned her to her rustic costume.

The underskirt was long and white, the skirt short, cut from green camlet stuff and rose-edged. The bodice, cross-laced from neck to waist with pink ribbons, and also green, enfolded Sophy's breast like leafage around a rose-bud. The billowy white sleeves of her blouse were laced in loose folds about her wrists; bright and full, they shone upon her shoulders like the wings of a butterfly poised to take flight. The collar fit snugly round her neck; a rose-colored bow secured it. Her earrings were artfully scored cherry pits, the proud handiwork of Sack Dobrzyński (they were his gift to her while she was still the object of his addresses; etched on the pits were two little hearts with a dart and a flame). A double string of amber beads hung about her neck and a garland of green rosemary bound her temples. The ribbons of her braids hung tossed over her shoulders, and over her brow, as was customary among the field women, rested a curved sickle, well-polished from recent reaping and bright as the crescent moon upon Diana's brow.

The guests cheered and applauded. One of the officers drew a leather portfolio from his pocket; it contained a bundle of papers. Laying out a sheet of foolscap, he sharpened a pencil, moistened it with his tongue, and gazing at Sophy set down to draw. No sooner did the Judge spy the drawing materials than he recognized the artist, though the colonel's uniform, the glittering epaulets, the seasoned lancer's mien, the blackened moustache, and the Spanish beard had wrought a considerable change upon him.

"Why hello, dear Count!" exclaimed the Judge. "A traveling painter's kit in your cartridge pouch, I see."

It was indeed the young Count. He hadn't been a soldier for long, but thanks to his immense wealth, his fielding of an entire horse regiment at his own expense, and the splendid manner in which he'd acquitted himself in his first engagement, the Emperor had only today conferred upon him the rank of colonel. The Judge greeted and congratulated him on his promotion, but the Count scarcely heeded him and went on with his sketching.

Meanwhile, the second betrothed couple and their party made their entrance. It was the Assessor—formerly the Tsar's, now Napoleon's loyal servant—with a detachment of Polish gendarmes under his command. Though he'd held that office for barely twenty hours, he was already wearing the dark blue uniform with its distinctive Polish facings. In he strode, spurs jangling, cavalry saber trailing behind him. At his side, solemn and arrayed in her full finery, walked his beloved, Thecla Hreczecha, the Steward's daughter. The Assessor had long since washed his hands of Telimena and so as to wring the coquette's heart the more he'd turned his affections to the Steward's daughter. The bride was not young; indeed, she was said to be all of fifty years old. But she was a stout soul, an able housekeeper, and suitably dowered, since, apart from the village she stood to inherit, a tidy monetary gift from the Judge had increased the sum of her assets.

As for the third pair, the guests waited for them in vain. Growing impatient, the Judge dispatched his servants to fetch them. They returned by and by with word that the third bridegroom, the Notary, had lost his wedding ring in the hare course and was even now scouring the meadow for it. As to his lady, she was still at her dresser. Though she was making all due haste with her housemaids doing their best to bear a hand, there was not the ghost of a chance she'd complete her toilet in time; indeed, she'd scarcely have it done this side of four o'clock.

NOTES

1. [*Author's note*] A Russian historian describes in similar fashion the omens and premonitions of the Muscovite people before the war of 1812. [C. Z.: Exactly which historian has not been determined.]

2. The word used by the poet is *wyraj*. In his notes he explains: "In the popular dialect the word properly means the autumn season, when the migratory birds fly away. To fly to *wyraj* means to fly to warmer lands. Hence, figuratively, the common folk apply the word *wyraj* to warm countries and especially to some fabulous, happy region lying beyond the sea."

3. Jérôme Bonaparte (1784-1860), the youngest brother of Napoleon.

4. Two cities in the Hrodna province of what is now Belarus.

5. Kazimierz Małachowski (1765-1845) returned to France in 1804 with the remnants of the Danube Legion after the ill-fated Haiti campaign of 1803. In 1812, he was still a colonel and commanded a regiment under Dąbrowski. He lived to take part in the November Insurrection of 1831. In 1812, Napoleon named Romuald Giedrojć (1750-1824) inspector general of the cavalry of the Lithuanian Army, which was then forming. Michał Grabowski (1773-1812) commanded a brigade under General Kniaziewicz. He was killed at the siege of Smolensk.

6. [*Author's note*] A book, now very rare, published more than a hundred years ago by Stanisław Czerniecki. That embassy to Rome has been often described and painted. See the preface to *Kucharz doskonały* (The Perfect Cook): "This embassy being a great source of amazement to every western state, redounded to the wisdom of the incomparable gentleman Ossoliński as well as to the splendor of his house and the magnificence of his table—so that one of the Roman princes said: 'Today Rome is happy in having such an ambassador.'" N.B. Czerniecki himself was Ossoliński's head cook.

7. I.e. "Lady Day"—the Feast of the Annunciation, March 25.

8. [*Author's note*] Upon the arrival of the French and Polish armies in Lithuania, each province formed a confederacy and elected its deputy to Parliament.

9. General Antoine Richepanse (1770-1802) was commander of a French column, which was relieved in an emergency by Kniaziewicz and his Danube Legion. "It is a well-known fact"— notes Mickiewicz—"that at Hohenlinden [Bavaria] General Kniaziewicz's Polish corps decided the victory." The action took place against the Austrians on December 3, 1800.

10. Napoleon freely availed himself of Polish troops in his Spanish campaign. In 1808 Polish light cavalry units under the command of Baron Jan Leon Hipolit Kozietulski (1781-1821) captured Somosierra, a defile in the Sierra de Guadarrama some sixty miles north of Madrid.

11. *Miles* (Latin) refers here to a Polish nobleman of ancient lineage. *Skartabella* in old Polish law was applied to an individual recently elevated to the nobility. Until the third generation he could not enjoy equal privileges with the rest of the nobility.

12. A brand of deep disgrace (Latin)

13. Although Napoleon decreed the freeing of the serfs in the Duchy of Warsaw, he decided to postpone implementation of the law in Lithuania until after the war against Russia. Later in *Pan Tadeusz*, the eponymous hero enfranchises his peasants in an independent action.

14. The Polish lancers or uhlans (*ulany*) serving in the Napoleonic wars wore the distinctive *czapka rogatywka*, a high, square-topped peaked helmet derived from the four-pointed "confederate's cap" (*konfederatka*), which in turn derived from the *krakuska*, a hat traditionally worn by the peasantry of the Kraków region. The *czapka*, fronted by the regimental insignia embossed in metal, was adorned with braids, plumes, or rosettes.

15. Poland and Lithuania were united in 1386 by the marriage of Queen Jadwiga (Hedwig) of Poland (1373-1399) to the pagan Prince Jagiełło of Lithuania, who thereupon embraced Christianity. The Jagiellonian dynasty endured until the last of the male line of that house Sigismund August died without issue in 1572, and the throne became elective.

16. Remained pending or unsettled (Latin)

17. The reference is to the magnificent palace built in Jezno (Jieznas), in Lithuania, by Antoni Michał Pac (d. 1774).

18. This was a Polish escutcheon characterized by a golden crescent on a red field surmounted by six-pointed star. It was borne by the Soplicas.

19. A small town in eastern Galicia, the scene of a battle in 1665 between a combined Tartar-Turkish army and the Poles under Sobieski.

BOOK XII

Let Us Love One Another!

———

Argument

The last banquet in the grand old Polish style. The centerpiece. An explanation of its figures. Its transformations. Dąbrowski receives a gift. More of Jackknife. Kniaziewicz receives a gift. Tadeusz's first official act upon receiving his inheritance. Gervase's observations. The Concert of Concerts. The Polonaise. Let us love one another!

At last the hall doors swung open with a crash and in strode the Chief Steward, head capped and erect. He greeted no one, nor did he take his place at the table; today the Steward emerged in a new character, as Marshal of the Court. Using his mace of office as a pointer, he directed the guests to their places and seated them according to their station and rank. As the highest official of the Province, the Confederate Marshal (formerly the Chamberlain) took the post of honor, a velvet chair with ivory armrests. Next to him on the right sat General Dąbrowski—on the left, Kniaziewicz, Patz[1] and Małachowski. The Chamberlain's wife was duly seated among them; after her followed the rest of the ladies, lords, officers, manor holders, and members of the nobility. All took their places, men and women alternately, in the order assigned by the Steward.

The Judge bowed to his guests, and withdrawing from the banquet hall repaired to the courtyard where he was fêting a large number of his village folk. Assembling them around a table a furlong in length, he seated the parish priest at one end and himself at the other. Sophy and Tadeusz he did not seat. Their business was to wait on the peasantry; they ate on the fly. Such was the ancient custom: the new heirs did the honors of the table at their inaugural banquet. Meanwhile, awaiting the repast in the great hall, the guests gazed in wonder at the table's grand centerpiece, an exquisite artifact wrought of a fittingly precious metal. Prince Radziwiłł "The Orphan"[2]—so the story went—had had it made to order in Venice and embellished according to his taste in the Polish style. Plundered during the Swedish Wars,[3] the object passed who knows how to the Manor, and now, retrieved from the treasury, it rested in a mighty circle like a carriage wheel on the table.

Covering the vessel to the upper edges was a confection of snow-white sugars and mousses. The result was a marvelous simulation of a winter landscape. In the center bulked a dark forest made from fruit preserves; around it clustered sugar-frosted likenesses of cottages suggesting snowbound peasant hamlets and noble villages; and all around the rim of the vessel stood little blown-porcelain figurines in Polish costumes. Like stage players these figures seemed to be acting out some momentous event. So expressive were their gestures, so vivid their colors, that but for the want of voices you'd swear they were alive.

But what did they represent? asked the curious guests. The Steward raised his staff and addressed his audience.

"By your leave, most highly honored guests!" he began. (Here they served the vodka aperitif.) All these figurines you see here before you are playing out the history of our regional assemblies—the voting, the upsets, the quarrels. I worked out the scenes myself, so allow me to explain them to you. On the right you see a large gathering of the nobility. Evidently, they have been invited to the inaugural banquet, since a table stands set. No one has yet been seated; they stand around in small knots. Each group holds council. Now pay attention to the man in the middle of each group. By his open mouth, wide-eyed stare, and busy hands, you can tell he's an orator wooing his audience. Here he underlines his point by tracing with his finger on the palm of his hand. These are speakers vouching for their candidates, with mixed results, as you can readily tell by their brothers' expressions.

"True, in this second group, the nobility listen intently. Observe this fellow with his hands under his belt. See him straining to hear? And this one here, hollowing his hand to his ear and twirling his moustache. No doubt he's collecting the pearls of eloquence and threading them on his memory. The speaker looks pleased; clearly, he has won them over. He rubs his pockets. He knows that he has their vote in his pocket.

"But what a difference in this third group here! The speaker has to seize his audience by their belts. See them pulling away, averting their heads? Observe this listener bridling with anger. See? He raises his arm, threatens the speaker and stops his mouth with his hand; he cannot bear to hear his rival praised. And mark this other fellow lowering his head like a bull as if to toss him. Some reach for their swords, others take to their heels.

"One man stands silent apart from the rest; clearly, he hasn't thrown in with either side. He's fearful. He hesitates. He hasn't a clue whom to vote for! In his struggle with himself, he leaves it all to chance. He raises his hands, puts out his thumbs, and shutting his eyes tries to align the nails. Clearly, he has entrusted his vote to fate: if the thumbs meet, it's, 'yea,' if not, 'nay.'

"On the left we observe yet another scene. Here the nobility have converted the priory's refectory into an electoral hall. The older men sit on benches arranged in rows. The youth stand behind them, peering over their heads. Here stands the marshal with the ballot urn in his hand. He counts the votes; the nobility watch with eager eyes. He has just shaken out the last ballot. The ushers raise their hands and announce the elected official.

"One nobleman refuses to abide by the common will. See him poking his head through the kitchen window? Observe that insolent wide-eyed stare of his. His mouth gapes open; he'd swallow up the entire room! Easy to guess what he's vociferating. *Veto!* And now see how this voice of discord sends the throng charging through the door. Heading for the kitchen, I'll warrant! Their blades are drawn. Oh, there'll be bloodshed, I shouldn't wonder. But here in the corridor, ladies and gentlemen, you'll mark a priest in a chasuble, the old prior bearing a monstrance with the Blessed Sacrament. A surpliced altar boy clears his way with a bell. The nobility sheathe their sabers, bless themselves and genuflect. The priest turns to where the clash of steel persists. Soon he'll have the whole lot hushed and reconciled. Ah, but you youngsters have no recollection of how famously our self-governing nobility, armed and unruly as they were, got along without the benefit of a police force. So long as the true faith flourished, we respected our laws. We enjoyed liberty with order and glory with prosperity. Other countries, I'm told, keep bands of ruffians at hand—all manner of law officers, gendarmes, and constables. But if it takes the sword alone to guard the public security, then I refuse to believe true liberty exists in those lands."

Here the Chamberlain broke in, tapping on his snuffbox. "Come, Mr. Steward," he said, "put off these stories of yours. Granted, our regional diets are of great interest, but we are famished. Have them bring in the dinner!"

The Steward lowered his mace to the floor.

"Your Excellency, grant me this pleasure," he replied. "Allow me yet a moment to explain this final scene. Here you see the newly elected marshal leaving the refectory on his supporters' shoulders. See the nobility tossing their caps in the air? Their mouths are open. '*Vivat!* A long life!' they cry.' And there opposite broods the beaten contender. He stands apart from the rest, his cap pulled down over his brow; meanwhile, his wife waits in front of the house. She has guessed, poor thing! She swoons in her chambermaid's arms. Poor thing, she has been counting on the title 'Right Honorable,' and now it's another three years of plain 'Honorable.'"

With that the Steward closed his commentary and waved his mace. Footmen began filing in two by two with the dinner. *Borsch royale*[4] was the opening dish. Next came an old-Polish consommé prepared with masterly skill. To the marvelous secrets of its preparation the Steward had added the measure of tossing in the odd pearl and coin; the clear broth was said to purify the blood and fortify the health. Then followed the rest of the dishes. Who could tell them all?—and even if one could, who could make head or tail of specialties no longer known today?—*kontuz, arkas,* and *blemas,*[5] or dishes with ingredients such as burbot meat, forcemeat, civet, deer musk, gum dragon, pine nut, and sloeberry. And the varieties of fish! Dried huchen from the Danube, flounder, white sturgeon, caviar (both Venetian and Turkish), large pike, medium-sized pike—eighteen inchers at least!—large carp, noble carp! And to crown all, the chef's secret specialty: an entire fish, uncut, sautéed at the head, baked in the center, and the tail marinated in a sauce.

But the guests took no interest in the names of the dishes, nor did they take time to probe the mysteries of the fish; they dispatched the meal with military expedition and washed it down with ample drafts of Hungarian wine.

Meanwhile, the grand centerpiece was changing color. Stripped of its mantle of snow, it was turning green. The delicate layer of sugar icing had melted under the warmth of the summer to reveal a landscape hitherto hidden from the eye. A new season emerged—spring, with its burst of greenery and many hues. Various grains and crops sprang up, as if leavened with yeast: saffron-hued wheat nodding its golden ears; rye decorated with silver leaf; buckwheat artfully fashioned from chocolate; flowering orchards of apple and pear.

But the guests had no time to savor the fruits of summer. In vain they begged the Steward to stay its passing. Like a planet governed by her ineluctable motions, the centerpiece changed season again. Already the gilded grainfields were soaking up the ambient warmth. The grass yellowed, the leaves reddened and fell, as if blown down by autumn's winds. The trees, gorgeous a moment ago, now hung stark and leafless, blasted by gale and frost. These leafless trees were cinnamon sticks, and the pine trees sprigs of laurel sprinkled with caraway seeds, to simulate pine needles.

Wine cups in hand, the guests began to break off the branches, roots and stumps and nibble on them as tidbits; meanwhile, the jubilant Steward circled the centerpiece and watched his guests.

"My dear Steward," said General Dąbrowski, affecting great amazement. "Is this a Chinese shadow play before me? Or has Pinetti[6] put his demons under your spell? Do such centerpieces still exist among us in Lithuania? Do the people still feast in this grand old fashion? Tell me, for I've spent the better part of my life abroad."

"No, General," replied the Steward with a bow. "No godless arts these, but a harking back to those grand old banquets held in the halls of our forefathers[7] when Poland was happy and strong. What I have done I learned from this book. As to the custom being observed in the rest of Lithuania, alas! new fashions are making inroads even here. Many a young nobleman balks at such excesses. He eats like a Jew, begrudges his guests food and drink, and stints his Hungarian wine while draining drafts of that infernal bogus *shampanskoe* from Moscow which is all the rage. Then, in the evening, he loses as much gold at cards as it would take to feed a hundred fellow noblemen. Even the Chamberlain—and here I'll be quite candid, trusting His Excellency will not take it amiss—even the Chamberlain scoffed on seeing me haul this centerpiece out of the treasury. 'A tiresome old contraption whose day was done,' he said. 'A child's plaything, not fit for such illustrious folk!' Yes, Your Honor, even you thought our company would be unimpressed, and yet judging by the awed looks of our nobility here, I see it's a beautiful object eminently worthy of being displayed. Who knows if Soplica Manor shall ever again have the good fortune of regaling such a distinguished body of guests? General, I see you have a discerning eye for banquets. Please accept this small tome. May it serve you well when you come to throw banquets for companies of foreign monarchs—aye, even Bonaparte himself! But before I dedicate this book to you, allow me to relate the manner in which it came into my possession—"

A sudden disturbance broke out at the door. "Long live Weathercock!" cried out a chorus of voices. A throng invaded the hall, pushing Matthias Dobrzyński to the forefront. The Judge seized him by the arm, and leading him to the table seated him prominently among the generals.

"Matthias," he said. "How unneighborly of you to turn up so late. Dinner's almost over." "I dine early," replied Dobrzyński. "It's not for the victuals I came. A lively curiosity seized me to take a closer look at our army. One might say a lot on that score. Hard to make out just what it is. The nobility spotted me and fetched me in by force, and now you've seated me, for which I thank you, good neighbor."

With that he turned over his plate as a sign that he was not eating, and there he sat in moody silence.

"Dobrzyński?" said General Dąbrowski, turning to him. "So you're that celebrated hewer of men of Kościuszko times—Matthias styled *The Birch*? I know you by reputation. Why, look at you! So hale! So spry! Yet how many summers is it now? See how *I've* aged! Behold Kniaziewicz's grizzled locks! Yet here you are, holding your own among the youngsters. I'll wager your Birch still puts out its buds. I hear the Muscovites got a sound thrashing at your hand recently.

But where are your brethren? I'd give my right eye to see those Jackknives and Razors of yours, those last shining examples of old Lithuania!"

"General," said the Judge. "After our victorious battle almost all the Dobrzyński sought refuge in the Kingdom. No doubt they have joined one or other of the legions."

"Indeed, sir," spoke up a youthful squadron commander. "I have in my second company a whiskered giant of a sergeant major by the name of Dobrzyński. He calls himself *The Sprinkler*, but the Mazovians call him *The Lithuanian Bear*. On your command, sir, I could have him brought in."

"We have several other Lithuanian-born men in our ranks," added a lieutenant. "I know one they call *Razor*, and another who rides with the flankers[8] bearing a blunderbuss. Two other Dobrzyński riflemen serve with the grenadiers."

"Aye," exclaimed the General. "But what of their leader? I would hear of the one they call *Jackknife*, of whom the Steward has told me so many wonders. A veritable giant of fabled times!"

"Jackknife did not seek refuge across the border," replied the Steward. "But fearing the inquiry, he kept clear of the Muscovites. The poor fellow spent the whole winter roaming the forests and has only just emerged. In martial times like these, you may find him of service, for he's a valiant knight, though, alas, the years are starting to weigh heavily on him. But look, here he comes now!"

The Steward pointed to the entrance hall where the servants and rustic folk stood crowded together. The shining dome of a man's skull rose high above them like a full-orbed moon; thrice it rose and thrice it vanished in a cloud of heads. It was Gervase bowing as he addressed his way through the throng.

"Your Excellency Hetman of the Crown . . . or is it General?" he said, having got clear of the crowd. "Whatever the correct title, Rębajłło at your service! Aye, and this my Jackknife, whose fame derives not from its hilt or chasing but from the temper of its steel, so that even Your Excellency has heard of it. Could this blade but speak, perchance it would put in a word for this ancient arm of mine. By God's grace, long and faithfully has it served our land and the family of my Horeszko lords whose name lives on in the memory of men. Rare, old boy, the accountant that trims his goose quill as deftly as Jackknife trims a man's neck. Some reckoning that would take! As to the number of ears and noses lopped off—past telling! And yet the blade stands clean of nicks, unstained by murderous deeds. Open warfare and duels are all it has known. Alas, but once—may the Lord grant him rest—but once, I say, did it dispose of an unarmed man. But there, as God is my witness, it was *pro publico bono*."

"Show me that jackknife!" cried out Dąbrowski with a laugh. "Oh, what a beauty! A true headsman's sword."

And running an awed eye over the prodigious rapier, he passed it to his officers. All tried their fortune, but few were strong enough to raise it over their head. They said Dembiński[9] of the brawny arm might have hefted it, but he was not present. Of those who were, only Squadron Leader Dwernicki and Platoon Commander Lieutenant Różycki[10] succeeded in swinging that massy bar of steel; and so the rapier went from hand to hand for trial.

It soon became apparent that General Kniaziewicz, the most strapping man among them, also boasted the strongest arm. Seizing the rapier as if it were a mere fencing foil, he executed a series of lightning-fast flourishes over the heads of the guests. He recalled the maneuvers of Polish swordsmanship: the horizontal cut, the circular, the diagonal, the cleaving stroke, the counter thrust, the counter-time and tierce—maneuvers he'd learned as a cadet in military college. While Kniaziewicz laughed and swung away, Gervase knelt down, tears in his eyes, and clasped him by the knees.

"Splendid, sir!" he moaned at every sweep of the blade. "So were you in the Confederacy too? Splendid! Marvelous! That's Pułaski's thrust! And there! Dzierżanowski struck his pose that way. And there! Why, that's Sawa's[11] slash! And that one! Only Matthias Dobrzyński could have trained your arm so. And this one, I'll be bound! I'll not brag, but it's my own invention—a cut known only to us Rębajłos. They named it after me—The Old Boy's Cut. Who taught you that? It's my cut, mine!"

And rising to his feet, he embraced the General.

"Now may I die in peace," he declared. "Here stands one that shall take my darling child to his bosom. For years the thought has troubled me night and day that my rapier will be hung out to rust after I'm gone. Now it shan't rust away. Your Excellency . . . Sir . . . General . . . Forgive me, but have nothing to do with those puny skewers, those flimsy little German foils. A noble sire's child wouldn't stoop to grasp such twigs. Bear a sword worthy of Polish nobility! See, I lay my Jackknife, my dearest possession, at your feet. I never had a wife, I never had a child, but it has been both wife and child to me. For years I never let it out of my embrace. From dawn to dusk I caressed it. At night it slept by my side. But now that I've grown old, it hangs like the Decalogue above my bed. I thought I should be buried with it clasped in my hand. But now I have found an heir. Long may Jackknife serve you!"

"Comrade!" replied Kniaziewicz, half in jest and half in earnest. "If you give away your wife and child, you'll be left old and alone, childless and widowed for the remainder of your days. What can I offer you in return for such a precious gift? Tell me how I may sweeten your orphaned and widowed state?"

"Am I Cybulski," dolefully rejoined the Warden, "who, as the ditty goes,[12] gamed away his wife in a round of marriage with the Muscovite? It is enough to know my Jackknife shall flash before the world in a hand like yours. Only be sure to give it ample strap, well let out, as it's a bit on the long side. When cutting, always swing it with both hands from the left ear down; this way you'll unseam your foe from crown to gut."

The General accepted the rapier, but since the weapon was so long he was unable to wear it; his servants stowed it in the baggage wagon. As to what became of the rapier, several accounts made the rounds, but the fact is that no one knew with certainty, either then or later.

"Come now, comrade," said Dąbrowski, turning to Matthias. "You seem unhappy with our arrival. Why so dour and silent? Does your heart not leap at the sight of our gold and silver eagles, at the sound of our buglers trumpeting Kościuszko's reveille so close to your ear? Come, Matthias, I took you for a better fighting man. If you won't take up the sword or mount a horse, then at least join your comrades in a merry pledge to Napoleon's health and the hopes of Poland."

"Hah!" snorted Matthias. "I've heard and seen for myself what's up. Two eagles, Hetman, do not share the same nest. God's favor, sir, rides a paint horse. The Emperor a great hero? One might say a lot on that score. I recall what my comrades the Puławski told me after seeing the great Dumouriez.[13] Poland needs a Polish hero, they said, not a Frenchman, nor yet an Italian. What she needs is a Piast,[14] a Jan, a Joseph, a Matthias—basta! They call it the Polish Army, but just look at these fusiliers, these sappers, these cannoneers, and grenadiers. I hear more German names among them than native ones.[15] Who can sort it out? No doubt there are Tartars and Turks among you, schismatics even, who care nothing for God or the Faith. With my own eyes I have seen our village lasses raped, passers-by robbed, churches looted. The Emperor makes for Moscow. Some march for an emperor who sets out without God's blessing![16] They tell me he has fallen under the Bishop's ban. What a farce! But then they can all go and kiss my..."

And dipping his bread in the soup, Matthias ate, leaving the last word unuttered.

Matthias' words were scarcely to the Chamberlain's taste. The youth began to murmur among themselves, but at that moment the Judge broke in, announcing the arrival of the third betrothal party.

It was the Notary Bolesta; at least he announced himself as the Notary, but no one recognized him. Until now he'd always dressed in the Polish style, but in one of the clauses of their nuptial articles, his plighted lady Telimena had made him renounce the loose-sleeved Polish robe; so willy-nilly the Notary had assumed the French garb.[17] Evidently, the frock coat robbed him of half his soul. Loath to look either to the right or the left, he walked like a crane, stiff and erect, as though he'd swallowed a stick. Despite his composed mien, he was clearly in torments, unable to bow and at a loss what to do with his hands—he who was so very fond of gestures! He thrust his hands under his belt, but there was no belt, so he proceeded to stroke his belly. Realizing his gaffe, he grew flustered, and blushing red as a lobster dispatched both hands into the same pocket of his frock coat. Like a man running the gauntlet he bore the murmurs and the sneers, as ashamed of the coat as of some discreditable deed. But then catching sight of Matthias' stare he fairly blenched.

Until this moment the two men had enjoyed a robust friendship. But now Matthias shot Bolesta a look so fierce, so withering, that the latter paled to a parchment's hue. He began to clutch at his buttons, as if Matthias' gaze would strip him of his coat. Dobrzyński merely repeated the word "stupid!" twice. So much did the change of dress appall him that he rose at once from the table, swept out of the hall without excusing himself, and mounting up returned to his village.

Meanwhile, tricked out from top to toe in the very latest sartorial confection, the Notary's comely sweetheart Telimena was spreading her splendor all round. Idle to set down in words the manner of gown she wore! And the arrangement of her hair! No pen could portray it. A painter's brush was needed to limn those laces, tulles, muslins, cashmeres, pearls, and precious stones. And her lively glances! And her rosy cheeks!

The Count recognized her at once. Paling with astonishment, he rose from the table and felt about for his sword.

"So it is you?" he cried. "Do my eyes deceive me? You! Clasping another's hand in my presence? Faithless creature! Perfidious soul! Do you not hide your face for shame? Are you so unmindful of your vow so recently made? And I so easily gulled! Why have I sported this love-gage? Woe to my rival who treats me with such disdain! Over my dead body shall he mount to the altar!"

The guests rose to their feet. The Notary was horribly put out. The Chamberlain hastened to appease the rivals; meanwhile, Telimena took the Count aside.

"I am not yet the Notary's bride," she whispered. "If you have anything against our marriage, then tell me this, and let your answer be brief and to the point! Do you love me? Does your heart still hold the same affection? Are you ready to wed me on the spot, now, this very day? If so, I'll renounce the Notary."

"Unfathomable woman," said the Count. "Your sentiments once struck me as poetic, but now they seem quite banal. What are these marriages of yours if not chains that bind hands and not souls? Believe me, there are ways of avowing one's love without declarations, ways of being bound without plighting one's troth! Two flaming hearts at points antipodal can converse in the tongues of the glimmering stars. Who knows, perhaps this explains why the Earth finds herself so drawn to the Sun, and why she is ever the object of the Moon's desire.[18] Perhaps that is why they gaze eternally upon each other; why they come together by the shortest path yet never unite."

"Enough of this!" said Telimena. "I am not a planet, thank heaven. Enough, I say! I am a woman. I see where this is tending, so you can stop your twattle. Now heed my warning! Breathe so much as a word against my marriage and as sure as God's in heaven I shall fly at you with these nails of mine and tear—"

"Madam!" protested the Count. "I shall not stand in the way of your happiness." And with his eyes filled with sadness and disdain, the Count turned away; but to punish his faithless sweetheart, he took the Chamberlain's daughter as the new object of his eternal flame.

The Steward, seeking by wise examples to reconcile the youths, resumed his story of the boar of Naliboka Forest and Rejtan's quarrel with the Prince de Nassau.[19] But by now the guests had eaten their ices and were filing out into the courtyard to enjoy the air.

The village folk had finished their feast. Stoups of mead were making the round. The musicians tuned their instruments and called the folk to dance. They looked for Tadeusz who was standing some distance away, whispering something of pressing moment to his future bride.

"Sophy!" he said, "I must consult with you on an important matter. I've discussed it with my uncle, and he's not opposed. You know that most of the villages of which I'm to take possession belong by right of inheritance to you. These peasants are your subjects, not mine, and I'd be loath to dispose of their affairs against the will of their mistress. Now that we have our beloved land restored, shall this happy circumstance mean nothing more to our peasantry than a change of masters? True, we have always ruled them with kindness, but God knows to whom I should will them after my death. I am a soldier, and we are both mortal. I am a man and know my caprices. The safer thing would be to renounce my rights and entrust the fate of the peasants to the care of the law. Since we are free, let us enfranchise our peasantry. Let us grant them title to the land that gave them birth, the land they have earned by blood and toil and thanks to which they feed us all and make us prosper. But I must caution you that by giving up these lands, we shall be earning a smaller income. We shall be forced to live on slenderer means. Now, I, from my youth, am quite used to frugal living. But you, Sophy, spring from a noble family. You spent your early years in the capital city. Can you see yourself living in the country far from high society like a common village girl?"

"I am a woman," replied Sophy modestly. "Governing's not in my line. You shall be the husband; I am too young to give counsel here. Whatever you decide I shall agree to with all my heart, and should we be the poorer for freeing the peasants, then you, Tadeusz, shall be all the dearer to my heart. I know little about my family and scarcely bother myself about it. This much I know—that I was an orphan in need and the Soplicas took me like their own daughter into their home. Under their roof I was raised, and now I am being given away in marriage. I do not fear country living. If I lived in the great city, it was long ago and I've long since put it out of mind. But I've always loved the countryside. Believe me, my hens and roosters amuse me far more than any Petersburg you'd care to imagine. If I felt drawn to the amusements and the people there, it was mere childishness on my part. I know now that the city bores me. This winter, after my brief stay in Wilno, I realized I was born for country living. Despite the city's amusements, I longed once more for the Manor. Nor do I fear manual labor. I am young and strong. I know how to mind the household and take charge of the keys. You'll see how I learn to keep house."

Even as Sophy uttered these last words, an astonished, dour-faced Gervase approached the young couple.

"I know all about it," he said. "The Judge has talked to me of this liberty. But how it concerns the peasantry, I cannot fathom. Something un-Polish[20] in this, I fear. Why, freedom's a matter for the nobility, not the peasantry! True, we are all sons of Adam, but I was taught the peasants sprang from Ham, the Jews from Japheth, and we, the nobility, from Shem; therefore, as elder brothers, we lord it over the other two. But our parish priest preaches otherwise. Such was the case under the Old Covenant, he says from the pulpit. Ever since Christ Our Lord, of royal blood, was born of the Jews in a peasant's stable, he has put all estates on an equal footing and made them one. So let it be, since it cannot be otherwise; the more so, as I hear that even my gracious lady Sophia has consented to it. Hers to command, mine to obey. She is mistress! Only see we do not grant them an empty freedom, in word only, like that under the Muscovites. When the late Mr. Karp[21] freed his serfs, the Muscovites reduced them to starvation by burdening them with a triple tax. So my advice is to turn to ancient custom, enroll our peasants upon our lineage and let it be known that they bear our blazon. My mistress shall bestow the Half Goat on some villages, and my master his Star and Crescent on others. Then even Rębajło will recognize the peasant as his equal when he sees in him an honorable gentleman with a coat of arms. Indeed, Parliament shall ratify it!

"And now, my lady, let not your spouse fret that he will impoverish you sorely by giving up your lands. Heaven forbid that I should see the hands of a noble sire's daughter calloused by domestic toil. I have a remedy for this. I know of a chest in the castle containing the Horeszko family's table service along with an array of rings, necklaces, bracelets, rich plumes, caparisons, and splendid swords. It is my lord Pantler's buried trove, kept safe from the hands of pillagers. By rights it belongs to the heiress, my lady Sophia. All this time I have guarded this hoard like the apple of my eye against the Muscovite and you Soplica folk. What's more, I have a hefty purse of my own thalers saved up from past services rendered and sundry gifts I received from my former master. I'd hoped to spend the odd penny in repairing the walls once the castle was restored to us, but now it seems the new master and mistress will have need of it. And so, Master Soplica, I shall settle into your house, live on my lady's bounty, and rock the cradle of a third generation of Horeszkos. If my lady has a son, I shall train him in the use of Jackknife. And a son it shall be! Wars loom ahead, and wartime always begets sons!"

Gervase had scarcely uttered these words when a solemn-faced Protase joined them. Bowing before the couple, he plunged his hand deep into his robe and withdrew a great panegyric two-and-a-half sheets long. The piece had been composed in rhyme by a young subaltern who enjoyed high repute in the capital for his odes. Later, he joined the army where he continued to cultivate the literary arts. After declaiming three hundred of the lines, the Usher reached the part of the poem that went as follows:

> O thou! whose charms
> Rouse torments exquisite and cruel delights,
> Whose fair gaze, turned on loud Bellona's host,
> Shivers the spear-shaft, breaks the serried shields;
> Do thou oust Mars this day, bid Hymen in,
> And hew the hydra heads from Strife's fell coil![22]

Tadeusz and Sophy clapped throughout the entire recital, though, in truth, they had heard enough. At last, at the Judge's behest, the parish priest mounted the table and made Tadeusz's resolution known to the villagers. On hearing the news, they rushed over to their young master and fell at his lady's feet.

"Our patrons' health!" they cried with tears in their eyes.

"And yours, fellow citizens!" replied Tadeusz. "Fellow Poles, equal and free!"

"A toast to our Common Folk!" proposed Dąbrowski.

"Long live the Generals!" cried the peasantry. "Long live the Army! The People! All the Estates!"

A thousand voices thundered out the toasts in turn. Only Buchman refused to join in the common rejoicing. Though he supported the idea in principle, he moved for amendments: first, appoint a legal commission, then . . . but there was little time, and his motions were promptly relegated to the shelf.

Already pairs made up of officers and ladies, enlisted men and village girls were forming a line in the courtyard. "The *Polonaise!*" they cried with one voice.

The officers were fetching in the military band when the Judge whispered into Dąbrowski's ear:

"Pray hold off your bandsmen awhile. You know it is my nephew's betrothal day. We have an ancient family custom of betrothing and wedding our young couples to the strains of our village music. Look there! The dulcimer player, the fiddler and the pipers stand waiting. Honest musicians! See? The fiddler bridles, the piper nods his head, imploring us with his eyes. If I send them away, the poor fellows will be sure to cry. Our villagers know no other music to skip to. Let our boys go first. Allow the folk to have their fun. Then we can listen to your splendid band." And he gave the sign.

The fiddler tucked up his sleeve, seized firm hold of the fingerboard, and thrusting the chin-rest under his jaw sent the bow like a racehorse over the strings. Upon this signal, the two pipers next to him blew into the goatskins. Puffing up their cheeks, they began to flap their elbows like wings. You'd swear they'd fly away—like Boreas's full-cheeked babes! Only the cymbalon was missing.

Though the district boasted a good many players of the hammer dulcimer, none would play in Jankiel's presence. (Where the innkeeper had spent the winter was a mystery; now, suddenly, he'd turned up in the company of the General Staff.) All knew that in skill, taste and sheer talent he had no equal on the instrument. They brought in the dulcimer and entreated him to play. But the Jew begged off, protesting that his hands had grown stiff; he was out of practice, ashamed to play before so a distinguished an audience; and making a bow, he sought his escape. Seeing him withdraw, Sophy ran up and held out to him on her snow-white hand the hammers the old master used to sound the strings.

"Dear Jankiel!" she implored, stroking his silver beard with her other hand. "Be so good as to play. This is my betrothal day. Did you not always promise to play at my wedding?"

Now Jankiel was immensely fond of Sophy. He wagged his beard—clearly, he would not disappoint her. They led him into the midst of the assembly, drew up a chair, seated him, and bringing forth the dulcimer set it on his lap. With pride and delight Jankiel eyed the instrument. Just so an old campaigner, recalled to active service, eyes the sword his grandsons have hauled down from the wall. He smiles; many years have passed since last he gripped the steel, yet he is confident his hand will hold its own. Two of the Master's pupils knelt down to tune the dulcimer; they plucked the strings, tested the pitch. Meanwhile, Jankiel sat silent, eyes half-closed, the hammers resting lightly in his hands.

He brought them down and beat out a slow, triumphal measure, then he smote the strings more briskly until the hammers rained down like a torrential shower, amazing the guests. But this was only a test; he broke off, poising the hammers in the air. Again he lowered them. This time they struck with light, tremulous movements, brushing the strings like a fly's wing and producing a scarcely audible hum; meanwhile, the Maestro gazed upward, waiting for the moment of inspiration. At last, looking proudly down on his instrument, he raised both arms and let them fall. Both hammers crashed down simultaneously, astounding his listeners again.

A mighty sound burst forth from many strings at once; it was as if an entire orchestra of janissaries[23] had struck up with bells, zils, and pounding drums. *The May Third Polonaise!* The lively notes breathed joy, brought joy to the ear. The girls itched to dance, the boys could scarcely stand still. Among the elders the strains brought back memories of old. They recalled the happy days ensuing upon that momentous May Third, when Senators and Members in the assembly hall had fêted the King, now formally reconciled with his nation—those happy days when they'd danced and chanted, "Long live our beloved King! Parliament! The People! All the Estates!"[24]

The Maestro kept quickening the time, building up the sound. Without warning, he struck a discordant note; it was like the hiss of a snake, like iron grating on glass! A collective shudder ran through the guests. Dread infected their joy. Disturbed and alarmed, they wondered if the instrument had lost its pitch or the Maestro's hand had erred. But a Master never errs! He had a reason for sounding that perfidious string and marring the tune. Louder and louder he harped on that sullen chord which conspired against the commonwealth of tones. Suddenly, the Warden understood the Maestro. "Why," he cried, clapping his hand to his face. "I know that sound! It is Targowica!" And with a loud twang the ominous string snapped. Without missing a beat, the player turned to the trebles; then breaking up and blurring the measure, he abandoned the trebles and crossed over to the bass.

A thousand tumultuous sounds broke forth with increasing intensity. They heard the beat of a march, the clash of arms, a charge, the storming of a rampart, gunfire, children's cries and mothers' wails! So expertly did the artist convey the horror of the assault that the village women shuddered, recalling with tears of anguish the Massacre of Praga[25] of which they'd heard in stories and songs. Great was their relief when at last, after causing every string to crash like thunder, the Maestro damped the sounds, as if driving them into the earth.

Scarcely had the audience time to recover from their amazement when the music changed again. Once more the first notes were light and hushed. A few thin strings whined shrilly like flies struggling in the spider's toils. But the strings grew in number, the scattered notes rallied, grouping with legions of chords, until they marched in time and harmony, resolving themselves into the mournful strains of that popular song of the errant trooper. Over holt and hill he roamed. Hunger and hardship often laid him low until at last he dropped lifeless at his trusty mount's feet, and over his body the pony pawed the dust.

An old song so dear to the Polish soldier's heart! The men recognized it at once. The rank and file crowded around the Maestro, listening, recalling the harrowing time when they'd crooned this song over their country's grave then marched hence into the wide world. Their thoughts ran on those long, nomadic years when, strangers among strangers, they traversed land and seas, across blistering sands and frozen wastes, when, oft in camp, the song had cheered and warmed their hearts; and so, reminiscing sadly, they bowed their heads.

But they soon raised them again. The Maestro was striking higher notes with growing strength, changing the measure and introducing yet another theme. Again his lofty eye ranged over the strings; then joining his hands, he slammed both hammers down at once. The resulting blow was so strong, so deftly executed, that the strings rang out like brazen trumpets, and from these horns issued forth and aloft the famous triumphal march, *Poland Is Not Yet Lost!*[26] Onward to Poland, Dąbrowski! The guests, applauding, sang out the refrain, "Onward, Dąbrowski!"

As if overwhelmed by his own playing, Jankiel released the hammers and flung up his arms. His fox-skin hat slipped to his shoulders, his beard wagged solemnly, a strange ruddiness blotched his cheeks, and a youthful fire blazed in his inspired eyes. Turning to Dąbrowski, the old master covered his eyes with his hand whence a torrent of tears flowed between his fingers.

"General!" he said. "Long has our Lithuania awaited you. Aye, so have we Jews waited for our Messiah. For years the bards prophesied you to the people. Heaven heralded your coming with signs. Now live on and wage war, o you, our . . ."

And saying this he sobbed; clearly, the honest Jew loved his homeland as passionately as any Pole. Dąbrowski extended his hand and thanked him, and Jankiel, doffing his cap, kissed the General's hand.

It was time now for the *Polonaise.* With a flick of his flowing sleeve and a twirl of his moustache, the Chamberlain stepped forward, offered Sophy his hand, and bowing courteously besought the top of the dance. The other pairs formed a line behind them; upon the given signal, the stately promenade commenced.

The Chamberlain led the train. His red boots flashed on the greensward. The sun beat upon his saber, his lavishly wrought belt glittered. He marched slowly, with seeming carelessness, yet in his every step, in his every gest and gesture, you could read the dancer's feelings and thoughts.

He stopped, as if to inquire of the lady, and leaned toward her as if to whisper in her ear, but the lady looked away; she was bashful and refused to listen.

He doffed his cap and bowed deferentially. The lady vouchsafed him a glance but remained obstinately silent. He slackened his pace, all the while following her glances with his eye. At last, he laughed out, clearly delighted by the lady's reply. Quickening his step, he gazed down at his rivals, now drawing his egret-plumed cap over his eyes, now pushing it back on his head. Finally, he cocked the cap at a rakish angle and curled his moustache. He strode on; the guests followed jealously on his heels. He seemed intent on stealing his lady away. Now he marked time, politely raising his hand and entreated them to pass him by, now he stepped nimbly aside, reversing his path, as if to confuse the dancers. But they pursued him doggedly with swift steps and encircled him in the evolutions of the dance. Growing angry, he clapped his hand to his crossguard. "I care not," he seemed to say. "A plague on your jealous eyes!" With pride writ on his brow, defiance in his eyes, he executed an about-face and bore down on the throng. Loath to stand in his way, the dancers stepped aside, then regrouping set off in pursuit again. Meanwhile, shouts rang out on every hand: "Ah, he may be the last! Look on, you youngsters, and mark it well! He may be the last to lead the dance this way."

And so, pair after pair, they processed, boisterous and merry. Round and round went the train, uncoiling and coiling anew like the thousand spires of a monstrous snake. Enhanced by the golden glow of the westering sun and the greensward's swarthy nap, the smears of color of the men's, ladies and soldiers' costumes shimmered vividly like burnished scales. On and on they danced. The music played. The plaudits! The pledges!

Only Corporal Sack Dobrzyński held aloof. He neither listened to the music, nor danced, nor shared in the general merriment. Standing sullenly aside with his hands behind his back, he recalled the days of his courtship of Sophy. He recalled the gifts of flowers and bird's eggs he'd brought her, the baskets he'd woven for her, the earrings he'd carved for her. The little ingrate! Though he'd lavished those lovely gifts on her in vain, though she ran from his sight, and his father forbade him to see her, yet despite all, he loved her still. How many times he'd sat on the fence just to catch a glimpse of her in the window! How many times he'd stolen into the hemp to watch her weed the garden, harvest her cucumbers, or fatten her capons! Aye, the little ingrate! And he drooped his head. But then, whistling out a mazurka, he rammed his visored cap down over his brow and made for the camp where sentinels stood watch over the field guns. To distract himself, he struck up a game of canasta[27] with a few old campaigners, sweetening his grief with a cup. Such was the constancy of Sack Dobrzyński's feelings for Sophy.

Meanwhile, Sophy danced blithely on. Though she led the dance, a distant spectator could scarcely make her out in the vast overgrown courtyard. Clad in her green dress, with garlands around her neck and the floral wreathe binding her brow, she ranged unseen over the grass and flowers, governing the dance even as an angel presides over the roll of the stars. Only by the eyes turned her way, by the arms extended toward her, and the bustle of bodies pressed around her, could one tell her presence. In vain the Chamberlain clung to her side! Already his rivals had dislodged him from the first pair. Nor did the lucky Dąbrowski have long to gloat; he, too, was obliged to yield her up. A third rival presented himself, only to have Sophy snatched from him by a fourth, and so he, too, walked forlornly away. At last, Sophy passed back to Tadeusz, and here, weary of dancing, fearing yet another change of partners and anxious to be with her betrothed spouse, she closed the dance. She returned to the table and began serving out wine to the guests.

The sun was setting. The evening was warm and calm. Puffs of cloud dotted the dome of the sky. Overhead, it was still blue, to the westward, rosy. The clouds, foretokening fair weather, were airy and bright: here they floated drowsily like a flock on the village green; yonder, somewhat smaller in size, they suggested a flight of teal. A larger cloud drifted up from the west. Like a sheer lace drapery it hung, translucent, amply folded, pearly white on the outside, gilded around the marges, and mauve in the center. Still it glowed and flamed in the ebbing light, until, at last, turning yellow, it grew pale and gray, and the sun, sinking his head, drew down the cloud, and with one last warm and wafting sigh nodded off to sleep.[28]

Meanwhile, the nobility drank on, pledging Bonaparte, the Generals, Sophy, and Tadeusz. Next, they saluted all three betrothed couples in turn, then all the invited guests both present and absent, then all those friends remembered among the living, and last, those of sainted memory.

And I, too, was a guest on that occasion. I drank the mead and the wine, and all that I saw and heard stands set down here in this book.[29]

FINIS

NOTES

1. Michał Ludwik Pac (1780-1835) served as Napoleon's adjutant and was elevated to the rank of general in 1812. The poet later met him in emigration.
2. Mikołaj Krzysztof Radziwiłł (1549-1616) known as "The Orphan" was converted from Calvinism to Catholicism largely through the efforts of the famous Polish Jesuit, Piotr Skarga. In 1582-1584 he made a pilgrimage to the Holy Land, on which he wrote his book *Peregrynacja do Ziemi Świętej* (A Journey to the Holy Land). A Latin translation appeared as early as 1610.
3. The Polish-Swedish wars, 1655-1660. The historical novelist Henryk Sienkiewicz (1846-1916) made them the subject of his novel *Potop* (*The Deluge*, 1886).

4. *Barszcz królewski*, a slightly tart soup made from the juice of pickled beets and fermented rye bread.

5. *Kontuz* is a kind of smoked sausage or bouillon made from minced chicken or veal; *arkas*, a dessert consisting of sweet milk, saffron, lemon, and rose-scented vodka; *blemas* (blanc-mange), an almond jelly, laced with wine and seasoned with cloves, cinnamon, or musk.

6. Giovanni Giuseppe Pinetti (1750-1800), an Italian conjurer famous throughout Europe. Contemporary accounts describe his visits to Grodno in 1796 and to Wilno early in the nineteenth century.

7. [*Author's note*] In the sixteenth century, and early in the seventeenth, at a time when the arts flourished, even banquets were directed by artists and were full of symbols and theatrical scenes. At a famous banquet given in Rome for Pope Leo X there was a centerpiece that represented the four seasons of the year in turn, and that evidently served as a model for Radziwiłł's. Table customs changed in Europe about the middle of the eighteenth century but remained unchanged longest in Poland.

8. Napoleon's cavalry units made use of flankers for light skirmishes, scouting missions and the defense of their flanks. By 1812, flankers were always armed with light cavalry carbines, even if the rest of the unit did not have them. The reference to an antique blunderbuss among them is a typical instance of the poet's droll sense of humor.

9. Henryk Dembiński (1791-1864), a Polish general who took part in the Napoleonic campaigns, the November Insurrection, and the Hungarian Revolution of 1831.

10. Józef Dwernicki (1778-1857), a member of the Polish Legions, who in 1804 fielded a squadron at his own expense. In 1806, he was promoted to general and distinguished himself in the November Insurrection. Samuel Różycki (1784-1834) was an officer in the campaign of 1812; he held the rank of general in the November Insurrection and commanded an expedition to Lithuania.

11. The Pułaski family were among the organizers of the Confederacy of Bar. Józef Pułaski was the first commander-in-chief of its armed forces. His son, Kazimierz, won fame as a leader after his father's death. Later, in 1777, he came to America and distinguished himself by his services to the revolutionary cause. He was killed in 1779 in the attack on Savannah. Michał Dzierżanowski (d. 1808), a Bar confederate and adventurer famous in the eighteenth century; he took part in almost all the wars of this time. For a while, he was king of Madagascar. Józef Sawa-Caliński (d. 1771), a heroic Cossack, one of the leaders of the Confederacy of Bar.

12. [*Author's note*] The mournful song of Mrs. Cybulski, whose husband gambled her away at cards to the Muscovites, is well known in Lithuania.

13. Charles François Dumouriez (1739-1823), a general sent by France to assist the Confederates of Bar in 1770.

14. The Piasts were the first royal dynasty of Poland. In later times, the name was used to denote any candidate for the Polish throne who was of native birth.

15. All the preceding terms are of French origin, but in his simplicity old Matthias puts them all under the generic German umbrella. In common usage, the Polish word *niemiecki* (German) is often synonymous with *cudzoziemski* or *obcy*, meaning "alien" or "foreign."

16 Matthias had probably heard something about the excommunication of Napoleon by Pope Pius VII in 1809. The following line with its implied internal rhyme is the despair of the translator.

17. [*Author's note*] The fashion of adopting the French garb raged in the provinces from 1800 to 1812. A great number of the young men changed their style of dress before marriage at the request of their future wives.

18. The moon is masculine in Polish.

19. [*Author's note*] The anecdote of the quarrel of Reytan with the Prince de Nassau, which the chief steward never concludes, is well known in popular tradition. We add here its conclusion for the gratification of the curious reader:– Reytan, angered by de Nassau's boasting, took up position beside him at the narrow passage through which the beasts would be forced to make their egress. At that moment, a huge boar, infuriated by the shots and the baiting, made a rush through the passage. Reytan snatched the gun from the prince's hands, cast his own on the ground, and taking a pike and offering another to the German, said, "Now we will see who does the better work with the spear." The boar was on the point of attacking them, when Steward Hreczecha, who was standing at some distance away, felled the beast with a first-rate shot. Angry at first, the two gentlemen later came to terms and handsomely rewarded Hreczecha.

20. Here again the speaker uses the word "German" (*z niemiecka*) in the sense of "foreign" or "non-native" (*z cudzoziemska*). More accurately it is French, as, since the revolution, France was the chief disseminator of democratic ideas.

21. The reference is to Ignacy Karp, Ensign of Upita (Wilno Province). As early as 1803, he enfranchised all the serfs belonging to his domains, around 7,000 male souls. Later, as marshal of the nobility, he oversaw, over a period of three years, the entry of 18,000 peasant families into the rolls of the nobility. As the poet explains in his notes, "[The] Tsarist government recognizes no freeman except the nobility. Peasants freed by landowners are immediately entered in the rolls of the Emperor's estates and forced to pay increased taxes in place of dues to their lords. It is a well-known fact that in the year 1818 the citizens of Wilno Province adopted in the regional diet a project for freeing all the peasants and appointed a delegation to the Emperor with that aim in view; but the Russian government ordained that the project should be quashed and no further mention made of it. There is no means of setting a man free under the Tsarist government except to take him into one's family. Accordingly, many have had the privileges of nobility conferred on them in this way as an act of grace or for money."

22. Protase's poem addressed to Sophy is considered an excellent pastiche of the neo-classical panegyric ode.

23. The army of the Polish-Lithuanian Commonwealth had its own janissaries' division with a band that played a noisy martial music similar to that of the original Turkish janissaries.

24. This scene was later famously portrayed by Jan Matejko in his Romantic tableau, *The Announcement of the Constitution of May Third to the Nation* (1891).

25. The massacre of the inhabitants of the Warsaw suburb of Praga on November 9, 1794, when the Russian forces under Suvorov took the city by storm. The event marked the end of the Kościuszko insurrection.

26. Then the *de facto* national anthem of Poland; now, since the restoration of Poland's independence in 1918, her official anthem. See also note 8 to Book I.

27. The Polish text gives *drużbart* (from German *Drosselbart*, king of hearts); a game of Polish cards popular during the eighteenth and nineteenth centuries.

28. Although *Pan Tadeusz* ends on an upbeat note with the flame of Polish hope burning brightly in the year 1812, the poet's sublime image of the changing cloud contains a presentiment of the catastrophe that lies ahead. It is the crowning instance of the "theme of disenchantment," which runs like a *leitmotif* throughout the entire work.

29. These closing lines echo the standard ending of a Polish fairy tale.

About the Translator

Christopher Adam Zakrzewski—(born 1948)—literary translator, teacher, scholar. Raised in the UK and Ontario, Canada. Doctoral studies in Russian and Polish Literature at the University of British Columbia. Professor of languages and literature at Our Lady Seat of Wisdom College in Barry's Bay, Ontario. Now retired, he and his wife Wendy live in the village of Wilno, Ontario. They have five children and nine grandchildren.

www.ingramcontent.com/pod-product-compliance
Lightning Source LLC
Chambersburg PA
CBHW020101030726
47498CB00006B/1899